The Hogarth Conspiracy

The Hogarth Conspiracy

A NOVEL

ALEX CONNOR

SILVER OAK

New York / London

SILVEROAK
New York / London

An Imprint of Sterling Publishing Co., Inc. (New York)
and Quercus Publishing Plc (London)
387 Park Avenue South
New York, NY 10016

ISBN 978–1-4027–9006–5

Originally published in 2011 in Great Britain as *Legacy of Blood*.
First published by Sterling Publishing, Co., Inc., 2012

Distributed in Canada by Sterling Publishing
$^c/o$ Canadian Manda Group, 165 Dufferin Street
Toronto, Ontario, Canada M6K 3H6

For information about custom editions, special sales, and premium and corporate purchases, please contact Sterling Special Sales at 800–805–5489 or specialsales@sterlingpublishing.com.

Manufactured in the United States of America

2 4 6 8 10 9 7 5 3 1

www.sterlingpublishing.com

. . . from all the deceits of the world, the flesh, and the devil, spare us. . . .

—THE BOOK OF COMMON PRAYER

I have endeavoured to treat my subject as a dramatic writer; my picture is my stage.

—WILLIAM HOGARTH ON HIS WORK

I remember the time when I have gone moping into the city, with scarce a shilling in my pocket . . . but as soon as I had received ten guineas . . . sallied out again with all the confidence of a man with ten thousand pounds. . . .

—WILLIAM HOGARTH

Prologue

Under the whorehouses and the taverns lie London's dead. Beneath cobbles and alleyways, within the hearing of the molly houses and the sodomisers, cheek by jowl with the shadow of St Paul's, and within the summer stink of the Thames. Under flagstones and feet, under weather and sewage, lay the passageway I hurried towards. Shaken, I looked back many times to see if I was being followed—but there was only the creak of a dozen inn signs and the sound of a startled horse whinnying shrilly in Drury Lane.

Mischief made mumbles in the night, and my hands were sweating as I reached the entrance of the narrow alleyway. Expecting me, a guard, silent and surly, stood back to let me enter, handing me a rush light, and then moved into the street above. As the iron gate slammed to a close, I stared into the dank open womb of the chamber below. I could see shadows of two other men, distorted into ghouls, and placed my foot gingerly on the next step. God! My mouth was thick with panic, my pulse speeding up, blood yammering like a lunatic in my veins. Turning at a bend, I stumbled, and the buckle of my shoe struck the stone wall, gouging a white scar into the brickwork.

Hearing my approach, the men turned. One, a priest, a handkerchief held over his nose, a sprig of rosemary pinned to his vestments, regarded me with indifference. Obviously, he had been to an earlier funeral where the mourners would have handed out the nosegays—rosemary for remembrance. The other man, a doctor, stood in his brocade coat, blood stiffening his waistcoat; ladybird splashes on the gilded buttons. Corpulent, he made an awkward gesture towards the back of the room as I passed under an arch into a shadowed area beyond. For an instant I could see nothing, then raised the light I was holding and watched the shallow underground room shudder in the smoking flame.

I had known her living. Polly Gunnell, one of Mrs Needham's whores, from the best brothel in London. Pretty and plump enough for the bankers, the businessmen, the theatregoers; fresh enough not to have to work out of a room in Drury Lane; sweet enough to avoid the streets. And quick and clever enough for royalty—or so she had bragged to me as she coiled a sliver of dark hair around her index finger and bit her bottom lip into a bud with her small teeth.

'Sit for me,' I had said a while ago, and I had drawn an engraving of her—

Courtesan at Her Toilette—*which had proved popular enough to earn me money, and Polly Gunnell fame. Encouraged, my imagination had found much room for Polly Gunnell, willing board and lodging for her knowing appeal. Inspired, I had constructed a morality tale, using her as the model, and called it* The Harlot's Progress.

But Polly Gunnell was no longer sleeping or breathing or biting her lip. She was lying on a stone table, next to a pile of beer barrels stacked up against the wall like a dunghill. Apart from her shoes, laced with two ivory ribbons, the heels sullied with London mud, she was naked. Slowly my gaze travelled upwards. Both thighs had been slashed from the knees to the groin, and around her vagina were numerous tiny mutilations, much blood bearing witness to the ferocity of the attack. Dry-mouthed, I attempted to swallow and tried to look away, but instead I looked at the rest of her body: Polly Gunnell's nipples had been cut off, and a knife slash ran from her throat down to her pubic bone.

And within her corpse a terrible emptiness where once her womb, now torn out of her, had lain.

Unnerved, I turned to look at the others. The doctor was winding his fob watch, and the priest's straight dark hair framed an expression of dissolute indifference. Nothing was said to me as I turned back to the body. Overhead, I could hear someone rolling barrels on the floor, a door slamming closed. My lamp spluttered as I turned back to the corpse. Polly Gunnell's face—once pert with cleverness, soft with eroticism, a perfect countenance for longing—had been disfigured by a blatantly vicious criss-crossing of cuts, laced like the pastry topping of a pie. The muscles were exposed, the eyelids cut away, the nose severed. Blood, drying thick and dark, crusted the open wounds. Not an inch of Polly Gunnell's pretty face remained. Not a millimetre of the countenance which had smiled out from the canvas and the printed page.

I had known Polly Gunnel's face as well as I knew my own: had drawn it, painted it, engraved it. I had chosen her as the heroine of my morality tale, out to tender for the populace, plying her trade from the canvas and the metal plate, willingly whoring for me—the painter—William Hogarth. Whoring for me as she had done for the pimp and the procuress, clicking her fingers at the world as she swung her leg at the stupidity of men. She had laughed at the fate of the girl in the picture without ever realising it was her own future, a prophecy she could never deflect.

Turning away at last, I tasted the vomit in my throat and swallowed hard. The rush light I held momentarily illuminated a bunch of rags in a corner. Curious, I moved over and bent down, lifting a corner to reveal a dead newborn infant, its limbs white, its lips dark.

Shaken, my voice faltered. "Was this her child? Did they cut the baby from her whilst she was still alive?" I asked of the doctor and the priest, who were now moving towards the stone steps. Towards the street. "Sweet Christ, what did they do to her?"

The doctor shrugged.

I knew what he was thinking as he looked at me, a small, stocky man, standing in front of him. William Hogarth, satirist, vicious and sentimental by turns, and now obviously sickened and trying not to vomit.

"Look," the doctor said curtly, "The priest's a witness. I'm following orders, that's all. I was told to fetch you here and to pay you for your trouble. You're to see to this." He jerked his head to where the monstrously mutilated body lay. "I don't know why they killed the woman; I don't want to know."

"But I do," I countered, persistently, "Who did this?"

"I've told you, I don't know!" The doctor answered vehemently, straightening his wig, his fleshy hands shaking. "I was only ordered to bring you here."

"By whom?"

The doctor shrugged again, feigning ignorance.

"I was sent a message; that was all." Rattled, he reached into his waistcoat pocket, feeling around urgently, then took a snort of tobacco. When he sneezed, he wiped the snot off his nose with the sleeve of his jacket. "When I got here, I was too late. I couldn't do anything for either of them."

I nodded. "Very well . . . I'll see to it."

"You made her famous." The doctor assumed a mock sympathetic expression. "Everyone in London fell in love with Polly Gunnell, but no one would know her now. Just another dead hack." Straightening up, he looked back at me. "Mind you don't end up the same way, Master Hogarth."

Sighing, he pulled on his hat and followed the priest up the steps into the alley beyond. I heard the dull iron thud of the gate echoing behind them as they left. I was now alone with the dead body of Polly Gunnell and her child. I took off my coat and laid it over her face, then touched the top of her head and felt the spring of hair under my fingers. I knew why she had been killed. Hadn't my own safety been threatened when The Harlot's Progress was published?

I had known at the time that the potency of the series would be given an added frisson if the public could identify some of the models in the paintings. How scandalous to depict Mrs. Needham, the infamous procuress, and how titillating to recognise Colonel Charteris, a rake so dissolute that England had nicknamed him the Rape-Master General. I flinched at the recollection. If only I had stopped there, but unable to resist another jibe, I had gone too far, satirised the wrong person. Depicted with Polly Gunnell a man as her lover. An important, familiar man, a man known to everyone in Europe—Frederick, Prince of Wales.

When the painting was viewed, I at once realised my mistake, but it was too late. Manhandled and threatened in my own home, I was ordered to alter the features of the courtesan's lover. And so the man in the picture was emasculated by paint, turned from a hero into a vacant fool with a few deft brushstrokes.

But of course I could not vandalize my masterpiece. I had simply made a copy and hidden the original. The famous image still existed, the wicked satire hidden but not destroyed. I relied on the fact that a painter admired by King George II and feted across Europe had redoubtable allies. Polly Gunnell might have had no power to protect herself, but the fame of William Hogarth sheltered me.

But only so far.

Of course they would summon me to see to the body of Polly Gunnell and her dead child. What better way to send me a warning? Secure my silence? To make me realise that any threat to the throne would be ruthlessly obliterated. My arrogance had blinded me, but from that moment on fear would ensure my compliance.

I bent down again to the dead infant. Not wanting to leave its corpse for the rats to rip apart, I gently lifted it from the floor. I would lay it by its mother, have them buried together. But as I held the little body, I noticed a muted flutter and touched the child's neck, where I felt the faint beating of a thready pulse.

"Jesus," I exclaimed, panicking and looking round. "Holy God."

I was almost insensible with fear. I had to get away—and I had to take the baby—a boy, as I now saw—with me. Now! Before anyone came back. Perhaps the doctor had already sent for the undertaker; perhaps even now he was walking down the alley. Maybe someone from the public house above would come down for more beer and find me—and the child.

Wrapping the rags around the infant, I hurried towards the steps with my bundle. Tentatively I stepped into the street. As I moved further into the alleyway,

I looked around me, but the priest and the doctor were long gone. Overhead, a swollen white belly of moon followed my progress as I skittered through the ginnels and crossed Drury Lane. I kept the child pressed close as I passed drunks and road sweepers, lurking around the shortcuts I had known from childhood.

Unnerved and scared, I expected to be challenged, expected to be stopped. And then what fate would befall me? If they caught me, if they realised what I'd done, my life would be forfeit. They had thought that Polly Gunnell's child was dead, but he was still alive: the bastard son of the Prince of Wales. The child who had survived against all the odds, whose existence was a threat to the most powerful figures in the land.

And I had that child. The child who desperate, ambitious, and ruthless men would seek to find and kill.

But only if they knew he had survived.

Only weeks earlier I had had an unexpected late-night visitor: Frederick, Prince of Wales, was ushered in by my startled servant. His manner was exceedingly courteous, almost as though I had been the royal and he the commoner.

"Master Hogarth," he had begun. "I have something to ask of you, a favour, if you will, and, of course, your absolute confidence."

I had immediately nodded agreement. Who refused the Prince of Wales?

"This concerns Polly Gunnell," he continued, producing her name like a face card, sure to win the hand. "Dear Polly, your model, is carrying my child."

There had always been royal bastards, but seldom had their fathers admitted parentage.

"I think you know of our liaison?"

"Polly has not referred to it directly."

"But you guessed, of course—otherwise there would have been no painting."

His Royal Highness had seemed to bear me no ill will, had even been—dare I think it?—amused by my audacity.

"I need to give you something," he said, whereupon a substantial gold signet ring was dropped into my hand. It bore the inscription

To my secret child, from his father, Frederick, Prince of Wales.

Stunned, I gazed at him. "This is not wise, sir. This is proof that—"

"As was the painting." He held my look. "I ask you to watch over Polly. She

has no family, and she trusts you, Master Hogarth. If the child is a boy, you understand what that could mean?"

I nodded mutely.

"Polly was under my protection, but yesterday she disappeared," he said, then gripped my sleeve, imploring me—ME, William Hogarth—for help. "If she comes to you, assist her. Protect her. And keep this ring for the child. It is a testimony, proof of its lineage. Promise me, sir, you will do this?"

"I swear it."

Satisfied, he had then nodded and left.

But I hadn't kept my word, because she had not come to me, I had not seen Polly again. Until tonight, when what I saw was only her bloody corpse. . . .

Afraid, I kept moving, increasing my speed, threading my way through the night crowds, passing a gin seller and ducking out of the way of a hackney coming quick from St James's Street. I knew that at any moment someone could step out from an alley or a tavern doorway. Any man, every man. Some thug, some priest, some sergeant at arms, and ask, "What's that, Master Hogarth? What's that you're carrying? What's that, Master Hogarth?"

It's flesh and blood. It's breathing, it's alive. It's why Polly Gunnell is dead and my life is threatened. It's the reason I'm running and have to keep running.

Out of breath, I paused momentarily and leaned against a wall, looking around me. I had to get home, get help. I had to get the child to safety. Although near exhaustion, I pushed myself on and then began to run again, dipping out of the beam of an idiot moon and the scrutiny of lighted doorways.

But no one saw me. No one saw William Hogarth that night. No one saw me panting as I finally made my way to my house. Scrabbling for my keys, the man known to have the wickedest brush in Europe unlocked the door and slammed it closed. Expecting at any moment for it to be breached, I slid the bolts and, shaking, clung to the infant in my arms.

The child was warming up against me. I could feel its heartbeat, feel the slow return of life—and I knew that the murderers must never know they had failed. All that must be reported back was that William Hogarth, painter and engraver, had organised and paid for the burial of his onetime model Polly Gunnell. And her dead bastard.

No one must know the child survived and certainly not know who its father was: such a revelation would bring only tragedy, the reverberations of which could undermine history.

Remembering the hidden picture, I determined to hide the signet ring with it. For a fleeting moment I was shamed by my own conceit, considered destroying the damned work. What had been merely a satire, an ill-aimed joke, had found a target so dangerous and volatile it had already resulted in murder.

Only I had caused it. Only I could make amends.

It was the year of Our Lord 1732.

Part One

STUMBLING IN THE AISLE OF THE PRIVATE PLANE, SIR OLIVER PETERS grabbed the back of the nearest seat and righted himself. He wondered for a moment if his medication was making him unsteady as he concentrated on making his way along the narrow aisle to the restroom. Entering, he leaned against the sink gratefully, catching his breath.

Over the last few months he had hidden his illness so adeptly that no one—not even his wife, Sonia—knew about it. His weight loss he had attributed to his new gym membership, his shortened hours at the gallery to a lull in sales that nobody had anticipated. His tailor, in his confidence, had discreetly altered his clothes to conceal any telltale slackness, and a smaller shirt-collar size prevented the giveaway gape at the neck.

But in truth cancer had infiltrated Sir Oliver Peters's plush life with all the viciousness of an arsonist setting fire to a child's nursery. The disease had attacked suddenly, hijacking the confines of his good luck with squatter's rights and aiming to take over each organ consecutively as it worked its way through the rotting majesty of his body.

Hearing a noise from beyond the door, Oliver stared into the mirror and winced. The noise was faint, but it was the unmistakable sound of sex, coming from the back of the plane and just audible through the restroom wall. There was female laughter too, then a man moaning. Oliver turned on the faucet to try to drown out the sound. He had never liked Bernie Freeland, finding his Australian camaraderie at odds with his own British reserve, and suspected that Freeland's friendliness covered a brittle, unstable personality. Admired as a hedonist and a determined collector, Freeland had bludgeoned his way into the art world, using connections bought by his wealth. Bullish and affectionate at the same time, he had sucked the life out of lesser personalities and intimidated many dealers.

The Australian's sexual greed was legendary. His private plane was a personalized brothel, servicing him as he traveled the world. From London to New York, the Far East to Dubai, and back to his home in Sydney, Bernie Freeland conducted his business with frequent interruptions for sexual gratification, using Viagra for longer trips and vials of amyl nitrate for a shorter hit—even, on occasion, crystal meth.

All this Oliver Peters knew from the gossip over the last decade. And all this was the reason why he normally never would have accepted a journey in Bernie Freeland's plane. The cancellation of the flight home from Hong Kong and the prospect of waiting over twenty-four hours for another had persuaded Oliver—feeling weak and desperate to keep his illness a secret—to accept the proffered invitation.

Once on board, he had found two other art dealers availing themselves of Freeland's generosity. Both men were known to him. Kit Wilkes was the illegitimate son of James Holden, MP, and Lim Chang, a Chinese dealer in ceramics, was an enthusiastic buyer of British art. Oliver had suspected that Lim Chang was as keen as he was to get back to London and as uncomfortable with his surroundings. But Kit Wilkes had been another matter. Sleek as a water vole, with pale green eyes and a full Cupid's bow of a mouth, Wilkes was a languid bisexual whose constant travels and hops over the equator made short work of the world. Often accompanied, Wilkes paraded his boys in their Ralph Lauren uniforms or his nymphets in all their prim pubescence, but he was more of a voyeur than an active participant. Wilkes had an obsession with hygiene and was known to demand a full examination of every male or female he hired; a certain Texan, Dr. Eli Fountain, provided the service from his offices in Wimpole Street. No one slept with Kit Wilkes who hadn't been examined thoroughly first.

A jolt in the plane made Oliver grab the edge of the sink to steady himself. Despite his reputation, Kit Wilkes was traveling alone—had even refused an invitation to watch Bernie Freeland and the three girls on board, preferring to try to sleep, resting his narrow head against one of the plane's windows. At one moment, caught in sunlight, his gaze had flickered briefly over to Oliver, his green eyes momentarily as yellow as the skin of a gecko.

The plane jolted again. Oliver heard the sound, louder now, of the women laughing and screaming playfully.

"Why don't you have some fun? I won't tell anyone," Bernie Freeland had said earlier, pointing through an open door to the girls sitting on the huge divan in a cabin that was decked out as a bedroom.

Wretchedly embarrassed, Oliver had smiled his regal smile and shaken his head. "I don't think so."

"No one would know."

But they would, you bastard, Oliver thought, suspecting that Bernie Freeland might have the bedroom taped, every sound recorded. What a splendid way to secure business: provide the services of a call girl to sweeten the deal. Or, if the client was unwilling to deal, blackmail him into submission afterward.

"No thank you, Bernie. The lift home is more than enough."

He had seen Bernie Freeland's expression shift as he looped one arm around Oliver and guided him to a seat beside the bar at the far end of the plane. Surprised, Oliver had felt the weight of the Australian's arm and winced inwardly, wondering if Freeland could feel his loss of body tone, the giveaway wasting of muscle.

But Freeland's mind had been elsewhere. Sipping a tonic water, Oliver had glanced around. Kit Wilkes was asleep, and Lim Chang was talking to one of the call girls, a redhead perched on the side of his seat.

"You okay?"

Smiling stiffly, Oliver had nodded. "Fine, thank you."

"You buy anything in Hong Kong?"

"No." Oliver studied the man's broad, tanned face, the dark mustache that disguised a corrected hair lip. "Did you?"

"A Corot. Nothing else." He jerked his head toward the private compartment, knowing he was embarrassing his companion and enjoying it. "That redhead, Annette, gives the best blow job in Europe. And the brunette in the back is at this moment going down on the other girl."

His expression unreadable, Oliver had stared at the Australian. *I'm being eaten alive by cancer*, he had thought, *medicated so heavily that sex is a memory. I can't get an erection even if I wanted to. So I can look at you with your big, pumped body and your private plane—and not envy you in the least.*

But he hadn't said it.

"You're married, aren't you?"

Oliver had nodded.

"Are you happy with her?"

"Of course."

"*Of course*," Freeland repeated. "I've got no one to share my life with. Well, whores, but no one special. And I'm thinking that if this plane crashed now, no one would really care if I died."

Oliver had been more than a little worried that the conversation might slip into mawkishness.

"I'm sure you have many friends."

"In *this* business?" Bernie had exclaimed. "You are fucking joking! You can't have friends in the art world. Too many people trying to get their hands in the same till at the same time. I was offered a Turner in Dubai—*Dubai*, of all bloody places—but before I got back to the broker, he'd sold it. Whole deal completed in an hour." He sniffed. "That's technology for you. That son of a bitch was on his BlackBerry faster than the naked eye could follow."

"It's not like the old days," Oliver replied, shifting in his seat. "You took your time then—"

"Time's money," said Bernie, cutting him short. He threw a glance in the direction of the "bedroom" and continued. "These whores, for example; their madam—Mrs. Fleet—knows almost as much about art as we do, but instead of running a gallery, she runs flesh. Uses the girls as bait or to close a deal. You talk about contacts? Fleet has contacts in the art world you and I could only dream about. All the dealers use her, but you won't find one who'll admit it."

"Well—"

As Oliver attempted a reply, Bernie carried on, warming to his theme. "Imagine the kind of pillow talk that goes on between the girls and their punters. Imagine how much Fleet tucks away for use at a later date or to sell on to the highest bidder. Her and her girls are like the fucking Resistance in the war, except the girls don't do much resisting."

After that conversation, Bernie Freeland had ordered dinner for himself and his guests before moving back into the bedroom—where he still was, judging from the sounds coming through the washroom wall.

Oliver urinated into the bowl, flushed the toilet, and rinsed and dried his hands. He didn't want to leave the bathroom, didn't want to reenter the hothouse atmosphere of the jet. But embarrassed and out of place, he slowly made his way back to his seat just as the call girls emerged and went over to the bar. In their underwear, they eyed the newly awakened Kit Wilkes—who instantly waved them away—then turned their attention to the other men.

The redhead, Annette Dvorski, began talking to Lim Chang as the brunette, Marian Miller, sat down next to Oliver.

"Can I do anything for you? Can *we*?" Marian Miller asked, taking in

Oliver's expensive clothes and rightly assuming him to be married and rich. "Anything you want?"

" Er . . . no. Thank you, no."

The girl—tipsy and smelling of sex—rested her hand on Oliver's thigh. She pouted when he removed it, saying, "You're not like Bernie's usual friends. In fact, you don't even like him, do you? He could turn out to be a real fly in the ointment."

Unnerved by the remark and wondering what she was implying, Oliver took a moment to reply.

"We aren't friends," he began tentatively. "We're colleagues."

Shifting in his seat, he listened to the plane's engine and began to feel the rip of pain building inside his stomach. Before long he would have to take more medication, then wait for fifteen minutes. Fifteen minutes in which the pain would build, the race on to see how severe it could become before the medication took effect, curtailing the message traveling from Oliver's stomach to his brain, crushing the synapse telegram and muffling the spasm.

While he waited for that relief, the journey began to seem interminable as a slight blond girl slid into the seat beside Marian. She took a sip of wine, then ran her tongue over her bottom lip; the third girl, Liza, sat down opposite Oliver. They were both pretty and knowing and wanting to talk to stave off the boredom of the long flight. And they both realized that Sir Oliver Peters wasn't going to be screwing anyone.

"You an art dealer?"

"Yes."

Marian Miller nodded. "It's worse than politics, isn't it?"

"Sorry?"

"The art world. You're all so nice to each other's faces, but you stab each other in the back at the first chance." She had a faint Scottish accent and a tight line about her chin. Oliver realized she would lose her looks quickly as her face hardened with age. "I've never heard about your gallery, though . . ."

Oliver tried to smile but failed.

". . . I know about Kit Wilkes's place. And about him. Everyone knows about him." She beckoned for Annette to come over. Reluctantly the redhead moved toward the group.

"Hey! Why drag me away?"

"That prick's not up for it," Marian replied, jerking her head toward Lim

Chang. "Why waste your time? We're just having a few drinks and a chat here. I was just talking about Wilkes. The bastard's pretending to be asleep again, but he's listening. Doesn't miss a trick." She turned back to Oliver. "I did a party with him a while back, rough stuff. He likes—"

"I don't think you should tell me."

"Suit yourself," she said, continuing anyway. "He was celebrating some deal in Russia, said they'd seeded a painter. Built up a whole history about some artist that doesn't even exist. He was laughing about the killing he'd made and said that the Russians were stupid and ignorant—which he said was even worse."

Surprised, Oliver glanced at Kit Wilkes. Underestimating the Russians was folly. Twenty years ago they hadn't known much about the international art trade, but now they were as well versed, as ruthless, and as rich as everyone else.

"He's a bastard," Marian said flatly, turning her attention away from Wilkes and back to Oliver. "So I take it that you've never been on one of Bernie's hunting parties," she said.

Oliver frowned. "Pardon?"

"When there's a big international show on in London or New York, he gets a group of dealers together with a group of whores and then gives the girls money to buy a painting. If the painting the girl buys turns out to be more valuable than the dealer's, she gets to keep the money." She smiled, taunting Oliver. "That's what it's all about, isn't it? Money? Liza pulled off a real coup last year. Not bad for a whore. But then again, whores get to hear and find out all sorts of things."

They both watched Liza walk over to the bar, where she ignored the young male attendant and accepted a tray of snacks from the older man who had attended to Bernie earlier. Un-self-conscious in her bra and panties, she returned to the group and passed the platter around.

Liza sat down and then stared intently at Oliver.

"Jesus," she said, sounding alarmed. "Are you all right?"

Two

OLIVER FLINCHED, WELL AWARE THAT THE GIRL HAD SPOTTED something, some intimation of illness. Or was it just his wretched unease with the conversation?

"I'm fine."

"You just look so pale. Are you sure you're okay?" Liza persisted. She helped herself to a couple of prawn canapés and crossed her legs in the lotus position, revealing the crotch of her panties. Oliver glanced away, and Marian turned to Liza. "I was telling Sir Oliver about Bernie's hunting parties. How you'd gotten really lucky last year,"

She turned back to Oliver. "God, you should see your face!" she exclaimed, her expression defiant, her tone confrontational. "You think we're just whores, don't you? We are, but we're also the best, most cultured whores. I've a degree in the history of art, with honors, and I worked in a gallery on Cork Street until I realized I could make more money on my back than behind a desk." The alcohol didn't seem to have had the slightest effect on Marian's brain; she was sharp as a tack.

"We all work for the same woman: Mrs. Fleet. Bernie hires her girls because we fuck the best *and* we can talk about art—because most of her clients are dealers. We fit in, you see. We impress the collectors, make them feel at home. We know all about the auctions and the reserves and the prices raised on different works. We know dealers on the way up and those on the way down. We make it our business to know who bought what where and for how much."

Discomforted, Oliver smiled but said nothing. Undaunted, Marian continued.

"We're an open secret, part of the haggling, the extra on the side. We can *make* a deal. Straight sex, blow job, anal, girl on girl, S&M, golden showers. . . . You want it? We deliver. It's a perk some of the biggest dealers use, an added incentive." Her expression was cold. "So before you wonder again how some hooker knows about art, *that's* how."

She glanced over to the bar, where Lim Chang was sipping a glass of wine, out of earshot. In the window seat, Kit Wilkes was immobile, a cashmere rug over his knees.

"Remember Arnold Fletcher?" Liza asked. Marian shot her a warning look. "I was just about to say—"

"Fletcher's no worse than the other dealers."

"Maybe not, but you have to admit he was desperate to get hold of that Gauguin," Liza went on. Addressing Oliver, she said, "You're in the business; you know how it works. Dealers are always plotting something."

It was true, Oliver thought. Collectors always plotted—always *had* plotted. In the Renaissance, they murdered to steal masterpieces, to procure the power that priceless works afforded them. In modern times, the Nazis had looted galleries, and many a dictator had bought works—through anonymous brokers—from respectable auction houses. Stolen artworks had created a feeding frenzy of their own, a rivalry as ruthless as the people drafted to run it. Since the middle of the twentieth century, Mafia connections and, later, the Russian mob had perpetuated the demimonde of the art dealing fraternity. Works were thieved to order, exorbitant prices paid to move valuable works from England to collections abroad.

In the two decades he had been trading, Oliver Peters had been privy to many of the secrets of dealing and fakery. Collectors would show a genuine work to a buyer in a gallery and then instruct the collector to mark the back of the painting. When the picture was brought to him or her later, the collector would check it, never questioning that it was genuine because it had his or her marking on the reverse. Few ever discovered that a false back had been put on the original painting and they had in fact marked—and *bought*—a fake.

And it wasn't just pictures. Stone statues had been buried in lime and coated with urine to age them; exquisite, dainty pieces of ivory were secreted in women's cleavages, where sweat gradually turned the material to an aged yellow. The tricks of forgery had been handed down the centuries. In trading church statues, false heads had been put on the dismembered figures in order to sell them for the highest price. The fakers—knowing that under x-ray the joins could show up as recent material—ground stone off the original statue to make a join appear genuine.

Like many dealers, Oliver had heard of masterpieces being stolen and disappearing from sight to reemerge decades later, having hopped flealike around the globe. Copies frequently were made by master fakers, something all artists of all times had had to come to terms with. But in the reckless art world an unscrupulous dealer would pass on a fake and retain the original to sell to an anonymous collector, who would keep it out of public view. As for the runners who undertook the transportation of stolen goods, the fences who were cheated by their bosses, the myriad people who populated the fuggy underbelly of the art market, they had often been jailed or disappeared. And no one asked questions.

Slowly, Oliver reached into his inside pocket and took out a small bottle of tablets. Liza, noticing, offered him a glass of water and fetched it. Gratefully sipping it, he swallowed two more diamorphine.

"You *sure* you're all right?" Liza asked.

"Just a headache."

"You look awfully pale—"

"No, really; it's nothing."

Nodding, she moved off to the bar, where Annette and Marian joined her for a drink. Pleased to be relieved of their company, Oliver glanced over his shoulder. Lim Chang was typing something into his BlackBerry, his concentration absolute.

"Are you working?" Oliver asked, interrupting the woodpecker tapping.

The man looked up, his lean features composed, his black hair punctuated by a precise parting, one narrow hand suspended, immobile, over the BlackBerry.

"Pardon?"

"I asked if you were working," Oliver replied, realizing how stilted the sentence sounded coming out of the blue after hours of silence. "Did you buy anything at the auction?"

"You were there, Sir Oliver."

"I was, but not all the time," he replied, trying to recover his usual confidence. "I bid for the Gainsborough but lost it to the Getty Museum."

Lim Chang's hand was still suspended above the BlackBerry.

"I bought a Sisley."

"Sisley . . . good, good," Oliver responded idiotically as the pain jabbed at his stomach. Smiling, he took the seat opposite Lim Chang. "Long journey, hey?"

"Long journey," Chang agreed.

"Kit Wilkes has been asleep most of the time. Not as active as our host," Oliver went on, smiling as though they shared a joke. "I can't say I feel very comfortable."

There was a protracted pause. Oliver wondered if he had said the wrong thing and if Lim Chang would turn out to be a close friend of the Australian's—and a willing passenger. But after what seemed several minutes, Lim Chang laid his BlackBerry on the small table in front of him and nodded briefly.

"I also feel a little . . . out of place."

Oliver sighed, thinking of home and how much he wanted to be in bed— Sonia next to him—nursing a glass of brandy and a copy of *The Burlington Magazine*.

"I was talking to the girls."

"I only spoke to one girl," Lim Chang offered, as though that minimized the offense. "What were they saying to you?"

"They were just talking about their work. Well, about who they worked for. . . . I didn't know they'd be like that. Well read, intelligent. It's not what you expect." Uncomfortable, he slid off the subject. "We've still got hours to go before we get to London. Are you going to work until then?"

In answer, Lim Chang looked at the BlackBerry and then glanced back at his fellow passenger. He seemed to be toying with his answer.

"I think," he said finally, "that perhaps I've worked long enough."

Two more awkward hours passed, Oliver in an agony of physical pain and mental unease and Lim Chang reserved, difficult company. Sleeping most of the time, Kit Wilkes barely stirred; the stewards attended to the passengers' needs with quiet efficiency. Back in the private cabin, the girls were back to amusing Bernie, only occasionally tripping through to fetch drinks or go to the bathroom. Their lack of both clothing and any kind of inhibition was unnerving, and when the pilot announced that the plane would be landing in ten minutes, Lim Chang and Oliver Peters breathed a genuine sigh of relief.

Then, just when the passengers were getting ready to prepare for landing, a befuddled Bernie Freeland, his eyes bloodshot, suddenly staggered and stumbled into the main cabin. Although a known teetotaler, to all appearances he was very drunk.

Lurching toward Oliver, he leaned forward.

"Jesus, I feel ill," he said, wrenching open the top of his shirt. "Listen to me," he whispered between short, rasping breaths, and leaned closer to Oliver. "If anything happens to me. If anything happens—"

"What are you saying?"

"Just listen," he urged, his voice hoarse, his breath foul, "I can trust you. I know that. . . . I've got the Hogarth, the painting the art world's always talked about. Guy Manners stole it; then he panicked and offered it to me."

"What are you talking about?"

"The missing Hogarth—I've got it."

Three

OLIVER WAS HAVING TROUBLE HEARING OVER THE NOISE OF THE engines, but it was obvious to him that Bernie Freeland was close to panic, and the other passengers were turning around and straining to listen.

"Bernie, sit down."

"*NO! Listen to me!*" His voice was almost a hiss. "It's the famous Hogarth . . . the picture with the Prince of Wales in it."

Startled, Oliver gripped the arm of his seat; the plane was lurching, and the older steward came and hurried Bernie to his seat and put on his safety belt. His eyes wide, Bernie stared imploringly at Oliver across the aisle, then slid off into a drugged torpor.

"What's wrong with him?" Oliver asked Malcolm Jenner, the steward, who was bending down toward his employer.

"I think someone's spiked his drink," Jenner replied, his voice low. "One of the girls probably, for a laugh. They know Mr. Freeland can't handle it. Any alcohol has a really bad effect on him." He nodded toward Oliver, all brisk competence. "Don't worry; it'll wear off. Mr. Freeland won't remember a thing later."

Mr. Freeland won't remember a thing. . . . Oliver hoped not. Leaning back in his seat, he was suddenly aware that both Kit Wilkes and Lim Chang were staring at him. He closed his eyes, Bernie's Freeland's words echoing in his head:

I've got the Hogarth painting. The one the art world's always talked about. . . . It's the Hogarth with the Prince of Wales in it. . . .

Oh, Jesus, why? Oliver thought. *Why now?* He felt a queasy terror, his blood running faster, his brain pumping. Was it true that Bernie Freeland had the painting of the Prince of Wales with his whore, Polly Gunnell?

Oliver tried to keep calm. How *could* the Australian have the Hogarth? And what had he said about Guy Manners selling it to him? Manners, a notorious gambler who hung around the art world like a ghoul. Adopted by a wealthy banker, he had been a troubled child, expelled from Eton for theft and later disowned by his family. Oliver thought about the Hogarth, the third picture in the lost series of *The Harlot's Progress*, which was the artist's damning criticism of his society—of prostitution, of the whorehouses, the pimps, the lechers of his time. The world had believed it long destroyed, and it was imperative that everyone continue to believe that.

Because only he, Oliver Peters, knew the painting still existed—*because he had it.*

Or did he?

Four

THE CAR PARK WAS QUIET. OLIVER LEANED BACK IN HIS SEAT, remembering the last minutes of that fateful plane journey. He knew that soon he would begin his drive home, but not until he had composed himself. Closing his eyes, he could picture the events as though they were taking place again. The jet had been circling, coming in to land at Heathrow, while Oliver stared at Bernie Freeland in open shock as the Australian's words reverberated in his head. Guy Manners had stolen the Hogarth, then sold it? If that was true, it would matter more to his confidant than Freeland realized.

Because they had stolen the painting from him.

Oliver knew that it hadn't been taken from his gallery—the Hogarth had never been housed there—but from the bank where he had a safety deposit box. The same bank where the Hogarth had been placed over fifteen years ago when his elderly father had passed it on to him.

"Guard it with your life," his father had urged. "The painting has incredible power. Men would kill to own it." His father had paused and then told him, "There is also an inscribed ring with a message from the Prince of Wales. Together, they prove the existence of a royal bastard. For safety's sake, the ring must *never* be hidden with the painting. It *must* be kept separate." He had clutched Oliver's arm tightly. "If this evidence fell into the wrong hands, it could bring down the monarchy. But of the two, the painting is the more important because no one knows of the existence of the ring."

Oliver had looked at his father in astonishment and disbelief. "Why hasn't the picture been destroyed?" he'd asked.

"Because it's proof. Like the ring. Without them there's no evidence; with them there's confirmation that there's an alternative successor to the English throne. One day it might be useful. If the House of Windsor faltered after the queen's death, there would be an alternative." He had paused again, an old man passing on an inheritance he revered and feared at the same time. "No one must ever know about Polly Gunnell's child. And no one must *ever* find out that there's a living descendant."

Oliver's mind went back to the flight. He had sat in his seat, rigid, thanking God that they were coming down to land before people could use their BlackBerries or cell phones. No one, he had reassured himself, could have made contact with his or her cohorts on the ground. No one could have passed on the damning news about the Hogarth. Or maybe, he had thought hopefully, none of them had overheard Bernie Freeland's garbled, panicked confession.

Then again, maybe they had. . . .

He relived those minutes, sitting in the plane, his mind churning. Had Freeland *really* got the Hogarth, or had he been duped? Perhaps the work was a fake . . . perhaps there was nothing to worry about. Maybe the Hogarth *hadn't* gotten into Bernie Freeland's hands. It was intolerable to imagine how the painting's secret might have been exposed, touted around by the likes of the Australian: the scandal fanned for the sake of publicity, the royal family humiliated, and, worse, the line of succession threatened. Freeland wasn't the type to act nobly, not when there was money in ignominy. *At least the ring hadn't been stolen*, Oliver thought with relief. *That* damning piece of evidence had been hidden elsewhere and remained safe.

Thinking back, Oliver remembered how he had turned to look at Kit Wilkes, thinking, *Please, God, don't let him be in on it.* If Wilkes knew the secret, it would be exposed as soon as they arrived at Heathrow. Realizing that he was being watched, Wilkes had looked up and caught Oliver's gaze. A knowing smile had flickered around the fleshy lips before he had turned his attention back to his magazine. *What had that been about?* Oliver had wondered. *Had he been intimating that he had heard what Bernie Freeland said? Or had it just been that ambiguous smile of his, which only just managed to be this side of a sneer?* Unsettled, Oliver had leaned back in his seat, staring out of the window as the airport came into view. If it was the real Hogarth, he had to get it back. *He had to.* He had breathed in, trying to steady himself.

Just as he was breathing in now in the confines of the airport car park, locked into his Daimler, unable to move, to go home, to think of the repercussions of one explosive remark. If the news came out, everyone would be after the picture. To own it—or to destroy it. Unbidden, his thoughts turned to Lim Chang, recalling the man's placid expression as they had landed. God, had *he* heard what Bernie Freeland had said?

He knew the extent of the task that faced him. He would be up against interested parties who would vie ruthlessly for the masterpiece for their own reasons. Some would want to expose and profit from the royal scandal, a scandal that could have changed the course of history and that might still undermine the House of Windsor. And then there were others who would want to make sure the painting was *never* seen, the truth of the alternative succession forever suppressed.

One thing was for certain: the picture would be worth a fortune on the open market. Every country on earth would scrabble to own it. And its secret. But to what lengths would some interested parties go to make sure the secret was kept? Oliver shuddered, remembering his maternal ancestor, the sly courtier Sir Nathaniel Overton. The man who had used the painting like the sword of Damocles, suspending it over the heads of the unsuspecting royals. But gradually, over the generations, the weapon had changed its use, finally becoming a treasured and protected secret. Oliver sighed. If the real Hogarth *was* waiting to be sprung, it could turn out to be the most pernicious jack-in-the-box in history. Worth stealing.

And well worth killing for.

The secret discovered by Overton so long ago *had* to be kept at all costs. But the only man who knew the whole truth was he, Oliver Peters. He and he alone. From choice he had cultivated no confidants. There were no advisers, no other relatives privy to the truth, and his son was still a boy, too young to inherit the secret. There was only he to succeed or fail. To protect or neglect.

And he was tired to the bone, mortally afraid, and riddled with cancer. He, Oliver Peters, had only weeks left to live.

Five

WHEN HE FINALLY RETURNED HOME, OLIVER PARKED THE CAR IN THE garage and walked out into the garden. The lights were on in an upstairs bedroom, but otherwise the house was in darkness. As he had hoped, his wife was preparing for bed. He could imagine her taking off her clothes and hanging them in the walk-in closet, dropping whatever needed cleaning into the white laundry hamper for the housekeeper to deal with. She would step out of her shoes and pad into the bathroom, her narrow feet making imprints on the carpet. Whatever the fashion, Sonia liked carpet under her feet, liked the feel of the wool, the give of the luxurious pile.

Oliver was in love with Sonia. He had *always* been in love with her. For all the oppressive duty of his inheritance, his love for his wife had always been calm, steady, graceful. Staring up at the bedroom window, Oliver let himself imagine Sonia's nightly routine, the silly vanity of products that promised a reversal of experience, a wicked rubbing out of the marionette lines around the mouth he had watched develop over years, along with the slight lengthening of the earlobes, the hardly discernible pigmentation under the eyes that darkened in summer. The measured, minute infractions of her beauty that to him were beautiful in themselves.

In a few minutes he would enter the house and act normally. Just as he had withheld the gravity of his illness from his wife, he would withhold the theft of the Hogarth. It was his only comfort to know that by keeping her in ignorance he could retain a pretense of normal life for a little longer. Before exposure. Or worse, if he failed—before disgrace.

The royal bastard, the offspring of Polly Gunnell and the Prince of Wales, had been a rumor in the art world since Hogarth's day. But it was nothing substantial, merely gossip to be shrugged off as just another salacious tidbit. To the general public it was one of the many romantic storylines about the English royalty, but Oliver knew otherwise. The royal bastard *had* existed. And had survived. In fact, his descendant was now living and working in Europe, blissfully unaware of his parentage.

Only a handful of people at the time of his birth and subsequently had ever known the secret of the royal bastard, and all of them had been loyal servants of the Crown—especially the opportunistic Sir Nathaniel Overton, admired and feared in equal measure. Overton's hold over the Georgian court had been legendary, his means ruthless, his protection of the royal family absolute. Although thinking that some of his ancestor's methods were suspect, Oliver recognized that Overton had been perfectly placed when the scandal broke. Acting quickly, he had forced Hogarth to remove the image of the Prince of Wales from his painting, and any mention of a bastard child had been ruthlessly suppressed. To all intents and purposes, Polly Gunnell and her child had simply disappeared, and the only proof of any liaison between the prince and the prostitute was the painting and the ring. The ring was safe, but the painting. Bernie Freeland claimed, was now in his possession.

The question of who had stolen the painting—and how—played relentlessly in Oliver's mind. But then it was surpassed by another, even more unwelcome, notion. If Bernie Freeland *did* have the Hogarth, how much did he know about its history? Was the lusty Australian just smug at the thought of owning such a prize, or was it the value of the painting that mattered? Perhaps there was more to it.Could Freeland possibly know the story *behind* the picture? And if he did, was he clever enough to keep quiet? Was he discreet? Honorable?

A whirlpool of questions flooded Oliver's thoughts: Could he get to Freeland before anyone else did? Could he regain the Hogarth before other factions intervened, factions Freeland would neither anticipate nor be able to control? Could he save the painting *and* the Australian, or would Bernie Freeland turn out to be a blundering fool? Would the man prove brave or reckless? If threatened, would he run? Or would he fight to protect knowledge that others had died for?

In short, did a loudmouthed man who ran with whores and couldn't hold his liquor know the secret? Know of the blood that marred the English throne?

Dear God, Oliver prayed, *let him be ignorant and stupid. Let him be a fool who knew nothing—and thus would live.*

Six

FLINGING HER CASE ONTO HER BED IN THE AIRPORT HOTEL AT Heathrow, Marian Miller flopped down beside it, staring at the light over her head. It was a godsend—if you believed in God—but it was fucking lucky anyway, and that was a fact. She touched her stomach with the index finger of her left hand, then jabbed it into her flesh. What a mess! What a bloody mess! Getting pregnant; what a fucking screw-up that was, she cursed. Well, she knew that she had to get rid of it, but until the Freeland trip, she had been short on cash. She'd recently spent her savings buying and furnishing a new apartment, and it would normally take at least a couple of weeks to raise enough to pay for a discreet abortion in a private clinic.

Of course, if Mrs. Fleet happened to find out first—which she well might, as Marian's checkup was due with the obnoxious Dr. Fountain—there would be hell to pay. Every one of Mrs. Fleet's girls was warned never to get pregnant, but Marian had always been told that she was infertile, rendered sterile by one too many abortions in her teens. However, now that her hormones had pulled this peevish, inconvenient little stunt, it appeared that the condition had been temporary,

Luckily, she had a way out. Her little jaunt on Bernie Freeland's jet had made her a pile of welcome—and quick—money. Enough to get her sorted out within twenty-four hours—if she tipped Dr. Fountain a bit of cash on the side for arranging it.

Putting in a call to Mrs. Fleet, Marian Miller got straight down to business.

"You won't believe what I just heard on Bernie Freeland's jet."

Mrs. Fleet was all glacial poise. "Is that you, Marian?"

"Yeah, it's me—with some news which is worth real money. And don't say you're not interested; you're always interested. I'll sell you the information."

"Really?"

Confident, Marian crossed her legs as she sat on the edge of the bed, kicking off her shoes and rubbing her left foot. For the last two years she had been selling information to her madam, passing on tips and gossip that could be useful later or news about a painting that would be vital to interested parties. It didn't happen often because her johns were mostly discreet, but some liked to talk, to brag, and Marian listened. And passed it all on, which had made her indispensable to Mrs. Fleet. In fact, over time, Marian had created a lucrative little niche for herself as the perfect spy, an adept sexual quisling.

"It's worth good money."

"You expect me to buy blind?"

"I've never let you down before," said Marian, "and this one's big, very big. Worth a couple of thousand, at least."

"So what *is* this great piece of news?"

"It's about a famous painting."

"What about it?"

"Pay me first," Marian pushed her. "Put a couple of thousand in my account today and I'll tell you."

Surprised, Mrs. Fleet took a moment to reply. "You can have the money, Marian, if what you tell me is worth it, but pay you before you tell me? Never."

"I need the money today!"

"Why the rush? You're not short of funds, are you?" Mrs. Fleet probed. "Not getting a liking for cocaine again, I hope. I don't use girls who take drugs—"

"I'm not on drugs."

"So what d'you want the money for?"

"Look, Mrs. Fleet," she replied sharply. "I work hard for you. I make good money for you, and I pass on interesting information to you, but I don't have to tell you what I spend my fucking money on."

"Very well. But why'd you want the money today? Why can't you tell me the news before I pay you?" She paused and then, sounding amused, said, "Oh, dear, you don't trust me, do you? You think I'll take the information and refuse to pay."

Irritated, Marian spoke before thinking. "I could go somewhere else."

"Now that *would* be stupid," Mrs. Fleet replied, nettled. "I thought we had a good relationship, Marian. You don't want to go threatening me, do you?"

Marian caught the chill in her tone and backed down.

"Okay, Mrs. Fleet; Bernie Freeland's got hold of a Hogarth. The one which shows the Prince of Wales with his whore."

"That was destroyed a long time ago."

"No. He's got it. He told Oliver Peters on the jet."

"Sir Oliver Peters? He was a passenger?" She sounded surprised.

"Bernie offered him a lift. He was uncomfortable the whole journey, the stuffed shirt. Anyway, someone spiked Bernie's drink for a laugh—"

"You?"

"Nah, I think it was Annette. She loves practical jokes," Marian said, hurrying on. "Anyway, Bernie panicked, thought he was dying, and whispered something to Oliver Peters about having this painting—only it wasn't such a whisper, if you get what I mean."

"So other people could have heard what he said?"

"Yeah," Marian agreed. "They could have. And some *were* acting a bit twitchy afterward. But we were coming in to land, so no one could do anything."

"Who else was on that flight besides you girls and Peters?"

"Kit Wilkes."

"And?"

"Lim Chang."

"Odd bunch," Mrs. Fleet said thoughtfully. "So we have three of the biggest dealers in the art world. Wilkes representing Russia, Lim Chang representing Asia, and Oliver Peters representing the UK. It's almost like the United Nations." She paused, considering what she had just heard. "So *if* the other passengers overheard what Bernie said, they could already be passing the information on to their contacts?"

"Yeah, but—"

"So why should I pay you if it might be common knowledge within hours?"

"It might. But then again, it might not," Marian replied briskly. "It could just be Sir Oliver Peters who heard, and me, of course. We could be the only two who know."

"You could, yes."

"And if it's *not* common knowledge, it gives you a head start, doesn't it? I reckon my tip-off's worth a couple of thousand, don't you?"

There was a long silence before Mrs. Fleet spoke again.

"As it happens, I've got a meeting near the airport this evening. I'll come by around eight, Mariah . . . with your money. Will cash do?"

"Fine."

"I've also got a new client for you at the hotel later tonight."

"Name?"

"Sergei Ivanovitch," Mrs. Fleet replied, adding, "I don't have to tell you to keep this Hogarth information to yourself, do I?"

"I won't say a word."

"Good girl. No point letting the world in on our little secret, is there?"

Seven

For many, Victor Ballam personified luck. Lucky in his ability and his business acumen. Fortunate in his good looks, his brain, and his quick wits, he was neither showy nor arrogant and was not verbally cruel. He knew he was fortunate and never took his luck for granted, a trait that earned him friends even in the bullpen of the London art world. So it was obvious that Victor would fall in love with a woman of beauty and intelligence. She was a svelte Norwegian law student, and with such a consort Victor's rise continued unabated, a glossy future predicted, even confirmed.

Always careful not to antagonize people, Victor managed to navigate the sales and auctions with skill and had opened his own gallery on Dover Street at the age of thirty. For an uncommon man, he had the common touch. And bobbing in a suffocating soup of egos, he remained naturally humble. Without resorting to dirty tricks, sleazy deals, or baited gossip, Victor Ballam—an uncrowned potentate, an impassioned counsel for the wronged—was respected and admired for his fairness and circumspection. He spoke out about the grubbier side of the art world and had become a media pet. He was blessed in his work and in his personal life.

No one had expected him to lose it all.

No one expected him to spend three years, four months, and five days in prison. It should have been six years, but Victor Ballam got time off for good behavior, enabling him to return to his old life more quickly. But the old life had packed up and moved on, emigrated to some moral high ground without leaving a forwarding address. Alarmed by its association with a proven fraudster, colleagues from Ballam's previous existence had taken offense, and all but some loose change of them had disowned him.

He came out of Long Lartin Prison on a bitter Worcestershire morning with just a brown paper package and slid into the passenger seat of a waiting Volvo, watched by the driver, his older brother, Christian. Christian had practiced his welcome speech for days, tutored by his wife, Ingola. She had been Victor's beautiful Norwegian fiancée, but at Victor's insistence—a year to the day after his internment—she had married his older brother. They had investigated and exhausted every alternative way to keep her in England, but in the end the solution was simple. Painful but simple. And in some strange way the marriage kept Ingola close to Victor, still a part of his life albeit not his lover.

Victor had always known Ingola's faults, had accepted her ambition and a certain ruthlessness as part of her nature. She might love him with intensity, but her own interests were her first priority. If she was threatened, she assumed she would be protected. And she was. So, as Victor's star fell to earth, Ingola was persuaded to let Christian save her.

It had been summer. The wedding was held at the registry office, and Victor sent a letter to both of them, wishing them well, and another addressed only to his brother:

> Christian
>
> Look after Ingola as I would have done. You'll make a good husband, she needs that, she deserves that. She'll make a fine lawyer some day, and do a lot better without a husband with a criminal record.
>
> Don't feel bad about taking my place.
>
> Don't try to excuse me.
>
> Don't hurt her.

What he thought but did not write was different:

> She can stay in England as a married woman. I'd have done that for her, and now I can't, you can.
>
> Don't make love to her. . . . Of course you can, of course you must. . . . Don't listen to her. . . . About Norway, about the way she likes her eggs cooked, about how she knows all the tunes to *Les Misérables*.
>
> Don't let her down.
>
> Don't remind her, don't let her talk about me. Don't let her look back. I can do that for both of us.

"You okay?" Christian asked, breaking into his brother's thoughts. Surreptitiously, he looked him up and down as they stopped at some traffic lights, heading for the house where he and Ingola lived in the countryside.

He saw in Victor a little weight loss, a bit of unexpected, premature crinkling around the eyes, but the hair was still dark and the eyes darker. And for all his crumpled clothes—folded too long in prison storage, leaving creases in the wrong places—Victor Ballam still retained his glamour, which, allied to an alert brain and honed ambition, made him memorably appealing. Christian might have the intellect, the professional respect, and the striking wife, but Victor—even *this* Victor—had the charisma.

"The lights have changed," Victor said, winking at his brother, who drove on.

"I thought we would go out for dinner—or we could stay in. Ingola said she would cook, and you know what a good cook she is." *Of course he knows,* Christian thought, irritated with himself. Catching sight of his thinning hairline, he wondered why he had inherited the male pattern baldness. But then again, he had inherited Ingola too, so what right did he have to feel jealous? But he had always felt jealous of his brother. "Whatever you want to do tonight, Victor, is fine."

"I'm not staying."

Christian glanced over at him. "What!"

"You heard me; I'm not staying here. I'm going back to London. Thanks for picking me up, Christian. I appreciate that, but if you'll drop me at the station—"

"*London?*"

"That's where I live. I was only put in Long Lartin because of the *nature* of my crime. What's the matter—haven't they got a color you like?" Victor gestured to the traffic lights as they changed from amber back to red. Behind them, cars started sounding their horns. "I have to get home," he continued. "I can't stay here."

"Go back in a while, when you've had a rest."

"If I don't go back now, I'll keep putting it off," Victor replied. "Thanks, incidentally, for sorting everything out. I mean . . . you know what I mean."

Before being jailed Victor had taken the opportunity to sign over his London apartment and furniture to his brother for safekeeping. Everything else his talent and skill had earned him over the previous sixteen years had been taken away or repossessed. His personal belongings remained within the Ballam family, but they were to all intents and purposes no longer his. He knew that Christian would never make any reference to their arrangement, but the contrast between having total control of his life and being in tandem with his sibling was marked. And it irked Victor, made him all the more eager to leave Worcestershire and try to regain his old life.

"Thanks for keeping an eye on the flat, too."

"No problem," Christian replied. "Your neighbor was very helpful, and when I couldn't get down to London, Ingola called in. Picked up any letters and packages and sent them on to you."

"It must have been a lot of trouble."

"No, not at all." Christian's tone was strained. He wanted to say something that would break the tension between them, but the words floated above his brain, just out of reach. Instead, he came across as faintly patronizing. "It was the least we could do. I would have visited more, you know, if you'd let me."

"You did more than enough," Victor replied, changing the subject. "I have to get back to London. You understand, don't you? If I put it off, I'll never go back. Anyway, I don't have anything up here. All my things are in the apartment."

"You'll be lonely."

"Jesus," Victor said, moved and trying hard not to show it. "You sound like you used to sound when we were going back to boarding school. I had to go into another house, under another housemaster, and you said, 'You'll be lonely,' when you really meant *you* would be." He paused, remembering the past, then asked, "How's Mother?"

"Fine."

"Does she know I'm out?"

"She hasn't been well. . . ."

"I see. So she doesn't know."

"I thought I'd tell her when she's feeling a bit better."

"And pray for a relapse?" Victor asked, his tone light but with an edge underneath.

From the day he had been sentenced, the widowed Celeste Ballam had disowned her second son. Ignoring his existence was preferable to lying or trying to concoct a parallel universe where Victor was still trading as a London art dealer in Dover Street. He was always her favorite child, but the professional scandal that had turned him from a glittering scion of the Ballam clan to a thief with a criminal record had buckled her. To Victor she had entrusted the status of the family. From Victor she had expected an impressive career and an enviable marriage.

Celeste had possessed the maternal smugness that came from having an exceptional child, and so when Victor's fall came, it torpedoed her future and capsized her status absolutely. But that was not all. Her son the thief had done something even worse: his crime had forced Celeste into having to idolize Christian, the second choice.

"If you go back to London now, what will you do, Victor?"

"Work."

Christian didn't really want his brother close by, was afraid that Ingola might still have feelings for him, but at the same time he was trying to be supportive. He had been the winner, after all. He could afford to be magnanimous.

"Work? Where?"

"Not at the gallery; I know that's out of bounds." Victor opened the brown paper package and rummaged through the few possessions in it. "Don't worry about me, I'll survive."

"I was thinking. . . . I spoke to a friend of mine. He could get you a job in Chipping Campden."

"As an art dealer?"

"Well, not really. He has a restaurant."

"You want me to be a waiter?"

"It's a start."

"Of what? Penury?"

Christian sighed, slowing down to the thirty-mile-an-hour speed limit. "You might find it hard to get a job now. What with your having a record . . ."

"Well, I'm glad you pointed that out, because I'd never have thought of it."

"I'm just trying to help," Christian responded in an injured tone.

"By expecting me to be a fucking waiter?" Victor countered, then cooled his tone, ashamed. "I'm not running away from London, Christian. If I don't go back, I'll look guilty."

"You're not thinking . . ."

"Of what?"

Christian took a deep breath. "Of trying to find out who framed you, are you?"

"For over three years I've thought about nothing else. Every day and every night I've gone over everything that happened."

"D'you know who did it?"

"Oh, yes," Victor replied evenly.

"You do?"

"I did it to myself."

"What d'you mean? You weren't guilty!"

"I was guilty of speaking out. Guilty of going on record about the forgeries, the fixed auctions, the rigged sales. I named names and courted the press to further my own fucking bandwagon. I thought people wanted to know the truth, and I thought I could get away with telling it. I mean, I *was* right, wasn't I?"

"Victor—"

But Victor carried on. "Being right's not enough, though. I suppose they built up their case for years. In the end it wasn't one person after me; it was a whole coterie of dealers, all of them more established and a bloody sight more ruthless than I was."

"They framed you for fraud."

"Yeah," Victor agreed. "But I can't get my own back. If it was one person, I could go after him, but a group? Never. Like they say, there's safety in numbers. The art world doesn't appreciate being threatened, and if it is, it closes ranks and suffocates the threat."

He wiped the condensation off the window next to him and looked out to the street, which was desolate under a downpour. "The only thing they won't expect is my return."

Christian struggled to keep the impatience out of his voice.

"But why bother if you can't get revenge?"

"Jesus, Christian, what's the alternative? You'd have me *hide*?"

"I'd have you safe," his brother replied, driving off as the lights changed. "You know they won't give you work."

"*Who* won't give me work, Christian? The dealers, the brokers, the auction houses? You think I *expect* to get work there? You think anyone would trust me now? I'd be lucky if I could get in the back door, let alone the front, of anyone's gallery."

"So who are you going to work for?" There was a protracted pause; Christian stole a quick look at his brother. "Victor, who *are* you going to work for?"

"It's a crooked business. There's enough work to keep me occupied."

Pulling over, Christian parked, turned off the engine, and looked at his brother in disbelief.

"Please tell me you're joking, Victor. Please, Victor, don't get mixed up in anything dodgy. It would ruin your life."

"It isn't ruined now?"

Christian looked straight ahead, trying to form his argument without sounding like the paternal older brother.

"Don't give up. Don't go down the wrong road. They put you there; you didn't do it. You're not a criminal."

"In the eyes of the world I am."

"But you know you're not!" Christian went on hurriedly. "Just concentrate on keeping on the right side of the law now. I'm sure you could get it all back, Victor. I'm sure you could in time if you work hard, keep your nose clean. People will forget. In time they will." He blundered on. "You were popular, well known. People liked you; they couldn't help themselves. They always liked you. People will *want* to forgive you."

"You think I'm guilty, Christian?"

"No, no! I didn't say that."

"It sounded like that."

Christian, confused, blundered on. "No, that wasn't what I meant. I . . ."

"People will want to forgive you," Victor repeated and, tucking the parcel under his arm, got out of the car.

"Victor!" Christian called after him. "Don't rush off. That wasn't what I meant."

Bending down, Victor looked into his brother's face, his scrutiny making Christian flush. "Ask me."

"Ask you what?"

"You know. It's what you've wanted to ask me for years. What you've *always* wanted to ask me."

Christian squirmed in his seat. "For God's sake!"

"Ask me."

"There's nothing I want to—"

"*Ask* me!"

"All right! Did you do it?"

"Go to hell," Victor said quietly, "but don't take Ingola with you."

And with that he strode away.

Eight

THE HOTEL CHAMBERMAID KNOCKED ON THE DOOR, PAUSED, KNOCKED again, waited, then opened it with her passkey. The room was in darkness, so she flicked on the light and walked in, laying some fresh towels on the dressing table. Singing softly under her breath, she turned down the bed and smoothed the sheet, placing a mint on the pillowcase. She picked up the towels and moved toward the bathroom.

Still singing, she reached for the pull cord and blinked as the light came on, together with the rush of the exhaust fan. Pulling back the shower curtain, she replaced the used soap and then turned to the sink. She let out a strangled yelp and almost lost her footing as she saw, wedged between the sink and the toilet, the naked corpse of a young woman.

Nobody would have recognized Marian Miller. Her face had been bludgeoned to a pulp, her nose crushed, and her top lip driven into her teeth, giving her a rictus grin. Blood had matted her hair and dried on her breasts, and her left hand dangled in the toilet bowl, the fingers wrinkled from immersion in the water.

Terrified, the chambermaid backed away, trying to skirt the body without touching it, but as she rushed past, she caught Marian Miller's foot and tripped, sending her flying and the corpse sliding forward and falling across the entry of the bathroom door. It was as she picked herself up that the maid saw them—the silver coins. Coins that fell out of Marian Miller's gaping mouth.

The maid had not waited to count them, but later the coroner did. There were thirty coins. Thirty pieces of silver. All of them Russian rubles. And there was some hair under Marian Miller's fingernails. At first it was believed to be the hair of her killer, but under examination it turned out to be not human hair but fur.

Dog fur.

Nine

As Marian Miller's body was being discovered, Bernie Freeland was in New York City, turning the corner into Times Square, where he paused to look up at the poster of a seminaked girl advertising underwear. He felt a momentary frisson of sexual excitement but found it immediately dampened by the memory of the call girls on his last flight. *Why did they have to go and ruin everything?* he thought irritably. Of course he knew he would never be able to find out which one had spiked his flaming drink, but as soon as he had recovered, he'd phoned Mrs. Fleet. Any other practical jokes, he told her, and he'd never use her service again. Of course, she calmed him down in seconds, promising that she would admonish her girls and reminding Bernie that if he could find better whores anywhere, he was welcome to try.

But the spiked drink wasn't what most worried Bernie. He was nagged by a faint memory of confiding in Sir Oliver Peters about the Hogarth. He wondered if the memory had been merely a dream and prayed it had. Surely, even drugged, he wouldn't have confessed to having the painting. And yet . . . Bernie had always reacted very adversely to alcohol. He remembered the potency of the drink, the burning sensation as it hit his gut, the dizzying confusion of the brain that followed. He even remembered with embarrassment having thought that he was dying. That one of his rivals had heard of his coup and was murdering him.

The crushing sensation of panic had been very real. But had it been real enough to make him talk? Bernie stopped walking, trying to reassure himself. He was an astute businessman, used to keeping secrets, knowing when to keep his mouth shut. For all his outward bonhomie, he had always been professionally circumspect. Would he—even out of control—make such a stupid, reckless slip? He thought of the painting. The Hogarth could make him one of the most respected dealers in the world. Surely he wouldn't have told anyone about it. Surely, even drugged, he wouldn't have let that secret out—and to three whores and three rival dealers. Bernie shook his head. No, never.

But how could he know for sure?

Perhaps his half-remembered confession to Oliver Peters *had* been overheard. Perhaps Kit Wilkes was already spreading the news to the Russian dealers, trying to steal a march on Bernie's triumph. Wilkes was sly, clever with his acquisitions, only laziness keeping him out of the top rank. And then there was Lim Chang, the company man. The perfect, ruthless face of Chinese collecting. What wouldn't he do for the Hogarth?

Walking on, Bernie bent his head down against the wind. He felt a snuffle of panic coming on but stifled it. Tomorrow he would see Annette Dvorski again. She was to come to New York for the weekend. He had a present for her. His thoughts moved back to Hogarth. Never a fool, Bernie had had the painting authenticated by a discreet expert from Tokyo, a man he often used. Duly reassured, he returned to the seller, Guy Manners, who had a pressing need for money and a jumpy eagerness to off-load the picture. Manners had known that Bernie Freeland was greedy, ambitious, and keen to buy. The original series of *The Harlot's Progress* had been destroyed, Manners explained; only one scandalous picture had survived. The picture Bernie now owned.

His good temper restored, Bernie moved on. He could hardly believe his luck. Lucky Bernie Freeland. Serendipity had always been on his shoulder. Fate was good to him. Liked him. Even picked him out. Except that this time he wasn't *quite* as fortunate as he seemed. He had seen in the Hogarth painting an opportunity to own something rare and valuable, something any dealer would want. But he hadn't known the *full* history of the work.

Based in New York, Bernie Freeland dealt in European and American paintings from the nineteenth and twentieth centuries. In the past he had traded some Hogarth etchings but never a painting. His knowledge of and liking for the English painter's work were limited, so he didn't know why the painting had been hidden or why it could be so controversial. He didn't know why so many people, from the highest to the lowest in the land, would be after it. And he didn't know how ruthless they would be. He certainly didn't realize that what he had just bought was deadly and that his greed—greater than his learning—had made him vulnerable.

Deep in thought, Bernie made for the crossing and waited for the walk sign to come on. He was thrilled that he had managed to get the painting back to New York without declaring it. Smuggling was against the law, but he had chosen a clever hiding place. The don't walk light changed to walk, and Bernie stepped off the sidewalk. A woman brushed past him, and he muttered impatiently under his breath, feeling himself pushed along with the rest of the people crossing the road.

The lights changed, the traffic moved again, and Bernie—halfway across the street and looking out for a cab—felt a sudden and unexpected jab at the base of his solar plexus. The blow was so intense that it winded him and knocked him off balance, sending him spinning backward—right into the path of an oncoming cab. His arms flailing uselessly, Bernie saw the vehicle coming toward him and knew in a flash that it could neither swerve to avoid him nor stop in time.

The cab smashed into Bernie Freeland, sending him over the hood and into the path of an oncoming truck. Thrown under the massive vehicle, Bernie felt the first tires grind over his stomach, bursting his guts, and then roll over his legs. Screaming, he felt himself caught up and dragged along; the scream died in his throat as his chest was crushed, filling his mouth and throat with blood as his hands clawed feebly at the underside of the truck.

When the vehicle finally stopped, Bernie heard the low, guttural screaming of an animal and realized it was his own; he dimly saw feet gathering around the truck, a blur of horrified faces bending down to look at him. . . .

The skin of his chest had been stripped away, his top ribs were exposed, his twisted, partially severed right leg jerked uncontrollably. Blood poured from his burst eardrums and spurted from his jugular vein. The last thing Bernie Freeland was aware of as he left the world was the smell of burned rubber and the ominous drip of gasoline from the burst tank over his head.

Ten

I'm not sleeping. . . .

Victor Ballam turned over restlessly and reached out with his arm. He jerked his eyes open: his hand didn't touch the wall. *Where was the wall? Where was it? Of course! There* was *no wall!* He wasn't in a prison cell anymore; he was free. Yet for a moment longer his hand groped in the empty air, his glance moving urgently around the bedroom of his London apartment, searching for familiarity, reassurance.

But the early hours and the early light were making humped ghouls out of benign furniture. Which wasn't his anymore. It was signed over, given to Christian. Like the apartment. Like Ingola. Not his. Christian's.

He would ask for it back, all of it, Victor decided. He sat up and flicked on the lamp.

I'm not sleeping.

Who would he tell?

There was no one.

In the past, before disgrace, before jail, he would have turned to Ingola. He would have felt her warmth and rested his head on her thigh and said, *I'm not sleeping.*

Even in prison he might have said the words to his cell mate, but the apartment was empty. His apartment but not his apartment. His furniture but not his furniture.

Confused, his mind fuzzy from insomnia, Victor got to his feet and walked over to the closet. Pulling open the doors, he looked at the immaculate suits ranked in front of him. He stroked the fine wool and let his fingers run over the rows of silk ties and then closed his eyes, trying to remember how it felt to wear those expensive clothes. Tried but couldn't remember, because the man who had last worn them was no more. Gone with the headlines and the gossip and the fingers pointing. He had gone in the prison van. Gone. And he would never come back.

Frowning, Victor smelled the skin of his arm, convinced there was still the odor of jail about him.

I'm not sleeping.

Embarrassed, he felt the sting of tears begin at the back of his eyes and bit down on his lip. He thought about having a drink, then thought again. He searched for an old pack of cigarettes, then threw them away, unopened. Cartier, pearl-tipped, brought back from Paris.

Jesus, who was I?

Was that me?

Victor fought to control himself. He would talk to his probation officer, tell him that he couldn't sleep, that he felt disoriented, out of place. Tell them that he had been punished for something he hadn't done, that they had broken him, taken away Victor Ballam and left some alien in his place—a man who couldn't feel the walls around him and was afraid of space. A man making a prison out of his freedom.

I'm innocent, Victor told himself. *I didn't do anything.*

Perhaps he would do better talking to a shrink. But that would cost money, and he had precious little of that now.

His movements jerky, Victor returned to the closet. He picked out his most expensive suit and dressed himself, going through motions and rituals that required no thought, trying to put himself back into life through force of habit. When he had finished, he put on a little cologne and then turned to study his reflection in the mirror.

Who was this man? he wondered, staring at himself and seeing not the person who had stood there three and a half years earlier but some spirit brother. Some diminished, hollowed fraction of his whole.

Slowly Victor walked closer to the glass and touched it, tracing the line of his face on the mirror's surface.

I'm not sleeping.

The man in the mirror gazed back at him, sympathetic but bewildered. *You were me. . . .* Mesmerized, Victor kept looking at his reflection, then took off his suit and curled up on the bed, his knees touching his chest, his eyes closed against the waking light.

Eleven

SUNDAY. CITY BELLS WERE RINGING IN CHURCHES ALL OVER LONDON. Opulent bells on the Brompton Oratory, middle-class bells in middle-class postal codes, cheaper bells in the East End. Bells cracked by centuries, bells replaced, bells with clangers that had sounded every Sunday through outbreaks of war and coronations, Royal births and—every weekend—vicars' romps reported in the *People* newspaper. Rocking echoes of the call to worship clipped past the closed bars and clubs, the parked cars, and the Landseer lions in Trafalgar Square. Worn irritable by the asses of countless tourists, the lions remained fixed as ever, staring at the entrance doors of the National Gallery and the shuttlecock flippancy of the Sainsbury Wing.

Having spent the early morning walking around the center of London, Victor finally returned to his car and drove to the address he had been given in Mayfair. After coming within a hair's breadth of a nervous breakdown, Victor had slowly climbed back, and two weeks later he was unexpectedly approached by an old colleague, Arnold Fletcher. A historian and dealer with a paranoid desire for privacy, Fletcher was regarded as an oddity; his overweight and shambolic appearance disguised an impressive intellect, but no one really knew Arnold Fletcher or where and how he had accrued his erudition and contacts. He had simply appeared twenty years earlier, apparently having been living abroad, sliding into the art world like a plump gray eel.

And it was this unlikely savior who, having heard that Victor was out of prison and needing work, pointed him toward 96 Park Street.

"It's a job that might be up your alley."

"Thanks. I need to make some money."

"Look, Ballam, it's a whorehouse," Arnold had said, obviously on edge, "so you have to be very discreet. The madam wants someone to do some asking around for her."

"I can do that."

"Yes, well, I wish you luck—and not a word about me, hey?"

"Not a word, Arnold."

"It could be difficult."

Victor had hurried to reassure him, grateful for the work. "I won't say a word. Trust me."

Ninety-six Park Street was an unobtrusive white-painted townhouse on four floors, its walls morose with ivy and creeper, its windows shuttered. Ringing the anonymous doorbell, he waited, surprised when he was buzzed in without having to identify himself.

"Third floor," said a woman's voice, and the intercom clicked off.

In the silence, Victor climbed the stairs. A shadow fell from above as the figure of a woman moved out onto the landing to greet him.

"You're very punctual," she said, putting out her hand and shaking his. "I'm Charlene Fleet."

If Victor had seen her at a traffic light, he would have imagined her to be an attractive mother in her midthirties, driving her offspring to school. Well groomed but not flashy or obvious. A doctor's wife, maybe, or herself a lawyer in her well-cut pantsuit. Her hair was blond but not highlighted, her makeup faultless, her lipstick muted. A professional woman certainly. But a professional madam?

Mrs. Fleet showed him into her office, where a bull mastiff lay asleep beside her desk. She sat down and crossed her legs, and, seeing her face in the light from the window, Victor now judged her nearer forty than thirty. But nothing about her or her surroundings betrayed her profession.

"You were recommended to me," she said easily, her voice soft and accentless. "I have a problem that concerns my girls, and I believe you can help me. As you know, it was Arnold Fletcher who recommended you."

Victor nodded.

"Of course," Mrs. Fleet went on, "everything said between us is in strictest confidence."

"Of course."

"Mr. Fletcher is a client of mine, and when I confided a little of my problem, he said you'd be the person to talk to."

Victor was surprised but didn't show it. "Did he tell you anything about me?"

"He told me that you've served a prison term for fraud and your reputation's all but gone. He said no one would give you the time of day now, not in the respectable world, anyway."

"Did he say anything bad?"

She smiled, apparently amused.

"I'm afraid you're now in my moral postal code, Mr. Ballam. Life can be very comfortable here—if you make the most of it. Mr. Fletcher said that having been an art dealer, you—"

"I'm *still* an art dealer."

"But not trading."

"Not at the moment."

"I apologize if I've hit a nerve, Mr. Ballam. I understand that a change in circumstances takes some getting used to for anyone."

Her manner was sympathetic. Everything was there—the tone of voice, the right expression, the implied shared experience—but instinctively he was on his guard with her and responded cautiously.

"How can I help you, Mrs. Fleet?"

"Bernie Freeland hired three of my best girls. They went to Hong Kong with him for a conference and returned to London with him in his private plane. One of the girls—Marian Miller—was murdered later that evening in her hotel room at Heathrow." Her voice never wavered. "I'm giving you just the bare bones of the story, Mr. Ballam; I can fill in any details later. Because of a canceled flight, Mr. Freeland had kindly given a lift to three other art dealers: Lim Chang, Kit Wilkes, and Sir Oliver Peters."

"Mixed bunch."

"You know them?"

"I know *of* them, and I've done business with Sir Oliver Peters in the past. He's an honorable man."

She nodded, then continued. "I want to know who killed Marian Miller. Murder is bad for my business. For the clients, for the girls, and of course for me. I need to know who killed my employee."

Victor raised an eyebrow. "What do the police think?"

"That it was probably a client."

"Did she have a client that evening?"

"Yes, Sergei Ivanovitch."

"Do you know him?"

"No. He was a new client."

"He just rang you out of the blue?"

"He was recommended to me," Mrs. Fleet said evenly. "By another dealer."

"So this Ivanovitch was a dealer?"

"So he said."

"Where?"

"Russia. In Moscow. He said he deals in nineteenth-century European art."

"Who recommended him?"

"I can't tell you that," she said, almost amused. "Client confidentiality is everything in this business."

"Even if someone recommends a murderer?"

"The person who recommended Mr. Ivanovitch is a respectable—"

"But you didn't meet Mr. Ivanovitch yourself?" Victor persisted, cutting in.

"No; it was arranged over the phone. As is most of our business. That's why my employees are referred to as *call* girls."

Victor ignored the barb and pressed on. "Even if you won't tell me, the police will want to know who he is."

"Oh, they knew Marian Miller was one of my girls, but I haven't told the police that Mr. Ivanovitch was recommended by anyone."

"I see."

"I doubt it. The police rang the telephone number Mr. Ivanovitch gave me and had his address checked out, but they were false." She paused, her tone confident. "I know how to handle the police, Mr. Ballam. We get along nicely, have for years."

Victor smiled wryly. "So Mr. Ivanovitch is the chief suspect?"

"At the moment. But personally I don't think he's involved. Most new clients give us false contact numbers and addresses until they trust us, but to begin with they don't. Why should they? They have a lot to lose."

"It seems your girls have more to lose."

She let the comment pass.

"There's a good deal more to all of this, Mr. Ballam. The flight on Bernie Freeland's jet was uneventful until just before landing. Bernie apparently had his drink spiked—"

"Bernie Freeland was drinking? That's out of character."

"He was only drinking tonic water until someone put something in it, and then he reacted very oddly, panicking and mumbling to Oliver Peters about some Hogarth painting. The one with the Prince of Wales depicted."

Victor kept his face expressionless as she continued.

"It's valuable, obviously, and scandalous. Dangerous even." She paused. "Marian Miller overheard the exchange between Bernie and Sir Oliver Peters."

"She told you that?"

"Naturally."

"What about the other dealers on the plane? Did they hear?"

She shrugged. "That's something Marian didn't know."

"Did the other girls overhear what was said?"

"Only Marian admitted to it," Mrs. Fleet replied. "As to the others, I don't know, but since Marian's death they've both been jumpy."

"How was she killed?"

"Bludgeoned. The police found thirty pieces of silver with her body. Russian rubles."

"Russian rubles—bit obvious, but it points the finger at Ivanovitch."

"Too obvious," Mrs. Fleet said smoothly. "Of course the police didn't tell me about the coins; the chambermaid did. I later found out from other sources that Marian Miller was pregnant."

"So what's the relevance of the thirty pieces of silver?"

Mrs. Fleet smiled chillingly. "Do you think there's a point to the coins?"

"Thirty pieces of silver was what they paid Judas for betraying Christ," Victor replied. "Did Marian Miller betray someone?"

"That's what I want you to discover, Mr. Ballam: why Marian Miller was murdered, why she *needed* to be killed. Someone reacted very quickly and very brutally within hours of her returning to London. Why?"

"Because of what she overheard on the plane journey, perhaps."

"I think so."

It was now eleven-thirty on a cold Sunday morning, but Mrs. Fleet rose and poured them each a glass of white wine from her office fridge. The sleeping mastiff suddenly raised his head from his paws, glanced over to Victor, and snarled softly. Mrs. Fleet's reaction was immediate. Clicking her fingers at the dog, she watched as the animal dropped its head again, showing the whites of its eyes. It was patently afraid of her, and her own expression was fleetingly triumphant.

Unsettled, Victor pressed on. "You think Marian Miller was killed because she knew about the Hogarth?"

"I'm not sure; that's why I needed to talk to you. You're the art expert. What's your opinion?"

Victor paused as though he were thinking, but in reality he was wondering how much to tell the implacable Mrs. Fleet. He suspected that she already realized the tremendous impact the work would have on the art market. His dealer's instinct heightened, he stared into his wine. He had grabbed at the chance of work, knowing he would have taken on anything to occupy his mind and shoehorn himself back into normal life. But he hadn't expected this. Hadn't expected to be told about a painting that had such a huge cult reputation. For one scintillating moment he imagined possessing the Hogarth himself.

And then he realized just how dangerous the Hogarth might prove to be if it really *was* authentic.

"The Hogarth would be worth a fortune," Victor said finally. "It would also be a great triumph for its owner."

"Worth killing for?"

"People kill for loose change."

"Neither of us deals in loose change, Mr. Ballam," she said, her tone suspiciously soft. "I had three girls working that flight. Marian's been butchered. Liza Frith and Annette Dvorski believe they might be next."

"I don't suppose you've talked to the police about the painting."

She looked at him and then ran her finger down the condensation on her glass. "Let them continue to think Marian was killed by some john."

"The mysterious Sergei Ivanovitch."

She nodded. "I run an exclusive whorehouse. I can't risk my clients being investigated and exposed. You don't use call girls, do you, Mr. Ballam? You wouldn't have to. You're attractive; you don't have to pay for it. But some men do. And some men want things only a working girl will do for them. Some hate their wives or don't have time for relationships. Others can't get a woman because they're ugly, or shy, or they can't get it up. There are men who want to be humiliated and degraded in every way physically possible, and everything they want, we give them. For a fee."

He held her gaze as she talked on.

"There's a recession on. In Germany the brothels are offering discounts for clients who arrive on their bikes. Yes, seriously." Her laugh was short on mirth. "But I don't have any problem keeping my girls busy. The art world provides my best customers. Some dealers use us as a bribe, an extra to sweeten a deal, and who can blame them? If a buyer is reluctant, a weekend with one of my girls could be the deciding factor. In the art world, the flesh and the Devil are close runners."

"Annette Dvorski is a foreign name."

She blinked, wrong-footed.

"Are you asking me if I'm using illegal immigrants?"

"Are you?"

"No, Mr. Ballam. Annette came to London to study, then decided that she preferred to make money horizontally. My girls are never forced into prostitution; they are all at the top of their game, hired for their looks *and* their brains. They aren't—or ever will be—King's Cross whores."

"Do they work for you exclusively?"

"Absolutely. If I catch a girl working for anyone else, she's fired."

"Without references?"

"I'm sorry you don't approve of me, Mr. Ballam, but you're hardly one to sit in judgment."

The barb found its mark.

"So if you won't confide in the police," Victor said evenly, "what d'you expect me to do?"

"Let me make myself clear. I am very rich, and I have power because of my influential connections. My client list relies on my discretion to protect them."

She leaned back in her chair, the dog immobile at her feet. "I don't care about the painting; I decided long ago not to enter the art market directly. I work the dealers another way, so the Hogarth means nothing to me. Neither do the other dealers on that plane, and I don't care about the money. If you get hold of the picture, keep it and good luck." She raised her glass in a mock salute, her tone confusingly gentle. "I just want you to find out if my employees are really in danger, and if they are, I want you to get them out of danger."

"That's a lot to ask."

"I'm offering a big fee."

Victor paused, caught between two emotions: fascination and caution.

"Well," he said finally. "You're clever, Mrs. Fleet; I'll give you that. You knew that I'd be interested because the art world's what I know, and you knew that I needed work because there's no queue to hire me. I also think you relied on the fact that I'd probably want to get revenge, but what is *really* clever—and I take my hat off to you for this—is that you knew that the moment you told me about the Hogarth and made me complicit, I was screwed."

She smiled slowly.

"Like I said, Mr. Ballam, welcome to my postal code."

Twelve

LOOSENING THE COLLAR OF HIS ELEGANT SHIRT, OLIVER PETERS stared at his oncologist, his expression momentarily blank. On the wall was the x-ray viewing machine showing the images of his stomach, lit from behind and looming like Halloween ghouls. But they looked fine to him. No gaps, no huge black crosses, no signs saying "diseased."

He blinked, looked away, and, sounding confused, said, "But I haven't been having as much pain lately."

His doctor nodded as though that was almost expected. "That can happen."

"That *has* happened," Oliver insisted, his features slackening with shock, his good manners faltering. "You're wrong, Doctor Chadwick; you've buggered it up. You've got it wrong!" He banged his fists on the side of his chair. "YOU ARE WRONG!" Recovering his composure, he sobbed once, the sound catching in his throat. "I . . . I'm not getting as much pain."

Without looking at his patient, the doctor wrote something in his notes. "That's good."

"Yes, that's good," Oliver echoed, but without conviction. A wife, an apartment in Hampstead and a house in Surrey, three children at private school, and a disease that was killing him. "What about chemotherapy?"

"The cancer is too advanced, Sir Oliver. It wouldn't help you, and it's a punishing treatment."

"It's a punishing disease," Oliver replied drily, trying to sound in control but panicking inside. His profits had been falling; he had struggled to cover the school fees for the last term. What now? Sell the business? Who would buy a gallery in a market grown nervous and wary?

"Alternative medicine . . . D'you think that might help? I mean, it might—er—might it?" He stopped, forced composure, and got to his feet. "How long have I got left?"

"About three months."

"But you do hear about remissions. . . ."

"Yes, they happen sometimes."

"So I could go into remission?" Oliver said desperately.

"No; I'm afraid your disease is too far advanced," Chadwick replied, his tone gentle. "You have to tell your wife. She really should know."

"Know that I'm dying? Perhaps I should also tell her that when I'm gone, she might have to take the children out of school. Perhaps I should share my last few months unloading every burden onto her shoulders. Sonia can watch me die, but in case that isn't difficult enough, why don't I let her know that after I've gone she might have to sell the country house? Even the gallery—if she can find a buyer." He was overflowing with bitterness and despair. "How *exactly* is that supposed to help my wife?"

Embarrassed, the doctor was hesitant.

"I'm sorry. I didn't know you had financial worries."

Oliver buttoned his jacket, smoothing down his hair as though to smooth down his emotions at the same time.

"No, I'm not going to tell Sonia anything, Doctor. Not until I've made her and the children secure," he said, and turned toward the door.

"Can you manage that? You don't have very much time, and the pain will get worse. You won't be able to work or function as well as you could before."

Pausing at the doorway, Oliver looked at the oncologist.

"I have your word that you will say nothing to my wife, Chadwick? Even if she asks you?"

Reluctantly, the doctor nodded. "I have to respect my patients' wishes, but if you won't confide in her, you should try to get some other form of support. Some help."

"I don't need help," Oliver replied, his tone ironic. "I need a miracle."

It was raining when Oliver Peters walked out onto Harley Street. Pausing a moment, he straightened his tie again and began walking toward Marylebone High Street. His mind went back to the flight in Bernie Freeland's jet. Not for the first time, he wished he hadn't gotten on the bloody plane in the first place. He had hated lying to Sonia, her dark eyes curious as she asked about his journey. He could have told her the truth, but he knew it would mean an argument. What was he doing accepting a lift with three call girls? Was he insane? What if someone had seen him? He was a respected man who moved in the highest circles, a confidant of some of the most important personages in the land. Sir Oliver Peters had always led an exemplary life. Why risk his reputation—and that of his family—on a shortcut home?

He knew why. Because he had been desperate to get home. Hong Kong was no place for a dying man, and Oliver had been more than glad to leave. But he couldn't have told Sonia that, because then he would have had to explain everything else. Instead, he had taken the proffered lift and grown more wretched by the minute in that unfamiliar, overheated atmosphere until, unexpectedly, fate had tossed him the Hogarth grenade.

Yes, his bank had said that morning, there *had* been a robbery. Several of the safe deposit boxes had been broken into, along with his. They were incredibly apologetic but explained that there had been no way of getting in touch with him. For his own security and wary of any revealing documentation being available, Oliver had given them only his cell number and had forgotten to update them when he had changed it.

Their relief had been obvious when he had contacted them.

"We're very sorry—"

"But I saw nothing about it in the news."

"We're managing to keep the matter secret, sir."

"I had only two objects in my safety deposit box. You remember?"

"Yes, Sir Oliver. A diamond necklace and a painting, as I remember."

"Have both been taken?"

There had been a lift of hope in the man's voice. "Only the painting, sir."

Of course, Oliver thought; *the painting had been the only thing the thief had wanted. And then, when he understood the danger of possessing it, he had sold it. To Bernie Freeland.* Oliver swallowed, relieved that the inscribed ring had never been stored with the painting, relieved that the other evidence of the royal bastard had not been found. Nor would it be because no one knew where the ring was. Except him.

"You said that other safety deposit boxes were broken into. Were other customers robbed?"

"No, sir," the manager had replied, hoarse with embarrassment. "Only you."

Only you. Of course it was only him. The thief had been after the painting, nothing else. And Oliver had a good idea who the thief had been—Guy Manners, the adopted son of one of the wealthiest banking families in Europe. Oliver held his panic in check. Obviously he couldn't go to the court.

No one spoke directly of royal bastards. Such matters were passed over to courtiers to deal with. Like Nathaniel Overton, who had managed the secret and then passed it down to his descendants, who had in turn passed it on to Oliver. Any direct plea for aid from the royals would have been unthinkable. Oliver's family had served them and managed their secret for generations, as they were expected to. With complete discretion. Even if the royal family *did* come to hear of the theft, there would be no direct contact; instead, they would expect the matter to be solved without being involved in any way. It was tradition. Rigid, unbroken tradition.

Sir Oliver Peters was on his own.

Walking quickly down Marylebone High Street, he tried to shake off a portentous feeling of doom. But the conversation with the bank manager continued to come back to him, crystal sharp.

"Do the police have any leads?" he had asked. "Any idea who took the painting?"

"No, sir. We're truly very sorry about this."

"Did you ever look at the painting?"

"No, sir!" The manager was genuinely offended. "The safety deposit box was never opened by anyone but yourself. As you know, the picture was always kept in a sealed cylinder. Neither I nor any of my staff have even seen the painting. You always expressly insisted that no one should ever look at the work or handle it."

"Well, someone managed to *handle* it out of your bank. How do you explain that?"

He couldn't, of course. And the police couldn't. They told Oliver that the surveillance cameras had been short-circuited and for twenty minutes—the duration of the robbery—there had been no visual record of who had entered the bank or the vault. Forensic evidence had little more to add. Obviously, someone had posed as a customer, entered the vault, and broken into Sir Oliver Peters's safety deposit. When the manager and staff were questioned further, all anyone could remember was a small, apparently Middle Eastern man who had come with two bodyguards. The fact that he had arrived so ostentatiously had meant that the staff wasn't suspicious. After a part-time assistant had checked his credentials, the little man had been shown into the vault. When he had left, everything had seemed in order. In fact, the robbery might have remained unnoticed for a long time if it had not been for the break in surveillance that made a security guard suspicious.

Clever, audacious, and well plotted, Oliver thought bitterly. Yet the thief had soon rid himself of his booty—Guy Manners heaving off the Hogarth to Bernie Freeland. And the last time Oliver had seen Bernie, he had been in fear for his life, babbling in front of some of the most cunning dealers on earth about his incredible find.

Thirteen

WITHOUT REALIZING IT, OLIVER HAD WALKED ALL THE WAY TO OLD Bond Street. He turned into the Burlington Arcade, strode to his gallery, and buzzed to be let in. To his surprise, a familiar face greeted him: Lim Chang. He stood up as Oliver entered, his expression a *mélange* of courtesy and anxiety. Oliver, picking up on the atmosphere, invited him into his office at the back of the building. Observing Lim Chang take a seat, he noticed the familiar, precise parting and a waxiness around his eyes.

"Good to see you again," Oliver began with practiced courtesy. "I thought you were going straight onto Paris for the Courbet auction."

"Bernie Freeland is dead."

Oliver was momentarily frozen in shock and then sat down behind his desk, trying to steady his thoughts. He wanted to ask questions but hesitated, knowing that he wouldn't like the answers. Wouldn't want to hear them, to consider what they meant. *Oh, Christ*, he thought, *why did I take that flight? Why in God's name did I take that flight?*

"Did you hear what I said?"

"Bernie Freeland is dead." His good manners covered his shock. "I'm so sorry to hear that. What happened?"

"He was run over. In New York. By a truck. Apparently his injuries were terrible."

Taking a deep breath, Oliver calmed himself. Bernie Freeland was dead, killed in an accident. The same Bernie Freeland who had been so excited about the Hogarth painting. Bernie Freeland who had confided in him. Oliver stared at his visitor with suspicion. How much did he know? Another thought followed immediately. *Where was the Hogarth painting?* Now that Freeland was dead, it would be up for grabs. Oliver felt his heart palpitate; He was too tired—too sick—for this.

Baring his small teeth in a half smile, Lim Chang leaned on the edge of the desk, his expression unreadable.

"A girl has been murdered—"

"What girl?"

"Marian Miller, one of the call girls on the flight. She was killed at the airport hotel."

"How d'you know that?"

"Because unfortunately I was staying in the same hotel," Chang replied. "Naturally I checked out, but not before I had to endure an interview with the police. They implied that perhaps I had met up with Ms. Miller there. Apparently it had been one of her favored places of work. Of course I said no. In fact, I insisted that I didn't know the woman."

"They believed you?"

"Indeed they did. They apologized and said that they were asking the same questions of everyone who had been staying at the hotel."

Oliver's mouth was dry, his voice stilted. "Did they know about the plane journey?"

"No. And I certainly didn't offer the information. It would have been very uncomfortable for both of us. I know neither of us wishes to brag about the company we kept on that flight," he said, coldly efficient. "But now Bernie Freeland has been killed. A coincidence? Maybe, maybe not." He took out a silk handkerchief and wiped his long, narrow hands. "For two hours I've been walking the streets, trying to work out my thoughts, Sir Oliver. You and I were on that flight too."

Oliver was determined not to give anything away. He was trying to think clearly, to control the avalanche that he felt was about to engulf him.

"What's your point, Mr. Chang?"

"Bernie Freeland acted very oddly just as we were coming in to land." He glanced at Oliver, looked away, looked back nervously. "I heard the steward say that his drink had been spiked. That would explain his panic and confusion but not what he said to you."

The avalanche was coming closer; Oliver could hear the roaring in his ears.

"I'm sorry; I don't understand."

"You know to what I'm referring." Chang paused, staring at the top of the desk. "I am talking to you in the strictest confidence. I have to trust you, Sir Oliver."

Oliver said nothing.

"I think we both know something that is potentially lethal, and I think these deaths prove it. They were not accidental."

The words hung in the still air. Oliver heard the phone ringing in the gallery outside, heard the shrill of a police siren coming up Piccadilly.

"What are you talking about, Mr. Chang?"

"About the lost painting by William Hogarth."

Chang paused, his initial nervousness replaced with equanimity. Oliver recognized the expression only too well, the ruthlessness that had helped the Chinese man make many important acquisitions for his government, the intense determination that had earned him a formidable reputation. Oliver watched him carefully, remembering the rumors about Lim Chang's ambition, his craving for power in his own country, his desperate, intense desire to succeed.

"Bernie Freeland told you about the painting," Lim Chang continued, "but the question is, Who else overheard? Obviously Marian Miller. I suspect it was the reason she was killed. But what about the other two call girls? And what about Kit Wilkes?"

Oliver was finding it difficult to swallow. He had hoped—*prayed*—that no one else knew about the Hogarth. That the people who relied on his protecting the secret were still in blissful ignorance. That he would be able to recover the painting before its loss was discovered. And yet Lim Chang was already onto it, and possibly even the loathsome and vicious Kit Wilkes.

Glancing down at his hands, Oliver thought about Wilkes, about his notorious reputation. Wilkes was known to be capricious and immoral; his impecunious beginnings had shaped his character, leaving him distrustful and devoid of conscience. Never recognized publicly by his politician father, James Holden, he had a spiteful nature that had been temporarily sweetened by a trust fund, but that had proved to be only a damage control exercise. At every opportunity, Kit had given interviews to the press about how James Holden had rejected his mother and humiliated her, causing her to have a nervous breakdown, conveniently forgetting that Elizabeth Wilkes had been well provided for and had her own gallery in Chelsea.

If Kit Wilkes knew about the Hogarth, he wouldn't think twice about exposing it. Knowing how much it would embarrass his royalty-doting father, he would relish selling the story to the tabloids. Oliver could imagine Kit's face on the television and all over the Internet, spreading the old scandal of Polly Gunnell to a slavering new market. And while he was drip feeding his audience, the price for the painting would be driven relentlessly up. Oliver flinched. Perhaps Wilkes might decide to sell the picture to the Russians, thereby adding his own personal, vindictive footnote to English history. A decadent royalist afterword that a communist country would savor.

It was imperative that he get the Hogarth back, Oliver realized. Whatever it cost him personally or privately, it was his duty.

"No," he said at last. "I haven't spoken to Wilkes. Obviously you haven't either."

"I tried this morning. But I was told that Mr. Wilkes has been admitted to the Friars Hospital."

"Why?"

"He's been in rehab before," Lim Chang went on, his eyes never leaving Oliver's face. "But this time he was admitted only hours after he landed in London, after our eventful flight. James Holden arranged it."

"His *father*?" Oliver was stunned. "How d'you know that? Holden's never admitted publicly that Kit is his son. Why would he suddenly show his hand now?"

"I said that Holden *arranged* it. I don't know that he was present when Kit Wilkes was admitted." Lim Chang's attitude had changed; he was relaxed, in charge. "I have contacts, and they told me all they knew."

Yes, I imagine you do *have contacts*, Oliver thought, irritated by the man's confidence. Only the previous year a triad gang had succeeded in smuggling several stolen paintings out of the country to China. When the police went in to investigate, they found themselves faced with the triads in Chinatown and backed off. One of the most notorious of Hong Kong's criminals had even opened a gallery in Mayfair. Using the cover of being a collector of Asian art, he had gradually infiltrated the upper echelons of the art business, and whereas once he would have been blacklisted, he was now welcomed by some of the less discerning among the dealers in an expanding art market.

Cautious, Oliver studied his visitor. "Is Kit Wilkes in serious condition?"

"He's in a coma. He took a drug overdose." Lim Chang's expression was bordering on self-satisfaction. "His lover called for the ambulance. James Holden is intimating that it was a suicide attempt."

"I don't believe it. Kit Wilkes isn't the type to commit suicide."

Lim Chang shrugged his lean shoulders. "That's not really the point, though, is it? The question is, Did he do it to himself? Or did someone do it to him?"

"Why would they?"

"To stop him from talking about the Hogarth," Chang replied evenly.

"We don't know that he overheard Freeland."

"No, we don't. But Wilkes is the most indiscreet man in London and obsessed with publicity. And he's an ambitious dealer too, eager for an easy triumph. He would love to get his hands on that painting."

Unsettled, Oliver wondered how Lim Chang would behave if he knew that the Hogarth had been in the possession of his family for many generations. Chang wanted the painting as a personal coup and a way to expose the decadent West; he didn't know that the man sitting opposite him had dedicated his life to protecting its secret. Didn't know that Sir Oliver Peters was one of very few people who knew the identity of the *living* descendant of Frederick, Prince of Wales, and Polly Gunnell. If the painting were to be made public, it would spark questions, media investigations, and the inevitable allegations and revelations.

Oliver thought of the man who could be king but never would be. A man living in complete ignorance of his lineage who had to be *kept* in ignorance. Because if he was exposed, what might happen then? He might become a subject for blackmail, or kidnapping, or even murder. English history was littered with dead monarchs and pretenders. Oliver had no wish to have a man's murder on his conscience.

And what if the man, once in possession of his true identity, proved untrustworthy? Or greedy? Perhaps avaricious and malicious enough to go abroad and try to disable the English monarchy from a distance? Somehow maintaining his composure, Oliver realized that he had to keep very close to Lim Chang. It could be that this dealer was his best—possibly only—chance of finding the Hogarth.

"You said Kit Wilkes was in a coma—"

Lim Chang cut him off. "What if someone's killing everyone who knows about the painting?"

The mood in the room altered, shifting to something sinister.

"Think about it, Sir Oliver. Of the passengers on that flight, one of the call girls is dead, one of the dealers is in the hospital, and Bernie Freeland has been killed. Out of seven people, three are dead or near death. That should worry you, Sir Oliver, because it worries me. The only thing we all had in common was knowing about the Hogarth. I'd have fought to obtain it for

China, Wilkes would have gone after it, and you—don't say you wouldn't want to get your hands on it, perhaps to *prevent* it from being exhibited—I know you have connections in royal circles. Perhaps your illustrious friends might ask you for a favor." He paused expectantly, but Oliver's expression gave nothing away. "Aside from the value of that painting, you and I both know the effect it would have. After all, someone's already killed for it."

Oliver stared at the desktop, knowing Chang's theory was right. Oliver *would* want to suppress the painting. For the first time in his cultured, well-ordered life, Oliver Peters had nothing to lose. A dying man could afford to be reckless. He sighed, thinking of his options. Pray God no one discovered that the Hogarth had been stolen. But if they did, surely he would be rewarded when it was back in his possession again. Surely grateful and powerful people would pay their debt of honor by seeing to it that his family's future was secure.

He was dying, so what would it matter if someone came after him? Killed or dying from cancer, he would be dead within months. All he had to do was find the Hogarth and he could die in peace. Desperation was suddenly making Oliver a cunning and wily competitor.

"What d'you suggest?" he said at last.

Lim Chang relaxed, sure he had the whip hand. "We should join forces."

"Why?"

"To find the Hogarth."

A metallic thrill shot through Oliver's spine. Lim Chang had the contacts, was privy to a criminal underworld off limits to a man of his standing. For years Chang had flexed his muscles around the globe to secure acquisitions, had intimidated and flattered to purchase myriad works of art for a country eager to impress the world. He was and had always been a discreet thug. No one would mourn the downfall of this little Machiavelli. Sighing, Oliver kept staring at his desk. He was more than willing to go along with Lim Chang, use him, and then outsmart him. He appeared deep in thought, pretending indecision, but he had never been more certain of anything in his life.

No one was going to get the Hogarth. No one but Oliver Peters.

Fourteen

HAVING STOPPED AT THE CORNER SHOP FOR SOME GROCERIES, VICTOR juggled his shopping bags as he struggled to get his keys from his pocket. Pausing midway up the flight of stairs to his apartment, he put down the bags, took out the keys in readiness, and then caught sight of someone's legs on the landing above. Although the person was wearing trousers, it was obviously a female, and Victor frowned, wary.

Curious, he continued up the stairs, taking the turn at the bend and stopping as he recognized the figure.

"Ingola!"

She looked exactly as she had that day they had spent in the country, their last day together. Ingola wore her success lightly: with her hair freshly brushed but without any makeup on her face and her intelligent gray eyes, her prettiness was unexpected—as was the sudden and painful punch in Victor's heart.

"Where's my brother?"

"Christian's coming in a little while. He has to park the car and run an errand," she said, flushing and obviously ill at ease. The sexual tension between them was palpable.

"Come in, then," Victor said, opening the door and stepping back to ensure that they wouldn't touch.

He felt a longing for her that shook him. During his time in jail he had concentrated on forgetting Ingola, recasting her as Christian's wife and his ex-lover. And by the time three-plus years had passed—years in which he hadn't seen or spoken to her—Victor had convinced himself that he had adjusted to the situation. It was one more amendment to his altered life, a fine-tuning of his meticulous plan. Ingola, the woman he had loved more than anything or anyone else, was out of his life. He had given her up.

But his heart hadn't.

Awkwardly, he went into the galley kitchen and made two mugs of coffee, surprised that he could remember without asking exactly how she liked it. When he went back into the sitting room, Ingola was standing by the window, her back erect, her expression impassive.

He passed the mug of coffee to her, taking care not to touch her hand. She was now his brother's wife; nothing could erase that fact.

"Thank you," she said, sitting down, aware of the tension in the room, and found herself taking quick looks at Victor. Snatched glimpses, short enough not to stare but long enough to remind herself why she had never been able to forget him. He was slimmer than before, his dark hair punctuated by gray, his eyes slower to show emotion. But the hands and the voice were exactly as she remembered them, and the pull was stronger than ever.

When Christian had gone to collect Victor from Long Lartin but had returned home without him, Ingola had felt her life splinter all over again. For over three years she had tried to love Christian and had provided him with grateful affection. She had even hoped that when Victor left jail, enough time would have passed for Christian to usurp his brother's place in her heart. Nature thought otherwise. Persuaded to marry Christian—having been convinced by Victor that he could never marry her once he had been convicted—Ingola had concentrated on her career. But success made an impoverished bedfellow, and Christian was a penniless substitute for his brother.

When Christian returned home without Victor after his release from prison, Ingola felt anguished, cheated out of a meeting she had lived for. Her Nordic composure clicked into place, but it was halfhearted, and after only a couple of days she knew she had to see Victor.

"How are you?"

He shrugged. "Better than I thought I'd be. And you?"

"Fine."

"Is Christian a good husband?

"Very."

"And a good father?"

It was the first reference Victor had made to his nephew. A subject he had thought would be too painful to mention. Jack was the child *he* and Ingola should have had, but he was Christian's son, not his—the child he had wanted with the woman he loved . . . if he had never been imprisoned. If he had never been disgraced. If he had never given her up.

"Christian's a great father, yes," Ingola replied, smiling. "Jack thinks the world of him."

Victor changed the subject. "You're qualified, doing well. Congratulations. I know your career meant a lot to you."

"You meant more."

The words were out of her mouth before she could check them. She stared at the patterned carpet, her mouth dry.

"So," Victor said, ignoring her previous remark. "Christian's parking the car?"

"No."

"What?"

"Your brother isn't with me."

Unsure how to react, Victor put down his mug of coffee and frowned. "Why did you say he was?"

"Would you have let me in if you'd known I was alone?"

"No."

"That's why."

She returned her gaze to the carpet.

"You shouldn't be here."

"I know that."

"Ingola," Victor said evenly, "we made an agreement. I was finished, I was going to jail, and you wanted and deserved a good life. Fair enough; you wanted to qualify, to get on. I understood that. Marrying Christian was the best outcome for you." He sighed; speaking about it hurt. "We talked it out, remember? Your career would have been finished if you'd stuck with me."

"You didn't love me enough."

"Jesus," he said bitterly. "Couldn't I say the same about you?"

Standing up, she walked into the kitchen. He could hear her running the cold water tap and knew she was cooling her coffee. He didn't know if he should feel relief that she wanted to finish her drink and be gone or fear that she would leave. He wished fervently that she hadn't come, that he could have kept her forever locked in Worcestershire. In the past. Segregated from his future in an apartheid of memory. But she was here, and her hair was still as thick as a horse's mane, and her hands were just as white, and something very like regret made him react harshly.

"Why come here?" he asked as she walked back into the sitting room.

In reply she put down her mug and went to him. Gently she touched his cheek. He shook her off, but she was undeterred. She touched his face again.

"You have to go. You can't be here."

But her hand stayed against his skin, her fingers tracing the outline of his features, and he remembered her. Every nuance, every scent, every suppressed longing. But he also remembered her stubbornness, her emotional greed.

"Ingola," he said, his voice wavering. "I can't do this. You *have* to go."

She nodded, then shook her head, tears in her eyes.

"No," she said with a catch in her throat.

"This is wrong. I know it, and so do you. Come on—you don't want me anymore. You just think you do."

Her eyes took on a familiar look of determination, almost defiance. "I *do* want you. I've always wanted you."

"No—"

"*Yes.*"

"You have to go."

"I will," she replied, kissing him, "I will . . . later."

They made love as though they knew they would be punished. Every moment was guilty, with Christian the decent, good phantom in the bed between them. But even as he wanted her gone, Victor clung to her, and Ingola fed off the heady mixture of desire and deceit that both of them had created. Created and failed to resist. And somewhere in between, both felt the aching realization of love lost and hope sacrificed.

When Victor woke two hours later, she was gone.

Fifteen

LIZA FRITH WAS SITTING WITH HER LEGS CURLED UNDER HER, WEARING no makeup, her ash-blond hair hanging around her face. She looked unusually young—and very frightened—chewing the side of her index finger as she watched Mrs. Fleet. She knew that business would be brisk—it always was in the Park Street brothel—but she could hear no sounds from below. In the four-story house, the ground floor was used for the reception of the clients; the first floor housed lounges, and there were offices at the back. On the second floor were the sumptuous bedrooms—soundproofed and discreet—with a separate back exit on the landing. The top floor was off limits to everyone, a light, airy space converted into Mrs. Fleet's private apartment.

The third floor was for the girls. No men allowed. There were only four bedrooms because most of the fifteen employed girls were sent out to entertain clients in hotels, on trips abroad, or on private flights. Knowing that it was in the police's interest to turn a blind eye to her activities, Mrs. Fleet had enough sense not to provoke the undue curiosity of her neighbors and kept the in-house business to a minimum.

"Have you heard about Kit Wilkes?" she asked Liza, her tone remote. "He's in the Friars Hospital—"

"In a coma!" Liza blurted out. "He was on the plane with us! First Marian and now Kit Wilkes."

She sounded unnerved, but Mrs. Fleet remained cool, irritated that she should have to play nursemaid to an unstable whore. Determined that Liza shouldn't find out about Bernie Freeland's accident, she passed the girl a coffee and sat down. *Accident? Like hell it was,* she thought. *Bernie Freeland had been killed.* Calmly, Mrs. Fleet studied Liza Frith. The girl had always proved reliable and sweet-natured, with little temperament. Popular with the clients and sexually uninhibited even for a working girl,

Liza had chosen to go into prostitution because she liked sex, a lazy life, and even lazier money. Intelligent enough to win a place at the University of Manchester, she had left after the second term and drifted into the outer periphery of Mrs. Fleet's radar. A known party girl who loved clubbing, Liza had been recommended by a friend who had worked for Mrs. Fleet's competitor in Argentina. Within a week she was ensconced at the Park Street premises.

But if her employer had an instinct for talent, she also had an instinct about weakness. Mrs. Fleet was never a woman to succumb to a hard luck story or show generosity in supplying second chances; vulnerability resonated in her head like a bee humming against a locked window. And she could sense it now in Liza Frith.

"I think you should stay here for a while, Liza," she said simply. "Have a rest. Perhaps you're tired."

"Marian's dead, and Kit Wilkes is in the hospital!"

And you don't even know about Bernie Freeland yet, Mrs. Fleet thought. She would make sure that Liza remained in ignorance or she might react badly, even become indiscreet. And in a business run on discretion, any intimation of trouble—anything that took the client's mind off pleasure—was bad for the profit margin.

"Liza, don't get yourself worked up," Mrs. Fleet continued, staring at the girl calmly. "Accidents happen."

"Marian was murdered!" Liza snapped. "Her head was bashed in. What do the police think?"

"That it was a client."

"No!" Liza said, shaking her head.

"Someone left thirty pieces of silver with her."

"Meaning what?" Liza asked, her childish voice raised. "What's that supposed to mean? Marian didn't betray anyone—unless she told people what she overheard on the plane."

"Which was?"

"I don't *know*," Liza said vehemently. "I couldn't hear what was going on from where I was sitting. Annette was next to me, and we were talking, coming in to land. Bernie going off like that was a shock. I turned and saw him leaning down to Sir Oliver Peters, but I couldn't hear what he said, just caught the name Hogarth; that was all."

Mrs. Fleet studied the girl closely. "Nothing else?"

"No. Anyway, where *is* Annette?" Liza asked suddenly, glancing at her employer and wondering why she was so calm. Wasn't it obvious that something was wrong, that the flight had been jinxed in some way? "When we last spoke, she said she was coming here."

"So she'll come," Mrs. Fleet replied, composed. She had not seen or heard from Annette Dvorski, but she wasn't going to show concern. Not yet, anyway.

"She wouldn't have still gone, would she?"

It was Mrs. Fleet's turn to look surprised. "Gone where?"

"To New York to meet up with Bernie Freeland. She was planning . . ." Liza felt herself turning pale. Jesus, why hadn't she kept her mouth shut? She realized from the look on her employer's face, her hard, narrowed eyes, that Mrs. Fleet hadn't known about the assignation. "Maybe I got it wrong."

"*Annette arranged to see Bernie Freeland?*"

Liza was stammering, trying to cover up.

"I could have gotten the dates wrong." Liza now mistook the woman's fixed expression for anger. "Annette always gets her dates wrong," she babbled.

"Shut up!" Mrs. Fleet said, rising to her feet and looking down into the street below. At once the mastiff rose and padded over to her, sitting at her feet.

At any other time the fact that Annette Dvorski had deceived her would have incensed Mrs. Fleet, but not this time. If the stupid girl *had* arranged a secret meeting with Bernie Freeland, she was going to get more than she bargained for. If she was on her way to New York, she would soon find out that her rendezvous was with a corpse.

"You stay here at Park Street, Liza. Do you understand?"

The girl nodded. "I can work."

Mrs. Fleet considered this awhile, then said, "No, not for the moment." Perhaps it was better to keep Liza Frith under wraps, away from people and questions. "Just stay indoors."

"You think I'm in danger?"

"I think you're worried, and you're no good to me in that state."

"Do the police know about the flight on Bernie Freeland's jet?"

"No," Mrs. Fleet replied, her tone warning. "And you must not say anything."

"But—"

"The flight is *not* to be mentioned. Forget it; it has nothing to do with Marian's death. She died in the airport hotel. On her own. I don't want you muddying the water."

When Liza left the room, Mrs. Fleet stared down at Park Street, at winter trees bleak and bad-tempered against a blustering sky; early London rain had left the roads greasy. From her vantage point, she could see over the London rooftops toward the horizon, where watercolor clouds skittled after one another. Her mind ran over the facts. One of her working girls had been murdered; another was missing, apparently on her way across the Atlantic. And a third, without knowing even half the truth of her situation, was hiding at Park Street.

Mrs. Fleet had grown up in the toughest area of Liverpool, accustomed to violence and intimidation. By hard graft and ruthlessness she had risen to the top of her game, and she liked her status. Not respectable but pretty nearly untouchable. No bailiffs coming to her door, no pimps either, no whores running with sores and willing to blow two men for the price of a drink. It took determination to get away from Scotland Road, a place where there were pubs on every corner and a hooker in every doorway.

But she'd done it. Mrs. Fleet—once Charlene O'Dywer—had shed her accent, her name, and her morals to get to Park Street. To become rich and safe. And now a fucking painting was endangering everything. She had enjoyed her extended interlude of luxury and safety, but . . . She smiled to herself wryly, almost resigned. Perhaps she had always known it was too good to last. Perhaps she had even expected that one day trouble would come to her expensive door.

But she was buggered if she was going to give in without a fight.

Sixteen

WALKING UP THE NARROW STAIRWELL OF THE TOWNHOUSE, VICTOR rang the bell marked "*Thomas Harcourt*" and waited to hear the lock being slid to open the door. He knew from past experience that Thomas—Tully to his friends—already would have checked on his caller through the peephole, but he had the grace to smile effusively as though surprised when he opened the door.

"Victor, come in, come in," he said, stepping back and allowing his visitor to enter the spacious, high-ceilinged drawing room that overlooked the Thames Embankment. The windows were almost the height of the room, and French doors led onto a balcony that spied on the river and let in the sound of traffic and pigeons.

"Coffee?" Tully asked. His lofty figure moved over to the stove in the open-plan kitchen, where a pan of milk simmered on the stove. "I remember how you like it, milky and sweet."

There was no mention of Victor having been in prison, no surprise at the sudden reemergence of an old friend, just a genuinely affectionate welcome tempered with an old uncomfortable memory that neither of them would ever forget.

Years earlier, Thomas Harcourt had been in the running with Ian McKellen, Daniel Day-Lewis, and Jeremy Irons to become one of the greatest English actors of his generation, formidable in the theater and mesmerizing on the screen. His tall, rangy frame, loose-limbed and supple, had allowed him to take on many of the great Shakespearean roles, and his voice, never strident, could become intimate for the screen. His indeterminate looks and mobility of expression allowed him to convince an audience that he was whatever the character called for: handsome, virtuous, heroic, predatory. . . .

Tully's decline came not through any failure of his own but from the sudden and traumatic death of his wife. Returning to work a month after her suicide, he developed stage fright or—keen to make light of an affliction that was crippling him—*life fright,* as he explained it to interviewers. People believed it was due to grief, but it was not that Tully missed his wife; it was more that she obsessed him, her suicide a constant reproach, a subtle undermining of his confidence that rendered this most articulate of actors a mumbling tyro.

Victor had never known his friend's wife but had heard that she was jealous of his success. She had wanted a career as successful as her husband's, but the public didn't take to her, and her bitterness turned to resentment. Her suicide, although professed in her note to be an act of release for her husband, was in fact the opposite. From the moment she killed herself she never left him. On stage, on a film set, she was there, making gibberish of his lines or wiping his memory until there were no lines and no more work.

"Two sugars, isn't it?"

Victor nodded and sat down. The apartment was in perfect order, the valuable Georgian commode in precisely the same place it had always been, as was a faded Hogarth print of *His Servants* and the luscious Gainsborough portrait hanging beside a vertiginous spiral staircase.

But the sofa was showing signs of wear and tear, Tully's trousers weren't as expensive as they had been, and his slip-on shoes were scuffed at the toe.

"Here you go." He handed Victor his coffee and sat down next to him. "You look well. Older but good."

"You look the same."

"I *am* the same," Tully replied, "and my work's picking up. I do voice-overs now. Can't forget your lines if they're printed in big, bold letters in front of you, and the pay's pretty good, especially if you do voice for feminine products. Tampax has been very good to me." He laughed, the sound resonant. "I expected to see you when you got back to town."

Victor nodded. "I've got a job."

"Which side of the law?"

"Which side d'you think?"

"You had it coming, you know," Tully went on, sipping his coffee. He set down his cup on the table next to him. "Too much, too young," he said. "You'd have gotten away with it if you'd been your brother, but people resent charisma, Victor. They can't forgive a person for having it." He paused, "Charisma—everyone wants it, and everyone resents it if they haven't got it. Poor soul, you couldn't go on being lucky, rich, and well known—*someone* had to stop you."

The assumption that he was innocent pleased Victor.

"You still know everything that's going on in London, Tully?"

"Everything. It passes for real life. I'm a willing recipient of news—from all kinds. But you know that, don't you, Victor?"

It was no secret that after his wife's death and the demise of his career Tully Harcourt had dabbled in gambling. Mostly the horses, sometimes the dogs. Dabbled in drugs too, but not for long. As with sex, Tully heart wasn't in it. But he craved the thrill of the bet, and the capital's casinos welcomed him until his losses included a family Herring portrait and a Dutch still life.

But Tully, nobody's fool, came to his senses and sought alternative—and safer—ways to amuse himself. Having moved among the bookies at the tracks, he had made unlikely friends and been drawn to the peripheries of the London underworld. Mentally and morally adept, he had, however, picked his role and stuck to it. He was an observer no more. A sympathetic listener. The pastor of the dispossessed.

"So," Tully asked, "who are you working for?"

"Charlene Fleet."

Tully's shape-shifting face altered, his curiosity making him alert.

"Mrs. Fleet of Park Street?"

"The same."

"She runs whores."

"I know that."

"For the art world mostly. She's cornered the market there, I believe."

Victor nodded. "Three days ago, one of her girls died. All this is in confidence, Tully."

"You didn't have to say that."

"Marian Miller was murdered."

Tully drew a protracted breath. "Not the girl with the thirty pieces of Russian silver?"

Victor raised his eyebrows. "I'm surprised that part's come out."

"Not publicly, but I heard it on the grapevine. People always gossip about that kind of thing. They don't much care about a call girl getting killed, but they like the salacious details. What were the coins supposed to mean?"

"That her killer was a Russian?" Victor offered, smiling wryly. "God knows. But what *isn't* common knowledge is that before she died, Marian Miller had been on board Bernie Freeland's jet. There were also three other art dealers on that plane and two other call girls, as well as the pilot, the copilot, and two male crew members. One of the dealers was Kit Wilkes—"

"Who's in the Friars Hospital."

"Yes, for the last three days. In a convenient coma."

Thoughtful, Tully moved over to the windows and closed them. Sliding the brass bolts, he drew the drapes against the early winter evening and flicked on a couple of lamps. At once the Gainsborough portrait was illuminated, the walking woman suddenly an eavesdropper, her head to one side, her parasol red as a skinned fish.

"Why was the girl killed?"

"Because she overheard something she shouldn't have." Concisely, Victor outlined what he knew of the Hogarth painting.

Tully was intrigued. "You say there were two other dealers on the plane?"

"Lim Chang and Sir Oliver Peters," Victor replied. "I don't know if they heard about the painting; I haven't talked to them yet."

"And the two other girls?"

"One's staying with Mrs. Fleet in Park Place. The other's still working."

Leaning back in his chair, Tully studied his visitor. He knew why Victor had come to him—not just to find out what the gossip was but because he could talk to Thomas Harcourt about the art world. Tully's grandfather had run one of the most successful galleries in Paris, and Tully had inherited some valuable pieces. He was also knowledgeable enough to understand the implications of the rediscovered Hogarth painting.

But there was more to it than that. Tully Harcourt owed Victor Ballam. He owed him a debt that could never be paid fully. A debt of honor, professional and personal, an unspoken debt that bound the two men together more tightly than a rope. Without tugging on that leash Victor knew Tully would be there for him. Without question Tully understood that the bond was unimpeachable, unbreakable. And for life.

"Where is it?"

"The picture? Bernie Freeland has it."

"In New York?" asked Tully.

"I imagine so. That's where he is now."

"You know what this could mean, don't you?"

"I was an art dealer, Tully; I know *exactly* what it could mean. That Hogarth on the open market could cause a monumental scandal." He paused, then said, "A long time ago I heard an interesting theory from Fraser Heath-Lincoln—"

"That old bastard."

Victor smiled, amused. "He liked me, thought I had potential, so we used to talk. He was vicious and untrustworthy, but he adored the royals. He used to say that the English throne was the closest thing to God, which was why he was so interested in the Hogarth series *The Harlot's Progress*. It was Fraser who told me about Polly Gunnell and the Prince of Wales—and about the painting that gave the game away."

Tully pulled a face. "It was just a rumor. And besides, the whole series of *The Harlot's Progress* was destroyed in a fire."

"Maybe not. Perhaps it was convenient for everyone to believe that it no longer existed because the painting proved the rumor. If the Hogarth depicts the Prince of Wales with his whore, it would be priceless. And very dangerous. And because of that everyone would be after it." Victor paused. "There's a theory that Hogarth took the child in and that he later placed the boy with his friend Thomas Coram, who set up the Foundling Hospital."

"Hogarth took the boy in?" Tully was amazed. "How could he have done that?"

"Easily. He could have passed him off as the child of one of his servants. Hogarth was married, living with his wife and his in-laws in a spacious townhouse. No one was interested in what went on below stairs. The painter knew that; he could have secreted the baby there and then moved it later."

"But why?"

"Maybe he felt he owed it to Polly Gunnell, his model. I think Hogarth knew about her involvement with the Prince of Wales; perhaps she had confided in him. For a long time there's been a rumor that she was killed *because* she was carrying the Prince of Wales's child. Well, what if it's true? I don't say the royals had anything to do with it, but Frederick, Prince of Wales, was estranged from his parents. He was feckless and spirited, but if he *had* had a son out of wedlock, that boy would have been the heir to the throne."

"But that would mean that the line of succession—"

"Wouldn't have led to Elizabeth the Second. Yes, that's exactly what it would mean."

"Jesus!"

"There were always pretenders to the English throne, Tully. Bonnie Prince

Charlie, for example. But if the anti-German factions could have replaced George, Prince of Wales, with an English heir—albeit an illegitimate one—they would have jumped at the chance. And even if they'd failed, the attempt would have destabilized royalty and Parliament."

Unblinking, Tully stared at Victor. "Did the child live?"

"I don't know; no one does. But if his existence is proved, it would delight the republicans and give them some mighty ammunition. There's a growing backlash against royalty in this country. The public is irritated by the extravagance of the young royals, their arrogant entitlement to status. Now, just imagine if Lim Chang got hold of this Hogarth painting—further proof of the decadent West, of the corruption within the royal family. Some might argue the Windsors shouldn't even be in power. China would love to be the whistle-blower on that scandal. They've been flexing their muscles since the Beijing Olympics, and every month their power increases along with their influence. How thrilled would *they* be to expose the scandal?"

"And Lim Chang would further his career."

"He would be a national hero, a fully paid-up member of the laurel wreath club. And then there's Kit Wilkes. Spiteful, delighted to embarrass his social-climbing father—the Hogarth exposé would be a double whammy. He could prove his own skill as a dealer and kick the establishment in the crotch at the same time. James Holden is a Tory MP, desperate for a knighthood and a place in the House of Lords one day. He isn't going to want his bastard to ruin his life. God knows, Wilkes has sold his father out to the tabloids dozens of times; he's made a career out of malice. But Holden moves in royal circles, he's ruthless, and he's grafted to get where he is. Somehow he's managed to hold on to his status."

"Are you saying Wilkes could ruin his father if he got hold of the Hogarth?"

Victor nodded, walked over to the window, held back the curtain, and looked out.

"And Wilkes might like to sell it to the Russians," he said.

He could see the street lamps reflected dully in the Thames and a small boat huffing its way over the dark river, then disappearing under the shadow of a bridge.

"And then there's Sir Oliver Peters," Victor went on. "Dealer in English art, part of the establishment, in fact, everything James Holden wants to be." Victor let the curtain drop and turned back to Tully. "Oliver Peters is the only dealer I don't worry about. My only concern is that if he got hold of the Hogarth, he might destroy it to protect the royals. He'd put honor before his own triumph."

"A year ago I'd have agreed with you."

It was Victor's turn to be surprised. "What?"

"He's dying. And the unexpected beckoning of his god might demote the royals in Sir Oliver's eyes. He might want to make a splash before he goes."

"No, he's too much of a royalist."

"But he's *dying*, Victor, and that changes a man's attitude. Sir Oliver might need to secure his reputation, ensure he's not forgotten. Chivalry's all well and good, but for a dying man with a wife and three children at a private school, the money that a Hogarth could make would be a powerful temptation."

"How d'you know he's dying?"

"His tailor's discreet, dear boy, but they gossip in the workroom. The other day Sir Oliver passed out while he was having a fitting, and he's been getting his clothes altered to cover his weight loss for months now."

"So all the dealers on Bernie Freeland's plane have reasons to want the picture, that is, if Freeland's prepared to sell it."

There was a long silence, both men thinking. Victor was the first to speak. "Mrs. Fleet said that Liza Frith—the girl now staying with her—is terrified."

"But the other girl who was on the plane is still working?"

"Annette Dvorski, yes. She was unnerved, but she's made of stronger stuff than Liza. You know something, Tully? That flight was deadly."

"You have to go to the police, Victor."

"I can't do that. They wouldn't listen to me, and I can't expose Mrs. Fleet and her clients."

"But a girl was murdered."

"And you think the police will find out who did it? They're looking for some phantom Russian—Marian Miller's convenient john that night." He smiled wryly. "No, the police haven't got a chance. The ranks are closing, Tully; I can feel it. I know how the art world functions. They have a secret and want to protect themselves. Bernie Freeland was drugged, and he let something slip. The trouble is, I don't know who heard what he said, if it was some of the passengers or all of them. But I have a better chance of finding out than the police."

"It's risky."

"I know. The stakes are much higher, and the fighting's a lot dirtier."

"And you'd love to get your own hands on that Hogarth, wouldn't you?" Tully said, his face assuming a beatific expression. "See that image of the Prince of Wales with his whore. She's got a baby in her belly. Is that why she's smiling? Kicking over the table, breast exposed. Tits a little too full, perhaps? Already heavy with milk? Imagine Hogarth painting the scene. Wicked little fellow to be so very naughty. . . . Now, you imagine owning it, Victor, the proof in your hands. The power to make everyone sit up and take notice again. The art world *couldn't* ignore you after a coup like that."

Stung, Victor retorted, "You think I'm doing this for revenge?"

"I *know* you're doing it for revenge."

"The person who has the Hogarth is holding a loaded shotgun," Victor said calmly. "Yes, it's worth a fortune, but it's also dangerous. It could challenge the royal lineage and even change history. Everyone who knows about it's threatened."

"Which is why you can't do this on your own!"

"I have to find that painting."

Tully paused. He could see the danger, could feel the underlying current of tension. Victor was putting himself in a difficult position. But then again, he had no choice.

So Tully did what his conscience prompted him to do. "Let me help you."

"Why? You've just said it's dangerous."

"I like a bit of danger, Victor; I'm fucking bored. I'm getting old before my time."

"You *are* old."

"Not that old." Tully smiled. "Only sixty-odd, and all my limbs are still working. Apart from the knees, but then, I don't suppose there will be much ballet involved, will there? Let me help."

But Victor wasn't having it. "No; I can find it on my own."

"And when you do—*if* you do—then what? There's already been one death; you've said yourself it's dangerous even to know about the flaming picture. Walk away from it, Victor. Get out of it now, while you have the chance."

"A girl was murdered!"

"And I'm sorry for it. But someone deliberately went after her, and they could well go after everyone else on that flight. And now that you're involved, what's to stop them from coming after you? Listen to reason, Victor, the situation's lethal; only a fool would go ahead with it alone. A fool or a martyr." He looked hard at Victor. "Just who are you trying to save?"

"I suppose that depends on who needs saving the most."

What have I done?

Descending the steps to the basement, I found—as I had hoped—the door of the kitchen open. Taking in a long breath, I walked in. A great fire sparked under a cumbersome grate from which a copper pan hung suspended over the flames. The smell of hot jam seemed at once welcoming and sickly, but for me it augured well: Nell Bindy was still working. Moving into the firelight, I stole a closer look at the baby in my arms, pulling back the rags which covered it and waiting for Nell to return.

Children, born to the poor who could hardly feed themselves, left on the bank of the Thames for the coming tide, or simply dropped in the street with the sewage, had been a scandal in the London streets for many years. Many times I had seen putrid grey bodies crawling with rats or bobbing in the capital's stinking river. I knew that for the destitute there was little choice; only the workhouse and the misery of gruelling labour and crowded, unsafe surroundings. Every day the newspapers advertised nurses who, for a modest fee, would take on children and find them good homes. But the trade had become a public scandal when it was discovered that the nurses had left their charges neglected, often abused, and always unfed in the dying rooms of London.

The money paid by desperate mothers was easy profit. The nurses reported back about the fictitious country homes the babies had gone to while hundreds of unclaimed carcasses sank under the tide of the Thames.

But I knew that Polly Gunnell would never have deserted her baby. I thought back to the last time I had seen her. She had been obviously pregnant, shrugging off my increasingly anxious enquiries but accepting an offer to sit for me again. Back in the comfort of the studio she had relaxed and begged to see the painting. Her insistence finally wore me down, and I showed it to her. If I am to be truthful, I was inordinately proud of the work, Number three in the series The Harlot's Progress, *showing pretty Polly Gunnell flirting with the onlooker, her lover sneaking out at the back of the painting. A man with a face all London knew.*

She had smiled at the Prince of Wales's image. "Polly," I had begun nervously. "The baby you're carrying . . ."

And she had put her fingers to her lips, shaking her head slightly at me. Pretty, so pretty, full of mischief, clever, and sure of herself.

I knew then without her telling me. I knew—and from that instant I was in fear for her. And, God forbid, somewhat for myself. I truly believe Polly never understood how perilous her situation was. Perhaps there was a certain triumph in knowing the lineage of her bastard, but she was in love, and that took precedence over everything. If she ever did consider her future, I imagine Polly would have believed herself safe, and I take comfort in the hope that she had no portent of her terrible death.

I did not seen her alive again.

Staring at the baby, it was obvious even to me, a childless man, that it was newborn and too weak to cry from hunger. Shaken, I wondered if Polly had delivered her son just before she was killed or if the baby had been ripped out of her whilst she was still alive. What terror must she have felt! What pain as she bled, her child thrown onto the floor out of her reach while her murderers set about her with their knives, tearing into her face. Polly had been a streetwalker, clever in city ways, but not clever or quick enough this time.

When had she known that they were after her? She couldn't have had much time or she would have escaped. Her death had been brutal, and her murderers, in discarding the baby, must have believed—as I had done at first—that the child was already dead.

God knows, they would never knowingly have left it alive.

Nervous, I jumped as the inner door opened. A spare-framed middle-aged woman entered the basement kitchen.

"What the hell . . ." She stared, then recognised me. Openly amazed, she said, "You want something, sir? I heard no bell ring." Her bottom teeth had gone; the top row were uneven. She came towards me, pausing to stir the jam, which was beginning to overflow and hiss on the side of the hot pan.

"What you got there, sir?"

Dumbly, I remained stock still, the bundle in my arms, my short frame bullish.

"Is everyone retired for the night?"

She nodded, still stirring the jam. "All in bed. Your wife retired early, and later your in-laws, sir." Her head jerked towards the package. "Can I ask what's in your arms?"

"Can I trust you?"

Slowly she kept stirring the conserve. "I've worked for Sir James Thornhill over twenty years, sir, and he ain't never had cause to doubt me or my word." Another bleed of jam hissed against the hot metal of the pan. "I've known your wife, Jane, since she was a child. Kept all her secrets. You ask, sir; ask your wife if Nell Bindy's to be trusted."

"I didn't mean to insult you," I said hurriedly. "I need help with a matter of the gravest consequence. I cannot impress upon you enough how important secrecy is, how vital it is that no one know anything of this. What I say to you tonight, what I show you, what I ask of you, must never be repeated to another living soul."

She stopped stirring the jam, took it off the stove, and folded her arms.

"Is it dangerous?"

I paused, then nodded.

"Could cause me trouble?"

I nodded again.

"Sir, I'm widowed, but I've a big family and two daughters, both married. I don't want trouble coming to their doors. Is there no one else you can ask for help?"

"No," I said simply.

"Then, sir, might I have the chance to refuse?"

"You may." I replied, still clinging to the baby. "I cannot blame you if you do. I would understand and say nothing to anyone on the matter. It would be between us and us alone." My eyes met hers calmly. "But if I were to tell you that a terrible wrong has been done, that a good woman has been killed, then what? And if I were to tell you that I may well hold the future of the country in my arms, would you relent?" I laid the bundle on the kitchen table and lifted the rags off the barely breathing newborn baby.

"Dear God," Nell exclaimed, unfastening her bodice and placing the sick child against the warmth of her body. "This is a newborn. It needs feeding or it'll die."

Relieved, I watched her heat some milk in a shallow pan and test it with her finger. She dipped the corner of a cloth into it, making a cotton teat, and slid it into the baby's mouth, but it was too weak to suckle. Nell tut-tutted impatiently and put some milk on her finger, wiping it on the baby's mouth. Finally, the child began to take the liquid.

Only then did she look back to me.

"Don't tell me any more, sir. I don't want to know who this child is or who its parents are."

"Not me, Nell. I'm not the father."

"I believe you, sir," she replied, agitated. "And I believe you're doing right, but I can't be punished for what I don't know, and I don't want to know any more." The baby was slowly feeding now. "I couldn't stand before God and not help this baby, but it's the baby that matters to me, sir, nothing more."

I nodded, understanding. "I didn't know where to take the child, Nell."

"Like I said, I've a big family and one daughter living in Chiswick. In amongst her brood we can lose a little one, pass it off as a relative's child. God knows it happens often enough."

I nodded earnestly. "I'll pay for the child's every need. Let it want for nothing. And I'd welcome a regular report of his progress. I want him to have a simple life, with some schooling. A quiet life."

"Chiswick's far enough from the city to be safe," Nell replied perceptively. "Has he a name?"

"No, no name."

"You should give him a name, sir."

"No, your daughter can name him."

She nodded, stared at the baby, then asked, "Will they hurt the child if they find it?"

"They will kill him."

She flinched. "Why?"

Why? Because of my arrogance and ambition, I thought, remembering the steady rise of my career. Sir James Thornhill's acceptance of his bullish son-in-law had been slow after I had had the temerity to elope with his daughter, Jane. Only admiration of his son-in-law's abilities and his wife's persuasion had brought Thornhill round. But for a long time I had been wary around my father-in-law. I was known as much for my truculence as my talent, but I had tried to temper the excesses of my nature and had been determined to establish myself and validate Thornhill's confidence in me. And so I had worked hard and created a topical niche for myself with The Harlot's Progress.

I had relished the immediate and popular success of the work when it was exhibited to the public. My reputation seemed established within one London day, and the series was proving to be exactly what I had hoped for—a triumphant popular success, vindicated by a flurry of early fakes. My spiteful paintbrush, coupled with my sardonic moral judgements, had led me to create works which were exciting, outrageous, and titillating.

But I had gone too far, parodied the wrong person, and set in motion a series of events which I knew were only in their infancy. I could paint the villains, the whores, the debauched—but not the royal court.

Anxious, I turned back to Nell.

"Go to Chiswick tonight. Now. In the morning I'll explain to everyone that you had a bereavement at home and will return soon." I took some coins from my pocket and handed them to her. "Take a hackney cab all the way. Go now, Nell. Tell your daughter anything you want—but not the truth. Tell no one that. There was never a child brought into this house. If anyone asks you about it, you deny any knowledge. Remember this and remember it well—no child ever came here."

Seventeen

AT FIRST UNAWARE THAT HE WAS BEING WATCHED, JAMES HOLDEN, MP, muffled a yawn and continued to listen to the protracted speech on arable farming that he had been forced to attend in Brussels. He would have to remember to congratulate the speaker afterward and buy him a drink even though his performance had been execrable. He would flatter and schmooze—what he did best. He would attend the dinner dance too, leaving his jacket open to disguise the filling out of his waist.

His left hand moved to the top of his head, touching his thick layered hair. He smiled to himself: the best head of hair in Westminster, they had said in *Private Eye*. He had ignored the second part of the quote: "topping the dumbest brain."

It wasn't true. He might not match the intellect of some his colleagues, but he was by no means dim, and his grasp of the minutiae of protocol and funding was impressive. The trouble was that such matters were considered dull, and those who dealt in them even duller. He would never get a place in the cabinet even with the Tories back in power, but he made a nifty backbencher and he was reliable. That counted for a lot. People might be attracted to the highfliers, but they needed the steady workhorses. And besides, his hard, dull, mind-grindingly boring work was not going to go unnoticed.

James uncrossed his legs as he felt cramp starting in his right calf and reflected on how he had been in line for an honor for some time, indeed been promised one. A medal, a circle of beaten metal to make up for all the interminable meat quotas. A medal to say that the time spent with his head up the asses of his betters was worth it. Besides, he deserved it; it was owed to him, and before long everyone would know it.

Suddenly aware that he was being watched, James turned to see a woman standing by the door of the chamber. He knew she was a journalist immediately; he'd seen so many of them over the years that he could recognize one in a multitude. And he knew why she was there: to get a quote about Kit Wilkes.

The name acted like a hair shirt, running bristles along his nerve ends. His wife, Margaret, had long since forgiven his dalliance with his secretary, but his short-lived affair with Elizabeth Wilkes, which followed, had unfortunately resulted in a son. Even that had not been too much of a problem at first. In private, James had settled some money on Elizabeth and, after some acrimonious exchanges, had agreed that he would pay for the child's schooling. But on one condition only: he would not acknowledge the boy publicly, never admit that he was Kit Wilkes's father. And would not give him the Holden name. That was not for the bastard result of an ill-judged fling.

But for all his detailed and meticulous planning, Holden had not allowed for Kit Wilkes's character. How could he have? As the boy hit his late teens, he discovered the tabloid newspapers. Expelled from school and using drugs, Kit Wilkes turned his bitterness and spite onto his father through the media. There was easy money in selling his story to the Sunday papers, and after a while Kit didn't have to approach them; they followed him. Soon Kit was universally known as the illegitimate son of James Holden, and his camp vindictiveness and longing for attention soon elevated him to the role of minor celebrity. A spell on a jungle reality show—where his hysterical outbursts and unexpected seduction of an aging female singer increased the ratings astronomically—was followed by a nervous breakdown and a spell in the Harley Street Clinic.

Photographed supposedly crying for his father, Kit Wilkes then declared that he was going to take over the running of his mother's art gallery. As before, he surprised everyone. The gallery had been privately settled on Elizabeth by James Holden, but for years she had left its running to a manager. However, Kit had other ideas. Possessing a keen intellect and an entrenched desire to succeed, he collected English portraiture when Britart was at its peak. Choosing a genre that was not popular, Kit was soon able to attain a small but impressive collection. A success by default, he sold his works at the end of the 1990s and made a killing.

Accompanied sometimes by a man, sometimes by a woman, his androgynous, Sphinx-like face appeared as regularly in the papers as a car ad, effortlessly pulling in the kind of publicity his father had always longed for. Setting Holden up as his personal whipping boy, Kit taunted him at every opportunity, mocking his fleshy figure, his sea lion jowls, his flamboyant bouffant hair. He took swipes at his father's work too, ridiculing the cereal crops, the beet and grain quotas, and James's endless sycophantic flattery of the aristocracy.

As the permanent Iago to his father's ambitious Othello, Kit Wilkes had been a vicious, vocal tyrant. But he wasn't talking now, James thought with relief. No, Kit was quiet now, mercifully silent in his coma, his Cupid's bow mouth uncharacteristically shut. There will be no quotes from my bastard son—he nodded at the journalist politely—and none from me.

Back to looking at the speaker, James appeared to concentrate, but he was thinking about a new jibe he'd heard his son had been preparing. Another exposure to fire a crippling dart into his father's bloated backside. James Holden's eyes remained on the speaker, his expression encouraging, but his thoughts were in London, and he was wishing with fervent intensity that his son's coma would become permanent and that Kit Wilkes would never talk again.

Eighteen

SMOOTHING HIS HANDS OVER THE NEW LEATHER TOP OF HIS DESK, DR. Eli Fountain smiled, his cheeks dimpling and his capped teeth revealed. The furniture restorer had done a good job, the doctor thought admiringly; it was a very competent piece of work. But then money bought the best, Fountain told himself. The best furniture, the best workman. The best kind of life. He didn't dwell on all the whores he had to examine for venereal disease or the grubby running around he had done for Charlene Fleet over the years; such unpleasantness was forgotten at the sight of a perfectly restored piece of furniture or a dinner at Le Gavroche.

All those years earlier, back in Texas, he had been a figure of fun. Short and unprepossessing with a slow drawl and a pudgy body, Eli Fountain had made few friends and courted no lovers. Realizing early on that his bedside manner was more likely to cause a relapse than a recovery, he had changed focus, and when the local whorehouse needed a clap doctor, he had obliged. Whores were used to ugly men and required no wooing. In return for a favor, a drug prescription, or an abortion, Fountain had managed to get all the sex his body craved.

He discovered that he could buy respect too. At least to his face. But then, after a botched abortion, he left Texas for good. Holding on to his doctor's license, he came to London. The whorehouse in Texas had given him some contacts, and top of the list had been Park Street. Of course Eli Fountain had known that Chelsea was for the elite and that he had to assume a persona that would slide effortlessly into this new milieu. But then, no one had ever accused Eli of being a slow learner.

So he kept his drawl because it was considered amusing in London, gotten himself a Savile Row tailor, and bought himself an apartment in a respectable, tree-flecked part of Kensington. It took two weeks to pamper, buff, and shine his image to get it ready for his interview with Mrs. Fleet, and as he walked up the stairs to her private rooms, Eli Fountain felt like a man about to undergo an epiphany.

On his third knock, Mrs. Fleet had opened the door and stood back to let him in, and his life had changed in that instant. Of course she loathed him—Eli knew that; he wasn't a fool—but alongside the loathing was real admiration. Eli had known from the first moment he set eyes on her that Mrs. Fleet was a born whore. Her tasteful, expensive clothes couldn't hide her large peasant's hands. And her cool control couldn't camouflage her unfeeling venal nature. She was as well suited to her profession as he was to treating whores.

They were made for each other. And without ever exchanging one kind word or a single endearment, without expressing gratitude, compassion, or consideration, they built up a bond of mutual greed. Mrs. Fleet clicked her fingers; he did the running. For a fee. She called him in the early hours to patch up some whore who had taken a beating, and he sat with the girl until she was calm again. For a fee. Mrs. Fleet could demand drugs for some of her clients and expect them to be ready and waiting on the pillow, and Eli would oblige. For a fee.

Two depraved individuals who kept each other's secrets, with Mrs. Fleet always making sure she had the upper hand. And Eli Fountain kept his secret copious notes and listened to the call girls moan as he commiserated and slipped them prescriptions. He also obliged several well-known clients who needed treatment for an STD, not, of course, caught from Mrs. Fleet's girls but on trips abroad. They confided in Eli Fountain, and he kept their confidences. Along with all the other sticky, dirty secrets that came his way. There was always plenty of room to hide a scandal or cover up a disgrace. Always plenty of people needing a slick reptile of a man to bury their detritus. And Doctor Eli Fountain swore undying loyalty to all of them.

For a fee.

Hunkering down in his coat as it began to rain, Victor Ballam walked down Cork Street toward Piccadilly. He crossed at the lights and passed under the haughty sheltering colonnade of the Ritz, pausing to buy a copy of the *Evening Standard* from a street vendor. Reading the newspaper headlines, Victor was so preoccupied that when someone bumped into him, he automatically mumbled an apology.

"Sorry."

"Be careful."

Surprised by the man's tone, Victor stared at him. "I said sorry."

"You will be, Mr. Ballam, if you don't back off now."

"Back off? What are you talking about?"

"Mrs. Fleet, her girls. The Hogarth." The man paused, his well-modulated voice low. "I see you understand me." Slowly he glanced at the paper in Victor's hands. "You don't want to end up as a headline on the front page, do you? A murder victim?"

"Who the hell *are* you?"

"That's not important. I'm just a little cog in a giant wheel that can crush anyone in its way. Like you, Mr. Ballam. So please keep your nose out of this matter or at best you'll find yourself back in jail and at worst you'll find yourself dead."

With that, the man moved off, past the main entrance of the Ritz, and disappeared around the corner.

Shaken, Victor glanced around him, wondering if anyone else might have overheard the exchange. But they had been alone with no convenient witnesses to what he realized was an unmistakable threat.

The man was hardly a thug. Clean shaven and well spoken, he was around fifty and had worn glasses; he could have been any one of a million similar men crossing London Bridge every morning. Victor doubted he could even pick him out in a lineup, but then, there wasn't going to be a lineup, was there? Victor wasn't going to the police. He couldn't. Unless matters got out of hand.

But hadn't they just done exactly that? Hadn't his life just been threatened? The shrill ring of his cell phone broke into his thoughts, and he moved into a doorway to take the call. It was Mrs. Fleet.

Simply, without preamble, she said, "Bernie Freeland's dead. And in light of what else has been going on, I don't believe it was an accident."

"Neither do I." Victor looked around to see if anyone was watching him, if the man who had threatened him was waiting for him.

His unease was obvious even over the phone.

"Are you up to this?" Mrs. Fleet demanded, her tone imperious.

"I really don't know."

She laughed hoarsely. "An honest answer from an honest man. No wonder you were in jail. There's something else I should tell you. Liza Frith is safe here, but Annette Dvorski's missing. I think she went to New York to meet up with Bernie Freeland. Obviously she didn't know she's going to end up visiting him in the morgue."

"Couldn't you stop her?"

"Obviously not."

Victor was curt. "Is Liza Frith there with you?"

"Why?"

"Put her on the line, will you?"

"All right, but just one thing before you talk to Liza: I don't want her to know about Bernie Freeland. The less she knows, the better. I don't need her to panic."

Before Victor could reply, she'd left the phone. A lull was followed by muffled footsteps, and then a young woman's childlike nervous voice said, "Hello?"

"My name's Victor Ballam, Liza. Mrs. Fleet's hired me to look into what's been happening, and I want to ask you something. Was Marian jumpy on the plane?"

"No. She wasn't the type. Didn't get frightened of anything."

"So she was acting perfectly normally?"

"Yeah."

"How long had she known Bernie Freeland?"

"Four or five years, I think," Liza replied, her tone soft. "Marian had done loads of those private jet flights with Bernie."

Pausing, Victor picked his words carefully. "Did you?"

"Some; not as many as Marian or Annette."

"Did you know the pilots on the flight?"

"I knew one of them: Duncan Fairfax. He always flies Bernie's jet, but the other one was new; never seen him before. Tallish but a bit wimpy actually. Even a pilot's uniform didn't work for him." She laughed, momentarily lighthearted. "But Duncan Fairfax was showing off as usual, lording it over him. Pompous ass."

"What was the copilot's name?"

"I dunno," Liza admitted. "Sorry."

"What about the cabin crew? What can you remember about them?"

"One young guy, one older one with glasses. I'd see him before; he was always on Bernie's plane. His name's Malcolm Jenner, but I hadn't seen the younger one before. Bernie said he worked at his home in Sydney, but he wanted to travel."

"Did he make you feel uneasy?"

Unexpectedly, she laughed again.

"No; we made *him* feel uncomfortable when he walked into the cabin without knocking. Bernie teased him about it afterward. But he was nice enough, not more than twenty-five, twenty-six."

"You're very observant."

"After Bernie passed out, there were hours when there was nothing to do. A plane's got few amusements," she added.

"What about Lim Chang, the Chinese dealer? Did you talk to him?"

"Annette talked to him, but not me. I liked Sir Oliver Peters. He was nice—but sad . . . like some men are, you know? Seemed a bit lost, which was strange, but Bernie admires him. He thinks Sir Oliver's classy, told me he feels like an oaf when the Englishman's around."

"What did you and Sir Oliver talk about?"

"Something and nothing."

"Did you talk to Kit Wilkes?"

"Oh, no! He was pretending to be asleep most of the flight, and we hadn't been checked out by Doctor Fountain." She explained. "Wilkes won't sleep with anyone without a medical check from that weird little Yank before he performs—or we do. Mind you, I reckon that it's *his* partners who have to worry."

"So nothing out of the ordinary happened until Bernie Freeland's drink was spiked?"

"No, nothing."

"Did you put something in his drink?"

"No!" She laughed. "It was Annette. She loves her practical jokes. We were in Madrid once, and she sent a note over to the woman at the next table, pretending it was the waiter asking her out."

"After Bernie's drink got spiked, what did he do?"

"Got all sweaty and panicky and said something to Sir Oliver Peters. I was too far away to hear what it was. I just caught the word *Hogarth* and told Annette, but she wasn't interested. She was reading."

"Could Kit Wilkes have overheard what was said?"

Liza thought for a moment. "I reckon everyone on that plane could have heard if they were close enough and listening."

"Including the crew?"

"Maybe."

Victor paused for a moment before continuing. "One other thing. Did Bernie Freeland give you anything on the flight? Did he give you—or any of the other girls—a package, some kind of parcel?"

She frowned, baffled.

"No, just a bracelet. Bernie's always generous. Pays well and throws in gifts if you've pleased him. And he'd enjoyed himself; he told us that."

"Hang on," Victor said, tucking himself farther into the stone doorway as the rain increased. "So Bernie gave you a bracelet each?"

"No; he gave *me* a bracelet, from Cartier. And he gave Marian a ring, because that was what she'd asked for on the last trip." Liza paused, thinking. "But Annette's really into sports, so she asked for a set of golf clubs."

"You're kidding!"

Liza laughed. "No, seriously. But Bernie didn't like the idea and asked her if she'd like a baseball bat instead."

"A *baseball* bat?"

"I know, odd or what? Anyway, Annette said no. And he pushed her and said it would be a special bat. She still wasn't having it, but then she said a baseball bat was okay—if there was something *really* special about it. Maybe she wanted it gold plated or something," Liza said, laughing again. "I suppose she thought Bernie would wrap it in a fur coat. Who knows?"

Victor pressed her. "It was definitely Bernie who suggested the bat?"

"Oh, yeah; it was his idea. But I never saw it. . . . Oh, hang on; I remember now. Annette told me that Bernie was going to give it to her when she met up with him in New York."

"So Bernie kept it on the plane with him?" Victor was thrown when Mrs. Fleet's voice suddenly came on the phone.

"What's all this about baseball bats? Does it matter?"

"No, probably not," Victor lied.

He wasn't about to tell Charlene Fleet what he suspected. Years earlier someone had smuggled a painting in a walking stick, and it wasn't too big a jump to suppose that Bernie Freeland had suggested the baseball bat for the same reason: to smuggle a small rolled-up canvas. It would be easy to hollow out to make room, and with clever weighting, no one need ever know. What better way to transport the Hogarth secretly? But when Bernie had been drugged, he had panicked, certain that someone was trying to kill him. So instead of giving Annette the baseball bat on the jet, he had held on to it, promising to give it to her when she came to New York.

At first it must have seemed such a simple plan. Annette wouldn't know about it; she would simply keep her gift until Bernie visited her again and surreptitiously removed the picture. He would be the only one who knew where the painting was, so no one would be able to steal it while he found a buyer. That had been the plan *before* Bernie was spooked. But later, trying to shake off the effects of his spiked drink, he had watched the girls and the dealers leave the plane and then had the jet flown directly on to New York *with the baseball bat still in his possession.* He had already arranged for Annette to visit him a few days later. He would just give her the bat then. She would take it—and the hidden canvas—back to London on an anonymous British Airways flight.

Victor could imagine Bernie Freeland's panic when he was taken ill. He would have assumed that he was in danger, his usual cunning ousted by the sogginess of the ingested drugs. In a haze, he would have confided in the most trustworthy person—Sir Oliver Peters—hoping that if he was killed, he would have someone to stand witness for him.

"Victor," Mrs. Fleet asked impatiently. "Why does the bat matter?"

He lied without conscience.

"I don't know that it does, but one thing's for sure: Annette Dvorski's on her way to New York because she thinks she's meeting up with her client, but Bernie Freeland's been killed, which makes me wonder if someone's going to be waiting for your girl."

"Shit."

Ordering Liza to leave the room, Mrs. Fleet picked up the phone again.

"Are you still there?"

"Yes."

"I've been thinking about Marian Miller, about who might have killed her."

"I've been thinking the same."

"It had to be someone who knew about the Hogarth."

"Which could be a few people. Or dozens. After all, what was to stop any of them from spreading the news as soon as they got off the jet? They all had time. Kit Wilkes could have got on to the Russians, Lim Chang the Chinese, and Sir Oliver Peters was back on his own turf, with all his contacts in easy reach. Marian Miller told you about the Hogarth as soon as she landed, so why should she be the only one?"

"We don't know that everyone overhead."

"No, we don't. Yet," Victor agreed. "Of course, there's another possibility: one of your girls killed Marian."

"Don't be stupid! Liza isn't the type; neither is Annette. What about Lim Chang?"

"I don't know yet."

"Then find out!"

He bristled, stung by her tone. "I've only just started working on this."

"Work faster. I don't want anything else to happen. Annette might be in danger."

"Please don't tell me you care about them."

"I care about my little empire and my money," she replied, her tone expressionless. "What I've created, built up over the years. I don't write music or paint pictures; I use flesh, Mr. Ballam. Flesh is what I deal in. I buy it and sell it and do very well out of it. Trouble makes people pry. I don't like that. I don't want my business dealings exposed. So, in answer to your question, I don't care about what happens to my girls except inasmuch as it endangers me. I've never been the whore with the heart of gold. I can sense you don't like me."

"Do I have to?"

"Or perhaps you find the whole matter intimidating? A little too much for you to handle?"

He refused to show his irritation even though she had struck a nerve. Victor had never expected to leave jail and be immediately thrown into a murder inquiry; he had hoped to ease himself back into the art world, never anticipating this headlong plunge into the maelstrom. He knew how important the Hogarth was—and how dangerous. But he was only just realizing that the danger was coming straight to his door.

"So, *is* it too much for you?" Mrs. Fleet repeated.

Victor ignored the question. "I'm going to New York, so I'm going to need some help here."

"Which means?"

"That I need to hire someone in London. Which will mean more expense for you."

"And you have a suitable person in mind?"

Victor thought of Tully Harcourt. He knew that Tully had been reckless in his youth and still hankered after excitement—but *danger*? Wasn't that too much to ask? Did he really want to risk Tully Harcourt's safety to repay an old debt?

But then again, Tully Harcourt was the only person Victor *could* trust.

"Well?" Mrs. Fleet snapped. "*Have* you got someone who can help you?"

"Yes. Yes, I have." Taking her silence as confirmation that she had accepted the proposal, Victor continued.

"Where would Annette Dvorski stay in New York?"

"At Bernie Freeland's apartment. I haven't got the details next to me; I'll text them to you."

"Fine." His tone was deceptively polite. "Oh, and Mrs. Fleet . . ."

"Yes?"

"I'm *not* one of your whores. You can't buy me or sell me, and if something happens that I don't like—because, frankly, I doubt you've been straight with me about anything—I'll walk away from this situation, and you, without looking back."

"I don't think so, Mr. Ballam," she replied, her voice butter soft. "After all, you are *part* of the situation now."

Part Two

"Shiploads of Dead Christs, Holy Families
and Madonnas . . .
The connoisseurs and I are at war, you know,
because I hate them. . . ."

—WILLIAM HOGARTH

Nineteen

SLIDING THE KEY INTO THE LOCK OF BERNIE FREELAND'S NEW YORK apartment, Annette Dvorski pushed open the door and dropped her bag onto the hall floor, rubbing her stiff neck. The place was in darkness, which surprised her. Usually there was a maid in attendance when she visited Bernie; she had never been in the apartment before when it was deserted. Curious, she glanced about her, taking in the familiar surroundings, then went into the master bedroom, half expecting the Australian to jump out and surprise her. But she found herself alone and, disappointed, flicked on the plasma TV on the wall opposite the bed.

Bored and a little peckish, Annette moving to the kitchen and made herself a sandwich with some leftovers from the fridge. Tired and stiff from the flight, she ran a bath, pinned up her long red hair, and stepped into the warm water. *Perhaps Bernie has left me a note,* she thought idly. She'd look when she finished bathing. He'd left no message on her cell phone, not even a text. *Odd, because he always let her know if he couldn't make it. Maybe he was stuck in traffic,* Annette mused. The snow was bad in New York; that always held everyone up. But it wouldn't have stopped him from calling her. She closed her eyes, relaxing in the water. Knowing where Bernie kept his cocaine, Annette decided she would take a snort later. Well, why not? Bernie was always open-handed.

She soaped her legs, then her breasts, studying a mole near her left nipple and remembering the LA Dodgers baseball bat. Bernie had told her all about it, delighted that he had managed to get hold of all the players' signatures. It was to be a prize, if she won a point against him the next time they played squash together. *Hah,* Annette thought; *like he ever really beat me. I could hammer the hell out of him if I wanted to, but why humiliate a client? Especially one as generous as Bernie Freeland.* Kneading a knotted muscle in her left calf, Annette thought of Mrs. Fleet and felt a twinge of anxiety.

When her employer found out—and she would—about this extracurricular trip to visit Bernie, there would be hell to pay. The two women had always disliked each other, but Mrs. Fleet saw her profit in Annette Dvorski and

Annette knew that she could get the highest fees by working as a Park Street girl. So they tolerated one another, occasionally spitting invective and, once, Mrs. Fleet actually hitting Annette during a quarrel. The fact that the madam hadn't raised her voice once during the altercation had made the violence all the more unexpected and shocking. Stupidly, Annette had lifted her hand to hit back, but the dog that was always with Mrs. Fleet had started snarling, and she had been forced to back down.

Annette also knew that her background, her supposedly impoverished Polish origins, nettled Mrs. Fleet so much that the woman had even asked Annette to change her name. But the redhead's stubborn streak had come out. After all, she had said, how many of the johns were interested in a girl's surname? In fact, Dvorski wasn't her father's name; Annette had taken her mother's maiden name after she died, a sentimental, titular memorial to a woman she could barely remember.

Still soaping herself, Annette studied her body, thankful there were no signs of aging even though she was thirty-one. Athletic genes and playing sports regularly had kept her lithe, able to cheat her real age. Slyly she smiled to herself. Mrs. Fleet thought she was twenty-six; indeed, she often said that a whore's best earning days were over when she hit thirty. Well, perhaps *hers* had been, but Annette was relying on at least another couple of good years. Or less if she could just hook Bernie Freeland.

Getting out of the bath, Annette wrapped a towel around herself. She knew she was Bernie's favorite girl; that much was obvious, and it had certainly galled Marian Miller. Annette remembered the dead girl without affection. Marian had been cold, conniving, and self serving, but the news of her death had been shocking. Suddenly uneasy, Annette moved into the kitchen, where dozens of stainless steel doors reflected her image back to her. She turned up the central heating. It was getting very cold now, snow falling outside the window and landing on the balcony; the lights of the apartment building opposite shone like glowworms in the freezing night.

Of course, she had been a bloody fool to spike Bernie's drink. She had only done it for a laugh, but no one could have foreseen his reaction. Annette frowned, remembering how Bernie had leaned down to talk to Sir Oliver Peters, his face sweaty, panicked. Aware of what she had done and feeling guilty, Annette had turned away from the scene, but the word *Hogarth* had caught her attention. Cursing, she tried to hear more of the garbled conversation but could only just make out Bernie saying, *"I've got it."*

Which was interesting. Very interesting.

Of course Annette had told Liza that she had heard nothing. After all, what point was there in broadcasting the news? News that might prove to be very lucrative for her. She knew enough about the art world to realize what having a Hogarth painting would mean, how it would swell Bernie Freeland's already overflowing coffers.

Slumped in a chair, watching the snowflakes land on the balcony, Annette wondered idly when Bernie would get back to the apartment. With the hazy lights opposite watchful and unwelcoming in the falling snow, she suddenly felt isolated and longed to hear the key in the lock, longed for Bernie's arrival to break the suffocating dead silence. Annette's confidence faltered momentarily, but she rallied, remembering the baseball bat, the present she had been promised. Bernie had said that he would give it to her when she came to New York. *Well, I am here now,* Annette thought. Looking for her present would keep her occupied.

Beginning in the bedroom, she looked through the closets, then searched the bathroom, the kitchen, and finally the living room. Lifting the window seats, she paused, wondering where else he could possibly have hidden it. Not in the hall cupboard, so where?

A thought suddenly occurred to her, and, smiling, she left a note for Bernie. Then she pulled on a tracksuit and made for the back stairs that would take her down to the basement gym eight flights below. Annette's fingers slid along the icy handrail; her feet moved noiselessly on the stairs. She began to hurry, and her breathing accelerated. At the bottom of the steps she took a deep breath, then pushed through the double doors into the gym.

The manager nodded a welcome. "Can I help you?"

"Did Mr. Freeland leave something for me to collect?"

"*Mr. Freeland?*" He appeared surprised, staring at her for a long moment before taking something out from under the counter. "He left this for you, miss. I was supposed to give it to you." Bernie Freeland was no mug. He didn't want to leave the bat in his apartment, where anyone could find it, and knew it would be securely locked in at the gym. He'd even slipped the manager a heavy retainer to ensure it went only to Annette.

Annette's manicured hand took hold of the bat, which was still wrapped in brown paper. "Thank you."

"I'm really sorry, miss."

She frowned. "About what?"

"Well, you know. . . ."

"No. What?"

"Mr. Freeland," the man said uncomfortably. "He was killed yesterday. In a traffic accident."

She felt the strength leave her legs. She spoke in a faraway voice that seemed to belong to somebody else,

"Mr. Freeland's *dead*?"

"You didn't know, miss? I'm so sorry. Can I get you a glass of water?"

Shaking her head, Annette backed away, moving out of the lobby, and looked up the stairwell. The stairs seemed to extend upward indefinitely, the echoing gray concrete bitterly cold and hostile. Turning away, she moved to the elevator and pressed the buzzer, her mind a collage of images: Bernie and Marian Miller, half-remembered clips of experiences and conversations, and a name—Hogarth. *Hogarth. Hogarth.* At last the elevator came to a stop in front of her, the doors slid open, and she walked in. Luckily, it was empty, and she leaned against the wall, holding on to the baseball bat, her eyes fixed on the lighted numbers overhead. Two, three, four, five . . . Suddenly the elevator stopped, and Annette tensed, expecting someone to enter. But no one was waiting, and after another moment the doors closed again and the elevator restarted its slow ascent.

Six, seven . . . Her breathing jagged with anxiety, Annette watched as the doors opened at her floor, then she stepped out. Down the hallway, a young man noticed the striking redhead, and a couple leaving for dinner nodded politely to her as they passed.

She moved toward the apartment, unlocked the door, and walked in.

It was eight-thirty in New York. Winter snow was falling, the lights were on all over the city, and yellow cabs sounded their horns as they limped through the traffic below. As a shaken Annette Dvorski walked into the apartment, she noticed that it was warm again and that there was a light flickering on the answer phone.

But she didn't notice the footprints on the balcony outside, fresh footprints breaking into the smoothness of the silent snow.

Twenty

"Like I said, I'm up for it. Is the whoremonger general paying expenses?" Tully asked

"She is. I am now officially working for Mrs. Fleet." Victor, in a taxi on its way to Heathrow Airport, was talking fast into his cell phone. "I'm going to New York," he explained. "Catching the next flight, so I'll be away, and I need someone in London."

"Thrilling. When do I start?"

"You sure about this?" Victor asked. "I told you what happened last night. I was threatened."

"You were warned off."

"What's the difference?"

"If the man was attached to the royals, he was just sent to scare you."

"But what if he wasn't? What if he was working for someone else entirely?"

"If you believe that, why are you still working on the case?"

"I need the money."

"Not to mention that a Hogarth is involved," Tully commented perceptively. "Stop worrying about me, Victor; I've got friends in low places. And besides, I've got nothing to lose."

"No one has *nothing* to lose."

Ignoring the comment, Tully went on. "Did I ever tell you about my grandfather? He married his first wife, then fell in love with her sister and set her up as his mistress in another town. He died a happy man, having kept his secret for decades."

"So?"

"After he died, the two sisters congratulated themselves on having feigned ignorance for so long. You see, they knew about each other all the time; it was just that neither of them had liked my grandfather enough to want him around seven days a week. So they had shared him. And all along they had let him think he was Don Juan."

"What's your point?"

"No one's who they seem," Tully said enigmatically.

"Are you sure you want in on this?"

"Yes. And don't ask me again. Have you anything to go on?"

"I think I know where the Hogarth is," Victor said simply. "And if I know, someone else might know too."

"Be careful. You might not see them coming."

"I didn't see jail coming either," Victor said bitterly. "Listen, Tully, there were two men acting as stewards on Bernie Freeland's flight. One man's an old hand called Malcolm Jenner, always worked for Bernie, and the other's a younger man called Terry Shaw. He was new; it was his first flight." Victor paused. "Can you talk to them if I send their addresses through to you?"

"No problem."

Clicking off his cell phone, Victor leaned back in the taxi and gazed out the window, thinking of Tully, his mind wandering back, reliving a past memory.

"You and I will live here forever, of course," Ingola had said, that long flaxen hair flipping up on her shoulders, her eyes narrowing against the sunlight. Behind her a field of linseed had shimmered hotly against the blue crater of sky; a swallow made staccato flights between clouds. "We'll have three children, at least."

He doubted it but hadn't said so. He was sure that Ingola's career would postpone the birth of children for some time. He didn't mind; her ambition matched his, although her single-mindedness could be brutal at times. But that was her charm: a combination of the sensual and the savage.

"We'll have three boys."

"Triplets; then you can have them all at once," he had teased, pausing to look past her shoulder at the man approaching. His voice had tightened immediately. "I thought you said no one knew we were here."

She had turned in slow motion, her skirt making a half circle in the heat, one hand already raised in greeting.

"Oh, Victor," she had replied, almost laughing. "It's only Tully."

Only Tully.

"We're here, mate."

Jerked back into the present, Victor paid the cabbie and moved into the airport. His confidence had blistered, and memory was playing ghost chords in the back of his mind.

Twenty-One

DUCKING UNDER THE AWNING, TULLY PAUSED, STARING AT THE GROUP of men who were surrounding a shallow circular metal ring, like a child's wading pool. The tent was smoggy with cigarette fug and the overwhelming smell of beer; two dark-skinned men stood by the entrance taking money, one wearing a T-shirt with a DKNY logo. Staring at Tully, the younger man nodded in recognition and let him move farther inside. His eyes stinging from the thick cigarette smoke, Tully glanced into the circular pit and watched as a weedy man of about sixty, coughing, smoothed over the bloodied surface with a rake. From the back of the tent came the sound of dogs barking frantically.

"I thought it were you," the man said, looking up at Tully as he approached. "Seen you at the horses often enough but never seen you 'ere before."

"No, I don't care for it," Tully replied, offering the man a cigarette and lighting it for him.

He had no taste for cruelty but knew that Bernie Freeland's steward, Malcolm Jenner, was involved in illegal dogfighting in Hackney. Tully saw one dog—a white bull terrier—being led into the ring, the owner of its opponent still standing next to his animal's locked cage.

Raising his voice to be heard over someone shouting the odds for the next match, he asked, "Where's Malcolm Jenner?"

The man jerked his head toward the makeshift bar set up on a couple of trestle tables. A hard-faced woman was serving behind it, helped by a weasely looking youth in a baseball cap pulled low over his face.

"That's his wife."

"His wife?" Tully noted her fleshy arms, her flushed face.

"Yeah, she runs these fights." The old man turned away to continue raking the bloodied sand, saying, "She'll tell you where Malcolm is. She keeps him on a tighter leash than the dogs."

"What's he like?"

"Under her thumb. She tells the poor bastard when he can piss, but she's no time for him really. Besotted with that dim-witted kid of theirs." He nodded toward the bar. "Been in Borstal for setting fires, little bastard. No wonder Malcolm gets away working for Bernie Freeland whenever he can."

Nodding, Tully walked over to the woman. Her eyes were small in her puffy face; her acrylic nails clicked against the beer cans as she opened them to pass them over the bar.

"What can I get you, love?"

"McEwan's," Tully replied, passing her the money. "I want to talk to your husband."

Her voice hardened. "I run the business."

"It's not about the dogs; it's about Malcolm's day job."

Immediately losing interest, she shrugged her fleshy shoulders and pointed toward a man who was just approaching the ring. "If you want a word, I'd be quick; the next fight's on soon."

Moving back to the ring, Tully could feel the tension rising in the arena as a trio of burly men laid bets, with a man in a shiny trilby hat shouting the odds. "*Old Boy*" was called out, then "*Spital fields,*" with Tully taking a moment to realize that they were talking about the dogs. All around him were the unhealthy faces of men habituated to fatty food and cheap beer. Some were sweating, and some were hyper, their attention fixed on the coming fight; one elderly man in a wheelchair pushed his way to the front of the ring.

Turning to a narrow-shouldered dapper man of about forty-five, Tully tapped him on the shoulder.

"Are you Malcolm Jenner?"

He didn't look up from the ring. "Who's asking?" His voice had a rough tone, like someone with a sore throat.

"I just want to have a word with you."

"And I want to marry Penelope Cruz; looks like we're both going to be disappointed," Jenner replied sarcastically, and beckoned to a man across the ring.

"It won't take a minute." Tully persisted. "It's about Bernie Freeland."

Malcolm's interest was suddenly piqued. "Does Mr. Freeland want me?"

"Not exactly," Tully replied. "Can we go outside and talk?"

"I've got a fight on, mister. If you want to talk to me, you can wait."

Nodding, Tully watched as the two dogs were lifted into the ring, each catching sight of the other and both straining at their leashes, their eyes rolling, spittle dribbling from their mouths. Both animals had obviously fought before; one had half an ear missing, and the other was badly scarred around the muzzle. But Tully knew that once they were released, both of them would fight to the death. He also knew that pit bulls and bull terriers had a death lock, that once they locked their bite on muscle or bone, nothing could prize them off.

Having once seen a dogfight before and having sworn never to see another, Tully walked away from the ring before the bout started. He stood outside smoking and waited for Malcolm Jenner to come to him after the fight was over. He felt rather than saw the first slamming of the dogs' bodies into each other, heard their hysterical barking and yelps punctuating the silent ripping of flesh. He could smell the sawdust and the blood coming from the ring and kept staring ahead, lighting another cigarette with shaking hands. He knew that often one of the dogs was killed; sometimes the owner would bury the corpse, but more often it was thrown into a nearby dump. He also knew that even if someone had heard about the illegal dogfight, by the time he had contacted the RSPCA and an officer had been called out, the bout would be over. The tent down, the bar closed. A dog's carcass in a recycling bin the only evidence left.

"So," Malcolm Jenner said, emerging from the tent some minutes later, "what d'you want?"

"Bernie Freeland's dead."

Clearly shocked, Jenner took a step back, glancing over his shoulder toward his wife and son. Without being told, Tully could guess what he was thinking. No more escapes, no more exotic—blessedly distant—locations. Just the grinding drudge of life in Hackney with a few pints at the weekend and an apartment in the projects smelling of dog hair.

"Dead? When?"

"Yesterday."

"How?"

"Traffic accident. Mr. Freeland was run over."

"I don't believe it! He never walked anywhere. He had a driver, or he got a cab." Jenner's expression was wary, his mistrust obvious. "Where did this so-called accident happen?"

"New York."

"Jesus Christ." Jenner fetched himself a can of beer at the bar and then came back to Tully, pulling the ring tag and tossing it onto the ground before taking a long drink. Finally he spoke again.

"Who are you?"

Tully smiled; always easy around people, never threatening, always inviting conversation and confidences.

"Me? I'm just looking into Mr. Freeland's death."

"I bet you bloody are," Jenner replied coldly, "It needs looking into. You're not police?"

"No. Don't worry about that."

"I mean, what with the dogfights . . ."

"I'm not police."

Jenner seemed to be diminishing in front of Tully's eyes, his confidence evaporating as the news of his employer's death hit home. "So someone's hired you to take a closer look at this accident?"

Tully nodded. "Mr. Freeland was a well-known man, a very rich man, and he must have had some enemies."

"Not really. He was an Australian, spoke his mind. People liked him." He looked Tully up and down. "But you don't think his death was an accident?"

"Marian Miller's death was no accident either."

Jenner flinched. "I heard about that. Nasty business."

"Of course, everything I'm saying to you goes no further. Otherwise, I'd have to report the dogfights, wouldn't I?"

Jenner's eyes flickered. "I've got your drift."

"What did *you* think about Marian Miller's death?"

"She was probably killed by her john. It looks that way from what I heard. I mean, why else would anyone kill her?"

"Well, we've been thinking about that," Tully continued. "Marian Miller was on that flight with Bernie Freeland, and I was wondering if you saw or heard anything which might explain her murder."

"Like what?"

"Apparently Mr. Freeland's drink was spiked—"

"Yeah."

"—and he was babbling."

"It was nothing in particular."

"So you heard what he said?"

"No; he was quiet again when I got him to his seat." Looking around,

Jenner dropped his voice. "Have you spoken to the other people on the flight? There were three other art dealers apart from Mr. Freeland and three working girls. And there were the pilots and Terry Shaw as well as me. Have you spoken to them yet?"

"No. I'm talking to Duncan Fairfax later."

"Good luck. He's a prick."

Amused, Tully looked at his notes. "And then I'll have a chat with the second pilot, John Yates."

"He was a newcomer. Mr. Freeland said that he was replacing the usual copilot. Said he came with very good references."

"Did you talk to him?"

"Yeah," Jenner replied, nodding. "He had his work cut out with Duncan Fairfax. I even worried about him, you know, being young and Fairfax being a bit of a bully. But he seemed calm, let it all wash over him." His voice dropped. "Mr. Freeland always used Duncan Fairfax because he's the best there is. He made allowances for his superior ways because of that. Mind you, Fairfax might have treated us like dirt, but he always brownnosed the boss."

Tully pressed on. "What about the steward who was working with you, Terry Shaw? What's he like?"

"Ah, enthusiastic but thick. And young, not much more than a kid really," Jenner replied, finishing his beer. "Well, same age as my boy, but a bit more about him. Not into arson, anyway." His voice drifted. "You see these?" he said suddenly, pointing at his impressively even teeth. "Mr. Freeland paid for these. I had problems for a long time, but when I'd been working for him for three years, he sent me to his dentist and paid for the lot. He was a good boss. You looked after him, and he looked after you."

"Did he pay well?"

"What d'you think?"

"So how will you manage now?"

Jenner shrugged. "Christ knows. It's not the money; you can always get hold of money. It's the job I'll miss. The uniform—I looked good in that uniform. White jacket and black trousers with gold stripe down the sides. Had them handmade, Mr. Freeland did." He paused, suddenly angry. "If he was killed, *why* was he killed?"

"You tell me," Tully replied, feeling his way. "I wasn't on that flight; you were. You must have seen and heard what was going on."

"Marian was killed in a hotel."

"Yes, but she'd just been on the jet with Mr. Freeland. Who's also been killed. The flight's the only thing they have in common. Please, humor me, Mr. Jenner," Tully went on. "Just tell me what went on and what you remember of the journey."

Jenner shrugged. "The Chinese dealer was working most of the time, that poof Wilkes was sleeping or pretending to, and Sir Snotty Oliver was looking airsick. He spent a while in the washroom." He thought back, remembering. "The girls were with Mr. Freeland, but then his drink got spiked—"

"It was definitely spiked?"

"Yeah. I thought at first someone had just put vodka in his tonic, but when I took the glass away, I could smell something odd. Mr. Freeland was okay, though; he slept it off. About two hours into the journey to New York I heard he was normal again."

"You *heard*? You weren't there?"

"No," Jenner replied. "Mr. Freeland has—had—two separate crews. Both regular. But if we had to fly for a long time, we changed crews. The pilots and the cabin crew can only work so many hours, so that day, when the boss decided he wanted to go straight on to New York, the other crew came on and relieved us."

"Before you left, did Mr. Freeland ask you what had happened when he was doped?"

"No. He didn't remember a thing. It didn't seem to occur to him that he might have done anything out of ordinary."

Tully nodded. "Anything unusual happen *before* Bernie Freeland's drink was spiked?"

"No. Me and Terry Shaw took care of the girls and the other dealers."

"You can't have stayed awake the whole time."

"Sure I did," he said scornfully. "I'm used to long flights."

"What about Terry Shaw?"

"He was buzzing; no chance of sleeping. It was his first flight on a private jet, and he couldn't get over it. Kept telling me that his girlfriend wouldn't believe it. He was so full of it, he took some photographs on his cell phone. I told him Mr. Freeland would give him hell if he found out."

"Terry Shaw took photographs?"

"Yeah," Jenner agreed. "Just of the inside of the plane and the bar. You know what kids are like; they're easily impressed."

Tully frowned. "He didn't take photographs of the girls?"

"Nah; his girlfriend would have gone mad. Terry was just thrilled about being on the private jet with Bernie Freeland."

"But didn't he work for Bernie Freeland in Australia?"

"Yeah. Shaw's family's English, but they emigrated a while back. He's got an English passport, but he was brought up in Australia. Terry had been working for Mr. Freeland at his house in Sydney, so it wasn't surprising he came on the jet. The boss didn't like strangers; he would never have let someone he didn't know on board. You can bet your life John Yates had been thoroughly checked out."

"Why was Freeland like that? What was he hiding?"

"His life, his business? There were call girls on the flight; you know that. Mr. Freeland liked to know that his staff was discreet," Jenner answered, his tone curt. "Who are you working for?"

"Someone who wants to know what happened. And you were there; you had a bird's-eye view."

"I wasn't in the cabin every minute."

"But if you weren't, then Terry Shaw would have been."

Jenner shrugged. "I can only tell you that there was some kind of upset with Mr. Freeland."

"Was he angry with Marian Miller? Or one of the other girls?"

"You're asking me questions I can't answer. What went on in the private part of the jet was off limits," Jenner replied emphatically. "I can only tell you what I know."

"What about the other dealers? Did Mr. Freeland talk to them?"

"Not much," Jenner said. "He chatted to Sir Oliver for a while, Kit Wilkes wasn't talking to anyone, and as for the other guy, I don't remember my boss talking to him at all. Mr. Freeland had the girls for company."

Tully nodded. "D'you know where Terry Shaw lives?"

"When he's in London, he stays with his family in Peckham. Does he know about Mr. Freeland?"

"Not through me," Tully replied, changing the subject. "So there was nothing that struck you as strange about that flight?"

"Only what an odd bunch they were," Jenner said, "Everyone seemed ill at ease, a bit uncomfortable. Even that bastard Wilkes."

"You don't like him?"

"Come on, who does? That little bum's made a living out of being a professional shit. Now, if you'd come to me and told me that *he'd* been killed, I wouldn't have been surprised. In fact, I'm amazed James Holden hasn't done him in years ago."

"So it was just a fluke that these art dealers were thrown together on the jet? You'd never seen them mix with your boss before; they weren't friends?"

"No," Jenner replied firmly. "We gave them a ride because their flights were delayed. As far as I know, they weren't friends and didn't socialize with one another."

"Thanks for your time," Tully said.

"Is that it?" Jenner sounded surprised.

"For now, yes," Tully replied, passing him a card. "If you think of anything, ring me."

"Just like that? You're not bringing the police into this?" Jenner said, baffled.

"To the outside world, the deaths look unrelated," Tully replied calmly. "The police believe Marian Miller was killed by a john, and Bernie Freeland died in a traffic accident. And for the moment, that's the way it's going to stay."

Behind them Tully could hear the sound of dogs starting to bark, and a battered metallic 4 × 4 pulled up alongside the tent. As a thickset man got out of the passenger seat. Jenner called out a nervous greeting, then walked off, the sound of the dogs echoing eerily in the city night.

Twenty-Two

BACK INSIDE BERNIE FREELAND'S APARTMENT, ANNETTE DVORSKI noticed that her hands were shaking uncontrollably as she locked the door behind her. Throwing the baseball bat onto the sofa, she began pacing the room, trying to make sense of what she had just heard. Bernie was dead. Bernie Freeland, the man she was relying on for an easy life, was dead. *Jesus*, she thought angrily, *why? Why was he dead? What kind of fucking accident had killed him? He never walked anywhere, so what the hell was he doing getting himself run over? It was such an ordinary, stupid way to die,* she thought, flopping heavily into an armchair and staring ahead.

He might not have known it, but Bernie Freeland had been chosen to become Annette Dvorski's personal, lucrative pension fund. He had always liked her and had recently mentioned that he wanted to set her up in her own apartment, keep her available just for him. Not bad, Annette had thought, imagining Mrs. Fleet's face when she told her. Rehearsing and relishing the words she would say to her bitch of a boss: *I'm set for life, no more working for you, you cold freak. No more Park Street, no more Mother Fleet. I'm home free, landed one of the biggest fishes there is.*

But then a lovely, fat, unexpected bonus had dropped into Annette's lap. Not only had she dreamed of landing Bernie Freeland, but she also dreamed of getting her hands on the Hogarth painting. She had worked for many of the art dealers from London, New York, and the Far East, and her connections were legion. How better to escape the whoring than by buying herself out? After all, she knew Arnold Fletcher and still had tentative contact with the reckless and deviant Guy Manners. She would auction the Hogarth privately, setting up a bidding war and knowing that the art hyenas would gather for the kill. All she had to do was get hold of the painting.

But right now all Annette could do was stare ahead, unable to act. If Bernie had just managed to live a bit longer, she would have been able to tease the hiding place out of him. She knew how much he'd cared for her. When the moment had been ripe, she would have made her move, landing the Hogarth and her own personal big fish. Instead, the big fish had landed on a mortuary slab, not going anywhere. Rage and frustration overwhelmed Annette, and she hurled a glass figurine against the wall, heard it splinter into a dozen fragments. *Why now? Why did he have to die now? A traffic accident, a bloody traffic accident—*

Annette stopped short, her mind in free fall. *A traffic* accident. *But was it really? Bernie was dead; Marian was dead.* Unnerved, she shivered. *Two deaths happening to two people who had traveled on the same plane. Two people who had known about the Hogarth.*

The hairs rose on the back of Annette's neck. She hurried into the bedroom, changed out of her sporting gear, and began tossing her clothes into her case. Zipping up her boots, Annette paused, cold to the bone. She was in New York, alone in a dead man's apartment with no protection and with knowledge that had already cost two lives. Unsteadily, she stood and picked up the baseball bat. She thought of Bernie Freeland and was tempted to leave it behind, but she pushed it into her suitcase and slammed the lid closed.

She would run, she told herself. Go back to the airport and catch the first flight home. It would be safer hiding in plain sight, much safer than going to an unfamiliar hotel. And much safer than staying in a dead man's home. Suddenly remembering her cell phone, Annette took it out of her bag. There had been four missed calls but no messages, and she was just about to put it back in her pocket when it rang.

Surprised, she stared at it, not recognizing the number, wondering if she should answer. It rang again, piercing in the quiet apartment, the snow muffling the usual noise outside. Again it rang, and Annette finally answered.

"Hello?"

"Annette Dvorski?"

"No; she's out."

"I don't think so."

Her hand gripped the phone, terror welling up inside her, her mouth dry as dust. "Who is this?"

"My name's Victor Ballam. I'm working for Mrs. Fleet." He could tell that she was confused and pressed on. "Are you all right?"

"Bernie Freeland's dead."

"I know."

"You *know*?"

"Yes," he said, catching the imminent panic in her voice. "Where are you?"

"In his apartment," Annette said, looking around.

"On your own?"

"No, there's a bar mitzvah going on in here! Of course I'm on my own."

"I'm in New York. I'm on my way to the apartment now."

"*What?*"

"I thought you'd be there. I'm close, really close." Victor said, obviously running. "Just wait for me."

But even as he spoke, Annette heard a sound coming from the bathroom and tensed. Her voice fell almost to a whisper. "I can hear noises!"

"Noises?"

"Maybe . . . I don't know; it could just be the plumbing. Or someone in the next apartment."

"Get out of there, Annette."

She nodded, hardly breathing. "I will, I will," she replied, her ears straining for any other sounds. Silently, she picked up her case and tiptoed toward the door, but when she tried the handle, it was locked. *"I can't open the door!"* she hissed into the phone, "It's locked." Frantically she rattled the door.

On the inside, the bolts were all drawn back. *Which meant that someone had locked it from the outside.*

"Jesus, I can't open it!"

"Is there another exit?"

Desperate, she ran into the kitchen, looking around. "No, no other exit."

Terrified, she moved into the living room again. The light was dim from the heavy snowfall as she flicked on a lamp. And then she saw the footprints on the balcony outside.

"Oh, Jesus," she sobbed. "Oh, no. *No!*"

"What is it? Annette, what is it?"

Her eyes were fixed on the footprints, her voice hoarse.

"Someone's here." She ran to the door again.

He could hear the frantic drumming of her hands on the wood, her muffled sobbing coming desperately over the phone line.

"Annette!" he shouted. "Annette!"

But she didn't answer. Victor ran the rest of the way as fast as he could. Arriving at the apartment block just as someone was leaving by the back door, he took the stairs two at a time, pushing open the fire exit doors on the seventh floor and then racing toward Bernie Freeland's apartment. Expecting to hear Annette still banging on the door, he slowed as he approached, unnerved by the total, threatening silence. Silence in the hallway and silence coming from the locked apartment.

"Annette?" he called anxiously. "Annette?"

He grabbed the handle and, to his surprise, felt it turn and the door open. Inside the apartment the lights were turned off. Victor's shadow fell onto the pale cold carpet of the dead man's home. His heartbeat drumming in his ears, he stepped into the darkness, feeling for a light switch on the wall.

"Annette?" he called out again. "Are you in here?"

He groped in the darkness, urgently looking for the switch. Then he heard a soft muffled sound and turned. In that moment something struck the back of his skull with such force that he fell forward, the floor rising to meet him as he lost consciousness.

Twenty-Three

DOWNING HIS THIRD CUP OF ESPRESSO IN THE TASTEFUL SURROUNDINGS of the Ritz London, Lim Chang dabbed the corners of his mouth and paid his bill. Once outside on Piccadilly, he was struck by the freezing sleet of the early morning and dipped his head against the cold. The black and gilt entrance to the Burlington Arcade was enticing, but he wasn't going to see Sir Oliver Peters. At least not yet. Although Chinatown—his immediate destination—wasn't far, he hailed a taxi to take him there.

He knew that most of the residents he wanted to talk to would not be up and about so early. Most worked night hours and slept late, which might well give him a slight, if temporary, advantage. Dressed in a dark suit and coat, he fiddled nervously with the white collar of his shirt and wondered if he should have gone for less formal attire after all. But then again, he was an outsider; no point trying to pretend otherwise. Besides, his appearance would ensure that everyone noticed him. The cab pulled up outside the New World restaurant, and Lim Chang got out and paid the driver. He glanced at the red gates that signaled the entrance to Chinatown and thought, not for the first time, that they were looking shabby, the red paint a little chipped, the florid display too stereotypically Far Eastern to enchant. Or maybe he was just jaded.

He walked past the New World restaurant and turned into Red Lion Street, watched by a Chinese woman who had her arms folded and was talking to a male kitchen hand who was rolling a smoke. From the open back door behind them came a billow of kitchen steam and the sound of dishwashers slamming closed. Skirting the pavement trash cans, Lim Chang watched as a van pulled up; two agile men opened its back doors and slammed crates of fish onto the pavement, calling out loudly in Cantonese. He nodded as he passed by, and they stared curiously after the businesslike figure, seeing him turn into one of the most notorious side alleys in London.

Uninterested in the effect he was creating, Chang moved down the passageway, past two closed shops and a known gambling club fronting as a lap-dancing venue. When he reached the third doorway, he looked down into the basement. A light was on, and after pausing for an instant, he descended the narrow stone steps. Through the open basement door, he saw two men playing cards and a woman feeding a scrawny baby, her eyes unfocused as the child suckled. Against one window was a table piled with unwashed plates and a knotted glue of burned candle ends. On the wall beside it hung a poster of Hong Kong with an obscene image drawn on it.

Slapping down his cards, one of the men—grossly fat and sweating profusely even though the temperature was hardly above thirty-five degrees—turned and looked at Lim Chang hovering in the doorway.

"I need some information," Lim Chang said simply, introducing himself to both men. He could see that his name registered, and the obese man gestured toward a chair with his puffy hand.

Lim Chang took the plastic seat, keeping his gaze averted from the woman feeding the child, who seemed indifferent to the fact that both of her breasts were visible The room smelled unpleasantly of onions, cooked food, and the giveaway stink of bugs.

"Information?"

Lim Chang nodded. "Do you know of a painting coming onto the market?"

Suspicious, the fat man looked over to his thinner companion, who idly scratched his shoulder with long yellowed fingernails. He turned bloodshot eyes to Chang.

"A painting?"

Chang inclined his head. "I want to know where this painting is. The artist is Hogarth, William Hogarth."

"Why would we know?" he said, turning to the gross man.

"If the painting is in London, you'd know about it," Lim Chang replied. "The Chinese government wishes to own this work. They would reward anyone well for assistance in this matter."

"Was it stolen?" the thinner man asked, moving to the sink and running the water. As he did so, the woman seemed to come back to life as she shoved the infant into a grubby crib and went and leaned against him.

"What's going on?" she asked.

He ignored her and went back to the table, his bleary eyes hard as he looked at Lim Chang. "Well, *was* it stolen?"

"I'm not sure," Chang replied with awesome composure. "The Australian art dealer Bernie Freeland recently acquired the painting."

The fat man wiped his forehead with a cloth. "And?"

"He's now dead."

"And the painting?"

"No one knows where it is," Lim Chang said tonelessly. "Mr. Freeland's death was supposedly an accident."

The men exchanged a glance, both picking up on the word *supposedly*.

"You've not heard about this death? This accident?" Chang persisted. "But you know who Mr. Freeland was?"

The obese man nodded.

"This painting is of great significance. As I say, the Chinese government would be most desirous of owning the work." He rose to his feet, certain that they understood. "I would pay very well for information regarding Mr. Hogarth and his whereabouts. I feel sure you will want to assist me in this."

Both men watched him in silence as he walked to the door, then listened to his footsteps as he climbed the basement steps. After a second or two, the fat man jerked his head.

Moments later, a wiry little man with spatulate yellow nails was following Lim Chang through Chinatown, watching the smart figure move farther and farther from the welcoming red gates into the mire beyond.

Surprised that he hadn't heard from Victor, Tully considered the brief telephone conversation he had just had with Bernie Freeland's pilot. Arrogant and short-tempered, Fairfax had answered Tully's questions curtly, with no embellishment. Yes, he had worked for Mr. Freeland for a decade. No, he didn't know the whores on that ill-fated flight or any of the hookers who had come and gone over the last ten years. Yes, it was a pity Freeland was dead as it would be the end to his lucrative pilot contract. And no, Fairfax said firmly, he hadn't liked the man one iota.

"I was doing my job, for which I was very well paid," he'd said, his tone impatient. "I'm a pilot. I don't mix with the passengers, especially the types Mr. Freeland liked."

"But there weren't only call girls on that particular flight," Tully had said. "There were some very important art dealers too, one of them a distinguished peer. Weren't you tempted to talk to them?"

"I was flying the plane." Fairfax's tone was pompous, self-important.

"You could have handed it over to your copilot, John Yates."

"Hah! A novice. It was his first flight for Mr. Freeland. I'd hardly let him take over, even temporarily."

"But he must have done that now and again, if only to let you stretch your legs."

The pilot's tone was metallic. "Are you trying to imply something?"

"Should I be?"

"I don't like your tone—"

Tully cut him off, oiling his ego into good temper again. "Forgive me. I appreciate your talking to me. After all, one of the young women who had been on that flight was killed shortly afterward."

"It didn't happen on my plane, so it has nothing to do with me."

"I understand," Tully responded patiently. "I was just wanting information for her family. They just want to know about Marian Miller's last hours."

"As a whore?"

Inwardly boiling, Tully struggled to keep his voice steady. "Nothing happened on the flight? No arguments between the passengers?"

"No."

"I've talked to the stewards and everyone else. It seems cut and dried except for Bernie Freeland's death. First Marian Miller's death, then Mr. Freeland's fatal accident. Seems oddly coincidental, doesn't it?"

Duncan Fairfax took in a pained breath.

"Let me spell this out for you. I was paid a great deal of money to fly Freeland's jet, and I liked the lifestyle. If you're implying that I would do anything to endanger that—"

Tully took a shot in the dark.

"Did Mr. Freeland threaten to fire you?"

"*What*? Freeland never threatened anything like that!" Fairfax snorted, caught off guard. "He promised me that it was my job for as long as I wanted it."

"But he'd just hired a new bright young pilot. John Yates could have turned out to be your rival." Tully paused before changing tack. "Did you recommend John Yates for the job as your copilot?"

"No; Mr. Freeland hired him on a personal recommendation."

"What did you think of Mr. Yates?"

"Very little."

Tully shifted gear. "What about Marian Miller?"

"The whore?" Fairfax snapped. "What about her?"

"Did you know her?"

"No!"

"Did John Yates?"

His temper ignited. "Right, that's it! That's all I'm going to say. The matter's closed."

"Especially for Bernie Freeland," Tully replied archly, ringing off.

He was thinking about the conversation as he made his way toward Peckham and the address he had been given for Terry Shaw. Knowing that the area was rough and that many of the houses were boarded up in preparation for redevelopment, he was not surprised to have his car surrounded only moments after he had arrived. Sitting in the driver's seat, he stared back at the group of kids and then got out of the Volvo, picking out one boy and beckoning to him.

"You a pedophile?"

Tully sighed expansively, passing the boy a fiver. "Watch out for my car, hey?"

"Just a fiver?"

"Another one if it's still got wheels when I come back, all right?" He looked at the group of kids, then glanced over to one of the boarded-up houses. "D'you know which is number twenty-three?"

The boy with the money pointed down the street. "Next door to number forty-seven," he said with a smirk, to the sniggering delight of his companions.

"Of course it is," Tully said wryly, walking off toward the occupied houses. The sleet was working itself into a temper; portentous clouds overhung the dull streets. A dog barked at Tully as he passed.

Tully rang the bell of number twenty-three.

"No one home," a voice called from inside.

"Mrs. Shaw?"

"She's moved."

"Mrs. Shaw, you're not in any trouble; I just wanted to have a chat with you," Tully said soothingly, staring into an old whey-colored face peering through a gap in the net door curtain.

"Oh, don't listen to my gran," a young man said suddenly, ushering the old woman into the front room and opening the door to Tully. "Malcolm Jenner said someone had been asking around. I was expecting you. Said your name was Sully."

"Tully."

"Yeah, Tully."

Walking into a narrow hallway made even narrower by packing cases, Tully followed Terry Shaw into the back kitchen. A cat sat on the table next to a half-eaten can of sardines.

"Lunch," Terry explained.

"For you or the cat?"

He smiled, clearly cold in his thin, creased shirt, his bony hands thrust deep into his pockets. Unshaven, his hair greasy and uncombed, a patch of acne on his forehead, Terry Shaw looked as though he hadn't slept properly for days. And he certainly didn't look like the kind of man Bernie Freeland would have hired for his cabin crew.

"You heard about your boss?"

"Yeah." He pushed the cat farther along the table and sat down, indicating the seat next to him for Tully.

"I thought it was too good to last," he went on, sounding despondent, running his nail along the table edge. "People like me don't get chances like that every day."

"Won't you go back to Australia?"

"What for? Mr. Freeland's dead; all his staff will be laid off." He stared dreamily ahead. "I wonder what they'll do with the jet. You think the person who buys it will want to hire me? I know I look a bit skanky now, but I scrub up well. I was proud of that job, that uniform. People envied me when I told them what I did. My girlfriend couldn't get over it."

"Terry, I want you to tell me about the flight."

"I'm never going to do another one, am I?" he said as the old lady shuffled into the kitchen and put on the kettle. "It's okay, Nan; I'll make the tea."

She turned and stared at Tully. "I know you," she said. "I know your voice."

"You don't, Nan."

"I *do* too," she said emphatically, "You do adverts on the TV. I know your voice."

Amused, Tully nodded. "You're right, Mrs. Shaw. That is my pleasure."

"You an actor?" Terry asked, impressed.

"Sometimes."

Terry frowned. "So why are you doing this?"

"For money, dear boy. That's why we all work."

The old lady was watching him as though transfixed.

"Are you queer?"

Tully shook his head. "No, Mrs. Shaw; sorry to disappoint you."

"Then why did you call him 'dear boy'?"

"Just a figure of speech."

"Oh, I see," she said seriously. "I just wondered. You know, you hear about actors, and you wonder. So many of them on the television act feminine these days."

"*Nan.*" Terry's voice was almost a wail. "Go in the front room. I'll bring you some tea."

She ignored her grandson and stared at the newcomer.

"Say it for me."

Tully's eyebrows rose. "I beg your pardon."

"Say the advert for me," she repeated, humming the jingle tune to herself. "Go on. We don't get famous people here often. Say it for me."

Impatiently, Terry steered his grandmother into the front room. He came back to the kitchen and with a wary expression asked, "Why are you *really* here, Mr. Tully?" Tully didn't bother to correct the "mister." "Malcolm Jenner said you wanted to know about the flight, but I don't know any more than he does. In fact, he did most of the serving of the food and drinks and I was just helping him, learning how to do it. You know . . ."

"You didn't overhear anything? Any arguments?"

"Nah."

"And you didn't know the girls before the flight?"

He flushed. "How would *I* know them? They were all tarts, and anyway, they were like in the bedroom most of the time."

"What happened after you landed in London?"

"Bernie Freeland and another crew flew on to New York. I stayed here."

"When did you hear that Marian Miller was murdered?"

"Malcolm phoned and told me Mr. Freeland didn't need me anymore, and then he told me about her. You can imagine how I felt when I heard

Freeland had died." He stared mournfully at the tabletop. "I thought it was too much of a lucky break. I don't get lucky like that. None of our family is lucky. Not like that. And now I'm stuck here, back living with my mother and grandmother."

"Will you really never go back to Australia?"

"Dunno. Haven't made up my mind yet."

Tully sighed. "So you can't remember anything strange or suspicious that happened on that flight?"

"No. It was heaven, something I'll never forget. Like being a movie star." He leaned toward Tully. "As for Bernie Freeland . . . Malcolm said maybe his death was *not* an accident."

"What I said to Mr. Jenner was in confidence."

"Yeah, well, he told me. But I'm not likely to tell anyone, am I? I mean, what's to gain? Anyway, it's just gossip. Malcolm likes a good story to tell over a beer." He stroked the cat absentmindedly. "Besides, if you ask me, I don't think there's anything to it. Just people dramatizing things. People die every day, so why not them?"

"Marian Miller was murdered."

"She was in a dangerous business, wasn't she?" he said flatly. "I mean, I'm sorry her and Mr. Freeland died, but they just ran out of luck, that's all." He looked around the gloomy kitchen. "Happens to everyone."

"Can I see the photographs you took on Bernie Freeland's plane?"

"They didn't come out," Terry said mournfully. "New cell phone too. Maybe I couldn't work it, maybe I wiped them by mistake, I dunno. But they're not there now. My girlfriend thinks I made it all up about going on the jet. The photos were proof, but I haven't even got those. Typical; just my luck. Just my friggin' luck."

Twenty-Four

VICTOR BALLAM FELT THE BLOOD PUMPING IN HIS EARS AS HE ROLLED over. He stared blearily up at the ceiling and attempted to lift his throbbing head off the floor. It took him several seconds to remember where he was and another moment to remember Annette Dvorski. Using the sofa for support, he levered himself upright, flinching as he became aware of the blood that had seeped into the back of his shirt collar. The winter light in the room was dimming with another fall of snow; the sound of sirens rose morosely from the muffled street below.

As carefully as he could, Victor stood up, trying to breathe evenly as his eyes adjusted to the lack of light. The French doors were open, letting in freezing air that was chilling the apartment, and he realized that it was the cold that had brought him around. He heard a muffled sound coming from the back of the apartment and picked his way carefully toward the bedroom but realized that the noise was only the sound of a television coming from the neighboring apartment.

Disconcerted, he entered the deserted kitchen. The sidelights were on, turning the metal surfaces into a fleet of mirrors. Victor looked around and reached for one of the large kitchen knives next to the sink. Feeling more confident with a weapon in his hand, he went to the bathroom, pushed open the door, and looked in.

"Annette?" he whispered groggily, then, more loudly, "Annette?"

No answer.

Closing the door behind him, Victor walked back into the sitting room, then stopped short. *The French doors were closed.* Someone had been in the apartment. Thoroughly unnerved, he tightened his grip on the knife and looked around, spotting the suitcase by the door and then, from behind the sofa, a bare foot poking out.

"Oh, Christ."

Warily he nudged the foot with his own. There was no response.

He pushed the sofa aside to reveal a woman's naked body, her limbs spread-eagled. Blood was still seeping slowly out from between her legs, darkening the carpet beneath her. Around her mouth ulcers bubbled from burned skin and puffed-up lips, and her face was flecked with bloodied foam. Bending over the woman, her eyes fixed open in death, Victor recoiled from the pungent smell of ammonia bleach that came from her bared lips.

Bleach had been poured over Annette Dvorski's breasts and vagina and into her mouth. The corrosive liquid had burned through skin and tissue, tearing into her insides, devouring her flesh. She had been forced to ingest the bleach, and then, as her throat contracted, she had coughed up a spray of blood and foam in her last dying moments, trying to expel the liquid as it reached her lungs and killed her.

Stepping back, Victor stared in horror at the gruesome sight, his heart hammering wildly. He had to get away. *Now.* He couldn't stay there, couldn't be found in Bernie Freeland's apartment with a brutally murdered girl. Taking a rug off the sofa, Victor laid it over the remains of Annette Dvorski, getting a sheen of blood on his hand. Hurriedly he wiped it off with a handkerchief, stuffed the handkerchief back into his pocket, and tried to calm himself.

He had found Annette Dvorski too late. And although he hadn't killed her, it would look as though he had. Whoever had entered and exited by the French doors had locked them, setting him up for her murder. In fact, on a warm night, without the bite of winter cold to slap him back into consciousness, Victor would *still* be lying on the floor next to the dead girl.

Realizing that the killer might at that very moment be reporting a disturbance in Bernie Freeland's apartment, Victor took a deep breath, steadied his nerves, and composed himself. His instinct was to run from the apartment building, but that would look suspicious. He had to blend in, appear as though he belonged there, an occupant of the building. He had to appear so natural and relaxed that even if he passed the police on his way out, he wouldn't warrant a second glance.

His gaze fell on Annette's suitcase by the door. Confused, he considered his options. He couldn't very well leave the case behind and risk someone finding out who she was and making a connection—however slight—to him, so he'd have to take the suitcase with him. After all, who ever heard of a murderer trying to escape with luggage? Another thought occurred to Victor as he looked around for Annette's handbag. Finding it on the bed, he tipped out all the contents: makeup, letters, hairbrush, passport, and, to his surprise, her cell phone. *When had she had an opportunity to replace it in her bag?* he wondered. *Or had the killer put it there?* He put everything back, then crammed the handbag into the suitcase and closed it. He was hoping that without any means of identification left behind, it might take the New York police a while to find out who the dead girl was. And even longer to discover her connection to Mrs. Fleet, the doomed flight, or Marian Miller's murder in London.

Wiping his fingerprints off the knife, off all the surfaces he had touched, and finally off the front door handle, Victor left the apartment with the suitcase. He was finding it difficult to think clearly or move fast because of the blow to his head. Avoiding the back stairs in case that might look suspicious, he made for the elevator. Remembering the bloodstain on his neck, he turned up his coat collar and stood watching the yellow numbers as the elevator traveled up to his floor. Every nerve in Victor's body was urging him to drop the case and run, but he waited until at last the elevator arrived.

With relief, he got in—the only passenger—but the doors didn't close immediately, remaining open as the elevator next to his stopped. They stayed open just long enough for Victor to see two police officers step out. Rigid with fear, he held his breath as they passed. He was standing in plain sight, blood on his clothes, waiting for them to notice him. Then, slowly, agonizingly slowly, the elevator doors closed, sliding together, concealing Victor. Then, equally slowly, the elevator took him down yard by painful yard to the waiting freedom of the street below.

Twenty-Five

ONCE OUTSIDE, VICTOR PICKED UP SPEED, PUTTING AS MUCH DISTANCE as he could between himself and Bernie Freeland's apartment building. He was conscious of the weight of the case in his hand and the pain in the back of his head. *What on earth am I doing?* he asked himself. He wasn't a hard man. He'd been in jail certainly—but for *fraud*, cosseted in a little enclave of similar criminals, hardly coming into contact with the worst prisoners. His so-called crime had been trivial in the light of their excesses. Envy had been his worst enemy; fellow prisoners had mocked him for his culture, his status, his choice of career. Some had enjoyed a certain schadenfreude at his downfall. But Victor had enjoyed no gratification whatsoever for what he had done; he had simply been a white-collar criminal—if indeed he was a criminal at all—and had served his time.

Now here he was, on a Manhattan street in the snow, fleeing from a murder scene, with the victim's suitcase and passport in his possession. He was quite alone and seriously out of his depth. Naively, he had thought that the job for Mrs. Fleet would just involve the finding and passing on of information. A quick, reasonable service for a good fee.

But in truth, he'd been blinded by the idea of getting his hands on the Hogarth painting, so eager to secure his revenge that he had ducked reality. But that reality had come home to him now. It had jolted him as much as the blow to his head and the sight of the dead woman.

His own stupidity stunned him. He had placed himself at the scene of the crime and managed to set himself up as the main suspect. *You bloody fool,* he thought. *Where will you go now?* Annette Dvorski was dead. The police would be after her killer, and the killer was the only person who knew that Victor was innocent. The only reason he hadn't been killed himself was that he was the scapegoat.

Victor reached into his pocket, flicked on his cell phone, and called Thomas Harcourt in London.

"Tully, it's Victor. Annette Dvorski's dead."

"*What?*"

"I found her. It was set up to look like I'd killed her. I'm coming back to London right away. Don't tell Mrs. Fleet. Don't say a word."

"Are you all right?"

"What d'you think? I'm in trouble, and I want you to be very careful."

"The people you asked me to look at?" Tully said. "The senior pilot's an ass but clean, and I don't think Terry Shaw and Malcolm Jenner have the making of killers. I haven't spoken to the other pilot yet, John Yates, but I'm working on it. The stewards are really cut up about losing their jobs. Working for Bernie Freeland was the best thing in their lives. They wouldn't want anything to happen to their boss, let alone kill him."

"Neither of them had anything to tell you about the flight?"

"Not a thing. And the photographs Terry Shaw took on the plane he erased by accident. Not exactly a bright spark, our Terry." Tully could hear the distant sirens on the New York street. "It's all gotten a bit messy, hasn't it?"

"You can say that again. I'm going to the airport now; I'll get the next flight. Oh, and Tully . . ."

"Yes?"

"Don't talk to *anyone*. Not until I get back." Victor paused, his voice low. "This isn't what I thought it would be. This isn't one person acting alone; this involves others. Quite a few others. And I've just realized something else: Mrs. Fleet didn't hire me because of my connections in the art world. She played me, Tully, and I fell for it. She knew my history, that I had nothing to lose. She knew I'd take on the case to get my own back, and she hired me because she knew I wasn't up to it."

Still talking, Victor crossed the street, walking swiftly toward a line of yellow cabs. "I tell you, that bitch was relying on me to fuck up. She didn't hire me to find out what happened; *she hired me to fail.*"

Victor Ballam climbed into the first cab on line and leaned back in his seat. He lifted the case onto his lap and stared at it, wondering again if he had done the right thing in keeping it with him. He flicked open the lid. Under the handbag was a woman's jacket, a skirt, and a pair of evening shoes. Lifting them out, he put them on the seat next to him and then took in a sharp breath.

Hardly believing his eyes, Victor stared at the baseball bat. The bat Bernie

Freeland had persuaded Annette to accept as a gift. *Jesus,* Victor thought, *was he right?* Making sure that the bat was concealed from the driver by the upturned suitcase lid, Victor ran his hands over it. Noticing how light it was, he felt around the bound tape at the end of the handle, which was slightly loose. Victor unwound it and pulled out a small, rolled-up canvas. He closed his eyes and leaned his head back against the car seat. *He had the Hogarth painting!* A work of art so treacherous that it had already cost three lives. And threatened his own.

Unrolling the canvas, Victor stared at the painting Hogarth had created over two hundred years before. The picture the artist himself had hidden. It shook in his hands as Polly Gunnell smiled up at him, as he easily recognized the Prince of Wales. Carefully he rolled up the precious canvas and slid it back into the handle of the bat, securing the tape over the end, and placed it back among Annette Dvorski's clothes. He then closed the case, locked it, and rested his hands on the lid.

He had no idea what would happen next. All that mattered in the sticky, overdeodorized interior of the cab was that Victor Ballam, late of Long Lartin Prison, was back in the running. He had in his possession what every other dealer around the globe would want. He had the artistic Semtex that could blow the market apart and reestablish him. Nothing would give Victor back his lost status, but the picture could propel him to heights beyond social and moral judgment.

Weary but ecstatic, he held his arms around the suitcase. In among a whore's clothes, makeup, and shoes lay a baseball bat: the unedifying but temporary tomb of Hogarth's masterpiece.

Twenty-Six

WITH THE BILL AT THE FRIARS HOSPITAL IN LONDON RUNNING AT eighteen hundred pounds a week, Elizabeth Wilkes was thinking that if her son had *had* to take an overdose, he certainly had chosen to recover in comfort. After all, even if he was unconscious, his surroundings would matter to him. She smiled loosely at the two people on the opposite side of her son's bed: a young man of around twenty-five and a girl who looked no more than eighteen. Pale and part Indian, the girl was plainly dressed in black, but when she rested her hands on the bed's iron railing, her rings clinked against the metal. *Hardly* that *much of a child*, Elizabeth thought, mentally assessing the price of the largest opal.

The man, Ronan Levy, was already known to her as one of a succession of young men Kit had promenaded around London like a prize Pomeranian at a dog show. He looked distraught and had obviously been crying. Even in winter Ronan Levy was tanned, but the tan didn't disguise the pallor beneath and seemed only to accentuate the makeup on his face. Eyebrows, arched and tattooed into shape, stood out over his watery eyes like two black tadpoles fighting to return to the water.

"I tell you, it wasn't an accident," he said, his tone edgy as he looked at Kit's mother.

He had said it before, but again his words brought no response. Wondering if Elizabeth Wilkes had heard, Ronan then realized that she was simply ignoring him and slumped farther down in his chair. His eyes scanned her: the Prada suit, the sable coat hanging over the edge of the chair and brushing the side of her Blahnik suede boot. Faultlessly groomed, Elizabeth Wilkes had all the appearance of wealth without the confidence of someone born to it. Clothes that should have acted as a background to her good looks seemed to overwhelm her; even her hairstyle was too fashionable to be comfortable. Fit and well honed, she attracted admiration in most circles, but on closer inspection it was obvious how urgently her looks were fighting the aging process. So far it was a draw.

Ronan tried again. "The overdose wasn't an accident."

She hissed him quiet. "You don't know what you're talking about!"

"Kit said—"

"Kit says a lot of things," Elizabeth cut in. "Most are lies. He's my son; I should know."

"Something happened to him."

She snorted softly.

"*It did!*" Ronan turned to the girl next to him. "I told you, didn't I? We talked when he got back to London, and then this happened." He held Elizabeth's brittle look. "He never overdosed; he never used enough to overdose. He was in control of it."

"That's what every addict says."

"Kit isn't an addict."

"No, but you are," she said smartly, seeing him for what he was and challenging him. "How do I know it wasn't you who introduced him to drugs?"

"Kit was on drugs long before I met him," Ronan replied defensively. "He talked about it, let on like he used at lot more drugs than he did. But he was actually careful."

"Kit's never careful about anything," Elizabeth said, secretly proud of her son's infamous reputation. "He can't control himself." She picked up a card nestling among some flowers and read out the inscription: "'From all your friends at the *Daily Star.*' How tasteful. I suppose he'll sell his near-death experience when he comes around."

"He's your son!"

"And *your* lover!" she countered. "But I daresay I get top billing."

Falling silent, Ronan began chewing the inside of his lip; the girl drummed her fingers on the bed rail. Silenced by a look from Elizabeth, she left the room, and Ronan took his chance. Leaning over the bed, his tone urgent, he said, "Mrs. Wilkes, listen to me. Please. I really think something's going on. I don't think this was an accident."

Wearily, Elizabeth stared into the tanned face. "It's a publicity stunt."

"Kit's dying."

In an instant her expression shifted from cold hauteur to crumbling unease. "*Dying?*"

Ronan nodded. "I overheard one of the doctors talking."

"Dying? My son?" She sounded dazed as she leaned forward, the sable falling unnoticed onto the floor.

Frantically she took hold of Kit's hand, staring into the sphinx face, the child's mouth. Confusion and panic were scrambling her thoughts. How could she live without her beloved son? He was everything to her. They had always been so close; he had told her everything. And they had planned every step as soon as he was old enough to understand. Elizabeth remembered how she had coached him about his father, fueling Kit's resentment, encouraging his feeling of betrayal.

Although she manipulated him to believe it was his idea, it was actually Elizabeth who had put the tabloids to work. It was she who had first filtered through information about James Holden. It was she who had set in motion the beginnings of the publicity hunger that had served them both so well. She was not driven by any feelings of lost love or rejection but by a determination to be rich. And to use any means at her disposal to accomplish that.

When Elizabeth became pregnant with James Holden's child, she swung into action with the speed and force of a juggernaut. No intellectual, she had the guile of a hedonist and the will not to relinquish any of her power. So she battled, playing the child card with Holden and begging for support for his son. When pleading didn't work, she resorted to threats: She would inform his wife. She would inform the papers. She would make sure that his well-placed society friends deserted him, that the esteem he had courted so assiduously would sink without trace in the mire of scandal.

Her threats took a while to register but effected the desired result. In private, Elizabeth had an income settled on her and her son, together with a small gallery in Chelsea. And as Kit grew up, he surpassed all of Elizabeth's hopes. The chip on his shoulder, the personal affront he felt for himself and his mother, steadily grew under her poisonous guidance. Acting as a wronged and helpless woman, Elizabeth succeeded in turning her teenage son into her private avenger. By the time Kit Wilkes was fifteen, he was hopelessly in thrall to his mother and as bitter as a disillusioned old man. His main aim in life was to please Elizabeth, and in doing so he indulged his own hatred of his father.

And now her snake-clever son was dying? Elizabeth stared in anguish at Kit lying there. Without him, what would she do? Without him there would be no income, no gallery. If he died, what hold would she have over his MP father? The papers wouldn't care about *her* story; she was just one more middle-aged jilted woman. Without the persona and glitter of Kit Wilkes, she was nothing. Dear God, Elizabeth thought to herself, was this her reward? After her endless devotion, was she going to be left alone?

"He *can't* die," she said helplessly. "You heard the doctor wrongly."

"No, I didn't," Ronan insisted, his distress intensifying. "They said that it wasn't just the drugs Kit had used but the quantity. They said it was too much."

"Too much for what?"

"Too much for *him*—and that's what doesn't make sense. Kit knows his limitations. Oh, he acts like a madman, but he's not stupid; he's always in control. He looks after himself."

Elizabeth thought of her son's obsession with having every one of his lovers medically checked out by the unctuous Dr. Eli Fountain. And his own regular health checks, his attention to hygiene. She didn't want to admit it, but Ronan was right; Kit *was* too careful to risk himself. So if her son hadn't accidentally overdosed and it *wasn't* a publicity stunt, who was responsible?

"Someone did this to him?" she asked, her voice so low that Ronan strained to hear her.

"Someone must have done it."

"Why?"

"I don't know," Ronan admitted, suddenly wondering if he should have told her, if Elizabeth Wilkes might do something stupid and endanger all of them. "But Kit was a different person when he came back to London. To be honest, I thought it was because of Guy Manners—"

Her head shot up at the notorious name. "Guy Manners? What's he got to do with Kit?"

"Kit said he was going to do some business with him. I didn't like it. Everyone knows what a bastard Manners is, but Kit wouldn't listen to me. He said they were going to meet up after he came back from China."

"What *business* could he have had with Guy Manners?"

"I don't know, but Kit said something that's stuck in my mind, and I keep thinking about it. He said, 'Don't worry about me if I'm unavailable for a while.'"

"What the hell does that mean?"

Ronan shrugged. "It was just something he said when he got back to London. He'd been going to catch an earlier flight, but it was canceled, and he came back on a private plane after someone offered him a lift. Thing is, one of the passengers on the private flight was murdered the night they got back."

"*What?*"

"A call girl." Ronan's voice was just above a whisper as he went on. "And a strange coincidence happened only the day afterward. The owner of the plane was killed."

Having let Kit take charge for years, Elizabeth found that her mental processes took a little longer to kick into gear.

"What are you talking about?"

"The man who owned the plane died in a road accident in New York."

"So?"

"He was an important art dealer."

"So?"

"He was powerful, really powerful."

She shrugged. "Who was he?"

"Bernie Freeland."

As Elizabeth heard the name, she paled. Her whole body tensed as she rose to her feet, her glamour gone, her age suddenly showing.

And worse, she looked afraid.

Twenty-Seven

BREATHING IN, OLIVER PETERS CLUTCHED HIS STOMACH AND FELT FOR the pill bottle in his jacket pocket. Hastily he swallowed two painkillers and slumped onto one of the Tate Gallery's hard wooden benches, his thoughts turning to his brother-in-law, Ambrose Wilton. Oliver wondered fleetingly if Ambrose would help Sonia after his death but dismissed the idea immediately. Almost a recluse, Ambrose had no interest in family. Living in Ireland, he spent his days breeding wolfhounds and treated everyone like a lackey. The family money ensured that Ambrose could run his estate, but Oliver had had to bail his brother-in-law out on a number of occasions because of ill-timed or ruinous gambles. Ambrose had never offered Oliver any thanks for his pains; almost since birth he had felt entitled. Entitled to money, status, power. Unlike his gracious sister, he kept himself distant from a world he treated with complete disdain. *No,* Oliver thought, *Ambrose Wilton would not be of any use at all.*

Oliver fixed his gaze on the famous painting *Hogarth's Servants,* but the pain was ripping into him and he felt sweat dampen the back of his shirt. His hands shaking, his body trembling at the effort to remain upright in his chair, he stared at the young boy in the painting—the secret image of the Prince of Wales's bastard son.

Hal . . . Only Oliver and a handful of others knew the true identity of the youth. Hogarth, obviously fond of the child and guilty at being unable to prevent the terrible death of Polly Gunnell, had secretly incorporated the boy's image in the painting of his staff. Of course, Hal had never really worked in Hogarth's home—that would have been too much of a risk—but the artist had kept a constant eye on the boy and had wanted, notoriously sentimental as he was, to have a keepsake for himself. So the tender image of his staff and their precious cuckoo had remained with Hogarth for many years until finally taking its place on a wall in the Tate Gallery, where it was enjoyed by hundreds of unsuspecting visitors every day.

Many commented on the kindness of Hogarth's depiction of his staff in an era in which people seldom gave thought to the lower orders. But no one knew that the boy in the painting was the bastard heir to the English throne. Not even the few members of the royal circle who knew of Hal's existence realized that *this* was his portrait. The secret of *Hogarth's Servants* had remained just that—a secret—privy only to the royal family and Sir Nathaniel Overton and his descendants.

Maintaining the long silence, Oliver had made many pilgrimages with his grandfather, his father, and then alone. Now dying, he knew that before long he would have to pass on the secret to his own son, but not yet. When he had regained the painting, then, and only then, he would confide in Simeon about the painting and the ring. The covert inheritance would be passed down whole, not in part.

He gave a jagged sigh. The medication was taking longer to have an effect. At first he had been out of pain within fifteen minutes; now he knew he had at least twenty-five minutes of agony to live through. And during that agony, as his innards burned and contracted with the cancer, he wondered if he could give up, give in—if, morally, there was a way to let go and keep his honor. And then he would think of his wife and three children and know that however bad it became, he would never kill himself. Never leave his family the legacy of the stigma. A body could be removed, cleaned up, but dishonor was indelible.

Pushing a clenched fist into his stomach and gulping another breath, he continued to stare at the painting. It had never occurred to him that having a young family later in life could turn out to be such a gamble. He had been in excellent health, his parents still alive; who would have predicted a terminal illness coming so quickly and cruelly? He thought of his home, his garden, summer sun in the trees, the house in the distance. Closing his eyes, Oliver then thought of the stone wall with the little memorial tablets to the dead family pets. Perhaps he should leave something in his will to say that he would like to have a stone put next to the dogs. The thought amused him despite the searing pain.

If anyone had told him he could endure such agony, he would not have believed him. He would have argued that no one could live with such suffering. But the days, weeks, and months had passed, and his tolerance for pain had increased, much as an alcoholic can tolerate more and more drink before getting drunk. Pain that once would have felled him became normal, and he'd learned to time his medication to cheat the worst of the onslaughts.

But now the attacks were getting beyond control and erratic, catching him unaware and rendering him all but useless until they passed. Breathing out, Oliver forced himself to think of something else, but the matter that came to mind didn't relax him at all: Lim Chang. *Why,* he wondered, *hadn't the Chinese dealer been in contact for two days?*

Had he found out something about the Hogarth? The thought alarmed Oliver. Perhaps he never should have joined forces with Lim Chang, after all, never have trusted him. But then again, he had had no choice. Chang had come to him with what he knew and offered his help. Oliver had been in no position to refuse. But what if his rival had learned something to his own advantage and decided to ignore their arrangement? After many years as a dealer, Oliver well knew how the business worked; someone who uncovered something important was hardly likely to share that discovery with a competitor no matter what he previously might have agreed to.

At last the pills were beginning to work, and with the lessening of the pain, Oliver felt his strength and his clarity of thought returning. He *had* to get hold of the Hogarth, *had* to secure the secret *and* his family's future. And he had to do it before his death. If he had to fight for it, he would. He would deal with anybody and undertake anything to acquire it. All that mattered was that when Sir Oliver Peters let go of this world, he would leave his family provided for and his secret intact.

Twenty-Eight

Mrs. Fleet was trying to call Victor Ballam's cell phone, but it was turned off. Irritated, she tossed her phone onto the couch in her office and went downstairs to a smaller office where a glossy woman was talking on another phone. She looked up as Mrs. Fleet entered, gesturing to an appointment book beside her. Picking it up, Mrs. Fleet looked down the list of bookings, her expression unreadable, her jubilation concealed. In among the usual clients, she saw the name of a Marylebone magistrate and made a mental note that he might well be of use if her premises were ever investigated.

Business was as organized and profitable as ever; her decision to specialize was paying off, with her art-dealer clients recommending an increasing number of their colleagues and connections. Before long she would have her girls fucking someone in virtually every London gallery, Mrs. Fleet thought with pleasure, putting the book on the desk and returning to her rooms at the top of the building.

As a self-educated woman who had come up the hard way, Mrs. Fleet might have been a sympathetic mentor, but she had no pretensions to maternal feelings. She had no truck with idleness either and expected her girls to be hardworking, reliable, and dedicated. Shortcomings were met with glacial disapproval. Relieved that her own brief whoring days were over, Mrs. Fleet chose to forget the drawbacks of the profession and had no compassion for its victims.

She *was*, however, worried that she might be looking at a victim now: Liza Frith, sitting in front of the television watching a rerun of a talent show. Amused, Mrs. Fleet watched the judges walk onto the stage to the accompaniment of fireworks and triumphant music. How long, she wondered, before they had a show to pick the new Messiah? Not *American Idol* but *God Idol*? And why not start with the judges?

"Did you want me?" Liza asked, getting to her feet.

"I think you should be working again."

"Working?"

"I can't let you hang around indefinitely, Liza. You need to get your mind off things."

"Have you heard from Annette?"

"I'm sure she's fine," Mrs. Fleet lied.

"But you haven't heard from her?"

"No."

"What about Mr. Ballam?"

"No," she said crisply. "I've been thinking very carefully about the whole matter. Perhaps we overreacted."

"Marian was killed!"

"Which was very unfortunate, but why are we assuming that her death was connected with the Hogarth painting?"

"The painting *must* be important. Bernie Freeland wouldn't have been interested unless it was valuable."

Mrs. Fleet paused, surprised by the girl's challenging tone.

"I've known Mr. Freeland for a long time. He's very good at his work, a very competent dealer, but he isn't always right." She tried a smile, watching Liza carefully. "Thinking back, I remember how he was once duped by a dealer in Africa. He bought some works by a supposedly important painter. He was fed information and background, but it didn't check out. They call it seeding, laying down a false history of a painter who never even existed. Many museums and galleries have been caught out this way."

Curious, Liza wondered why her employer was doing such a sudden and unexpected about-face.

"Mr. Freeland was also tricked into purchasing a Matisse which turned out to be a fake. You girls are knowledgeable but hardly dealers. I think perhaps the whole matter has been blown out of all proportion."

Liza wasn't convinced. "Maybe. But when you talk to Annette—"

"I may not ever talk to Miss Dvorski again," Mrs. Fleet countered. "Any girl that makes arrangements behind my back is usually fired. You work for me exclusively or you're out."

In a baggy sweater and leggings, Liza looked vulnerable, even cowed. But she was suspicious of her employer's motives and anxious enough about her friend to challenge her.

"You don't care what's happened to Annette?"

"She's probably living the high life with Mr. Freeland," she lied, knowing that Liza was unaware of the Australian's death and wanting to keep it that way. A plan had come into Charlene Fleet's mind, and she was inching her way toward its inception. "Incidentally, Bernie Freeland is no longer a client of mine. I can't have people going behind my back. I can't have passengers either, Liza. So if you want to stay on at Park Street, I think it's time you went back to work."

Her expression was composed, her logic convincing. To all intents and purposes she was bothering an employee, no more. But she was really sending Liza Frith out as bait.

"Something's not right about all of this," Liza said nervously. "You weren't on that plane."

"No, I wasn't, but you've got too much imagination, and I've encouraged it," Mrs. Fleet said dismissively. "You're not a child; you shouldn't act like one."

"But I don't want to leave here, not just yet!" she pleaded. "Can't I just wait until we hear from Annette? Or Mr. Ballam? Just until we know everything's okay?"

"Poor Liza," Mrs. Fleet said, her tone honeyed. "You're one of my best girls; you know that, don't you? And as one of my best you have a responsibility. Clients have been asking for you. I can't keep on making excuses for your absence, can I?"

"But—"

"No, Liza, you have to work." She turned off the television and walked to the door. "If it makes you feel better, stay in London; I can always find girls for the trips abroad. Grateful girls who want to do well." Her tone flatlined. "Toughen up, Liza. Or get out of the business."

Twenty-Nine

Once at Kennedy Airport, Victor Ballam was able to clear his thoughts. In the men's room before checking in, he emptied Annette Dvorski's suitcase, junking everything that identified her. Realizing that leaving only a baseball bat rolling around in a suitcase would seem suspicious, he packed it in some of her clothes, locked the case, bought a couple of luggage straps, and affixed a label with his name and London address to the handle of the case. At first, he had been tempted to carry the painting in his hand luggage, but he was afraid of being robbed or attacked again. And, Victor reasoned, no one would suspect him of entrusting the picture to the hold.

Holding his breath, he checked his luggage in for the 4 p.m. flight to Heathrow. The beige bag passed through unchallenged. His mouth was dry and he could hardly speak as his passport was checked, but no one was after him, Victor reassured himself. Why would they be? No one could connect him to Annette Dvorski. He hadn't told anyone where he was going, and only Charlene Fleet knew the address of Bernie Freeland's apartment.

Victor watched as the ground stewardess stared at his passport before finally handing it back to him with his boarding pass. He was sweating even though it was cold, his shirt moist against his skin, his collar tight. In the men's room, he'd changed his bloodied shirt and jacket, pushing the soiled garments to the bottom of a wastebasket, and washed up. Of course he was leaving behind DNA and fingerprints, but what choice did he have? He could hardly keep the evidence on him, and he didn't have time to dispose of it in any other way.

But his clean clothes seemed too tight for him, his anxiety prickling like heat rash. *Mrs. Fleet,* he thought. *Mrs. Fleet. Had she had something to do with Annette Dvorski's death? She could easily have arranged it.* Knowing that Victor would turn up at the New York apartment, she could have planned for him to be the convenient scapegoat.

But why?

He sat at a bar in the airport lounge and ordered coffee, avoiding eye contact with other drinkers. Of course, setting him up would have been the perfect solution if Mrs. Fleet had wanted to get him out of the way, but hadn't she made it clear that she had no interest in the painting? Victor frowned. So why would she lie? Unless she had been bluffing, luring him in to take the bait. But if *that* was the case, she had failed because he now had the painting. Checking his cell phone, Victor found several messages from his employer asking how he was getting on. Genuine interest? Or would Mrs. Fleet take his silence to imply that he was *unable* to call her, perhaps because he was in a New York jail charged with the murder of one of her girls?

Enough, Victor told himself, and glanced at his watch. Two hours to wait until he could board his plane. He knew that he wouldn't relax until he was safely home in London, with the suitcase back in his possession. The suitcase that was at that moment piled onto a cart with other pieces of luggage. Every time an airport security officer walked past him, Victor tensed. Watching the police from across the concourse, he imagined that at any moment he would feel a hand on his shoulder. Arrested. For something he hadn't done. *Déjà vu*, he thought grimly, watching the airport clock.

His thoughts slid back to Mrs. Fleet, then Ingola, then Annette Dvorski's desperate hammering on the apartment door. If only he had been faster. If only he had been there a minute earlier.

"Have you got the time?"

Startled, Victor glanced at the Chinese man standing by his side, then looked at his watch. "It's just about three o'clock."

"Time drags, doesn't it?" the man went on. "When you're waiting, I mean."

Wary, Victor nodded and turned back to his coffee.

But the man wasn't about to be put off. "I'm flying to Paris. How about you?"

Victor ignored the question, and the man looked embarrassed. "Forgive me. I don't want to make a nuisance of myself."

"Then don't."

"Sorry to bother you," he said, and walked away. Victor stared straight ahead, watching him through the mirror behind the bar. He saw the man looking puzzled, then taking off his coat and sitting down under the departures board. A typical traveler, lonely and looking for conversation; his attention soon turned to a couple sitting beside him.

The waiting time seemed interminable until finally the London flight was called. Relieved, Victor joined the line for boarding, surprised to see that the Chinese man was still talking to the couple, the woman laughing. But why was he in the line for the London plane if he was going to Paris? Victor wondered, suddenly alert and suspicious. Glancing around, he kept his eyes on the airport police and guards, his muscles aching with tension and the wound at the back of his head throbbing. The line eventually shuffled its way forward until at long last Victor found himself on the plane and settled himself into his window seat to wait for takeoff.

Outside it was dark, only the lights from the terminal building and the runway making any impression on the concourse. Seeing the empty luggage cart pass, Victor imagined the suitcase lying in the hold below his feet, its priceless cargo snuggled down among the feminine ephemera of Annette Dvorski's brief life. He heard the engines start up. His breathing slowed, and he secured the safety belt across his lap with a sense of relief.

And then he saw him. The Chinese man. Taking a seat four rows ahead of him. Only now he was neither laughing nor talking, and the couple were no longer with him. Uneasy, Victor watched him take off his jacket and throw it casually into the overhead locker before sitting down. Then he turned and glanced over to Victor.

And nodded.

Thirty

RELUCTANTLY, LIZA FRITH PULLED ON AN EVENING DRESS AND SLIPPED into a pair of black stiletto heels. She had applied her makeup slowly and without enthusiasm, with Mrs. Fleet's words reverberating in her head.

Toughen up, Liza. Or get out of the business.

"I *will* get out of the bloody business," Liza said aloud, throwing her eyebrow pencil into her makeup case and brushing her hair. "Cow."

She had thought, mistakenly, that her employer understood her anxiety. But Mrs. Fleet—Mother Fleet as some of the girls called her sarcastically—was only interested in business. Still, Liza thought, she could hardly complain. She'd made money at Park Street, lazy money, enough of it to plan with. Having been a university student for a while, Liza had run up doughty debts that neither she nor her working-class parents could ever have paid off—if, that is, she hadn't worked as a call girl for the last eighteen months. But what had seemed like an easy way to earn cash had suddenly soured. Liza had never been troubled by the morality of prostitution, but the flight on Bernie Freeland's plane and Marian Miller's murder had scared her.

Liza could hear the sound of her employer's voice from the landing above, but checking that she was alone in the basement den, she locked the door and tried Annette's cell phone. As before, there was no reply. Hurriedly, Liza snatched up her Filofax and, bending back the leather binder as far as it would go, uncovered a slim inner pocket. Carefully, she pulled out a number of hundred-pound notes and a piece of paper with a number scribbled on it. Thoughtful, she stared at the paper.

Bernie Freeland—001 212-555-6000

He had given her his private New York number months before, swearing her to secrecy. But Liza had never really liked Bernie and had never followed it up. Until now. Now it seemed like a good idea to phone him and ask if Annette was there. What harm could it do? It would reassure her, and Bernie would hardly be likely to mention it to Mrs. Fleet.

Dialing the number, she waited for the phone to be picked up. On the fourth ring, it was.

"Hello? Mr. Freeland?"

There was a slow pause.

"Who's this?"

"I was asking for Mr. Freeland," Liza said cautiously. "Isn't this his number?"

"It is."

"So is he there?"

"Who's asking for him?"

"A friend," Liza said, worried and hesitant. "If Mr. Freeland's not there, can I talk to Annette Dvorski?"

"There's no one here with that name."

"She was supposed to be visiting Mr. Freeland," Liza went on, turning toward the door and checking that it was locked. "Annette Dvorski was coming to see him. I know she was; she told me."

"I'm very sorry to have to tell you Mr. Freeland's dead, killed in a traffic accident. I'm the manager of the apartment building. I was here when the phone rang, so I picked it up."

Liza was shaking uncontrollably. "*Dead?* Mr. Freeland? He can't be! He can't be!"

"I'm so sorry," the manager continued. "I wish I could have given you better news. Mr. Freeland will be buried tomorrow." For a moment he hesitated, wondering if he should mention Annette Dvorski's death, but decided against it. Why should he spread news that would become public all too soon?

"But she was . . ." On the other end of the phone, Liza was finding it hard to speak. "*When* was Bernie Freeland killed?"

"The day before yesterday."

So Annette had traveled all the way to New York to meet up with a corpse, Liza thought helplessly. She must have gotten there, found out Bernie was dead—but then what? Came back to England? But if so, why hadn't she been in touch? Clicking off the cell phone without saying another word, Liza collapsed onto the sofa.

It couldn't be a coincidence, she thought. Hadn't she known there was something wrong? Marian was dead, and now Bernie Freeland was dead, and Annette was missing. Frightened, Liza looked around the room, trying to collect her thoughts. Mrs. Fleet was sending her out to work, and that was the last thing she wanted to do. If there was someone after all the girls who had been on that flight, she wasn't going to let herself be the next target. So where could she go? Home? Up north? Looking down at her evening dress and coat, Liza realized that the day clothes she had been wearing earlier were upstairs, on the second floor. There was no way she could get to them without passing Mrs. Fleet and being questioned about what she was doing.

Suddenly she was even more suspicious of her employer. Did she know what had happened to Bernie Freeland? She had lost interest in Annette's whereabouts very suddenly after first appearing to be so concerned. Liza stopped dead, staring at the door. Surely Mrs. Fleet wouldn't have sent her back to work if she thought she was in danger. Surely she wouldn't have booked an eight-thirty appointment for her at the Hilton, Room 899, with a stranger who could turn out to be anyone.

Unless she was using her.

In that moment Liza didn't know who she was most afraid of, her employer or whoever was coming after her. Because she was sure that someone was. Someone was after all the girls who had been on that flight. But why? For a bloody picture? Was that it? Liza could feel her breathing speed up. Of course it was the painting; it was the only thing they all had in common.

Spooked, Liza reacted. Hitching up her skirt, she clambered onto the table against the wall and tried to push open the narrow window at street level. But the metal had been painted over and didn't give. She would have to find another way to get out of the house without running into Mrs. Fleet. And whoever was waiting for her at the Hilton. If she went up north, she could hide out for a while. All she had to do was get herself out of Park Street.

Composing herself, Liza put on her coat and walked upstairs. Unlocking the front door, she looked out into the street. Immediately, Mrs. Fleet came toward her, smiling approvingly.

"You look wonderful. You know where you're going?"

"Room 899, the Hilton. Do you have a name?"

"Mr. Gillow."

"Has he used us before?"

"No. He sounds young; that's why I thought you'd like him. Asked to book you for two hours. Make sure you get the money first." Mrs. Fleet paused, irritated. "What's the matter now?"

"He's new. The last client Marian Miller ever saw was new. And he killed her."

"We don't know that."

"The police think he did."

"They think it was a sex killing, yes." Mrs. Fleet thought of the thirty rubles and hurried on. "These things happen occasionally."

"I don't want them to happen to me!" Liza replied stubbornly. "They haven't caught Sergei Ivanovitch, have they? What's to stop him coming after me?"

"Why should he?"

"He might. If it all has something to do with the Hogarth."

"Oh, that bloody painting!" Mrs. Fleet snapped. "Marian Miller was a bitch. For all we know she might have tried stealing from the john. Or provoked him, pushed him over the edge. Or maybe she wasn't into sex as much as usual. After all, she *was* pregnant."

"Marian was pregnant?"

"You didn't know?" Mrs. Fleet responded. "Neither did I until the police told me."

"But she was infertile."

"Apparently not. Look, Marian was a difficult woman. I had several complaints about her. You know what she was like, jerked the men around sometimes. But I seriously doubt her death had anything to do with William Hogarth."

"But you don't know anything about the client I'm going to meet tonight."

"We hardly ever know about the clients. It never bothered you before."

"Marian Miller hadn't been murdered before! I'd rather go with a regular, someone I know."

"Listen," Mrs. Fleet said, moving closer to Liza, the dog as ever following close behind her. "I've had enough of this hysteria. You get your ass out there and do what you're paid for." She took hold of Liza's shoulder and pushed her out the door. "There's a taxi waiting."

With a resounding bang, the front door slammed shut in Liza's face. All her belongings, her clothes, and her possessions were on the second floor in the front bedroom she shared with Annette. Or *had* shared with Annette. They hadn't needed to share—there were enough bedrooms to house five working girls at any one time—but Liza and Annette had liked company and the camaraderie that came from sharing clothes and talking into the small hours.

Damn it, Liza thought helplessly. Everything she owned was at Park Street. Her life was there, her friends, her security. Or what she had taken for security. But now the smart black door looked uninviting, almost sinister, and as she walked to the waiting taxi, Liza knew Mrs. Fleet was watching her from a window above.

Getting into the back of the taxi, Liza noticed the driver looking at her. The address was notorious; he knew she was a working girl and gave her a lecherous look. Turning away, Liza reached into her bag and opened her Filofax, thinking of the money she had hidden there. As the cab pulled away from the curb, she waited until they were out on Park Lane before tapping on the partition glass.

The driver slid it open with his left hand, keeping his eyes on the traffic. "Yeah?"

"How much to drive me up north?"

"You what?"

"How much would it cost for you to drive me up to Manchester tonight?" She paused. "Well, how much?"

"Five hundred quid."

"I want a ride; I don't want to buy the bloody cab!"

"Okay, four hundred."

She nodded. "That's better. When we get closer, I'll tell you where to go."

"You sure about this?"

"I'm sure. Can you turn off the radio so that no one can reach you?"

"What the hell for?"

"I don't want anyone to know where I've gone."

Sighing, he picked up the radio handset and clicked it on, a crackling voice coming over the line. "Hello?"

"This is cab 459. I've dropped the Park Street passenger off at the Hilton and picked up some guy who wants to be driven home. Up north. I've taken the job, so I'll be off for the rest of the night." He flicked off the switch, watching Liza in the mirror. "All right?"

"Thanks."

"Are you in trouble?"

She hunkered down into her coat, flicking on the heating switch and ignoring the question.

"How long will it take?"

"Four hours if we're lucky." He took another look at her. "If you're in trouble, I don't want to get involved; you hear me?"

"I'm not in trouble," she lied, her voice steady. "I've just had enough of being on the game. I want to go home."

Unconvinced, he looked at her for another moment, then slid the partition glass closed and headed for the motorway going north.

Thirty-One

VICTOR WAS WAITING AT THE CAROUSEL IN TERMINAL FOUR AT Heathrow for his suitcase to come out with the other luggage from the New York flight. Although he had slept on the flight, he was stiff from being cramped, and his head ached. Gingerly he touched the back of his skull, feeling the swelling and a crust of dry blood. He looked around at the other waiting passengers, and his eyes lit on somebody just entering the arrivals area. It was the Chinese man, this time talking to another couple and appearing irritatingly jovial.

Victor turned back to the ramp where the suitcases were sliding down onto the moving belt. There seemed to be a flurry of luggage, then a lull, and then finally his case came into sight. Moving close to the conveyor belt, he grabbed the suitcase and made for customs, walking calmly through the green light. Within minutes, he would be out of Heathrow and home free.

But a voice stopped him. "Excuse me, sir."

Tensing, Victor turned. The customs officer beckoned for him to approach a desk that was segregated off to one side. Hesitating, he stared at the man and then moved across to join a few other travelers who had also been stopped: the middle-aged couple he had first noticed in New York and an irritable young woman chewing gum. She was listening to her iPod and tapping her foot as her suitcase was opened; the customs officer started rifling through it.

So this is going to be the end, Victor thought bitterly. Almost within sight of home. His case would be opened, and the officer would find a *woman's* clothes—and a baseball bat. He would find a woman's underwear and stare at Victor, and even before he asked it, he would be wondering what the hell was going on. The middle-aged couple looked on as their bags were searched; Victor would be next. He would say the suitcase belonged to his wife, he thought suddenly. Of course—they were *her* things. He was picking up her case.

There was only one flaw in the plan. Where was *his* case? And if he didn't have a case, why were there were none of his belongings among his wife's?

Dry-mouthed, Victor watched the customs officer, a burly man with a buzz haircut. Of course he might not have time to explain his apparent cross-dressing because the officer might already have been informed of Annette Dvorski's murder. Victor Ballam's description might have been circulated already, with the London police awaiting his return from New York.

Oh, Jesus, he thought desperately. *Should I make a run for it?* If they *did* know about Annette's death, how guilty would he seem, taking her bag? Who *but* her killer would have stolen it? And why? How long would it take customs to wonder about the baseball bat? Victor felt a sudden disabling wave of frustration coupled with fear. He had been so close, had had the painting in his possession. Had held history in his hands. His revenge, his triumph had been within reach if he could have just gotten through customs.

"Sir," the officer said politely, "can you please open your case."

Victor paused.

"Sir, can you open your bag, please."

Unfastening the securing straps, he could feel the officer watching him. Although only inches from exposure, Victor was amazed to find that his hands didn't shake, and when he clicked open the locks, he stood back calmly as the officer leaned forward. From where Victor was standing, his view of the interior was blocked by the raised lid. The officer looked at him curiously.

"Is this your case, sir?"

Victor was about to lie, to say it was his wife's. Then he was about to run. He did neither. Just stayed silent, staring as the officer dropped the lid back, exposing the inside of the case.

Victor stared in astonishment. There were no women's clothes; there was no baseball bat. Instead, a couple of freshly laundered shirts were lying on top of a pair of jeans; a copy of *Apollo* magazine lay over a laundry bag.

"Is this your case, sir?"

Confused, Victor wanted to laugh, to say no, it's not my fucking case. It's the wrong case. It's a switched case with my luggage straps and my label on it. It's no longer full of a dead girl's clothes, and there's no baseball bat. Putting Annette Dvorski's suitcase in the hold had been a gamble that had backfired badly. No, he wanted to shout; it's *not* my bloody case.

But instead he nodded. "Yes; yes, it's my case."

"Have you anything to declare?"

Only a murdered woman in a New York apartment and a hidden stolen painting.

"No, I've nothing to declare."

The man stared at him. "Do you mind if I search your luggage further?"

Victor shrugged. *Go ahead,* he thought. *Have a good look. God knows what's inside. Help yourself.*

As he watched the officer's meaty hands go through the innocuous, carefully packed contents, he wondered *how* the case had been switched. Was it the Chinese man? Victor thought back to his attempt at conversation, then the unexpected nod. Had *he* exchanged the cases? Had he also known about Annette Dvorski's murder?

Had he killed her?

"Thank you, sir; you can go."

Dumbly, Victor nodded and picked up the suitcase. Around him the noises of the airport buzzed in his ears as he stared blankly ahead, but relief gave way to frustration and despair. *He had lost the Hogarth.* He had been duped. Not only that: someone knew he had been in the apartment where Annette Dvorski died. Otherwise how would they know what was in the case and want to steal it back?

Victor kept moving. Was he going to be stopped again? Was he going to be arrested when he left Heathrow? Stiff-backed, he walked toward the taxi stand outside. *No one man could have pulled off such a clever switch with the luggage,* he thought. It was too organized, too planned. The airport's exit doors slid open noiselessly in front of him as he approached, the London air coming hard and cold against his skin as he slid into the backseat of the first waiting cab.

His confusion was compounded by his sense of being outnumbered. Obviously he was just one man against many, and the longer he spent on the case, the less he understood. Fear for his safety should have made Victor back off, but he had held the Hogarth in his hands, had—if only briefly—savored the frisson of revenge that had been long coming. The very people who had betrayed and cheated him before, the denizens of the art world, were not about to triumph again. Nor were their cohorts, the Chinese, the Russians, or the likes of Charlene Fleet. Whoever wanted the Hogarth and was prepared to kill for it was up against an unexpectedly formidable ally.

Victor Ballam would be a scapegoat only once.

Part Three

"... I am doing this for you. You are not fourteen years old yet, I think, but you will be twenty-four, and this portrait will then be like you. 'Tis the lady's last stake; see how she hesitates between her money and her honour? Take you care. . . . I shall give you this picture as a warning. . . ."

—WILLIAM HOGARTH ADVISING HESTER THRALE, A YOUNG FRIEND, TO WHOM HE GAVE *THE LADY'S LAST STAKE*, A MORALITY PAINTING

On the 5th of March, 1733, clutching my artist's materials, I was shown into a damp room off the condemned cell of Newgate Prison to meet with Sarah Malcolm.

In truth, I had no compunction in profiting from her crime and was ready to risk the danger of catching jail fever by visiting Newgate. But there was to be no invention or moral in this portrait: no pretty Polly Gunnell playing the whore. This time the likeness was to be exact, a replica of a woman who had titillated and terrified the populace in equal measure.

Sitting down and fingering a rosary, Sarah Malcolm turned her light eyes onto me, the deft application of rouge on her cheeks adding an unexpected, callous, touch. I noticed that her arms were surprisingly powerful. But then they had had to be. On Sunday, 4th February, 1733, Mrs Lydia Dunscombe, aged 80, and her companion, Elizabeth Harrison, aged 60, were discovered strangled in their beds.

Although pleading guilty to theft, Sarah Malcolm denied the murders but was found guilty and sentenced to hang at Newgate Prison. She ordered a pair of drawers for herself for her execution to prevent the crowd from looking up her skirts as she swung from the gibbet. Oddly, as I looked at this infamous criminal, another woman came to mind. Another fascinator. But whereas Polly Gunnell had been innocent, Sarah Malcolm was a convicted murderess.

Outside, I could hear a clock chiming the quarter and a prison bell ringing. From within came the clatter of metal dishes, the sound at odds with the careful, muted scratching of my pen. At that moment I could see Polly Gunnell as clearly as I saw Sarah Malcolm—but a Polly still flickering with energy, poking out her tongue at the world and all of London's hidden nastiness. Even pregnant, she had laughed at her situation, never expecting the route which would take her from a prince's bed to a stone slab under a public house.

Breathing in, I dismissed the memory of Polly and turned back to Sarah Malcolm. In two days she would swing from a rope to the hiss of the crowd, would kick her legs as she slowly lost consciousness—unless the drop killed her quickly by breaking her neck. I kept drawing, allowing myself—for the briefest of instants— to remember another death. And a life. A secret life. A child's life. And I thought of the grave that child had so narrowly escaped.

I knew only too well how the people of London would relish such a revelation. How they would bray and fight to see the Prince's bastard. How quickly the dead Polly Gunnell would become the penitent Magdalene for their times, another *victim of the rich and influential. It took no effort to picture how the rabble would gather for a child who could upturn a throne.*

Swayed by the popularity of Frederick, Prince of Wales, how easily they might swing their support behind his heir, the London mob challenging the power of the unpopular George III. After all, they would argue, was it not a fact that the King and Queen disliked their own son? Had the King not referred to Frederick as a "wechselbalg," a changeling? Well, here is the changeling's son. The mob's saviour.

At times my courage had wavered. For several months after I had saved the infant I was troubled by nightmares and imagined men following my progress on every street; imagined brutal hands knocking on the studio door, heard eerie tapping on the windows at night. I started at noises, avoided alleyways, and lit the candles as soon as the light began to fail. The men of my dreams were always the same: doctors and priests, like the two men who had been with Polly's body in that dank cellar. Yet as time passed, I had grown calm, my increasing success occupying more and more of my attention. Once or twice I had considered confiding in Jane but had stayed silent.

Knowledge was danger. In this case only ignorance ensured safety.

I quickly finished my drawings, collected them together, and slid them into my portfolio. I gathered my tools and signalled the guard that I was ready to leave. The governor showed me out of Newgate Prison into the feeble city sunlight.

I looked ahead, watching the gibbet being erected from which Sarah Malcolm would hang. And as I hurried from that terrible place I thought, for some unaccountable reason, of the villain Overton. I thought of the Royal court and was suddenly sick to my stomach.

Above my head a grey cloud slowly shifted. A portentous sensation of doom crossed my heart, and the London air was wicked with malice as the clock struck ten.

Thirty-Two

"I HAD IT," VICTOR SAID SIMPLY AS TULLY OPENED THE DOOR. "I HAD the Hogarth, and I lost it!" In silence, Tully passed him a whiskey as Victor, caught between confusion and rage, went on. "I've been set up. I was on my way to see Annette Dvorski—I was even talking to her on the cell phone, for God's sake—but when I got there, someone knocked me out."

"*What!*"

"When I came to—which I wouldn't have if it hadn't been as cold as hell in Bernie Freeland's apartment—Annette Dvorski had been murdered." He could see the image of her body and quickly shook it away. "*I* was supposed to be found there, Tully. I was supposed to be taken for her killer. Jesus, I only just got away."

"So you think someone set you up?"

Victor's expression was hostile.

"Of course. *Everything's* been set up. Everything. The only thing they didn't expect was that I'd recover in time to get away. Or that I'd take Annette Dvorski's case with me."

"You took her case? Why?"

"I wasn't thinking clearly. It was an impulse; I just grabbed it." He looked at his friend. "And you know what? The Hogarth was in it, smuggled into New York *inside* a baseball bat. It was a present from Bernie Freeland to Annette Dvorski. He was supposed to give it to Annette at their next meeting, but he was killed before he had the chance." Victor finished his drink, surprised that he still felt jumpy—and sober—and that the wound on the back of his scalp was still aching. "I don't suppose they realized what was in the suitcase or they would have taken it earlier. Maybe they only realized afterward, when they saw me with it."

"Who's *they?*"

"Whoever set me up. I took the case and went to JFK, got the first flight I could. But before I checked the bag in—"

An incredulous Tully interrupted, staring at him. "*You checked the bag in the hold?*"

Victor threw up his hands.

"I know, I know! But at the time I thought it was the right thing to do. I thought that if anyone was following me, they'd assume I had the painting on me, so before I checked the case in, I put new straps around it and a label with my name on it." He leaned back in his seat, feeling the first pull of the alcohol. "When I got back to Heathrow, I was stopped at customs. They opened the bag, and it wasn't mine! It had been switched. Someone put my strap and label on another case. Annette Dvorski's bag—and the Hogarth— have disappeared." Victor paused, looking intently at Tully. "You didn't tell Mrs. Fleet I was back in London, did you?"

"Of course not!" Tully replied, refilling both of their glasses. "Look, Victor, you *have* to go to the police now."

"Oh, yes; they're going to listen to me," he said bitterly. "Think about it, Tully. I was in Bernie Freeland's apartment. Annette Dvorski was murdered there. I haven't a leg to stand on."

"Do the police know you were there?"

"I doubt it. There's no connection between me and Annette Dvorski. I dumped all her identification papers. No one in New York should be able to tie me to Annette unless they find out what I'm investigating. She only had a pay-as-you-go phone." He held Tully's gaze. "Which is why I can't go to the police."

"But you had no reason to kill the woman."

"I took the Hogarth. How's that for a motive?" Victor said coldly. "They would assume that I killed her to get the painting. I'm a disgraced art dealer. A criminal with a record for fraud, remember? The perfect person to set up."

Tully was thoughtful for a moment. "Who else knew you were in New York?"

"Only Charlene Fleet."

"But why would *she* set you up?"

"To get me to find the Hogarth. As soon as I had the painting, I was no further use to her. Remember what I said on the phone, Tully? She didn't hire me to succeed; she hired me to fail."

"But you *didn't* fail. You found the Hogarth."

"Which was then taken from me." Victor stared into the glass of whiskey, finally feeling the effect on his empty stomach. "She said she didn't give a damn about the painting, that she only wanted her girls safe to protect her business. She was obviously lying."

"If it was she who set you up."

"There's no one else it could have been. Apart from you."

Tully's expression was bland.

"Victor, dear boy, don't even think about it. I'm on your side. I didn't tell anyone—either deliberately or accidentally—where you were or what you were doing."

"So it has to be Fleet," Victor concluded. "I haven't returned any of her messages; she doesn't even know I'm back in London. She might be thinking that I'm languishing in some New York jail at this very minute. Then she'd have the painting and I'd be blamed for Annette Dvorski's murder. It would be clever to hire me and pretend to have no interest in the painting, but one by one the passengers on that plane, the people who knew about the Hogarth, are being killed or silenced. Of course, she can't be doing it on her own, but Charlene Fleet has contacts everywhere and a lot of money. I know for a fact that her clients include Russian and Chinese dealers as well as Americans, not to mention the English. Think of Arnold Fletcher for a start. I suppose it's no coincidence that he brought me in on this case."

"Arnold's not a criminal," Tully replied firmly. "He's not the type. Too careful, too private, too cagey. Everyone wants to know where his money came from, where *he* came from, but no one ever finds out. A very dark horse is Arnold."

"He's not like Fleet's usual clients."

"He probably gets lonely, like we all do." Tully said, changing the subject. "Can you imagine how much that woman knows?"

"And how many people owe her, how many secrets she's hogging. Fleet could buy any amount of help." Victor paused, thoughtful. "There was a peculiar Chinese man at the airport; I think he might have switched the suitcases."

He touched the back of his head and grimaced.

"What is it?" Tully asked.

"I told you; I was knocked out."

"You should get a doctor to look at that." Tully was wondering if the blow to Victor's head had confused him. "You could have a concussion, you know. I remember an actor I worked with once was struck by a piece of scenery which hadn't been erected properly. He was in a dreadful state, couldn't remember his own name. Concussion can scramble your thoughts terribly."

"Don't humor me, Tully. There *was* a Chinese man at the airport, behaving oddly. Said he was going to Paris, then got on my plane to London. And someone *did* force bleach down Annette Dvorski's throat, and I *did* run for my bloody life. So please," Victor said wearily, "do me a favor and believe me. Because frankly, I need someone to believe me."

Thirty-Three

IN AN EXPANSIVE WHITE-FRONTED HOUSE SET BEHIND CLIPPED YEW hedges in an exclusive enclave in Connecticut, Louis Freeland sat alone in his room. For a while he had been staring out the window and wondering when it would rain. The sky had been temperamental with clouds since ten that morning, but not a drop had fallen. He would, Louis promised himself, walk in the rain. When it finally came. He would not wear a hat but walk to the very bottom of the lawn and stand by the lake, feeling the cold water falling on his hair.

He liked the lake, had sometimes imagined that his mother might come there. That if he concentrated, he might catch a glimpse of a whitewater creature hiding in the long green reeds. It was an image that had shimmered throughout his childhood dreams: the accidental drowning of his mother. So long had he lived with the image that it had assumed a psychotic intensity. He could picture her clothes, always green in color, her drowning dress filled with water, her hair sleek to her head like a statue's. And the reeds, waving under the weight of the lake, taking her down.

None of Louis's doctors realized that he understood how his mother had died because he had the gift of listening, not of talking. He was often dumbly uncommunicative, but it wasn't through stupidity, just unwillingness to speak. For Louis, there was too much talk. People did it all the time, throwing out words like dry seeds on rocky ground, dead before they struck earth, making no impact. Sometimes he had wanted to put the words back into the speaker's mouth and get him or her to swallow them. To take them away again.

But he had been a child and knew that he had little power in a world of professional medical people or among the glistening cleverness of his father's acquaintances. Thinking of his father, Louis felt a thrill of expectancy that had never left him since he had been six years old. The joy of it! The joy of knowing that he—a solitary child, left alone, without a mother—possessed the whole of his father's attention. Louis felt a hum of satisfaction. Who had need of a mother with Bernie Freeland as a father?

Still looking up at the sky, Louis heard footsteps along the passage and turned to his computer. He would appear to be busy and with luck would be left alone. With studied concentration he stared at the wide screen, his searching brown eyes focused on the game he was playing. His narrow hands, small as a boy's, worked the computer keyboard like a concert pianist; only the sound of his soft intermittent cough broke the silence.

For all his insight, Louis had never realized that his life was a virtual secret. The staff and his doctors knew who his father was, but Bernie had been ashamed of his son, always ill at ease in his company. He had wanted the perfect heir to his hard-won fortune, but Louis had fallen short of his father's emotional and professional mark. Conceived as a result of a brief marriage, the boy had been born with learning difficulties. His mother had died in a freak drowning accident when he was six, and he had been raised by a nurse and Mrs. Sheldon, the housekeeper.

Louis was given the best treatment, the best therapy, and his difficulties gradually lessened as he grew into his teens until he was noticeably different only in his social diffidence. Emotionally awkward, he lacked his father's easy, boisterous charm but was devoted to him, a devotion that Bernie found it increasingly difficult to deal with.

At first Louis had lived with Bernie in Australia, his father's peripatetic lifestyle suiting them both. Louis spent his time either with his adored father or longing to see him. For a child with a limited emotional range, he existed in a state of continuous expectation that was heightened when he was moved to his father's home in Connecticut. Although Bernie insisted that he had found better tutors for his son, which had necessitated the move, his prime motive had actually been selfish.

With one failed marriage behind him and no other children, Bernie Freeland had found Louis's devotion unpalatable as he grew from a child into a young man. What had been affectionate, at times touching, in a child was embarrassing in an adult. He didn't understand that his son's whole existence was centered on him. Seldom demonstrative with anyone else, Louis would run to Bernie and sit adoringly at his feet, listening to every word. He was a constant appreciative audience of one.

But he wasn't what Bernie wanted. A woman's admiration was fine, flattering, but Louis's uninhibited attachment made him cringe. And worse, it gave him guilt. So Bernie put distance between them. Spending more time on his own in Australia, he emotionally segregated his own son. Every privilege was provided for Louis. He had the best surroundings, conditions, and schooling. He had friends who were paid to play with him, friends chosen by his private doctors. But Louis's devotion to his largely absent father did not weaken.

Then, to everyone's surprise, the awkward boy turned into an attractive young man. Sometimes Bernie would look at Louis and wonder why his personality did not live up to his appearance. If only he had been born with normal social skills, he could have brought him into the business, showed him off, set him on the natural route of inheritance. But although good-looking and to all intents and purposes outwardly normal, Louis Freeland was never going to be the gilded child. Still, all he wanted was his father's love and approval, and, thankfully, Bernie was a good liar.

The footsteps Louis heard had paused at his door. A doctor looked in and turned to the woman beside him.

"Does he know yet?"

Mrs. Sheldon shook her head. "No; you said you were going to tell him."

"I don't think I would be the right person." He paused, uncomfortable. "I don't know how he'd take it from me."

Uneasy, Mrs. Sheldon stared at Louis. He was too far away to hear her conversation with the doctor but close enough to sense something was wrong. He turned and caught the woman's eye. She smiled warmly at him and then turned back to the doctor.

"Louis is far more capable than you give him credit for. He can look after himself—with a bit of help."

The doctor seemed unconvinced. "According to the lawyer, Mr. Freeland's left instructions for his son's future in his will. I don't know the details, but no doubt Louis will be a very rich man."

"*If* his father left him the money," Mrs. Sheldon countered brusquely. "Frankly, I hope he didn't. Louis doesn't understand money; it doesn't mean much to him."

"It'll mean a lot to the person looking after him. His assistants and his doctors should be well provided for . . . to care for Louis, I mean."

Ignoring him, Mrs. Sheldon kept watching Louis. She had cared for him since he was six years old and had watched the minor and major triumphs of his child's life, but she had often been the only audience. She could never accuse Bernie Freeland of neglect or unkindness. Just a lack of empathy. She had lost count of how many times she had tried to tell Bernie about his son's progress, but instead of being encouraged, the father had seemed to want Louis to remain a child. A boy. A boy could stay in the background. A boy's faults would not make for social awkwardness. No questions about any career he might follow. No sexual urges to control or fulfill. Louis, even at twenty-two, was expected to remain the eternal uncomprehending infant.

It did Mrs. Sheldon no good to try to tell her employer that Louis was taking computer classes and going to the city on his own. Or even, later, that he had started a friendship with a girl at the college. Her excitement had been met with deaf ears, and as time had gone on, she had become aware that Bernie Freeland was one day going to be forced to face up to his son's true condition. And worse, he was going to have to see that Louis could lead a normal life. Limited, small, contained, yes. But normal.

But normal was never going to be enough.

"You have to tell him," the doctor repeated. "Or course, Louis worshipped his father; he could withdraw into himself entirely when he hears that Mr. Freeland's dead."

She nodded slowly. "I'll tell him. He'll be all right."

"Well, if you need me, call. I can always give him a sedative."

"He was talking about his father only this morning," Mrs. Sheldon said. "He knows Mr. Freeland was due for a visit. You think he has no conception of time, don't you, but you're wrong. Louis *senses* time. Louis senses a lot of things." She looked at the doctor, her expression challenging. "We get along very well together. I can manage him."

"You might find yourself expected to manage Louis for the rest of his life."

"No; he's not a child," she replied with certainty. "And his father's death might be the only way anyone will allow him to grow up."

She walked into the room, hearing the doctor's footsteps fade into the distance. In a few moments he would drive away. Later he would ring her and ask how the patient was, adding today's fee to the hundreds of bills he had submitted over the years for treatment that had been unnecessary, excessive, an intensity of care to assuage Bernie Freeland's guilt.

"Are you winning?" Mrs. Sheldon asked, walking over to Louis and putting her hand on his shoulder. She felt him relax; he was always grateful for physical contact.

"I like this game."

"That's good, Louis." Her voice was gentle. "I have to talk to you."

He swiveled around in his chair, looking up at her, taking in the familiar features and noticing the serious expression.

"I know you love your father very much," Mrs. Sheldon began, straining at the words, "but there's been a terrible accident, my dear." She paused, trying to read any expression in the young man's face. He seldom showed any emotion except with his father, and Mrs. Sheldon had grown used to Louis's facial blankness. But for once she found his neutrality unnerving and pushed on. "I'm sorry, Louis. Your father's been killed—in a car accident—in New York. I'm so sorry." She squeezed his shoulder. "I'm so very sorry."

His large brown eyes remained fixed on her as he tried to assimilate her words. For a moment he picked up on her anxiety, but it was fleeting. Far away, from over the horizon, there came the faintest echo of a thunderclap. Then silence. Immobile, Louis sat in his seat, Mrs. Sheldon's hand still on his shoulder. A few moments passed in silence.

Then, as the first drowning drops of rain began at last to fall on the ledge outside, Louis Freeland sighed.

Thirty-Four

RETYING HIS TIE, LIM CHANG STARED AT HIS REFLECTION IN THE bathroom mirror of his hotel room. His fury was almost uncontrollable. Banging his fists on the side of the sink, he felt a jolt of pain that was momentarily soothing. But only momentarily. In his rage, he wrenched at the tie around his neck and flung it onto the floor. Dark and curled, it lay like a night snake against the bath mat. Lim Chang ground it underfoot, his anger a muted growl at the back of his throat.

Back in the bedroom, he poured himself a Scotch from the minibar, downing it in one swallow. His usual habit was never to drink before noon, but he was desperate to find some way to prevent any further loss of control. He slumped into the chair by the window, marginally more relaxed thanks to the whiskey. In all his time as an international dealer Lim Chang had never lost control. His expression, whether he was attending a private view or outbidding a competitor, did not alter. He liked to imagine that he was upholding some long-held Chinese tradition of inscrutability, something fast disappearing as Western culture took hold.

It was obvious that in the new China the old principles of control and order were crumbling. Children and young adults resented the discipline of their parents and grandparents, and under the influence of the USA and Europe, a slow homogenization of Chinese culture was taking place. It was inevitable, Chang knew, if the country was to be a world leader. China could not remain forever culturally alien if it wished to be accepted in the West, but he missed the obedience he had been able to command. He loathed the questioning of his power and felt that he was watching not so much the advance of a nation as its mutation.

His rage still burning, Lim Chang felt his control finally regaining the upper hand. He would solve the problem; he always did. His superiors expected it of him and he would not disappoint them, but he was very relieved that he hadn't told anyone about the Hogarth. No point bragging about a coup before it was executed. His prudence and inherent modesty, which amused some, would now prove his greatest protection. He would obtain the painting, and he *would* take it back to China, but no one needed to know how he had managed it. And if for some inconceivable reason he failed, it was better that his country remain in ignorance. Better the discreet hero than the flashy failure.

That they had had the nerve to talk to him like that! Lim Chang was outraged. To try to deal with *him*, a spokesperson for Chinese culture. To try to bring him down to their level. He winced at the memory of his visit the previous night. He had received a message that there was news on the painting and that he should return to Chinatown. Back through the evening streets he had walked, past tourists and night workers and security cameras, their metal noses poking out from under the red awnings of Chinese restaurants, until he reached the dingy basement again.

This time a third man—angular, well dressed, and no more than thirty—had joined the original two. He had bowed in mock salutation as Lim Chang entered the crowded room, the smell of cooking oil strong in the air, an unfinished card game still set out on the table by the window. From behind the thin curtain that separated the room from the back of a club, he heard loud Western music playing, its sound vibrating under his feet.

"May I ask who I'm dealing with?" Lim Chang had said, looking from the sweating man to the younger stranger.

"I don't think we need names," the newcomer replied.

"But you have mine," Lim Chang said not unreasonably. He waited a moment, then continued, realizing that the man was not going to identify himself. "Do you have the Hogarth painting?"

Sitting down and jiggling his leg, the young man rubbed his eyes, the lids pink. "It'll cost you—"

Chang was outraged. "I work for the Chinese government!" he blustered. "I have to organize money with them."

"I don't care who you fucking work for." The man sounded amused, but he rapidly shifted to a threatening tone. "It was very difficult getting hold of the painting. You have to pay for it."

"I don't have the means at this moment."

"Then you don't have the painting," he replied, unfazed. "I want half a million pounds."

"Half a million!"

"It's cheap." The young man rubbed his eyes again, then took a small plastic bottle from his pocket. Carefully he put a couple of drops in each eye, blinking repeatedly until his vision cleared. To Lim Chang he seemed hyped with frantic nervous energy.

"So," he had said, still blinking, "do you want it or not?"

Desperately, Chang played for time. "You really expect me to buy it without seeing it?"

The young man had hesitated, then reached over to his bag and pulled out a cylinder. Lim Chang's pulse quickened as he watched the canvas being drawn from its hiding place. Knocking the card game off the table, the man had laid out the painting, the neon light from the street overhead illuminating a masterpiece that had been painted over two hundred and fifty years earlier. Staring open-mouthed, Lim Chang examined the work, looked at the pert face of Polly Gunnell smiling up at him, recognized her handsome young lover in the background: Frederick, Prince of Wales.

So it *was* real. What had been a select and garbled rumor in the art world for so many years *had* existed. Not a rumor but—as Lim Chang realized while fighting unaccustomed light-headedness—tangible damning proof that the royal bastard had existed, heir to the English throne. Then another thought struck him almost instantly: what a dangerous piece this was, what a priceless acquisition. What a political lever. What a coup to take home to Communist China . . .

Surprised, Chang had suddenly felt faint, a sensation he had never experienced before. He gripped the table for support.

"Watch out!" the young man had said angrily. "I didn't say you could touch it."

Recovering himself, Lim Chang had bent farther toward the canvas. The neon light flickered alternately red and green over the oil painting, and the overhead basement light bled out the colors under its dim wattage. But the genius had been there. The confidence and bravura of the work were obvious. At the left corner there had been a small tear, but there was no other fault apart from the darkening of the varnish.

Slowly Lim Chang had picked it up.

"Hey!"

"I have to examine the back," Chang had said firmly, turning the work carefully and noting a watermark in the grain of the canvas, along with expected and natural signs of wear.

"So?" the young man had said impatiently. "It's genuine."

"I believe it is," Lim Chang agreed, doubting that the seller would know whether it was authentic. "However, this painting is not for myself; it's for the Chinese people."

"Then ask them for the money."

"The government will buy the painting, but it will take a little time for them to organize the funds. And besides, these are rather unusual circumstances."

The young man's eyes had narrowed.

"Dealers trade works of art every day. What's so different about this?" he said. "I've asked around about you. You've bought enough paintings; you know how the business runs. No one gives the stuff away, do they? They sell it."

"But I buy through the proper channels."

The sweating man had laughed then, flopping into a seat behind Lim Chang. The younger man said, "If I was sitting in a gallery in Bond Street, you wouldn't give this a second's thought."

Watched by the three men, Lim Chang had realized that he was in a very precarious position. He wanted the Hogarth but was reluctant to approach his superiors for half a million pounds without telling them from whom he intended to purchase the painting. But then again, he could hardly let the opportunity slip through his fingers. The solution was obvious. He would have to lie. If lying was the only way to secure a notorious masterpiece, so be it.

Outwardly calm, he appeared to be considering the proposal, but he had actually been weighing his options. If he didn't buy the Hogarth, who would? He was worldly enough to know that many art purchases were suspect, even illegal. The young man had been right. To all intents and purposes, he was just another dealer.

Who also happened to be a gangster dealing from a basement in Chinatown.

"Where did you get it from?" Chang asked.

"You don't need to know that," the young man replied, his left eye running. "You asked for help finding it. We found it."

"Where?"

"Do you want it or not?"

"I'll need some time to raise the money." Lim Chang stood up, catching the young man off guard.

Surprised, he had risen to his feet. "I need a decision now!"

"Why? You have another buyer?"

"You're too fucking smug," the young man said coldly. "I could find a dealer in a minute. Just walk a few streets and into any gallery off Piccadilly."

"No, you couldn't," Lim Chang had replied, for the first time feeling confident. "You'd never get away with it. They'd have the police on you in an instant. And even if they didn't, you really think you'd see any money? You know as well as I do that you can't get rid of a painting as famous as this one without everyone wanting to know where you got it from. Every dealer in this town or any major city would recognize the work." He had carried on, his equanimity impressive. "People have always believed this Hogarth was destroyed, but everyone's actually hoped that one day it might reemerge."

"I don't need a lesson in art history. It's just a fucking painting that I want money for."

Lim Chang paused. He had to be careful; if he said too much about its importance, the triads might decide to keep the work for themselves. He couldn't afford for them to realize what they had. So he decided to tell them enough to scare them, to make them want to get the Hogarth off their hands as quickly as possible.

"Perhaps I should warn you that there have been two deaths already because of this painting. And for all I know, there might have been others."

The young man had sat down, rolling up the canvas and sliding it back into the cylinder.

"You trying to scare me?" He had looked at his colleagues, amused. "I think this little government ass licker is trying to scare me."

Chang had taken in a breath. "You don't want this painting."

"*Yes, I do!*" The young man's violent tone reverberated around the basement room. "Only *you* want it more, Lim Chang. You want it *much* more. Then you can run home and get a pat on the back from your superiors." He had sneered, provoking him. "What a little hero you'll be then. They might put a note under the painting to say that you obtained it from the Western despots. You're the perfect company man, Chang. A product of old China, born to serve." He had paused, letting the words take effect. "Find a way to get that half a million or I'll find another dealer. You really think there's only one route to sell this?"

"You have to give me some time."

"You've got a week," the young man had said dismissively. "Now get out."

Remembering the devastating humiliation he had felt, Lim Chang walked back into the bathroom and picked up the creased tie, returning it to his wardrobe and picking out another. Slowly he finished dressing, then walked out of the hotel, leaving his key card at reception, and headed for Hyde Park. In the bitter winter morning, he moved through the underpass and then came out into the greenery of the park, taking a route that eventually would lead him to Piccadilly.

But the morning was spoiled by the memory of the previous evening. Chang bristled at the thought of the young man with the sore eyes calling him an ass licker, born to serve, then wondered why he had felt the insult so acutely. Hadn't he always been proud to serve his country? Proud to have risen up the ranks to a position of some authority and respectability? Hadn't he devoted his life to duty? His wife had played only a minor role in his existence, and his son was a shadowy figure; he had left them very much on the periphery of his life, both of them largely ignorant of Lim Chang's true nature.

Over the years, he had learned to excuse his ruthlessness, his venality, by referring to his successes. Having acquired many important pieces of art for his country, Lim Chang had assuaged any guilt with his belief that all was forgivable in the service of the people and the people's country. But slowly, seeing how China was becoming a major player in the world, he had realized that he must become more flexible.

Still smarting, Lim Chang walked toward Piccadilly, finally turning into the Burlington Arcade. Checking the time on his wristwatch, he silently rehearsed his speech one more time, then pressed the buzzer at the entrance to Sir Oliver Peters's gallery. He could see movement inside, and an attractive female secretary opened the door for him, smiling a welcome.

"Can I help you?"

"I've come to see Sir Oliver Peters," Chang said confidently.

"Have you an appointment? I'm afraid he's very busy today."

"He'll see me. Just tell him Lim Chang wishes to have a word with him."

Thirty–Five

As Lim Chang cooled his heels in the gallery, Oliver was on a call to his brother-in-law, Ambrose Wilton. Although he had expected little in the way of help, anxiety for his family finally had forced him to approach the recluse. But even after he had confided that he had terminal cancer, there was only a muted, grudging response.

"How long have you got?" Ambrose asked imperiously, as though the whole matter was an inconvenience with which he never should have been troubled.

"A couple of months," Oliver replied, hearing the dogs barking in the background as an accompaniment to Ambrose's regal tone resonating down the line from rainy Ireland. "Sonia's your sister."

"I know who my family members are."

"Then have some concern for them!" Oliver snapped. "God knows, I've helped you often enough in the past."

"You like helping people," Ambrose replied loftily. "You always have. I'm not like you, Oliver. I don't feel the need to dig people out of holes. You have a social conscience; congratulations. I'm sure your obituary will be effusive."

Taking in a breath, Oliver dropped his voice. "I'm not asking for myself but for your sister."

"You have money; you'll leave her well off," Ambrose retorted. "Sonia and I were never close."

"That wasn't her fault."

"I like dogs," Ambrose said curtly, "not people."

"Without my help you'd have been on the streets."

"You can't force sympathy out of me," Ambrose went on. "It's not in my nature. I don't care about you or Sonia. I live alone because I like it, so please don't expect anything from me. You would only be disappointed."

And that was that.

Oliver leaned back in his seat, reflecting bitterly on the conversation. He was so angered by Ambrose Wilton that it was a relief when Lim Chang was shown into his office. Oliver's manners were as graceful as ever as he showed Chang to a seat before regaining his own behind the desk.

"I have some news," the Chinese dealer announced without ado.

Oliver concealed his relief. It had been three days since he last had seen Lim Chang, and he'd begun to wonder if he had been cheated, even dreamed of Chang finding the Hogarth and returning to China with it, with him learning the mortifying news from the *Daily Telegraph*.

"News?" Oliver repeated. "Good news?"

"The Hogarth has been found."

Touching his mouth with the tips of his fingers, Oliver took in a breath. The Hogarth was safe.

"In London?"

"In London."

"Who has it?"

"That's not important," Lim Chang went on. "They want half a million pounds for it."

A laugh bubbled up in Oliver's chest. Half a million pounds. Where was he going to get half a million pounds? Of course, he *appeared* to have that much money; he had all the outward trappings of wealth, but it was a sham. He had assets but a paltry bank account.

"Half a million pounds?"

Chang nodded.

"You think that's a fair price?" Oliver asked, watching Chang intently.

The Chinese man raised his eyebrows. "It's a fair price for someone who wants to get rid of it fast."

"Won't you please tell me who has it?"

Chang ignored the question. "We both know, you and I," he said, "that the picture would raise a lot more at auction. Possibly fifteen million, perhaps more."

"But half a million pounds." Oliver mused, the strong scent of the tea roses on an occasional table making him momentarily queasy. Could he perhaps raise it? Could he make such a big sale? And even if he could, how long would it take? Or could he borrow so much? Time—and the lack of it—was pressing hard on him. "It's a bad market to raise finance."

"I thought perhaps you would have the funds available to you."

"Half a million pounds?" Oliver said, smiling. "Those days are gone. Like many others, I'm struggling."

Lim Chang covered his surprise as Oliver asked, "Where did they find the painting?"

"I don't know." Lim Chang met his gaze evenly. "I honestly don't know."

"You're being very cagey," Oliver remarked, unsure of his own ground and feeling anxious but pressuring his visitor nevertheless. "Why won't you tell me how you got hold of the picture, Chang?"

At any other time Oliver would have obeyed his instinct and retreated. As one of the London dealers who had always been above reproach, all his deals legal and fair, he had avoided any smear on his reputation. He had seen many dealers overreach themselves or try to steal a march on their competitors by underhanded means. Some had profited by misattributed works, dummy auction lots, and seeding, but several had been caught. If the dealer was old school, he would be given a slap on the wrist, but any newcomers, upstarts, or foreigners were drummed out. The art world had a long-standing code of tacitly protecting its own but crucifying any greedy infiltrator.

But Oliver Peters was now a desperate man, and his usual caution deserted him.

"I thought we trusted each other," he said quietly. "I thought that was why we joined forces."

"Which is why I've come back to you with news of the Hogarth," Lim Chang replied, somewhat annoyed. "I could have returned to my country with the painting and reneged on my promise. Some dealers would have done just that."

"I apologize," Oliver said, shamed by his unspoken suspicions. "My remarks were uncalled for. But I simply don't have half a million pounds at my disposal. I could certainly try to raise it, but it would take time."

"I've been given a week."

"A week." How long a week seemed in business, he thought, and how short when your life only had weeks to run. "I can try."

Silent, Lim Chang studied the Englishman. He had thought that Sir Oliver Peters would be able to raise the money immediately and was shocked to find he was unable to do so. It irked Chang that his plan had been summarily overturned. The Chinese government wanted the painting and was prepared to buy it, but bureaucracy impeded the process and Chang knew it would take much longer than a week to secure the money from Beijing. He had been relying on Oliver's funding; that was the reason—the only reason—he had joined forces with him. With Sir Oliver Peters's money he would have obtained the Hogarth immediately and then done exactly what the Englishman had suspected and taken the painting back to China.

Now his plan was coming unstuck, and anger flickered beneath his impenetrable exterior. "We *have* to obtain this painting."

"I know. I *do* know," Oliver agreed emphatically, glancing over at the family photograph on his desk. His imminent dishonesty shamed him, but Lim Chang's discomfort hardly ranked alongside his own inherited responsibility to the secret of the royal bastard or the future security of his family. Besides, the Chinese man's record was far from impeccable; he had had many guilty dealings in his past, many ruthless deals. Would it be so unforgivable to cheat him to regain what was, after all, his own property?

Afraid that his intentions would show on his face, Oliver kept gazing at his family photograph. He had had no other means of finding the Hogarth, he told himself; he had been forced to use the Chinese dealer. And it had worked; the painting had been found. All that remained was to raise half a million pounds and the painting would be back in his possession. He needed Lim Chang to get the picture, and Lim Chang needed him to supply the funds. They needed each other, and both resented it.

Oliver vowed to himself that no matter what happened, Chang would not get the Hogarth. He didn't know how much the man knew about the history of the work, but to have the royal family in any way besmirched was intolerable. Or worse, if the surviving descendant was found and exposed . . . Oliver swallowed, barely able to contemplate such a catastrophe, but one thing was certain: he *could not* fail. All he had to do was somehow raise or borrow half a million pounds.

"I'll get the money," he said at last, raising his head. "Did you see the Hogarth?"

"Yes," Lim Chang replied. "And it's genuine. I would bet my life on it."

"Do the people who have it . . . Do they know what they have?"

"No," Lim Chang said curtly, "but they know it's valuable; nothing more than that."

"So no other dealers have seen it?"

Lim Chang shook his head. "None."

"Then we know what we have to do," Oliver replied, standing up to indicate that the meeting was over.

He did not extend his hand; his conscience at least prevented that. Instead, he showed Lim Chang to the door and out into the Burlington Arcade. Deep in thought, Oliver was still staring ahead when his secretary interrupted him.

"You're about to have another visitor, sir."

Surprised, he stared at her. "I made no appointments."

"I know, but the gentleman said he wanted to talk to you about a Hogarth painting because you were one of the best dealers in English art in London. I told him that you were in a meeting, and he said he would call back in half an hour." She glanced at her watch. "He should be here any time now."

Taken aback, Oliver stared into the secretary's pretty face. "Did he give you a name?"

"Mr. Victor Ballam."

The name caught Oliver off guard. So much so that for an instant he was uncertain how to react. Then he nodded and walked toward his office. He paused at the door, turning back to his secretary.

"*Victor Ballam?*"

"Yes, sir."

"I see. Well, when he comes back, show him in, will you, and we'll have some coffee, please. Oh, and Margaret, don't disturb us and don't put through any calls while Mr. Ballam is here."

Thirty-Six

BACK AT HIS DESK, OLIVER PICKED UP HIS PEN AND ROTATED IT IDLY, thinking about his imminent visitor. A man who had come into the art world like a pistol shot, catching everyone off guard. A glamorous, attractive man with a quick mind, a connoisseur's taste, and a dealer's skill. Brave, occasionally reckless, but smart enough not to overreach himself too soon. Victor Ballam had had a background in advertising, and fellow dealers initially had sneered at his confidence, but his talent was soon obvious to all, attracting admiration and envy in equal measure. By the time Victor had worked in Dover Street for eighteen months, he had been poached by a gallery in Cork Street and feted for his unerring, almost uncanny predictions on the market.

He had been one of the few who had sensed the first struggles of Britart and spotted the growing appreciation of Russian and African painting. As cunning as a market trader, Victor allied his skill to a God-given instinct for art. The self-taught upstart outsider was viewed with awe as his fortunes rose faster than a helium balloon. No private view was complete without the dark-haired figure of Victor Ballam. No gallery opening was a success without his presence. And he wore his success well. Another man would have become arrogant, pompous; Victor did not. He defended what he believed in and stood his ground, but he was easy to deal with. Within another year he had become a partner in the Cork Street gallery. He was wanted and accepted, one of the few outsiders to have penetrated and impressed the art world.

But for all his predictive skills, thought Oliver, still twisting the pen in his fingers, Victor Ballam had not foreseen his own downfall. When he was charged with fraud, Oliver had been the only person to speak out in his defense. To no avail. When Victor was sentenced, his fallen star left a crater so deep that it buried him for years in Long Lartin.

"Sir Oliver?"

He looked up to see his secretary in the doorway.

"Mr. Ballam is here now."

"Show him in, Margaret," said Oliver, watching as the familiar figure entered the room. Familiar but different. Victor Ballam was older, of course, but his carefree charm had been tested and it was a noticeably more chary individual who sat down in the proffered seat. Waiting until Margaret had brought in the coffee and left the office, Oliver finally spoke.

"It's good to see you after so long, Victor." He paused, his manners serving him well. "Are you working back in London?"

"Not in the gallery. That option's closed to me now. I'm doing some investigative work."

"Indeed." Oliver sipped his coffee. "In this area?"

Victor smiled, trying to ease the tension.

"I'm sorry to just turn up like this, Sir Oliver. It's good of you to see me. Most dealers would have shown me the door."

"Most dealers were very jealous of you," Oliver said honestly. "I always liked you."

Unaccountably pleased, Victor smiled again. "I learned a lot from you."

"Maybe, but I'm old school, while you were the bright new hope. I'm sorry; I shouldn't have used the past tense."

Victor shrugged. "We both know I'm finished as a dealer. My reputation's ruined. Now I could uncover a new Van Gogh and everyone would swear I'd stolen it." He paused. "But when I was in trouble, you spoke up for me. You didn't have to do that. I owe you."

"You don't owe me anything."

"Don't you want to know what happened?"

"No," Oliver said simply, shaking his head. "If you didn't do it, no amount of my sympathy will make it hurt a jot less. If you did do it, then you've paid for it. Not just by your sentence but by being in the position you are in now."

He wanted to say more but kept his counsel. He never believed that Victor would have deliberately dealt in fakes. It would have been too clumsy, too crude for him. And besides, why would he have threatened a career that was progressing so well? Other dealers might say that Victor Ballam had dealt in forgeries because he was greedy for the money, but Oliver had never believed that. *They* might have been greedy, but Victor? No; greed had never been one of his vices.

Instead, Oliver Peters had long believed that Victor had been stopped deliberately. But why? The answer was obvious. His ascent had been too fast, too glittering, for some of the art world grandees. He was too ripe for the age: photogenic, media-savvy, always the first to be called on for a sound bite when some sale hit the news. And he was incorruptible, brave enough to speak out about some of the less savory aspects of the art business. He made speeches. He made points. And he made enemies.

But there could be no murder, no dramatic disappearance. Victor Ballam had to be silenced by being disgraced. And what better fall from grace for the whiter-than-white dealer than to be exposed as a fraud? At his trial, people derided Victor's hypocrisy, his hubris, and he got three-plus years in jail. The art world could have tolerated his success, but his judgment of them? Never.

"I didn't believe that you did it," Oliver said. "I want you to know that. I think you were set up."

Victor nodded. "I know I was."

"You know who did it?"

"No. Do you?"

"No; I would have told you."

A moment passed between them.

"It was unjust."

Oliver didn't miss a beat. "Many things are in life."

Victor held his gaze. Among all the dealers, he had always sought Sir Oliver Peters's respect. And now, as he looked at him and saw the signs of illness, he felt a debt of honor he wanted to repay. If he *was* involved in anything dangerous, Victor wanted to protect him.

"I've been hired to investigate what happened to a call girl called Marian Miller. Just before her death she'd been traveling on Bernie Freeland's jet."

Oliver leaned back in his seat, cautious. "You know I was also a passenger on that flight?"

"Yes. That's why I'm here. I'm talking to everyone who was involved. Did you know that Bernie Freeland was killed in New York?"

"Yes."

"And that Kit Wilkes has been admitted to the hospital with a drug overdose?"

"I heard about that too. A tragedy," Oliver said. "I have to be honest with you: I don't really socialize with Mr. Wilkes; we move in different circles. Of course I know of him as a dealer, but we've never worked together."

Victor hesitated for an instant before continuing.

"One of the other girls who were on that flight is now missing. And another's been murdered in New York."

Shaken, Oliver reached for his coffee cup and took a long drink. Victor could see the shock on his features, the twitch of a muscle in his left cheek.

"I'm sorry to have to tell you all this," Victor went on, "and I'm relying on your discretion."

"Yes, yes; that goes without saying."

"It's unlikely to be coincidence that so many of the passengers are now dead."

"Kit Wilkes is still alive."

"Yes, but his condition's critical. Bernie Freeland's dead. Marian Miller's dead. And now Annette Dvorski's been murdered."

"Good God."

Victor held Oliver's glance. "I was surprised to hear that you'd been on that plane."

"My scheduled flight was canceled and I wanted to get home, so Bernie Freeland offered me a lift. We'd all attended an auction in Hong Kong."

"You, Bernie Freeland, Lim Chang, and Kit Wilkes?"

Oliver nodded, but he was uneasy, wondering what else Victor was going to say. Why he was in his office, talking about dead passengers. So many dead passengers.

"Apparently there was mention of a painting, a lost Hogarth," Victor began. "Did Bernie Freeland talk to you about it?"

Oliver fielded the question.

"I was out of place, uncomfortable. As you say, there were call girls on the jet. Bernie Freeland was a brash character, and he lived in a way that was alien to me. Most of the time I was regretting accepting the lift and just wanted to get home."

"But you two talked during the flight?"

"Bernie Freeland's drink was spiked," Oliver replied, on the defensive. "He wasn't making much sense."

"But he *did* mention the Hogarth, didn't he?"

Oliver winced.

"He did say something, but I dismissed it out of hand. All the paintings of *The Harlot's Progress* were destroyed by fire a long time ago." Oliver laced his fingers together, almost as though to contain the cat's cradle of lies he had begun to spin. "You were in the art business, Victor; you know it runs on stories. There's always talk of a new Raphael, a suddenly discovered Michelangelo—usually that tiresome cherub he was supposed to have faked."

"But *this* painting was special, important—and dangerous," Victor said carefully, catching a brief flicker crossing Oliver Peters's face. He knew the story and suspected that the man facing him knew it too even if he wasn't about to admit it.

"Dangerous?"

"It's supposed to depict the Prince of Wales and Polly Gunnell, his whore who bore him a bastard son."

"Oh, that old rumor," Oliver said smoothly, flicking the words away with his hand. "A rumor isn't a fact."

"Well, someone's taking it very seriously. I've already been threatened. Someone warned me off as soon as I got involved in this case."

Oliver's mind was working overtime. *Who knew that the Hogarth was missing?* He had prayed that the fact would remain secret until he could recover the painting. His mistake—his bad luck—he had hoped would never be exposed. *But someone knew.* Someone had warned Victor Ballam. How long before they threatened him too? How long before someone came, sent from the royal advisers? How long before he was reprimanded, relieved of his position, demoted, his reputation and his family's security destabilized?

Oliver's mouth was as dry as ash. "Who threatened you?"

"I don't know."

"*Why* would someone threaten you?"

"Come on, Sir Oliver; we both know it's because of the Hogarth."

"All this for a painting? Never." He paused, uncertain if he was sounding convincing and piteously ashamed at having to lie. But what was his choice? To tell the truth? And to Victor Ballam? Hardly. But once the lying had begun, Oliver was finding its acceleration breathtaking. "Bernie Freeland didn't really know much about art. He was a lucky dealer, not an accomplished one. Not in English art, anyway. I doubt he would have known if the Hogarth painting was genuine. He might have been taken in by a fake."

"What if he wasn't taken in?" Victor replied. "True, Freeland was a businessman who *became* a collector; he didn't have a connoisseur's instinct. But he had a lot of money, and he could easily have paid to have the painting authenticated. I doubt he'd have bought a Hogarth unless he *knew* it was genuine."

Victor broke the silence that followed. "When he mentioned the painting to you, what did you think?"

"That he was babbling. I thought he was ill."

Victor changed tack. "My client—"

"Who is?"

"That's confidential," Victor countered, elastic with the truth himself. "But it's someone who wants to find out why so many of the passengers on that flight have been killed and hopefully prevent the remainder from ending up the same way." This time he saw Oliver flinch and pressed on. "You were such a disparate bunch, people with so little in common. True, four of you were art dealers, but not friends. You lived in different countries, had different nationalities, and moved in different circles. As for the working girls, they were simply hired by Bernie Freeland for the trip. Or did any of the last-minute passengers have sex with them?"

Outraged and showing it, Oliver snapped his answer. "No!"

"I had to ask."

"No one had sex with the girls except Bernie Freeland."

"So the *only* thing all of you had in common was knowing about the Hogarth."

"That's ridiculous!" Oliver said sharply, trying to put Victor off the scent. "Bernie Freeland was just rambling."

"Freeland *had* got hold of the Hogarth, hadn't he?"

"I don't know," Oliver replied coolly. "You seem to know a lot about what went on in that plane. Why don't you tell me?"

Surprised, Victor wondered why Oliver was being so confrontational and then remembered Tully telling him that Peters was terminally ill. Perhaps no longer able to remain honorable, perhaps driven to getting the Hogarth himself and making a fortune to secure his family's future. Remembering how he had had lost the Hogarth, Victor suddenly wondered if, indeed, *Oliver Peters* knew where the painting was. Perhaps it was in his gallery, behind the next wall. Perhaps in his bank.

Poised, Victor studied the elegant man in front of him. How many people *really* knew about the Hogarth? Had anyone had time to pass the information on? Had Lim Chang spoken to the Chinese? Kit Wilkes to the Russians?

Oliver Peters to the British contingent? Kit Wilkes couldn't have kept the secret for an hour. Could Lim Chang have resisted broadcasting such a coup? In the minutes after they left Bernie Freeland's plane, how many busy little fingers texted messages and made phone calls?

Victor wondered whether the information became public property or remained contained. Whether knotted tendrils of communication reached out across the Internet from that tight little coterie, humming over phone lines and cable connections. From one manageable little bunch, did the news then snake its prolonged reach around the globe?

And if it did, could any one dealer, especially a man as sick as Oliver Peters, grab the prize for himself?

"Have you been in touch with Lim Chang?"

Oliver blinked. "Why should I be?"

"He was on the flight, and he must have heard about Bernie Freeland's death," Victor replied. "It would be natural for you two to talk."

"Who authorized you to ask all these questions?" Oliver asked, suddenly taking out a small vial of pills. Without attempting to disguise what he was doing, he shook out two tablets and swallowed them with what was left of his coffee. "You sound like a policeman, Victor. Although the force doesn't hire anyone with a criminal record, do they?" Ashamed of the jibe, he said, "Forgive my manners; I'm in a little pain."

More than a little, Victor thought. "No one wants to bring the police into this, Sir Oliver. It would come out about the prostitutes and who was on the plane. I don't think anyone wants that kind of publicity."

"Guilt by association."

Victor nodded. "I understand why everyone wants to keep it private, and with the Hogarth back on the market—and we both know it *is*—secrecy's paramount."

Oliver was listening, surprised and wary. Was this man on his side? Was this convicted criminal, this ex-dealer, just grubbing about for information, or was he genuinely aware of the painting's significance?

"Sir Oliver, there are many dealers who could make a fortune out of the painting. Others would want to destroy it to defend reputations—royal reputations, the line of succession itself."

"I don't have it," Oliver said.

He had decided to fabricate his own version of events, at the same time appearing to help Victor. In this way he hoped he would find out more about what was going on and keep tabs on Lim Chang, whose request for money had played on Oliver's mind. What if it was a trick? What if Chang took the half a million and returned to China with the Hogarth *and* the money? Perhaps his only protection was to throw in his lot with Victor Ballam.

Weary with anxiety and pain, Oliver said, "I don't have the Hogarth. I was just an innocent party in this whole sordid mess. I was unlucky when I accepted Freeland's offer of a lift. I had nothing to do with the death of the call girl."

"I'm not suggesting you did."

"They said she was killed by a client."

"The police think so."

"But you don't?"

"No. I might have, but after Marian Miller's death, when Bernie Freeland was killed and then Annette Dvorski was murdered, it was just too much of a coincidence. You all knew about the Hogarth."

Still cautious, Oliver refused to be drawn.

"And even if you didn't, people *believed* that every passenger did. Sir Oliver, I need to know exactly what went on, who said what. And who you've spoken to since."

"Only Lim Chang."

"He's in London?"

Oliver was straining to concentrate. "Yes, he told me about Bernie Freeland's death."

"Does he know about the Hogarth?"

Oliver blinked slowly, thinking, then sighed, shaking his head. "There's really no point in my lying anymore, is there?"

"No."

"Anyone on that jet could have heard about the Hogarth."

Relieved, Victor nodded. "Bernie Freeland *did* talk to you, didn't he?"

"Yes. What he said was garbled, but he told me he had the painting. Someone had stolen it."

"From where?"

I don't know," Oliver replied, wanting to shout out, *From my bank. Stolen from me. My family. The Hogarth is my property, my responsibility, and I want it back*. But he didn't say any of it, because he knew he had to concentrate on recovering the painting. The thief was almost a secondary matter. "I just know that it was stolen and the thief wanted to get rid of it in a hurry. He sold it to Bernie Freeland."

"What else did he say?"

"He was scared, worried that something might happen to him. He was right; something did." Oliver paused, holding Victor's gaze. "But you have to remember how it was. We were just coming into land. The journey had been stressful; we all wanted to leave the plane and go home. And then suddenly Bernie Freeland started lurching around and saying these peculiar things to me. He was whispering, but loudly, if you know what I mean. And at first I didn't know what he was talking about." Oliver paused, remembering. "By the time the steward had settled him in his seat, we were landing. He said that Mr. Freeland's drink had been spiked but that he would be fine later. It was all so hurried, so odd."

"But anyone on the flight could have heard about the Hogarth?"

"Well, some passengers were closer to us than others," Oliver conceded, "but yes, I suppose everyone *could* have heard."

"What about the staff on the jet?" Victor asked, remembering what Tully had told him. "Did you notice anything unusual?"

"I don't remember the pilots. I didn't exchange a word with them. Oh, wait a minute. One pilot came into the cabin briefly, but that was all. He was busy, preoccupied. Young."

"That would have been John Yates," Victor said, thinking aloud. "What about the stewards?"

"The younger steward was a bit embarrassed because of the way the girls were behaving. They were flirting with them, walking around in their underwear." He paused, regarding Victor intently. "I'm very happily married, which is one of the reasons I'm trying to help you as much as I can. I don't want my wife to find out who my fellow passengers were."

"I understand."

"It would be embarrassing for her and for my children. You of all people know how mud sticks," Oliver said softly. "You asked me about the crew. I hardly remember the pilots, but I recall the stewards quite well. The older man was very efficient, seemed at home on the plane. I imagine he was someone who had worked for Freeland for a while. The younger man seemed excited, interested in the plane." Oliver sighed. "But was there anything unusual about them? No, nothing."

"What about the passengers?"

"Lim Chang was working most of the time. He was sitting across the aisle from me."

"What was Kit Wilkes doing?"

"Reading, sleeping . . ." Oliver turned his thoughts back to Wilkes. "At least he pretended to be asleep, but I remember thinking that no one could sleep for so long."

"Did he seem drugged?"

"Not to me. As I said, he was quiet. I always imagined people on drugs became very vocal."

"But he looked well?"

"Yes, he looked perfectly well. Mind you, I was talking to the girls for a while." Oliver took in a breath, unnerved. "You said that one of them has gone missing. Which one?"

"Liza Frith. She's very slim, blond."

"I remember her; she was kind," Oliver replied without elaborating. "Is she in danger?"

"She knows about the Hogarth, so yes."

"And Kit Wilkes is in the Friars Hospital with a drug overdose. You think he was stopped before he could talk about the Hogarth?"

"I'm sure of it," Victor replied. "Whoever did it worked fast. But were they fast enough?"

"I don't understand."

"Before Kit Wilkes was hospitalized he might not have had enough time to meet up with someone, but he *did* have enough time to pass on the news about the Hogarth."

Breathing deeply to steady himself, Oliver looked at Victor. "Are you sure all this is about the painting?"

"Oh, yes; I'm certain."

Troubled, Oliver fell silent. Should he confide? No, not yet. Perhaps later, when he might need Victor Ballam's help. For the time being he would work alone, try to raise the half a million to buy back the Hogarth. *One step at a time,* Oliver told himself; *take it one step at a time.* Momentarily forgetting that Victor was there, he remembered the call girls, alive and talking. He could see Lim Chang working on his BlackBerry as clearly as though he were still sitting next to him. And he felt the same dizzying fear at hearing the name *Hogarth*.

He could imagine the towering disappointment of his grandfather and father and the contempt of the redoubtable Sir Nathaniel Overton. Was he, Oliver Peters, to be the man who failed? The keeper who dropped the flame? The trusted confidant who was found wanting? Had generations of his family protected the royal secret only for him to fail now?

Watching the man he had admired for years, Victor knew Oliver Peters was holding back. There was a sense of despair, of palpable regret, that hung over the dealer like a shroud.

"Is there anything else you want to tell me, Sir Oliver?"

Slowly he shook his head.

"Too many deaths, too many accidents for it to be a coincidence," Victor repeated.

Unwilling to risk his voice, Oliver nodded. There had been too many deaths, and he was in the middle of the stew, trying to do a deal for a painting that had blood all over it.

Finally, he looked up. "I'm in danger, aren't I?"

"Yes," Victor replied sadly. "I rather think you are."

Thirty-Seven

ELIZABETH WILKES STARED AT THE STILL-LIFE PAINTING ON THE WALL of the office, her expression blank. She hadn't visited Park Street for many years and found it changed. For all the discreetly new wallpaper and furnishings, there was the same distinct and palpable aura of sex. The pictures might be tasteful, but she knew that behind the soundproofed doors men were being relieved or humiliated; all the muted lamplight in the world could not romanticize the humping of paid sex.

Uneasy, she touched her hair several times as though to reassure herself that the expensive cut was in place, not cheapened by her surroundings. She even wondered momentarily if she should leave, then realized she couldn't. Her son was dying. Or so his consultant had told her that morning. Her beloved Kit was barely alive, and without him there was nothing. No life, no future. Hearing a sound overhead, Elizabeth tensed, but no one came into the office, and after another moment she sat down, sighing nervously.

Perhaps she had been foolish to stop James Holden on the street in that way. But seeing him, portly and prosperous, had reminded her of her past. The disappointment of her failure underlined the anxiety she had over her son's condition—*their* son's condition—and she hoped desperately that Kit might activate some belated paternal response.

"What on *earth*" James Holden had expostulated, feeling someone touch his arm and turning to see who. "Elizabeth! I don't wish to talk to you."

Piqued, she had nonetheless fallen into step with him as he pounded toward Marylebone High Street. "We have to talk about Kit. I have to thank you—"

"Hah!"

"—for what you did. Getting him admitted to the Friars Hospital." She had to hurry now, almost running to keep up with him. "How did you know he was ill?"

Arriving at the traffic lights, James had been forced to stop walking but had kept his gaze averted from his ex-lover.

"A friend of your son's—"

"*Our* son."

"—contacted me. Look, I only acted out of common decency, not paternal concern. I did what I thought was for the best."

"And what would look right if it came out in the press."

"Oh, think what you like!" he had snapped, "but I don't want to be drawn into this anymore. You know that, and if you don't, you should. I don't want any contact with you *or* that young man."

"He's dying."

"I doubt it," James had replied, pulling down the bottom of his waistcoat and staring ahead. "He's just taken an overdose. Addicts do that, I hear. Doctor Fountain is hopeful that he might recover in time. No doubt he'll soon be back to talking to the press about this latest scandal."

"Kit is dying," Elizabeth had repeated. "He's in a coma."

Exasperated, James had finally turned to face her. He saw a handsome woman but felt no attraction to her. Her demands and the appalling behavior of her son had made him loathe them both. How he had been made to pay for his affair; how he had danced to the mockery of the tabloids and the eternal postings on the Web. No one—not even his most bitter political enemies—could have employed such determined and constant battery. That he was still respected in some quarters, still in the running for an honor, was little short of a miracle. And now Kit Wilkes—the tick that had burrowed under his skin for decades—had been silenced.

And he was supposed to care?

"Elizabeth, there is nothing more I can—or am willing—to do."

"But if Kit dies . . ."

"It will be a tragedy, but a self-made tragedy," he'd said coldly.

Remembering those words, Elizabeth shuddered. There had been something in James Holden's tone that had worried her. Nothing obvious but something under the words that prickled and tickled like a burr. Had it been relief? She cringed. Had she overplayed her hand? Had her encouragement of her son's vitriol backfired? Surely a father couldn't welcome his child's death. Surely not even a harried, humiliated father could see it as a deliverance. Elizabeth stared at the handbag on her lap. Bottega Veneta; so expensive, so divinely exquisite. If Kit died, how would she afford such luxuries? How could she run the gallery without his input? His punishing skill? How could she maintain her livelihood or her status if Kit perished?

And just *who*, she wondered, had told Holden about her son's overdose? Elizabeth should have asked him for a name, demanded one. Who had been with Kit when he was taken ill? Ronan Levy? Her thoughts tangled themselves as she remembered what Ronan had said at the hospital, how insistent he had been that Kit's condition was not accidental.

"He knows his limitations. . . . Kit's always in control. He looks after himself."

"So someone did this to him?"

"Someone must have. Kit was a different person when he came back to London."

When he came back to London . . . on a private jet owned by Bernie Freeland, the same Bernie Freeland who had been killed so coincidentally a day later. Unnerved, Elizabeth jumped as the door opened and Charlene Fleet walked in. Behind her came the dog, which settled beside her at her feet as she sat down opposite Elizabeth. Having not seen her for many years, Elizabeth was struck by her confidence and her looks, subtly assisted by surgery. Her hands were the only clue to her hard beginnings. Always rather large, they were clumsy for a slim woman and bare of jewelry as though any ornament would draw attention to them.

Elizabeth remembered Charlene Fleet's hands well.

"How are you? I haven't seen you for a long time," Mrs. Fleet said.

"My son is very ill, in a coma."

"Really? How sad."

Elizabeth faltered for a moment, then drove on. "I've been hearing some very strange things."

"You should never listen to gossip."

"Apparently my son was given a lift on a plane owned by Bernie Freeland."

Nothing changed in Mrs. Fleet's expression. "Poor Mr. Freeland. He was killed in a traffic accident, you know."

"I heard."

"But then you knew him rather well, didn't you?" she asked, looking coolly at Elizabeth. "When you were working for me. You were one of my best girls, you know, always very popular. It was a shame you left the profession."

A chilly silence descended and hung over the two women before Elizabeth replied.

"I wanted to get out of the business as soon as I could."

"With as *much* as you could."

"I won't deny it," Elizabeth said, conscious of the other woman's hostility. "I wanted to make money. We both did, Charlene."

Smiling, Mrs. Fleet looked around the room, her gaze settling briefly on the view outside the window. She was inordinately pleased with her success, with her power even more than her money. Long gone were the days when she had been at the mercy of others—men and women. Long gone, left in Scotland Road and Liverpool, where she had kept a knife in her pocket for protection. No one knew where Mrs. Fleet had originated. Her past had been obliterated by a series of clever moves and meticulous attention to detail. With savage ruthlessness, she had cut off any ties to her earlier life and perfected her cover. No one knew who she was, where she had come from, or what she had done.

Except the woman sitting opposite her now.

"So why are you here, Elizabeth?"

"Something happened on that flight, and you had girls working it."

"So?"

"I want to talk to them."

"Really!" Mrs. Fleet replied, shocked by the sheer nerve of the request. "Well, they're unavailable."

"Are they here?"

"No."

"Well, where are they?"

Mrs. Fleet took in a long breath.

"If you must know, one of those girls has been murdered."

Elizabeth blinked, her mind processing the information. But she knew enough about Mrs. Fleet to suspect the account and she immediately questioned it.

"When?"

"The evening after her trip with Bernie Freeland."

"Odd, isn't it, that Freeland was killed too?" Elizabeth parried. "And that my son was admitted to the hospital just hours after he got off the same flight." She held her nerve, facing up to Mrs. Fleet. "What really happened on that plane?"

"Nothing as far as I know."

"Liar." Elizabeth was afraid of Mrs. Fleet but more terrified of losing her son. "Kit is dying."

"That has nothing to do with me. You had a good run, God knows. You and I worked out a very clever plan which you've benefited from for years. I organized a life for you, Elizabeth—a cushy life. Don't come crying to me now that your luck's run out."

Elizabeth was losing her grip. She fought to keep control but couldn't stop herself from hissing, "I know about you."

"And I know about you. All the things you wouldn't want other people to know," Mrs. Fleet replied. "Remember that."

"I know where you came from, who you are."

"Yes, you do." Her composure was terrifying. "Well, Elizabeth, you blackmailed me once and I went along with it, but I didn't have the same power then. Didn't have much power at all—*then*. It was lucky that James Holden was a client of mine. You got a good living out of him by passing your bastard off as his. It's a shame that Bernie Freeland never knew he had a son *without* learning difficulties."

Flushing, Elizabeth gripped the bag on her lap, her nails scraping the leather.

"You can't tell anyone now!"

"I don't need to," Mrs. Fleet replied. "If your son dies, your life's finished anyway. You're nothing without Kit Wilkes. Nothing without your hold over James Holden. I wonder what he'd say if he knew that he'd been cheated? That Kit Wilkes, who's tormented him for years, isn't really his son? It could turn a man's mind, something like that. To think of all he's suffered, all the humiliation. His wife's tolerance, his party's pity, his ambitions constantly thwarted by embarrassing disclosures and mockery. And for what? *A lie.* Poor James Holden, suffering—and paying—for another man's kid." She sighed, the sound empty, lethal. "Don't get in my way, Elizabeth. Not this time. You're out of your class."

But Elizabeth, her voice shaking, still pushed her. *"What happened on that flight?"*

"Nothing more than I told you. Your son overdosed; that's all."

"I don't believe you," Elizabeth said. She rose and moved toward the door. "I'm going to get someone to look into this."

Mrs. Fleet was on her feet instantly, catching hold of the other woman's arm and tightening her grip. Her face was only inches from Elizabeth's, her voice threatening.

"Take me on and you'll lose," she hissed. "You think you know me? You did when we were children, when I was young. Well, now I've had years to learn how this world runs, and there's no one I'm afraid of and no one who can touch me. People *fear* me now. I have power you can't imagine, Elizabeth, so don't begin a fight you can only lose." She let go off her arm and stepped back. "Now, get out."

"My son—"

"Needs you. So I'd go back to the hospital right away, Elizabeth. Sit at his bedside, be the good mother." She paused, all the malice of years in her voice. "After all, you were never much of a sister, were you?"

Thirty-Eight

"**Does it *look* like you can talk to him?**" Ronan Levy asked, turning from Victor to the immobile figure on the bed. "Kit's in a coma."

"I know. I didn't want to talk to him; I wanted to talk to you."

"*Me?* Who the hell are you?"

"Someone who isn't convinced about Kit Wilkes's overdose."

"Did his mother send you?"

"No. I've never met Elizabeth Wilkes."

"She was here a few days ago, but then she backed off. Until this morning, and then she was fussing over him like she cared. Some mother, hey?" Ronan was fiddling with the gold ring in his ear, wary, suspicious. "Are you police?"

"No."

"Thought not. She wouldn't call the police in even after what I told her." He paused, suspended between disbelief and anger. "I care about Kit. *Really* care. More than she does."

"How did you two meet?"

"I was in a band, and Kit saw us playing some club." Ronan paused. "He just came over and said he'd like to fuck. Then he passed me a card with the name of a Dr. Eli Fountain on it. I went to see him and got the all clear."

"You didn't mind?"

Ronan shrugged. "The gay scene's dangerous. In a way I was glad to know he was careful. Kit never takes chances. Which is why he'd never overdose. He's too cautious."

Following Ronan's gaze, Victor stared at the inert figure in the hospital bed. *How you would have crowed about the Hogarth,* he thought. *What a brilliant way to embarrass your social-climbing father. And what a coup for your own career.* Staring at the closed eyelids, Victor found the ambiguity of the figure, his stillness underlying the menace of his character, compelling and fascinating.

"Can you see how extraordinary he is?" Ronan asked, sighing. "There's always one person like that in your life, isn't there?"

Like Ingola, Victor thought uncomfortably. On his return to London,

Tully had told him that she had called twice, asking where he was. Tully hadn't seemed surprised. But then, why should he be? They had known each other for years.

Hurriedly he pushed the thought aside.

"Did Kit mention any new purchase he had made? A special painting?"

"No, nothing. He said Hong Kong had been a waste of time." Ronan paused, remembering. "But he did seem a bit hyped up. I didn't press him about work. I was just glad he was home."

"And he said nothing about the flight?"

"No, although I don't believe that Bernie Freeland's death was an accident."

"You know about that?"

"Oh, yeah. But it's all too much of a coincidence, isn't it? What with Kit being drugged . . . Look, I want to help you; I want to help *him*. But I don't know anything. I don't know what happened. I just know *something* did. Kit wasn't the same since he came back to London. He mentioned Guy Manners, said they were going to talk about doing business."

Victor had known Guy Manners and his florid reputation in the past. No one was surprised when his adoptive family had disowned their ungrateful cuckoo; his enthusiastic criminality had been almost expected. Yet for all that, Victor had always thought of Manners as a lost soul, believed that under the bravado was a drifter, a misfit in the art world.

Victor frowned. "What kind of business?"

"Kit didn't say, but he took his so-called *overdose* only hours after he got home. I thought he was sleeping, and when I went in to unpack his bag, I found him." He scrutinized Victor, then asked, "Were you on that plane?"

"No," he replied, and changed the subject. "D'you know someone called Mrs. Fleet? Charlene Fleet?"

"I only know *of* her. Don't tell me Kit's used her services."

"I'm not suggesting that, but three of her call girls were on the flight with him, and two are now dead."

Ronan tipped his head to one side, looking quizzically at Victor. "Who are you working for?"

"Myself. I *was* hired by someone, but I'm on my own now."

He thought of the two latest messages left by Mrs. Fleet, which, like all the others, he had ignored, and wondered how long it would be before she heard he was back in London. Would she come after him or send someone? Victor didn't know, but he wasn't going to report back personally. Let her discover that her plan hadn't worked. If she was after the Hogarth and determined to get rid of anyone who knew about it, he was going to stay as far out of her reach as possible.

"Someone did this to Kit," Ronan said suddenly. "Someone injected him."

"He was *injected*?"

Ronan nodded. "He'd never inject himself; he's too squeamish. That's another reason this doesn't feel right."

"Have *you* injected him?"

He shook his head violently. "No! I'm not the one who hurt him. You think I could?"

"No, I don't."

Thoughtful, Victor turned back to Kit Wilkes. Someone who was adept at using needles had gotten to the dealer. Someone had made sure Kit Wilkes wasn't going to talk.

"Did you meet him at the airport?"

Ronan nodded. "Yeah; then I drove us back to the flat."

"He didn't stop off anywhere? At the gallery, perhaps?"

"No."

"So you both got back to the flat, and then what?"

"He went for a quick shower, and then he said he was tired and went into the bedroom to lie down. He was asleep when I looked in about ten minutes later. Then I tidied up the flat, watched part of a DVD—"

"No one came to the door?"

"No."

"No one telephoned?"

"No!" Ronan replied emphatically. "It was just me and him. I didn't hurt him."

"Someone did. Someone got access to him. Did you fall asleep?"

"I was tired. I'd been up early, so yeah, I fell asleep for a bit," Ronan admitted timorously. "But I'd have heard someone come in."

"Is there a back entrance to the flat?"

He stared at Victor, openly hostile now. "Yeah, but they'd have to have a key. And besides, I'd have heard."

"How bad was your hangover, Ronan?"

Ronan flinched. "Oh, you *are* good, aren't you?" he said, his tone sarcastic.

"I'm learning."

"How did you know I was hung over?"

"I guessed."

Ronan was pale now and slightly sweaty. "No one could have gotten into the flat without me knowing."

"But you didn't expect anything to happen. You couldn't have known that anything would."

"I *should* have known!" he said, anguished, and gripped Kit's hand.

"Who were you with the night before?"

"Friends. Guys I've known for years. It was just a night out at a bar. Nothing happened, nothing was said; it was just normal." Ronan was still holding Kit's hand, his voice tremulous. "You'll find out who did this to him, won't you?"

"Yes."

"Why won't he wake up? If he'd just wake up and tell us what happened. That flight was deadly, and I want to know why."

I had known him for years. Thomas Coram, retired sea captain, philanthropist, and humanitarian, although I doubt he would have owned the words. When I walked into the Foundling Hospital in Bloomsbury that day in 1745, he caught me up in a spontaneous embrace. He was shimmering with achievement, his heavy face damson around the jowls. Finally, after a number of frustrating years, laden with official delays—during which he had endured much carping as he chivvied, bullied, and badgered the authorities—he had established his Foundling Hospital for the wretched, abused, and abandoned children of London.

We had spoken of it many times over the years; indeed I had become a founding governor, raising capital by installing a permanent art collection at Bloomsbury Square. Flattered and cajoled by Thomas, I was persuaded to design the children's uniform and the coat of arms. We two men—ironically, both childless—stood up against the callous indifference that prevailed. The capital had little regard for its weakest offspring. I, who could not bear to see an animal flogged, wondered at the depravity of cruelty meted out to infants who had been inconveniently born.

Even in the midst of good work, wickedness thrived. When it became known that the Foundling Hospital had announced that it would receive ALL who were needy, a veritable torrent of children came to London from the country workhouses—and with them came the sinister "Coram men."

Using the name of the benefactor whose good work they betrayed, these rogues were paid to collect, and then deliver, unwanted children to the Foundling Hospital. But on the way from the countryside to the capital, many of the infants were abused and many died. Only a percentage of the country children ever made their way through the gates of the hospital in Bloomsbury. Seeing so many such wretches, I and my wife took over the care of several children. Jane had always wanted a family, as I had. But in this God was not listening—or perhaps I had offended him too, as I had so many others.

Naturally, Thomas knew of Hal, the infant I had hidden thirteen years earlier. But not his heritage. He didn't know that the child's life—which had so far been mercifully without incident—was about to change.

"I wanted to talk about Hal," I said, sitting down opposite Thomas as he lowered his great bulk into an oversized chair, the springs of which sighed like a diving whale. "He's old enough to start work. He needs to be apprenticed and learn a trade, and"—how I baulked at the sentimentality—"I would like to see more of him. Not directly, of course, but indirectly."

I faltered at the words but was only voicing my long-held thoughts. Thomas raised the great arcs of his eyebrows in surprise.

"We could give him a job here, William. God knows he wouldn't stand out among so many others. Just one more lad. Besides, he could learn a trade at the hospital."

Damn me, but I was never clever at gratitude and blundered on.

"Well, if you could . . . we could . . . yes, yes, that would serve."

I should mention here that I had followed my ward's history closely. From the moment Hal was taken to Chiswick into the Binny household, I had paid for his upkeep—more perhaps than was necessary—to smooth his existence and that of his surrogate family. Nell kept her word, and no one knew of his beginnings. Neither was I personally known to Hal, but I had been made aware of every step of his progress from infancy to boyhood. He was, it must be said, an engaging child. Strong but not stocky. Tall but not so tall as to draw attention. And his colouring was middling, made remarkable only by the fierce interest in his eyes.

How do I know all this? From watching him at a distance and being quick with my pen to record his looks at many stages. By the time Hal was ten, I had several sketchbooks filled with images of the boy. Images that reminded me of Polly Gunnell.

Of course I felt guilt for the loss of his mother. Time and time again I remonstrated with myself, telling myself that I should have halted the affair, that I should have followed up on my suspicions—but it had been Polly's life, and she was not the first whore to bed a son of the nobility. I had presumed she was clever enough. I had not realised that in some instances no one is clever enough.

When I watched Hal, it was easy to read Polly's expression in her son's visage. But there was also a spectre of his father in him. Thankfully too slight to invite comment or notice. After all, we had spent thirteen years avoiding such attention.

But now the newborn I had rescued was taller than I. Much taller. But then, most are. Although the romantic notion had occurred to me over the years, I would never have risked bringing Hal into my home and endangering Jane and the others I hold dear. For the innocent, thirteen years is a long respite. For the guilty, thirteen years is too short for determined people to forget. To those who had wanted his death, Polly Gunnell's bastard son had been long in the grave. Some clumsy emotional gesture on my part would not be allowed to resurrect him.

As though privy to my thoughts, Thomas said suddenly, "Sir Nathaniel

Overton progresses rapidly up the ranks at court. I hear he has the King's ear, although the Queen is still suspicious of him."

Sir Nathaniel Overton, one of the most mendacious men in England. A man who supported the King but was also rumoured to be on convivial terms with the Young Pretender. A man so unreadable, so cunning, he had to be welcomed into the royal circle, his machinations kept close by and observed minutely. A man no one really knew, whose motives were unfathomable, whose true intentions were opaque. Sir Nathaniel Overton, the courtier I had long suspected to have had some hand in Polly Gunnell's death.

And over the thirteen years since her murder how his comet rose. How he was feted and praised, flattered into a silky keeper of secrets. For what reason? For his skill? Or the Court's gratitude? How better could a subject prove his loyalty than by killing any threat to the crown? And how cleverly Nathaniel Overton wore his disguise of the benign.

I feared him as I feared no other man. I knew him through my own connections at Court, although my royal patronage had been halted prematurely by my rival, the villain Kent. But on the few occasions I had talked to Nathaniel Overton there had always been—under the courtly manners—the scintilla of a threat. He looked at me as though he was reminding me of what he knew. He looked at me as though he was reminding me that I had once been his shit-clearer, his minion. That I had buried his victims to secure my own safety.

I daresay he would have killed me if he realised what I had really done.

"Hal could be trained as a farrier," Thomas suggested, returning to our original topic. "God knows, there's enough horses need shoeing and work here to keep him busy for life. A boy brought up in the country should be good with animals."

And I nodded, pleased by the thought. And I wondered if tonight was the time to tell Jane about the child. But why now, after so long? And anyway—as I had always believed—surely safety lay in ignorance.

But ignorance—like a candle flame—lasts only so long.

Thirty-Nine

CROSSING LINCOLN'S INN FIELDS, INGOLA DIALED A NUMBER ON HER cell phone and waited impatiently for it to be answered. When it was, she began talking without a greeting, saying, "Victor won't return my calls! I know he's back from New York; he called his brother last night."

Tully sighed. "But not you?"

"No, not me! Did you give him my messages?"

"I did."

"I see." She let the inference hang. "We slept together, you know."

Tully picked up his coffee and drained the cup, staring out of the window as a bus passed. On the top level he could see several huddled figures, their faces pink, indecipherable blobs looking out onto the passing street.

"D'you *really* want to tell me this, sweetheart?"

"Yes, I do, *sweetheart*," she replied acidly, then muted her tone. "Don't tell Victor I told you, will you? He'd be furious, and if Christian found out . . ."

"I won't tell Victor. And your husband won't hear about it from me," Tully replied, glancing at his watch and then holding it to his ear to check that it was still ticking. "What a very silly girl, you are, Ingola. Whatever possessed you? It's not fair to screw up Victor like this, if you'll pardon the expression. He let you go; you should stay gone."

He could sense her contrition even before she answered.

"No one else is like him, Tully. I try to get on with my life, to carry on and make a life with Christian, but now Victor's out of prison, he's—"

"Available?"

"Well . . ."

"No, Ingola, he's not available," Tully admonished her. "Not to you. You know it, and you should back off. Besides, he's got other things on his mind right now."

"Is he okay?"

"Yes, but he's under pressure. He's working on a difficult case."

"Working on a case? What kind of case? He's not a lawyer or a cop. Nothing illegal, is it?"

"Nothing that can affect your burgeoning legal career."

"What's Victor involved in?"

"Detective work," Tully replied, relishing the words. "I'm assisting him. It's all very 221b Baker Street."

"Detective work? What the hell does Victor know about that?"

"He knows about the art world, and it's a case which involves the business."

"Victor's an art *dealer.*"

"Victor is whatever people will let him be," Tully retorted deftly. "Which isn't a dealer, my love. His days of being the hotshot are over."

"You're such a bastard."

Tully shrugged. "I see life as all men should, without muddying sentimentality. Victor needed to work; this work came along. He's been floundering a bit, but I imagine he'll prove to be rather good at it. Victor is clever and resourceful; he always was. He'll stick with it however hard it gets."

"There's no risk, is there?"

He thought of what he knew and lied. "Only a little."

"Look after him, will you? I want to know you have his back."

"I always have his back."

"Oh, Tully," she said quietly. "You and I both know that's not true."

A moment of thudding silence fell between them. Tully was the first to break it.

"I was wrong in the past; I admit it. But everyone's entitled to make a mistake."

"Entitled to make one, yes. But not entitled to repeat it."

For once Charlene Fleet's immense control was threatening to desert her. Enraged at having her messages ignored, she had driven over to Victor's apartment and was sitting outside in a resident's parking space, almost willing a traffic warden to come along and try to move her. In the backseat sat the mastiff, alert but as ever cowed by his mistress. Nursing a cup of Starbucks coffee she had bought around the corner, Mrs. Fleet turned on the car heater and felt the warm air nuzzle against her calves. It was one of the things that always impressed her about her car. How the best German engineering could ensure almost immediate heat, not like the clapped-out freezing Mini she had driven for years up north.

Mind you, back then she had been proud of the Mini. Back then, it was something to have a car in Scotland Road, something few people had. Or if they did, it had been bought on credit and was repossessed as soon as they defaulted on the payments. Or vandalized by kids or one of the innumerable drunks who spilled out of the pubs nightly. She had seen cars with tires sticky with vomit, graffiti smeared on the windows and the hood. The drunks wrote on anything, even the police cars when the cops went in to sort out the pub fights.

She took off the lid of her cup and watched the windshield mist up with steam from the coffee. A memory came back of a woman throwing hot coffee at a man. The liquid had caught him on the side of his face and blinded him in his left eye. Her father had always been a mean bastard, but becoming partially sighted had made him worse and given him an opportunity to avoid dock work. He had died two years later of a burst appendix; her mother had refused to go with him in the ambulance to Bootle Hospital. A month later her uncle came to the door and told her mother what he thought of her, and she told him that if he said another word, she'd get the coffee and do him the same.

Wiping the mist off the windshield with her hand, Mrs. Fleet stared into the street, waiting for Victor, but her thoughts slid back to Liverpool, and, irritated, she got out of the car. Almost as soon as she did, Victor walked up to his front door.

"Ballam! What the hell are you playing at?" she called out.

"Can we talk inside?" he replied. "I'm afraid dogs aren't allowed."

Throwing her coffee into the gutter, Mrs. Fleet moved past Victor into the hallway and started up the stairs.

"First on the left," he said, watching her pause uncertainly. Unlocking the door, he let her in ahead of him. Standing in the center of Victor's living room, she seemed immediately to lay claim to the space.

"I've been trying to get hold of you since—"

He cut her short. "Enough! I need the truth from you, although that's probably the last thing I'll get. What happened in New York?"

Her eyes widened.

"How the fuck do *I* know? You were there, not me."

"Have you heard from Annette Dvorski?" he asked, waiting for some reaction in her eyes.

Which didn't come.

"No! You were going over there to see her, remember? Well, *did* you see her?"

"Oh, yes; I saw her." Victor took off his coat and sat down. "She'd been murdered. I've never seen anything like it, and I don't want to see anything like it again."

In silence, Mrs. Fleet sat down opposite Victor and stared at him for a long moment. It was difficult to tell whether she had known already.

"Murdered?"

"Yes. In Bernie Freeland's apartment," Victor replied. "I was about to meet up with her when I was knocked out. When I came to, she was lying dead next to me. It was obviously meant to look as though I'd done it." He was trying to read her face, but there was nothing beyond a fleeting expression of distaste.

"Tortured?"

"The killer poured bleach over her breasts and genitals, then made her drink it."

Again no response.

"I only just got away before the police came. I ran."

"Yes. Of course you would," she said finally, taking out a tissue and blowing her nose. Victor couldn't tell if she had a cold or had actually been about to cry. "I noticed that they're doing some building work next door. I'm allergic to dust."

"I'm allergic to being framed," Victor replied. "What's going on?"

"That's what I'm paying you to find out."

"Stop lying to me!" Victor snapped. "No one else knew I was going to Bernie Freeland's apartment in New York. No one but you knew that Annette Dvorski was going to be there."

"Your assistant knew."

"Tully? No; he wouldn't set me up."

"So did Liza Frith, if it comes to that." She sneezed violently, blew her nose, and tucked the tissue into her pocket. The gesture made her seem oddly vulnerable. "Before she ran off, that is. In fact, it was Liza who told me about Annette and Freeland meeting up. You know that, Mr. Ballam; she told you on the phone. Don't deny it; I stood next to you and heard the conversation. So before you start throwing accusations my way, I suggest you look at Liza Frith. She's left Park Street."

Victor raised his eyebrows. "Where is she?"

"I don't know. She came from up north somewhere. Maybe she went back. Or maybe she was after the Hogarth for herself."

Victor shook his head.

"When I spoke to Liza, she was afraid for herself and for Annette. Obviously she was so scared, she went on the run." He paused, staring at Mrs. Fleet. "And why would Liza do that if she was involved?"

"A bluff?"

"Come on; you can't believe that!" He stared into the composed face. "Liza's just another working girl. You're the one with the contacts and the power. You're the one with the money, Mrs. Fleet."

"Meaning?"

"You could be behind all of this."

"Well, I could, but I'm not. Besides, I want all this to be over as quickly as possible. The police"—she said the word with contempt—"have been asking me some questions. Nothing I can't handle, but an irritation nevertheless. I'm afraid I lied, denied that any of my girls had been on that plane with Bernie Freeland. To all intents and purposes, the late Mr. Freeland had been traveling alone."

"And they believed you?"

"I told you before, Mr. Ballam; I have a certain *arrangement* with the police." She smiled. "I've also had a word with Malcolm Jenner, the steward. He seems more than willing to agree with my story, even embellish it. We thought it might be better for everyone if there was no mention of call girls. Or art dealers."

"How much did you have to pay Jenner?"

She raised her eyebrows. "You should be grateful to me. I've gotten you off the hook. Now no one will make the connection between me, my girls, the dealers, and you. You're out of the woods."

"Funny, it doesn't feel like that."

"You worry too much."

Victor laughed sardonically. "Like you say, Mrs. Fleet, you have a lot of contacts. If you can control what the police know and get Malcolm Jenner to say what you want, why stop there? You could be running the whole show."

"Really? And what would I get out of it?" she said dismissively. "I told you I don't want the painting."

"You could just be saying that."

"Oh, so now *I'm* bluffing, am I?"

"Why not? You hired me knowing I'd take the bait and also knowing I'd fail. You relied on that. You realized I'd follow whatever information I had, knew that I'd blunder into that apartment in New York—and you knew how easy it would be to set me up for Annette Dvorski's murder."

She sighed, sounding almost bored. "How exactly would I profit from another of my girls being killed?"

"To get the painting."

"I don't want the fucking painting!" she said emphatically. Then, her eyes fixed on him, her tone sly, she said, "Why? Did *you* get it?"

"Where from?"

"Don't be irritating. Did Annette Dvorski have it?"

He lied without conscience. "I don't know."

"Don't underestimate my intelligence. You want that painting, Mr. Ballam; you ache to get your hands on it. Don't tell me you didn't search that apartment for it."

"I didn't see any painting."

"Maybe Annette had hidden it."

"Maybe Bernie Freeland had and Annette didn't find it," he offered. "Or maybe her killer tortured her to tell him where it was."

Thoughtful, Mrs. Fleet rubbed her left knee, her expression unreadable. "I think you have it."

"I don't. But if I did, why would it matter to you? You said you didn't want it."

"But if the painting is the reason for all these killings, we should find it."

Smiling, Victor put his head on one side, watching her. "What if I was to tell you that I did know where the painting was?"

"Do you?"

"That knowledge would be my protection, wouldn't it? I mean, if you— or anyone—wanted the Hogarth, they'd have to come to me."

"Or simply kill you for it," she said, her tone eerily blank. "After all, they've killed all the others, haven't they?"

"But they haven't got the Hogarth," Victor said, baiting her and waiting to see if she would take the bait. "After killing three people and damn near killing Kit Wilkes, they still haven't got the painting. Not very successful, are they?"

"Not as art thieves. But as murderers, extremely."

He couldn't fathom her. *Was* she was masterminding the whole episode or merely watching from the sidelines?

"You could sell the Hogarth privately, you know."

He waited for the reaction, but there was none.

"And share the proceeds with you, Mr. Ballam?" She walked over to him, standing very close, the scent of Chanel faintly perceptible on her skin. "No, I don't think so. I don't share; I never have. And attractive as you are, no man has ever made me lose my head." Slowly she fastened her coat, her hands steady. "I want only one thing from you—find Liza Frith and bring her back to London."

"Because you think she has the Hogarth?"

She smiled distantly.

"No, because she walked out on me. And no one does that, Mr. Ballam. She owes me a good lifestyle and a great career. She owes me loyalty. When it's time for someone to go, I tell *them*, they don't tell me. No one ever leaves me. You would do well to remember that."

Out in the chill of the night, Victor paused on Park Street, glancing up at the window of Mrs. Fleet's apartment. He wondered if she was making herself a drink or something to eat or if perhaps she would suddenly come out to take the dog for a walk. Then he realized that he was giving her normal habits, a routine existence. Whereas in fact she was hermetically sealed in her own world, fighting to control everyone who came within her sphere.

Hearing his cell phone ring, Victor glanced at the unfamiliar number, then answered it.

"Hello?"

"Is that Victor Ballam?"

"Yes. Who's this?"

"Elizabeth Wilkes," the voice said crisply. "Ring any bells?"

Forty

Walking through the Arundel Centre, Liza stared into the window of Boots the Chemist, checking to see if anyone was following her. When she had first arrived in Manchester, she had decided not to go to her parents' home, worried that she might bring trouble to their door. She had gone to a friend, another working girl, who was happy to get the additional rent from a roommate and not interested in asking too many questions. All Liza offered was a story that she had left her pimp in London and come back to the north for a break. Don't worry, she told the girl. I won't be competition; no working up here. I just want a few weeks off.

The first night she had slept on the sofa in the shabby front room of the apartment, listening to the sound of someone's television, and when she finally dropped off, a car alarm woke her around one. Disoriented, Liza had gone into the kitchen, the apartment empty, a note pinned on the fridge—get some milk and bread. Homesickness had overwhelmed her as she looked around at the squalor. This was how she once had lived, the life she had fled when she grabbed the chance Mrs. Fleet had offered.

That was still on the game, yes, but on the game in comfort. Liza studied her reflection in the Boots window and thought of Marian Miller. Then she thought of Annette Dvorski and the flight in Bernie Freeland's plane. It seemed like another existence, another time, so different from the bleak northern afternoon that she shivered and pulled her coat around her. Her fear was always present, intensifying as the days passed.

She had believed herself to be under threat at Park Street, but since leaving the familiar surroundings, she found herself startled even by shadows. Increasingly desperate to make contact with Annette Dvorski, she told herself that if she could just talk to Annette, she would calm down. Just talking would help; after all, they had been on the same flight. Not knowing where Annette was or if, God forbid, something had happened to her was unbearable. The cell phone number Liza had used so many times before kept ringing out unobtainable. But that morning, after one more queasy night,

Liza remembered something: years previously, Annette had handed her a note with another cell phone number. "Don't use it unless it's an emergency," she had said. "If you need me, you can call it, but *only* in an emergency."

Liza dug out the faded Post-it note from her Filofax and looked at the number. Well, she thought, this was an emergency, wasn't it, and the only way she could get to talk to Annette—if the number was still valid. She knew how often working girls changed their cell phones, sometimes to avoid suspect johns and sometimes to drop out of sight for a while. It was a familiar ploy to give a client the number of a phone you would dump later, so Liza knew that the chances of Annette keeping the cell phone for over three years were less than slim.

But still, it was worth a try.

Glancing once more into the window of Boots, Liza searched the faces in the crowd. Nobody looked obviously suspicious, although there had been odd phone calls late at night at the apartment when her friend was out working. And the previous week she had been followed by a couple of men. Liza realized that her courage was disappearing fast; every day was taking her farther away from London and the familiar, into the shadowy and threatening life of streets she no longer knew. Comforting landmarks from the past— roads, shops, houses—had all gone. She'd found herself in a city that had changed beyond all recognition. Killing time, she had passed boarded-up churches and job centers, walking without knowing where she was going, the memory of the flight in Bernie Freeland's jet replaying constantly in her head. And along with the images, there was the knowledge that something was terribly, terribly wrong.

Taking a deep breath, Liza punched in Annette's emergency number on her cell phone but missed a digit and had to start again. She tensed, expecting to hear the disconnected tone or a mechanical voice telling her that the phone was no longer in use. But instead the number rang.

Hopeful, Liza felt her heart racing, her mouth pressed to the phone as it was answered.

But instead of Annette's voice, she heard a man's.

"Hello? Who's this? Hello?" he snapped irritably, his voice hoarse. "Oh, for fuck's sake!"

And then silence, the connection severed.

Shaking, Liza leaned against the wall and stared at the phone in her hand.

She didn't wonder why she hadn't spoken; she was just glad she'd stayed silent. Because there was something wrong about the man who had answered the phone. Something familiar. Something that made her breath catch in her throat. Of all people, she had not expected *him* to answer Annette Dvorski's cell phone.

Fighting panic, Liza rang another number. "Victor Ballam?"

"Is that you, Liza?" he asked, relieved. "Are you all right?"

She wasn't all right; she was terrified. "I need help. I'm in Manchester."

"Are you on your own?"

"Yeah. I don't know what to do. I don't know what to think anymore. It's all muddled up, and I'm scared; I'm so scared."

"Get the next train back to London. I'll meet you at the station—"

But Liza was past reason. "I shouldn't have rung the number! He shouldn't have answered."

"What are you talking about? What number, Liza? Who shouldn't have answered?"

Her mouth was pressed against the cell phone. "You have to help me!"

"I will."

"People are *dying*. They're killing all the people on that flight."

She stopped talking suddenly. "Liza? Are you there?" Victor asked, anxious.

"I don't trust that bitch Fleet. I don't trust anyone. I shouldn't even be ringing you; I don't know who you are really." Her voice speeded up; her hand gripped the phone tightly. She sounded confused, childish almost. "I tried to ring Annette Dvorski," she said, explaining about the emergency number.

Victor's stomach turned over.

"I rang the number," Liza went on, "and a man answered. *I knew him!*" She sounded almost hysterical. "The man who answered Annette's phone? I know who he was; I recognized his voice. It was Malcolm Jenner."

"Malcolm Jenner?"

"The steward who worked for Bernie Freeland!" Liza went on blindly. "He was on the jet! He was on the flight we were on. He was there; I remember him. I remember his voice. Jesus," she said, her voice plummeting. "Why did *he* answer? And why has he got Annette's cell phone?"

Forty—One

EVERY DAY IN LONDON, EARLY RISERS WALK THEIR DOGS IN THE PARK. There are numerous plastic doggy bags attached to bins so that no one leaves a souvenir of his or her animal on the large verdant expanses where the dogs run. While cabs and buses begin to crawl down Park Lane and up Piccadilly, buses empty out groups of tourists, and rain falls on the shop windows and concrete pavements—while all this is happening, the dogs in the park bark for bones, for balls, for attention. They bark enthusiastically at passing horses or aggressively at airplanes overhead. The dogs bark early in the mornings and in the cold gray winter afternoons before night falls.

And they bark when they are afraid.

This morning in Hyde Park, a young woman ran toward the sound of her dog barking. She called him, but he didn't respond, remaining a little way off and snarling. As she approached, the woman saw her pet and peered over to where he was looking and barking. She thought for some moments that she had happened upon some discarded Guy Fawkes left over from the fifth of November, but when she drew closer, she stopped, a hand covering her mouth to prevent a scream. The dog had stopped barking. He was now whimpering, down on his haunches, staring at the tableau in front of him.

Lim Chang was bound tightly with rope around his chest and ankles, his head bent at an odd angle on his shoulder. He was propped up against a water fountain, and his left arm was depressing the nozzle so that a steady stream of water had soaked his scorched sleeve and run down into the blood around his feet. His clothes had been stuffed with straw and Chinese firecrackers had been pushed deep into his ears and mouth, and both were set on fire. His trousers were undone, and around his private parts there was a smearing of what looked like some kind of food paste; what was left of his penis was little more than a bloodied gnawed stump. There had been no clean, surgical cut—just a jagged tearing of the flesh, an eating away of the organ. An animal attack. A hungry animal going for the scent of food, eating away at flesh and muscle that had been prepared for it. As the woman stared, immobilized with horror, she saw to her disbelief Lim Chang's eyes flicker for an instant, then roll upward, the whites exposed as his body gave a sudden ghastly shudder before death.

All the time he had been tortured, Lim Chang had been alive.

No one had seen or heard a thing.

He had died within walking distance of Piccadilly, of Bond Street, of the many London galleries and auction houses he had dealt with for decades. Later the police would find in his inside jacket pocket an airline ticket to Hong Kong dated the following day. They would also find, behind his bare feet, a briefcase, now empty.

Nobody knew what had been taken from the case or why he had been tortured to death. Nobody knew that of the six passengers who had taken that ill-fated flight in Bernie Freeland's plane, only two were still around.

And the painting that had led indirectly to their deaths was on the move again.

Part four

WITHOUT INGOLA REALIZING THAT HE WAS WATCHING HER, CHRISTIAN studied his wife's blond hair and the line of her cheek. He thought, as he had so often over the years, that he had been a very lucky man—even though it was only because of his brother's fall from grace that he was able to claim Ingola as his own. Guilt, as it did often, nudged Christian. And, as he did often, he reassured himself that it had been Victor's wish for him to marry Ingola and take care of her. And he had been more than willing to do so. When his son was born, Christian had felt himself blessed. By default, but blessed nonetheless.

He knew that if Victor had continued his spectacular rise, Ingola would have been married to his brother now, living in London, a talented couple, inviting admiration and provoking envy. Ingola would not be leading an unremarkable life in Worcestershire. Still staring at his wife, Christian wondered if she regretted her decision and realized that of course she did. Ingola had been very much in love with Victor. Christian's devotion, however much needed, would have come as a poor substitute.

"What is it?"

Christian blinked, realizing that she was talking to him. "I was thinking . . . about Victor."

He waited for a reaction, but she answered very calmly, "What about him?"

"D'you think he's all right?"

Turning away, Ingola reached for the evening paper, her heart speeding up. *Guilt* was hardly a big enough word for what she felt. How could she have cheated on Christian? This man who loved her and looked after her. Who did everything in his power to make her happy. It wasn't his fault that he wasn't Victor. It wasn't his fault that life had shunted her off the path she had wanted. And it wasn't his fault that she didn't—couldn't—love him enough.

It was *her* fault that she had lacked the courage to stand by Victor, putting her own career before him. That she had ducked out of the shadow of his disgrace and sacrificed their future for her security. Feel all the guilt you want, Ingola told herself; it was your choice, and you have to make the best of it.

"Are you worried about him?"

Christian nodded. "I just wonder what he's doing. For a job, I mean."

She feigned ignorance. "I don't know. Ring him if you're anxious."

"We didn't part on good terms last time we spoke," Christian admitted. "I said something which annoyed him. Without meaning to, I implied that I thought he was guilty."

She put down the paper. "*What?*"

"I didn't mean it. It came out wrong, and he jumped down my throat." Christian flushed under his wife's scrutiny and wondered what to say next.

She saved him the trouble. "It's funny, but in all this time we've never actually talked about Victor being guilty or innocent. You never wondered about it?"

"What?"

"The case. The fakes, all of it." She paused, eager to hear what her husband really thought. "We presumed Victor was innocent, of course, but did you never wonder?"

Angrily, Christian rounded on her. "My brother did nothing wrong!"

"I know that. You know that. We care about him, of course, and we believed in him, but he was found guilty. There was so much evidence, so many witnesses."

Astonished, Christian could hardly believe what he was hearing, yet he felt a kind of giddy relief. In the past Ingola would never have doubted Victor, never have said a negative word about him. But time had gone on, and obviously her affection had waned. The fierce love had dwindled. Now she had reservations, and to his shame, the thought pleased him.

"Are you saying that you think Victor did it?"

She shook her head impatiently. "No, I'm just wondering. Oh, it doesn't matter."

"It does matter," Christian persisted. "You were in love with Victor; you knew him better than anyone. Do you think . . . do you *really* think he did something wrong?"

Pausing, Ingola wondered how she would sleep that night. How she could rest with a quiet conscience, having manipulated her husband so deftly. By intimating that she had doubts about Victor, she was suggesting that her feelings for him had cooled, a suggestion that would certainly throw off any suspicion that there was still a bond between them.

"I could never suspect you of doing anything wrong, Christian," she said gently. "But Victor? To be honest, I'm not sure."

Picking up the paper again, she began to read, but the words buzzed in front of her eyes and she knew with terrible certainty that Christian was watching her and counting his blessings. It would never occur to him that she had recently slept with his brother—or that she now longed for Victor Ballam more than she ever had.

Cursing, Tully got out of bed and walked over to the table, flicking on the lamp. Sleep was being capricious. He would doze, then wake suddenly, his heart hammering, his skin sweaty. Wondering if he was coming down with flu, he took two aspirins and sat at the table, pulling his notes toward him. He had to admit that he had been enjoying his detective work; it appealed to him, and he found it easy to draw confidences out of people. But since Victor had returned from New York, the atmosphere had altered, and Tully realized that the part he had so readily assumed was not for evenings and matinees only. As the death count rose, grim reality had set in, and the headline on the *Evening Standard* that afternoon had unnerved him to the point of panic:

MURDER VICTIM FOUND IN HYDE PARK

The name of Lim Chang had reverberated from the page as Tully read the details of the killing, his unease growing when he couldn't contact Victor on his cell phone. Finally, around seven, he had received a text from him. It was simple and to the point:

> Coming back to London.
> Will call and see you tomorrow. Don't
> talk to Charlene Fleet.

Rubbing his forehead, an already nervous Tully jumped when the phone rang next to him.

"Yes?"

"Is that Tully Harcourt?"

"Who's this?"

"A friend."

"It's two in the morning. Who rings at two in the morning?" he said warily. "No friend of mine—"

"You have dangerous friends, Mr. Harcourt. Like Victor Ballam." The voice paused and then went on. "Friends like that could get you into a lot of trouble, but a friend like me could help you.

Although uneasy, Tully affected a nonchalant tone. "I don't think so, old boy. Thanks for calling—"

"Stop fucking around!"

"I beg your pardon?"

"You help me, and I'll help you when things get rough. And they will get very rough. Where's Victor Ballam?"

"What business is that of yours?"

"Where's Victor Ballam?"

From below, Tully could hear the main door close softly at the street entrance. Still holding the phone, he moved to the front door of his apartment and checked that the locks were bolted, peering through the peephole into the corridor outside. He could hear footsteps but see no one. The space was empty. Silent.

Suddenly the voice came over the phone again. "I can see you, Mr. Harcourt."

Unnerved, Tully spun around, looking at the windows. But the curtains were closed.

Calmly the voice continued. "Just tell me where Victor Ballam is."

There was a long pause, then Tully—to his horror—smelled gasoline. Glancing across the room, he could see a thin trickle coming under his door, the odor intensifying by the second.

"Jesus!"

"I can just walk away," the voice went on, "or I can put a match to this, Mr. Harcourt. The choice is yours. Where's Victor Ballam?"

Sweating, Tully shouted into the phone. "In New York."

There was a long silence, then Tully caught the unmistakable sound of someone striking a match. A moment later, he could smell fire as smoke began to leak under the door. Crossing the room and throwing open the patio windows, Tully gulped in the fresh air and stared down into the street below. A figure was just leaving the building. A huddled figure who paused on the opposite side of the road and pointed to the cell phone in his hand.

Snatching up his own phone again, Tully listened.

"That was the wrong answer, Mr. Harcourt. You and I both know that Mr. Ballam's no longer in New York. I was just trying to find out which side you were really on." The voice sighed. "People burn in their beds all the time, Mr. Harcourt. They say fire is the most painful way to go. Back off now. While you still can."

Forty-Three

EVEN ON SUCH A COOL DAY, THERE WAS SWEAT ON HER TOP LIP AS SHE caught Victor's eye, and for a moment she looked as though she might bolt. Victor moved quickly across the concourse of Euston Station toward her.

"Liza Frith?"

She nodded, recognizing his voice and looking around nervously. "The train was late. I kept thinking all sorts of crazy things, like someone was holding it up deliberately. I was hoping you'd wait for me."

Taking her bag, Victor guided her toward the taxi rank.

"Are you okay?"

"Yeah. Where are we going?"

"Somewhere safe," he assured her, helping her into the cab and sitting beside her. She smelled faintly of apples, the scent curious and out of place. "I've got a friend who's got a flat in Little Venice. He doesn't use it much, just rents it out in the summer for tourists. But it's quiet and surrounded by neighbors."

She smiled, shrugging. "Thanks."

"You'll be safe, I promise," Victor reassured her, checking that the partition between them and the driver was closed. "Now tell me about Malcolm Jenner. You said it was he that picked up Annette's phone?"

"Yeah, but why did he have it?" she asked urgently. "Why him of all people?"

"I don't know."

Suddenly suspicious, Liza studied Victor. "Why are you helping me? You work for Mrs. Fleet. Did she send you to find me?"

"No; I sent myself."

Her expression was lost, then troubled. "Annette's dead, isn't she? I knew it the moment that man picked up her phone. She's dead, isn't she?"

He didn't deny it. "Yes."

"Did Malcolm Jenner kill her?"

"I don't know yet."

Liza's tone hovered between panic and resignation. "Ma Fleet thinks

I don't know about Bernie Freeland's death. She thinks I'm stupid. Well, maybe I'm not that interested in most things, but the murder of my fellow passengers certainly caught my attention." Her tone edged on bitterness. "I bought a paper on the train, and I saw Lim Chang's photograph. One more of the dealers dead. How many does that leave, Mr. Ballam?"

"Oliver Peters."

"And Kit Wilkes?"

"In the hospital."

She sighed. "Dying?"

"Probably."

"And out of the working girls, there's just me." She sighed raggedly. "Well, I don't want to die, Mr. Ballam; I don't want to be next." She pressed her hands together, her suitcase at her feet. "I don't want to die because of some painting. I don't see why I should; it's got nothing to do with me. I was just working on that flight. I'm not involved. I don't care about any picture!"

"Liza—"

She brushed him off. "I'm not going to let anyone kill me. You hear me? No one's going to kill me."

He touched the back of her hand. Its coldness startled him.

"The paper said that a dog attack was involved," she went on, "that Lim Chang had been mauled by an animal," Liza paused. "Mrs. Fleet has a dog."

"I know."

"I wouldn't put it past that bitch. She was sending me out on a job when I bolted. I didn't trust her, didn't want to end up with some stranger at the Hilton. Didn't want to end up like Marian Miller in a hotel or on the front page of the *Evening Standard* like Lim Chang. I think Ma Fleet's capable of murder." Liza stared out of the window a while, then turned back to Victor. Her pupils were dilated.

Shock or drugs? he wondered.

"What d'you know about Charlene Fleet?"

"Nothing," she replied. "No one does."

"She has no family? No man in her life?"

"Not that any of us know about. She isn't the confiding type. If Ma Fleet's got a private life, she keeps it under wraps."

Victor nodded. "Okay. So what d'you know about Malcolm Jenner?"

"He was a steward on the flight."

"He had no connection to Annette?"

"No."

"They didn't seem particularly friendly or act as though they knew each other?"

"No," Liza repeated, shaking her head. "I don't remember them even talking. She never said she knew him or recognized him, so why did he end up with Annette's phone?"

"Perhaps she left it on the plane and he found it."

"Why wouldn't he have given it back to her?"

"Maybe he tried to."

"But she was already dead?" Liza asked softly.

Victor skirted the question. "Did Malcolm Jenner overhear the talk about the Hogarth painting?"

"I don't think so. The stewards were moving about a lot, and when they weren't busy, they were in the galley. The copilot only came into the cabin briefly, the chief pilot even less. He spoke to Bernie a couple of times, but he kept away from us. Bernie doesn't—didn't—like any of the staff near the bedroom." She tapped the side of her suitcase with the toe of her left shoe. "I left Park Street with only the clothes I was wearing. I bought this case in Manchester and some cheap stuff from Peacocks. The kind I used to despise. Funnily enough, I don't care anymore. Fashion doesn't matter so much if you're going to get murdered."

Victor could sense she was close to panic. "I'm surprised you didn't leave the country, Liza."

"I would have, only Ma Fleet's got my passport. I told you: I left everything at Park Street." She turned to him, her voice soft, childlike. "Is she after the painting?"

"She says not."

"Have you got it?"

The question caught him off guard. "Why d'you want to know?"

"I was on that flight, Mr. Ballam. I have a right to know."

"No; I don't have the Hogarth."

"D'you know where it is?"

"If I did, do you think I'd tell you and put you in even more danger?"

She shook her head. "All right, let me put it this way. If you know where that painting is, can't you give it to the person who wants it so badly?" She gripped his hand suddenly, her fingers bloodless. "I don't care why they want it! I don't care if they want to splash the news about some painting with a whore and her bloody prince in it! I don't care if people close to the royal family get it and burn it. I don't *care*! But I'm not dying for it, Mr. Ballam. I tell you here and now. I'll do whatever I have to do to protect myself. *Whatever* I have to do."

He could see that she meant it.

Forty-Four

AS HE LET VICTOR IN, TULLY POINTED TO THE SINGED BASE OF HIS front door. "I didn't know I was signing up for this, old boy."

"What happened?" Victor asked. "Are you all right?"

"Someone wanted to know where you were."

"And you told them?"

"No, which was why I had my front door char-grilled. It gives a whole new meaning to *flame mahogany.*" Tully poured them both a coffee and perched on the edge of the table by the window.

"I never thought it would get this dangerous."

"Liar! Of course you fucking did. But I've got no one to blame but myself. I wanted to help you, and I still do. So is Liza Frith in the flat?"

"Yeah; I've just left her there. Thanks."

Tully nodded.

"The place is registered in my mother's name, so no one should be able to trace it back to me. And I rent it out through an agent in the summertime. It's definitely secure. Got an alarm and what they call *decorative* bars on all the windows and doors, although frankly, if you didn't have bars on a basement flat, you'd be asking for trouble. If she doesn't go out or let anyone in, she'll be safe." He paused, then asked, "Why's she there?"

"I need to keep an eye on her."

"So, now *she's* in danger?"

Victor caught the tone in his voice. "I had to get Liza Frith somewhere safe. I'll move her as soon as I can. I'm sorry, Tully, really I am, but I had no choice."

Tully kept his gaze averted. "This is all getting a bit much, isn't it? I mean, now Lim Chang's been killed and I have a hooker in my late mother's flat. You should go to the police."

"I can't."

"You're still reporting back to Mrs. Fleet?"

"Up to a point. But now I've put some distance between her and me."

"So who's paying you?" Tully replied, raising his eyebrows. "You need funds, Victor."

"I'll see you get paid."

"Oh, you're such a fucking prick at times!" Tully emptied his cup and then refilled it. Irritated, he sat down at the table. "Listen, Victor, I'll be frank with you. I'm worried. You were hired to investigate a call girl's death and protect Charlene Fleet's business; that was all. But now the whole thing's mushroomed. How d'you know Fleet isn't behind it?"

"She might be," Victor admitted "Did you see who did that to your door?"

Tully glanced over his shoulder. "Some nut."

"Man or woman?"

"Man."

"Did you get a look at him?"

"Not clearly," Tully replied, "but after he'd scorched my door, he was on the street looking up at me. Wearing a hoodie, with a scarf over the bottom half of his face. But I *did* see his eyes, and I think he was Chinese."

Chinese. Like the man at the airport. Nothing in his features betrayed what Victor was feeling. The overwhelming sense that he was drowning, capsized, his lungs riddled with holes. He had no idea what was happening or where the next threat might come from. Tully and Liza Frith were relying on him to keep them safe, and he couldn't even protect himself.

"It said in the paper that the police think Lim Chang's death is related to the triads," Tully offered. "Some revenge killing. Personally, I wouldn't be surprised; it's always revenge with them. The triads are such excitable little people. I remember them when I used to gamble. Fascinating, very quick, prodigious memories, nasty tempers if they were crossed. There was a basement club in Chinatown where I used to go." Tully paused, memory taking a snapshot of an earlier time. Of the time he had been broke, panicked. Of the time he had gone to Victor for help. "Anyway," he hurried on, "the regular Chinese are all in awe of the triads—like the Italians with the Mafia—because the triads pretty much run Chinatown."

"So?"

"I'm saying that it could well be a revenge killing."

"For gambling debts? No, not Lim Chang; he was an upright company man."

"Who was after the Hogarth. Maybe he double-crossed someone. Promised them the painting, then reneged on his word."

"Or perhaps it's just convenient for the police to blame it on the triads,"

Victor replied. He wanted to confide in Tully but was on his guard. There was only the faintest odor of burned wood still present in the apartment, but it was in the air and in the furnishings, the threat hanging over both of them. "You don't have to go on with this, Tully."

"I owe you, remember? What I did was wrong. My bad conscience will make sure I keep helping you." A shudder of an old unpleasant memory drifted between them. "But I still say you should go to the police."

"And what if they think I'm behind all of this? There's a Hogarth in the mix. Even if they didn't take me in, they'd keep an eye on me. I don't want that."

"You'd rather get killed?"

"Why would I get killed?"

"For the same bloody reason the dealers and the call girls have been— because they know about the painting."

"You know about it too."

"But I don't know where it is."

Victor held his gaze. "Neither do I. Now."

"You've forgotten one other person who knows—Arnold Fletcher. I've been thinking about him. Perhaps you were right; perhaps he is involved. He got you and Mrs. Fleet together. Perhaps he knows there's a Hogarth up for grabs."

Victor leaned back, thinking. Arnold Fletcher . . . He could picture his old colleague easily. Overweight, erudite, private. But criminal? A killer? No, not Arnold.

His attention shifted back to Tully.

"You interviewed Malcolm Jenner. What kind of man is he?"

"On the make. Enjoyed his job. Hag of a wife who thinks the world of their ghastly rough-ass son." Tully shrugged. "Jenner's no mastermind, but I'd put money on it that he's no killer either."

"So why would he have Annette Dvorski's phone?"

"Jenner was the chief steward; he was responsible for the plane. He'd pick up anything left behind."

"Why not give it back to the girl?"

"Was it an expensive phone?" Tully asked archly. "Because if it was, I imagine Jenner might think lost property counted as one of the perks of the job. After all, a call girl would hardly be strapped for cash, would she? More than capable of buying herself another cell phone, especially if she was one of Bernie Freeland's favorites."

The explanation was plausible. "So what's Malcolm Jenner planning to do now?"

"He didn't say. Like Terry Shaw—the other steward—he was shell-shocked."

"And the pilots?"

"Duncan Fairfax is a pompous prick," said Tully. "Puffed up with himself, full of it. Didn't mix with the passengers. His copilot was new, a man called John Yates." Tully thought back over what he knew. "I haven't managed to get in touch with Yates yet, but I asked around. He seems well thought of, nothing suspicious."

"What about Fairfax?"

"No gossip. Apart from him being unpopular, he's respected. Jenner said that he's the pilot for another hotshot with his own plane, so I imagine he'll carry on working for him."

Victor pricked up his ears. "An art dealer?"

"Apparently. One thing I *did* find out that was interesting . . ." Victor looked up, watching Tully as he continued. "In the twenty-two years he's been a pilot, Duncan Fairfax's only ever worked on private jets. Mostly for art dealers."

"So he has to know about the business," Victor said. "Some knowledge must have rubbed off along the way."

"I doubt it. You see what you think of him, but to me Duncan Fairfax is ignorant, money-grubbing hired help. All the pomposity in the world can't cover his true nature. He wasn't even slightly bothered about Bernie Freeland's death or the girl's. He only cared about losing the job. In fact, the only time Fairfax showed any real anger was when I suggested that Freeland might want to fire him."

Victor raised his eyebrows. "Why did you say that?"

"I don't know; just a hunch. Fairfax made no secret of despising his employer, and I suppose I just wanted to rattle him. But he *wasn't* being dismissed, and he certainly wouldn't have killed the golden goose."

"The numbers are dropping," Victor said quietly. "Marian Miller, Annette Dvorski, Bernie Freeland, now Lim Chang—all dead. And Kit Wilkes critical in the hospital. The list is getting shorter by the day."

"Of people who were on the plane," Tully reminded him. "Not of suspects. *That* list keeps growing."

"You asked around about Sergei Ivanovitch?"

"No one's ever heard of him."

"Someone said that Kit Wilkes might have been doing business with Guy Manners."

Tully smiled. "Rumor."

"And like you said, there's always Arnold Fletcher to consider. He *did* have dealings with a gallery in Moscow about four years ago; he was doing very well, and then suddenly it all fell apart. I don't remember the details—it was during my trial, and I had other things on my mind—but someone said Arnold had tried to cheat them." He frowned, remembering. "The Russians stopped trading with him and moved on to Kit Wilkes."

"Interesting."

"Very," Victor agreed. "It would take a tough man to stand up to the Russians. Wilkes is cunning, but tough? Who knows?"

"So Oliver Peters is the only dealer left," Tully said, musing. "I remember him from when I was a boy. My father knew his father quite well, but I've only met him a couple of times since. He came to see a play I was in. Said his wife was a fan of mine, and we had dinner at the Ritz afterward. He paid, naturally; I was only twenty-four." He smiled at Victor. "My father used to say that Oliver Peters was a very clever man, very well thought of in the highest circles. The kind of man who'd want to protect those who'd honored him."

"Meaning?"

"He's dying," Tully said quietly. "He could afford to sacrifice himself. After all, he's got nothing to lose."

"You're wrong. Dying, Oliver Peters has options. If he has the Hogarth, he can destroy it in an act of royalist loyalty. Or sell it to protect his own family after he's dead."

"Which would go against everything he stands for."

Victor shrugged. "Maybe what Oliver Peters stands for doesn't matter so much now. Of course, there is another choice he could make. He could up the stakes and bargain."

"With the *royals?*"

"With those close to the royals," Victor said. "Oliver's time is short.

He might throw caution to the winds. If he went to the royal advisers and told them he had the Hogarth, he might ask them to buy it. He might also mention that he had already spoken to other interested parties, like the Chinese or the Russians."

"No! He wouldn't dare."

"He's close to death, Tully. He might dare anything. If the murders were done by a dealer, Oliver Peters is the prime suspect. After all, he was on the plane. He knew who heard about the Hogarth. He knew what had to be done to secure that painting. Perhaps he would go to any lengths to do just that."

"But blackmailing the royal family . . ."

"Their advisers might think it was worth a fee to stop the Hogarth from ever seeing the light of day, which would prevent any question mark over the validity of the House of Windsor. After all, what would be the alternative? For Oliver Peters to sell it elsewhere? Those close to the royals wouldn't want a foreign power using Hogarth's painting as leverage."

Shaken, Tully held his gaze. "You *really* think the picture is that powerful?"

"Yes. It was powerful when it was first painted, and it's just as potent now. Perhaps more so if it brings into question the line of succession." Victor turned to Tully, his voice low. "There's blood on this painting. To the ruthless, a little more will count for nothing."

Forty-Five

SMILING, OLIVER PETERS SAT IN THE FRONT OF HIS RANGE ROVER AND watched the rugby match. Although he had wanted to spend the weekend in London, his family had pleaded with him to stay with them in the country, and he had relented. Oliver might want—might *need*—to be in London, but he was more than a little aware that he had few weekends left.

As usual, Sonia's arrangements had been extensive: a dinner party, a visit to her parents, and a shopping trip for an antique desk. A normal if busy weekend, but with one difference: Simeon, their son, was playing his first rugby match. Sonia couldn't go, but Oliver had promised he would attend, and even though the day was cold and he was in desperate pain, he made the journey: he knew it might be the last time he would watch his son play.

In the drizzling rain, he could make out his heir in the distance: tall, mud-splattered, and tough. A son to be proud of. A son who would in time have a great responsibility to carry. Oliver swallowed some pills with a little bottled water, turned on the radio, and listened to a snatch of Rossini. The music cheered him, as did the sight of Simeon waving to him from across the field as the sides changed at halftime.

In his youth he too had played rugby. *In his youth* . . . when he'd been fit and well, when running was easy, movement fluid. That morning Sonia had again commented on his weight loss, and again he had avoided the truth, telling her that it was due to an ulcer and that he was getting treatment. She had no reason to doubt him; he had never lied to her before, so why now? She had stroked his hair and told him she would look into a better diet for him, food that would be easier to digest. How he had longed then to cling to her, to tell her that no diet on earth could help. Tell her he that was mortally afraid and that he didn't want to leave her and didn't want her to go on alone. That every moment with her was now doubly precious. He wanted to ask if she believed in life after death. If there was some comfort she could offer that would make their parting bearable.

But he said nothing. He refused to unburden himself only to burden her. And yet, at the same time as he longed for the cancer to halt its indecent progress, Oliver wanted the end to come quickly, before he had to put his family through the anguish of seeing him decay. But no matter how hard it was, he *had* to live a little longer to secure their futures. When he had done that, he could go with a quiet heart.

He stared into the drizzle, thinking of the murdered Lim Chang and the half a million pounds he had managed to raise. It had surprised and flattered him to discover that his blameless reputation had stood him in good stead. He had managed to get the money relatively easily, ready to hand over to Lim Chang in return for the Hogarth. *His* Hogarth.

But Lim Chang was no more. It should have been so simple.

Oliver's stomach clenched in agony, his eyes watering as he stared ahead. Slowly the pain subsided, leaving him with shaking hands and a sweaty brow. But his mind was clear. Sir Oliver Peters's body might be decomposing by the second, but his brain was working perfectly.

So much had been riding on the Hogarth that he hadn't trusted Lim Chang to keep his word. Instead, he had suspected that his Chinese colleague might pass over his money, take the painting, and disappear. And if he did, God knew how many people would be affected by the fallout. Oliver couldn't possibly allow that; he had to safeguard those who relied on him. *All* those who relied on him. Whatever it took. And so the distinguished Sir Oliver Peters had found himself assuming a new role, that of watcher. He had given the money to Chang, but he wasn't going to let it or Lim Chang out of his sight for a moment.

In the cold morning he had pulled on his gloves and turned up the collar of his coat, shivering in the unexpected wind as he followed the Chinese man. For a time Oliver had waited outside a row of shops, trying not to look too conspicuous; then, when he had seen Lim Chang leave, Oliver had followed him. An hour earlier Oliver had handed over a briefcase containing half a million pounds to Lim Chang. This time the briefcase held the Hogarth. Following Chang from a distance, Oliver saw him enter Hyde Park and realized that he was heading for Piccadilly and therefore—or so he believed— for Oliver's gallery.

He was going to keep his word. He was bringing the Hogarth back!

Oliver, eager to get to his gallery before Lim Chang arrived, began walking through the park as swiftly as he could manage. It was still very early and very quiet, and he hadn't gone far when he heard the distant sound of a dog barking hysterically.

The park was empty of people, but the barking was incessant and getting louder, so unsettling that Oliver began hurrying toward the noise to see what was going on. The unsettling incessant barking increased in volume as he approached. As Oliver, his heart pumping, paused for breath at a clump of trees that blocked his view, the barking stopped. Hidden behind the trees, he peered through the leaves to be met by a sight so horrific that for a few seconds he couldn't breathe.

What he saw was Lim Chang tied to a water fountain under an overhang of trees. A Chinese thug was pummeling his bloodied face, and another was pushing firecrackers into his ears. One of the men lit them, and both of them were convulsed with laughter as Chang struggled hopelessly, making a gurgling, choking sound as a third man approached, struggling to hold onto a dog that was snarling and straining at its leash. Chang's eyes bulged with terror as one of the men unfastened the fly of his trousers.

Rooted to the spot behind the bushes, Oliver saw the dog released and flying at Lim Chang's genitals. Sickened, he turned away, retching. Forcing himself to look back, he had seen the attackers reach for the case; they had the money but had come to steal back the Hogarth.

Instinctively, without thinking, Oliver shouted, "STOP! POLICE!" as loudly as he could, praying someone would be drawn to the scene.

Panicked, the men tried unsuccessfully to open the triple locked case. Desperately they tried to snatch it away, but Lim Chang had fastened it to his wrist by a chain, and as they tugged, they pulled the bloodied man half over. Chang slumped against the water fountain, the bone of his wrist breaking from the force.

A police car siren sounded, and, defeated, the men ran off. But the car didn't come into the park; no one did. Instead, Oliver Peters stood alone, immobile, staring at the body of Lim Chang. He knew that before long the corpse would be found, just as he had known that the killers had made a point of killing Chang in the open. They could easily have killed him earlier, when he gave them the money in exchange for the painting, but why murder him covertly in a basement when they could send out a warning signal to everyone with such a vicious and public killing?

Hardly believing what he was about to do, Oliver had taken a key from his pocket, unfastened the lock of the case, and taken out a small package. Bundling the precious Hogarth under his arm, he had begun to run. He had left the park, left the mutilated body of Lim Chang. Clutching his picture, Oliver Peters disappeared instantly into the back streets of Mayfair.

The rain was drizzling down the windshield as Oliver looked out into a dismal sky. Simeon was still playing rugby. Sighing, Oliver thought of the painting hidden in a safety deposit in an obscure bank in Henley-on-Thames. The safe at his gallery would have been too obvious a target, and he certainly wasn't going to risk his usual safe deposit box that had been robbed in the first place. Not for the first time, he prayed that the triads would be content with half a million pounds. They might have lost the Hogarth, but they were considerably richer. *Please God, it would be enough.*

Had he really gotten away with it?

His first responsibility was to the royal family, but *his* family's security was vital. The line of succession might be imperative, but he also had to protect his own kin. Waving to Simeon, Oliver smiled at his son through the rain, thinking of the kink of fate that had made him accept the lift on Bernie Freeland's jet. Then he thought of the others on the flight. Remembered them. And the way they had died.

Fear dug its claws into him.

The previous day Oliver Peters had been followed. And the private phone in the gallery had rung a few times, but there had been only silence when he answered. He felt threatened by shadows he would never have noticed before, and noises could make his stomach lurch and his heartbeat quicken. He knew that he wasn't being watched by any members of the court circle. If they had discovered his error, they would also know that the Hogarth was safe again and would have had no reason for further surveillance.

It was now obvious to Oliver that the people after him were those who wanted the painting not for its incendiary secret but for its market value. But they would *not* get it. Who cared if the Chinese came for him? Who cared if the Russians killed him? He was dying already. All that mattered was that he should fulfill his duty.

Then Oliver remembered the half a million pounds he had borrowed and felt his spirits fold. He had safeguarded the royals but left his own family vulnerable. How could he repay the money before he died? How and where could he find it? He could hardly leave the burden of debt with his family. He recoiled from the thought of selling off any of his children's inheritance, but he *had* to raise money. And quickly.

Then a profoundly shameful thought entered his mind. *He could sell the Hogarth.* And he had the ring: the ring with its damning inscription, its existence kept hidden for so long. But the Hogarth . . . *What a fortune it would fetch*, Oliver thought. He could pay back the half a million loan easily and put the remainder of the money in the bank in his wife's name. His family would be provided for, and no one would know. To all intents and purposes the painting would be hidden as it always had been. Who would know if he sold it? No one had ever asked to see it. No one spoke of it.

Oliver clenched his fists as his conscience shifted. Why, he asked himself, had his first duty always been to the royals? He hadn't asked to inherit the Hogarth legacy; it was foisted upon him, passed down with the family silver and the country house. It was a fact known to only a handful of people, a rumor known to only a handful more. So why should he be expected to put the royal family before his own family? He was soon to die, owing a fortune; surely the rules couldn't remain the same.

Still staring at his son, Oliver let his thoughts drift. An idea, shocking and unthinkable only minutes earlier, had begun to seem reasonable. Ten minutes later, he'd made up his mind. He would drive back to London, to the gallery in the Burlington Arcade, and begin making some discreet phone calls.

But first he would stay and watch his son for a little while longer.

Focusing on the rugby game, on Simeon, Oliver silently addressed his son. *When I'm gone*, he thought, *you'll think of me well, as a good man, a good father, a good provider. You'll never know what Hogarth's reckless painting cost me. Or what it made me—a man I would never have suspected I could have become. It corrupted me, Simeon, made me a little mad. But you won't know that. You'll never know I robbed a dead man. You'll never know what amount of blood was spilled for that painting now and in the past.*

You won't know. And it won't matter, because thank God, it will all have been worthwhile.

Forty–Six

WATCHING FROM HIS CAR, VICTOR RUBBED HIS NECK AND KEPT HIS eyes fixed on the back entrance of Charlene Fleet's Park Street premises. Having checked that Liza was safe in the apartment, he had driven over to Mayfair and waited, watching throughout the evening and into the small hours. Scared but willing to help, Liza had given him a list of Mrs. Fleet's clients. As Victor had expected, there was a smattering of prominent figures in law and medicine, but most were art dealers. Many, like Arnold Fletcher and a number of Japanese and Chinese connoisseurs, were known to him. As for the Russians, it was no surprise that Marian Miller's last assignation had been with the mysterious Sergei Ivanovitch or that Mrs. Fleet had nine Russian dealers on her books.

So had it been a clumsy ploy of hers to plant the name and the rubles on Marian Miller's body? Victor doubted it. It seemed too crass for Mrs. Fleet, but then again, maybe that was what he was *supposed* to think. And then there were the dog hairs found on Marian's body. What did they mean? Were they a clue, pointing to someone with a dog? Or someone who handled dogs? Victor sighed, wondering if he was missing the obvious. Marian Miller *could* have been killed by the Russians. After all, she had contacted Mrs. Fleet about the painting as soon as she had gotten off the jet. Maybe she had called someone else as well, set in motion a backup plan in case her employer wasn't interested.

Another name on the list had caught Victor's eye: Dr. Eli Fountain. The same Eli Fountain who was paid by Kit Wilkes to examine any potential lover. The same Eli Fountain who was at that very moment walking out of the back entrance of the Park Street premises. Leaving his car, Victor followed the dapper little figure to the corner of Curzon Street, where Dr. Fountain suddenly turned and addressed him.

"Can I help you?" His accent was Texan, slow in the vowels, peculiarly oily.

"I beg your pardon?"

"You've been following me. Why is that?" he asked, his head tilted slightly forward, his eyes challenging. At only five foot five, he was oddly aggressive. "I don't like being followed. By anyone."

"I wanted to ask you some questions."

Fountain waved a manicured hand. "Phone my office."

"I thought you might like to talk discreetly."

"I only *ever* talk discreetly," he replied, amused. "Why are you hanging around in the dark to talk to me?"

"You know Kit Wilkes."

"Who are you?"

"Victor Ballam."

"Oh . . . Mrs. Fleet talks highly of you. Or rather, she did. I gather you've really pissed her off. You should always return phone calls, Mr. Ballam."

"About Kit Wilkes, Doctor Fountain."

"Why should I talk to you?" the doctor said, his hands deep in the pockets of his cashmere overcoat. "Especially out here, in the cold. Now, if you were to offer me a drink, I might find myself a little more chatty."

A few minutes later Victor was ordering two whiskeys in the lounge of a nearby hotel. It was very late, and the room was virtually empty other than one man with his luggage waiting to depart and a woman in the corner talking on her cell phone. Smiling as he raised his glass, Dr. Fountain took a long drink and then leaned back in his seat, studying Victor. His hands were smooth, his nails trimmed and buffed to a satin sheen.

"I believe you're helping Mrs. Fleet find out who's killing her girls. Murder is so off-putting for the clients."

Victor didn't miss a beat. "Is that what she told you?"

"Poor Marian and Annette; such *talented* girls."

"Did you look after them?"

"Like I always say to Mrs. Fleet, you can't be too careful. Any STD would be so bad for business. Of course, murder's worse. I know all her girls. Liza Frith, who you spoke to, I believe, ran off. Did you know that, Mr. Ballam?"

Victor ignored the question and pressed on. "Have you known Mrs. Fleet for long?"

"Centuries."

"But you're not English."

"I suppose the accent gave me away," he said, smiling, oddly sinister. "You really shouldn't mess with Mrs. Fleet, you know. She is a very powerful woman with many influential friends. I know for a fact she would look upon it kindly if you were to return Liza Frith."

"I don't own her."

"Everyone owns everyone else, Mr. Ballam. We just pretend otherwise to get along." He finished his drink, his eyes steady. "We owe people or they owe us, and we remind them of that when we need them."

With a stab of discomfort, Victor thought of Tully. "I don't know where Liza Frith is. I wanted to ask you about Kit Wilkes."

"He's not likely to recover, poor boy."

"I believe his father, James Holden, arranged for him to be admitted to the Friary."

Doctor Fountain's eyes flickered. "He did."

"That was unusual, seeing as how he usually avoids any connection with his illegitimate son."

"Must have been paternal concern."

"Or a cover-up?"

"I beg your pardon?"

Victor chose his words very carefully. "How much d'you know about what happened on Bernie Freeland's plane?"

"Probably as much as you do," he replied, coldly charming. "But please ask away, Mr. Ballam. I don't sleep well and find the early hours tedious, hard to spend alone. Talking is a relief."

A silence, and then Victor asked, "Why do you think the girls were killed?"

"I thought you were hired to find that out."

"But if you're so close to Mrs. Fleet, you must know."

Leaning forward, Dr. Fountain stared into Victor's face, his tone one of suppressed anger. "Don't talk to me like some tight-assed Sunday school teacher. I know about the Hogarth."

"Mrs. Fleet told you?"

"Maybe." Fountain relaxed again. "Or then again, maybe someone else told me."

"Kit Wilkes?"

"Now, how could I break doctor–patient confidence?"

Smiling faintly, Victor stared at the bottom of his glass. "You couldn't. But speaking hypothetically, of course, if someone had news that was potentially dangerous and certainly profitable and confided this to their doctor, how easy would it be for this doctor—who would know the patient's full medical history—to silence them? Make it look like a drug overdose, perhaps. Something which wouldn't seem suspicious in a known drug user."

Victor put down his glass and gazed at the odious little man in front of him. "Does any of this sound familiar?"

"I think I might have seen the movie."

Victor smiled. "How did it end?"

"The hero got killed."

Draining his glass, Victor stared at his companion. The atmosphere between them was thick with the odor of malice that was emanating from the little man.

"Did you know Lim Chang?" Victor asked.

"Only by reputation."

"Which means?"

"He was an art dealer; I'm allied to that world. That's all I meant."

"So you knew Bernie Freeland?"

"Oh, yes; I knew him. I used to accompany him on some of his flights."

"Giving the girls drugs?"

"You should be more careful what you say, Mr. Ballam. Running off at the mouth like that is so un-English, like a little baby bird fluttering its little wings as it tries to fly." He flicked his hands weakly, mocking Victor. "But it doesn't have the strength, you see, so the poor little mite crashes to earth. Sad, but that's what happens when people overreach themselves."

Unperturbed, Victor continued. "James Holden is one of Mrs. Fleet's clients. Is that how you met him?"

"Your research is letting you down, Mr. Ballam, so let me help you out. James Holden is a client at Park Street, and yes, I do take care of his son, Kit Wilkes. I have also on a couple of occasions attended James Holden myself."

"For a medical condition?"

"I'm not a plumber; it wasn't for a burst faucet."

"Would you say you two are friends?"

"Friendship is a pretty concept," Fountain continued, "but James Holden and I are not close."

"So he wouldn't feel able to ask you for a favor?"

Suddenly Dr. Fountain's cell phone rang. He took it from his pocket, looked at the caller ID, and answered.

"Hello there, Mrs. Fleet. I'm just having a nightcap with Mr. Ballam. . . . Oh, yes; he's going to call you back anytime now. . . . What? . . . He's been asking me all kinds of questions." Unexpectedly, Fountain glanced over to Victor and winked. "About what? About James Holden and Kit Wilkes." He paused, listening. "No, Mr. Ballam says he doesn't know where Liza Frith is, and I believe him, I really do." He listened, then smiled smoothly. "Bye; call you tomorrow."

Shutting off the cell phone, he slid it back into the inside pocket of his jacket, then looked hard at Victor.

"I've just lied to one of my oldest friends," he said simply. "Now, why would you think I'd do that?"

"Because lying would serve you better than the truth, perhaps."

Fountain smirked. "You see through me like a pane of glass, Mr. Ballam. I have nowhere to hide." His expression changed to one of cold intent. "Where's the painting?"

"You know something?" Victor asked, playing for time. "I wasn't expecting you to say that."

"Where is it?"

"I don't know."

"I think you do," Fountain insisted. "Let's put it this way: *I want that Hogarth.* I may well have a buyer for it."

"A dealer?"

"I can't say, Mr. Ballam. I mean, if I were to confide in you and you had the Hogarth in your possession, then what would stop you from going to my contact directly and making a deal without me? I just want to make this sale and retire. I'm tired of nursing whores and villains, and I want money. Lots of it." He put his head on one side. "That, my friend, is the only reason I lied to Mrs. Fleet. I need to be on good terms with you more than with her, because I need you to find that picture. Mrs. Fleet can't do that."

"Who told you about the painting?"

"Kit Wilkes."

Surprised, Victor kept his face expressionless. "Just before he fell into that convenient coma?"

"An injection isn't that hard to give, Mr. Ballam. You're a novice if you think you'd have to be a doctor. Anyone used to having or giving shots could use a needle." He paused, steadied his tone. "Kit told me about the Hogarth."

Victor shook his head dismissively. "No, I don't think so. Kit Wilkes is an art dealer; he wouldn't confide in someone who wasn't in the business."

"Usually I'd agree with your logic, but poor Kit was running scared. I was there, and he needed to talk, to have a witness."

"To what?"

"Kit phoned me as soon as he got back to his flat from the flight. He told me about the Hogarth and how important—even dangerous—it was. He said that if anything happened to him—"

"Why did he think something might happen to him?"

"I don't know. Maybe because he'd just been talking to Guy Manners."

"Now there's a name that keeps cropping up. The elusive Mr. Manners. D'you know him? Where he is now?"

"Like you say, he's elusive, a will-o'-the-wisp." Fountain paused. "But I wouldn't read too much into it. Kit lies, makes up all kinds of stories. He's also a very suspicious man, chary of everyone. Doubts everything he sees and even what he doesn't. He's very smart, loves plotting and setting people up against each other, but he's got one big failing, Mr. Ballam: he doesn't let his right hand know what his left hand's doing, and that can be lethal. Sometimes I think Kit's too clever for his own good."

Victor stared into the man's cold eyes. "Did he know where the Hogarth was?"

"He said it was hidden in New York, that Bernie Freeland had it." He smiled slowly. "Oh, I see I have your attention now. Kit then went on to tell me that he'd arranged for someone to collect it."

"Who?"

"I don't know," Fountain said, slumping back into his seat. "We were talking, and suddenly the line went dead. When I finally got an answer—about two hours later—I was told that Kit Wilkes was in a coma . . . unlikely to recover." He paused. "Now, *you* tell *me:* would I silence him *before* I'd found out where the painting was? That would make nonsense of my plan. Surely you can see that."

Victor thought of Annette Dvorski. She had gone over to New York, to Bernie Freeland's apartment. She had had the Hogarth in her bag. Had *she* been sent by Kit Wilkes? Had she been the elected courier?

"Was it one of Mrs. Fleet's girls?"

Dr. Fountain looked at Victor and then laughed softly, wiping his hand across the back of his mouth before he spoke again.

"A *whore*? Don't be absurd. Kit Wilkes hates women; he'd never have used a woman. He thinks all females are stupid and doesn't trust any of them. No; whoever it was, it wasn't a woman, and certainly not a hooker. It was a man, Mr. Ballam. That's all I know." He stood up to leave, buttoning his cashmere coat. "Find that man and you've found the Hogarth."

"Then what?"

"Call me. I'll make it worth your while. I'll do the deal and give you a piece of the proceeds."

Fountain smiled, seeming genuinely amused. "Oh, Mr. Ballam, don't you go worrying about my hurting you. I'm no killer; I don't have the balls for that. I'm a charlatan and a coward, and above all I'm greedy. Greedy to get away from this city. From the dealers and their call girls, from the likes of Charlene Fleet and James Holden and Kit Wilkes. I've spent too long following the muck cart. Take me up on my offer, Mr. Ballam. After all, that painting's unlucky. Dangerous even. If I were you, I'd want to get it off my hands as soon as I could."

"You're not worried that it might be dangerous for you?"

"I'm prepared to take the risk for the money. It's the only thing that works for me. Money makes me tall and handsome. With enough money I can retire, stop pandering to whores and whoremongers. Start going in front doors instead of back entrances. Find the Hogarth, Mr. Ballam. I reckon you're clever enough to pull that off." He turned to go, then turned back. "But don't be tempted to keep it. You're not smart enough to get away with *that*."

Forty-Seven

RETURNING TO HIS CAR, VICTOR WAS SURPRISED TO SEE MRS. FLEET watching him from the back entrance of her house. With a jerk of her head, she gestured for him to enter. Victor followed her up to the apartment at the top of the townhouse. Her makeup was immaculate, the lip liner even, not a trace of oiliness or imperfect finish to her skin. Her appearance was a triumph; only her voice betrayed her underlying anger.

"I'm paying you for information. What's the latest?"

"Lim Chang is dead."

She faced him, unmoved. "I know; I read the papers. What else?"

"I've been looking into everyone on that flight. The pilots, the cabin crew, trying to find any link between any of them. There's nothing—apart from the Hogarth, that is."

"What about Liza Frith?"

"I don't know where she is."

She laughed without humor. "Really? I don't believe you. I think you know exactly where she is. The question is, Why would you be keeping her from me? Did she say something that worried you? Did she intimate that I might have threatened her in some way?"

"Did you?"

"Liza Frith works for me, Mr. Ballam. She is of interest to me only as an employee who is very good at her job and makes me a lot of money. Money I am not making at the moment because of her absence." She shivered and turned up the thermostat on the radiator. "Liza is the nervous type, highly imaginative, but running off like that was ridiculous. Her life was hardly in danger at Park Street."

"Maybe she thought it was," Victor replied, noticing that the increase of heat was hardly touching the chill of the room. "She was very scared because of what she knew."

"Maybe I should be afraid," Mrs. Fleet responded. "I know about the Hogarth too, but you don't see me panicking. Or is that because you think I'm somehow involved in all of this?"

"I really don't know," Victor replied, keeping his tone neutral while becoming aware of a subtle change in Mrs. Fleet's frigid self-control. He didn't know exactly why or how, but he sensed that she wasn't as indomitable as usual. She seemed—could he believe it?—afraid.

"If anything happens to Liza Frith, I'll hold you personally responsible."

"Why should anything happen to her?"

"She should be back here, where I can keep an eye on her."

"Like I said, why should anything happen to her?"

"The other two were killed!" Mrs. Fleet snapped. She quickly composed herself, but the effect wasn't wholly convincing, and Victor saw her hand shake slightly as she gestured to him. "I don't want you working for me on this case any longer."

"What?"

"I'm firing you."

"Forget it! Somebody wanted to frame me for Annette Dvorski's murder, Mrs. Fleet. If the police find out I was in Bernie Freeland's apartment, I'll be their prime suspect, and—"

"Just let it go! I'm not going to tell them you were in New York, and your associate's hardly likely to give you away. The only other person who knew was Liza Frith, and I doubt she'll turn on you. What would be the point?" Mrs. Fleet leaned across the desk toward Victor. "Get Liza to come back here, will you? I can take care of her at Park Street."

"She doesn't trust you, and neither do I."

The room had warmed up, but the heat was making no impact on Mrs. Fleet, who, shivering again, sat back in her chair with her arms folded and studied Victor. From the floor below Victor could hear noises: indistinguishable, disembodied, fainter than the street sounds beyond. He found the effect confusing. The noises outside were familiar, commonplace; the muffled sounds within were eerie, almost threatening. Anything could be happening in the rooms below his feet, he realized. A person could be suffocated, injected, killed, and no one would know. Suddenly the Park Street brothel seemed more like a charnel house.

Mrs. Fleet spoke. "I won't pay you to continue with the investigation."

Victor shrugged. "Suit yourself. You can stop paying me, but you can't stop me investigating. I want to know what happened for my own reasons. I want to know about the Hogarth, and I certainly don't want to see anyone else killed."

She smiled, but the effect was unnerving. "Who cares if the painting is exposed? Who cares about the royals?"

"I certainly think the House of Windsor would care."

"And we should protect them?" she queried. "That girl in the painting wasn't the first—and won't be the last—to have fucked a prince. Royalty's a busted flush. Some say they're good for tourism, but when the old queen dies, what then?" Mrs. Fleet raised her eyebrows. "You think people will follow the next king? No chance. The time and place for royalty is dying out. Celebrities are the new kings and queens; movie stars are the Knights of the Round Table. No one wants to be a minor royal when they can make a million with a film or a line of cosmetics. Or by kicking a football around. Royalty was everything—in the old world. Your painting, Mr. Ballam, might not have the power you think."

"Or you hope," Victor parried, unconvinced. "The wealth and status of the monarchy counts for more now than it ever did. It's not long since the last royal wedding. The whole world watched that; don't tell me no one cares about the monarchy."

"Hah!"

"People want to be honored; no tin-pot president can rival a king. This country's admired for its royal family and its traditions. Others envy us the pomp and ceremony. Republics and communist states resent our traditions, but they covet them. They might not admit it, but they do. The House of Windsor still wields huge influence in the world, so yes, I believe that the Hogarth painting is still lethal."

Mrs. Fleet's eyes were fixed on Victor's, unblinking, as he said, "You know as well as I do that the killing won't stop."

"Lim Chang—"

"Was mauled to pieces by a dog."

Unsettled, she turned away, her hand momentarily covering her mouth.

"Someone set a dog on him. A big dog, vicious, trained to its owner's command."

With one quick movement, she turned back to face Victor, her expression frantic. "Go on, say it! You want to, so say it. You think *I* did it. You think I set my dog on Lim Chang. I hired you to find out what happened to my girls, not to start accusing me of murder! Would I be that stupid to have you working for me if I was involved?" Her hand drifted to the edge of the desk, then fluttered momentarily in the dead air. "Let it be, Mr. Ballam. It's gone too far. For my sake—and your own—let it be."

"I can't do that."

"They killed my dog," she said, her voice breaking for one brief moment. "They ran a car over him. They killed him and left him in the road. They killed my dog." Her shaking increased; her eyes dimmed. "He meant everything to me. More than my girls or my business or any damn painting!"

Surprised, Victor stared at her. He had been so sure that she had used the mastiff, that she was involved in Chang's death. But here she sat, shaking in her chair, a yawning empty space at her feet, and he realized why the atmosphere was so eerie.

"Before you wonder," she went on. "Before your limited brain conjures up the thought, my dog was killed *before* Lim Chang died. If you don't believe me, call the vet. He'll confirm everything I've said." She tossed a phone book across the desk. "Go on, ring him."

Victor glanced at the book and then back at Mrs. Fleet. "Who killed your dog? *Why* would they kill your dog?"

"As a warning, Mr. Ballam."

"You should take it."

"No. They've gone too far. They killed the one thing I cared about, and someone will pay for that, believe me. Someone will *really* pay for it." Her voice was deadly. "No one takes what's mine. *No one.*"

Forty-Eight

LIZA COULD HEAR A RADIO PLAYING IN THE BASEMENT NEXT DOOR, then the sound of a child laughing. The noises soothed her, and she opened the curtain over the window. High over her head, the lofty white townhouses shimmered under the winter lamplight. A man rode past on a bicycle. Turning away, Liza made herself some cereal, then took out her wallet and counted what was left of her money.

Worried, she slumped down on the sofa, flipping the wallet onto a cushion. How long could she go on without earning money? She had hardly anything left and no one to beg a loan from. She could hardly ask Victor Ballam; he had done more than enough for her. She thought wistfully of how much she could have made in one night working for Mrs. Fleet, then remembered the flight on Bernie Freeland's plane and jumped when someone tapped lightly on the basement door.

"Hello?" a friendly female voice called. "Hello? I know there's someone in there."

Looking through the peephole, Liza saw a smiling face looking back at her.

"I live next door. We're neighbors. Can you open up; I want to ask you something."

Cautiously, Liza opened the door as far as the chain allowed and peered through the gap. "Sorry to disturb you, but the cat wandered off this morning. A big ginger tom we got from the rescue center. I just wondered if you'd seen him."

Liza shook her head. "No. But I haven't been out today, and I didn't see him in the backyard."

The woman shrugged. "I suppose he'll come back," she said with a smile to her daughter, who was standing beside her. "He *will*, darling; he's just having a look around his new territory."

"Cats wander all the time," Liza added, her tone reassuring. "He'll probably come home when he's hungry."

"Speaking of which," the woman said, "we're going to have dinner now, and I've made loads. D'you want to join us?"

"No; no thanks."

"Oh, come on," the woman said. "My family want to meet you. We heard you moving around and thought you might be lonely."

Tempted, Liza looked at her. She was a mother with a child in tow. They lived in the house next to hers. How dangerous could it be to have a chat? Liza hesitated. Victor hadn't called for hours, and the night promised to be another lonely one. Suddenly she hankered after company.

"Please, do come," the woman urged. "This is my daughter, Shauna, and I'm Jayne. I've made far too much food for us. You're very welcome to share it."

"Well—"

"Come on!"

The decision was made at that moment. "Thank you, Jayne; I *am* hungry and a bit lonely," she said, grabbing her bag and undoing the chain. "I'm Liza, by the way."

Showing Liza into the basement of the house next door, Jayne busied herself with the food. "Are you working in London?" she asked, her tone warm and interested.

"No; I've come down from the north."

"Looking for work?"

"Yes, in a while." Liza smiled at the little girl beside her, who was nursing a doll on her lap. "Have you lived here long?"

"No, not long," Jayne replied easily.

Liza glanced around and noticed a photograph on the shelf by the window. A picture of a middle-aged couple. With no children.

"Is this your flat?"

"Oh, yes. It's not very big, but you make do. I think your flat might be a bit larger than this one. But then, if you're on your own, you've got more space, haven't you? No family to clutter it up. Still, although this flat's a little cramped, I like the area."

Slowly, Liza continued to look around, noticing another photograph of the same middle-aged woman, who was nothing like her hostess. In the cramped confines of a small central London apartment, why would someone put out pictures of other people? And not just one but a few of them. Slowly she kept scanning the room, noticing that the furnishings were old-fashioned for a young mother and that there were precious few children's toys. Suddenly nervous, Liza felt the hairs rising on the back of her neck and stood up.

"The food's nearly ready," Jayne said.

"I have to go. I can hear my cell phone ringing."

"Have your meal first," Jayne replied with just a tinge of irritation in her voice. "They'll leave a message."

Liza shook her head. "I think I should answer it. It might be important—" She stopped short as a man entered the room. A thin Chinese man with yellow spatulate fingernails.

Finding the address that Tully had given him in the backstreets, Victor walked into the large covered area. But this time the place was quiet. There was no dogfight taking place, only a group of men talking at the back. As he entered, they all looked over to him, but only one approached.

"Can I help you?"

"I want to talk to Malcolm Jenner."

"That's me."

"I'm Victor Ballam."

"Congratulations," Jenner replied sourly. "What d'you want?"

"I want to talk about a cell phone. Annette Dvorski's cell phone."

He could see Jenner's eyes flicker and followed as he led him farther outside. Jenner lit a cigarette and stared at Victor.

"I don't know what you're talking about."

"I think you do. Annette Dvorski was on Bernie Freeland's plane. You talked to my colleague about it, Tully Harcourt."

"Okay, so I talked to him about Mr. Freeland. I don't remember talking about any girl, though."

"Did you know her?"

"Who?"

"Annette Dvorski."

"She was a hooker on the flight."

"Nothing else?"

"What else is there?"

"So why have you got her cell phone?"

"I found it," Jenner replied, but he was clearly uneasy, unable to look Victor in the eye. "I can't tell you any more than I told your colleague."

"You know that Annette Dvorski's dead?"

He paused, took a long drag of his cigarette, and stared hard at the ground. In the building behind, several of the men were moving, bringing out dogs. The animals were pulling at their leashes and snarling, their hackles raised. Fighting dogs. Killing machines. Animals that could easily tear a man to pieces.

Victor's breathing quickened as he gestured to them. "You run dogs here?"

Jenner looked up, half regretfully, half resigned. "My wife does. Your friend said he'd keep it quiet."

"He certainly did. He didn't even tell me."

Victor watched as the men came closer; the dogs were focused, alert.

"Like I said, Mr. Ballam," Jenner went on, aware of his backup. "I've got nothing more to say about that flight."

"Why are you so scared?"

"Don't pretend *you're* not."

Victor smiled ruefully. "Oh, I admit it; I'm bloody terrified. But you—why are you so afraid?" He reached out and gripped Jenner's arm. "Look, I'm past caring, and frankly, if you want me to beg, fine, I'll beg. I'm involved in something I don't understand. Everywhere I go people are telling me to back off or they're threatening me." Fear was making him angry. "Well, I won't back off. Not now, not ever. But I'm floundering, and I need some help."

"I can't give it to you."

"You know something," Victor persisted, glancing at the dogs and then back to Jenner. "You *have* to help me. Four people on that flight have already been killed."

"Yeah, and I don't want to be the fifth."

Victor increased his grip on Jenner's arm. "Neither do I. I want to put a stop to it, but I can't unless someone helps me out. Give me something. *Anything.*"

The dogs were only five feet away from Victor now, surrounding him. Jenner stubbed out the cigarette butt with the heel of his boot.

"Leave now, before you get into any real trouble. I only have to say the word and they'll set the dogs on you."

"I don't doubt it," Victor said quietly, letting go of Malcolm Jenner's arm. The dogs were so close, he could smell them. "But I want you to remember those girls and what happened to them. I want you to close your eyes at night and think of what they suffered. Marian Miller's head smashed in, Annette Dvorski tortured and forced to swallow bleach."

To Victor's surprise, Jenner suddenly gestured for the men to back off. For a moment they hesitated, then moved away, walking the dogs back into the building beyond. In the grim, chill daylight, Malcolm Jenner reached for another cigarette, his hands shaking so much that he could hardly light it. His color had faded, his eyes were watery behind his glasses, and a cough rasped from the back of his throat.

"She was tortured?"

"Yes."

"How d'you know?"

"Because I found her."

Jenner nodded, struggling for breath. "She suffered?"

"More than anyone should."

There was a pause as Jenner stared upward into the dead sky. Finally, he looked back to Victor.

"It was supposed to be so easy. She had a plan, you see. She said we could pull it off, that it would be a breeze. Annette told me she had Bernie Freeland eating out of the palm of her hand."

Stunned, Victor stared at the man in front of him. "A plan?"

"She was all lit up, excited. She said she was going to get her hands on some painting that was worth a fortune. She'd been larking around, spiking Mr. Freeland's drink for a laugh, but then she overheard something he said. When we landed, she phoned me and told me all about it." He smiled at the memory. "Annette said we'd be living like royalty. Said we were really onto something, that we could sell the picture for millions."

"But you didn't even know her."

"We *pretended* we didn't know each other. It stopped people from asking questions. But we'd known each other for a long time." Jenner paused, his voice hardly audible. "Annette Dvorski was my niece."

Forty-Nine

RACHEL FAIRFAX, BELOVED WIFE OF DUNCAN, WAS TRYING TO WORK out a recipe for that evening's meal. Having spent half an hour in the butcher's choosing the right cut of beef, she was now frowning as she read the instructions for St. James's stew. She was the only person who didn't think her husband was a son of a bitch. In all the years they had been married, Duncan had worshipped his wife, and the fact that they had no children had not weakened but strengthened their bond. In Duncan, Rachel had found a protective admirer. In Rachel, Duncan had discovered an uncomplicated, endlessly affectionate—and undemanding—consort.

He was not a man to offer information, and she was not a woman to ask questions. Her mind held no room for suspicion or doubt, whereas his was a pot roast of secrets seasoned with a garnish of *folie de grandeur.* Coming from a comfortable and respected army family, Rachel was at ease with the world. Born into poor stock and having lied about his lowly beginnings, Duncan felt unsteady in life. At any time he was liable to fall, to have his humble origins revealed and laughed at.

Rachel was terrified of only one thing: losing her husband in an air crash. He was terrified of being exposed, being brought down to earth and viewed as a social calamity, the bogus puffed-up liar that he was. But for all Duncan Fairfax's failings, his love for his wife was genuine. It was the only genuine thing about him. There was no straying from the marital bed, no accepting any of the sexual treats on offer. He could have added adultery to his many failings, but Duncan was a moral hypocrite. Lying to prop himself up was justifiable; lying to deceive his wife was unforgivable.

And over their eighteen years of marriage Rachel had nurtured an image of her husband that he saw reflected in her eyes and in everything she did for him. It was a false image but a precious one. An image not of the man he was but the man he *pretended* to be. Rachel was his mirror. The uncritical, loving reflection of his importance.

Hearing the kitchen door open, Rachel looked up and smiled as her husband entered. "I'm making your favorite."

"Everything you make for me is my favorite, darling." He kissed her cheek. "How are you feeling?"

"You worry too much about me."

"You need looking after, and there's no one better to look after you than me. Did you check your blood sugar?"

"I can cope with my diabetes, darling; you know I can," Rachel replied, turning back to the recipe. "I thought we could eat around seven?"

"Good."

"You could watch the golf on BBC2," she offered, "or go out and play a few holes."

He shook his head, weary as he sank into a chair in the open-plan kitchen. For once he had a week off. Bernie Freeland's death had given him an unexpected break. Naturally, Duncan had told his wife about his employer's death, but not about the gruesome murder of Marian Miller. He glanced at Rachel, knowing how much the news would upset her, send her blood sugar through the roof. Why tell her when there was nothing to be gained from it? Wasn't it enough that she got anxious every time he flew?

Rachel had never demanded that Duncan stop flying, but she *had* hinted at an early retirement. He had ducked the suggestion because he liked his work and *loved* the money he made. Flying for a regular commercial airline would never have been as lucrative as piloting a private jet, and for a snob like Duncan Fairfax, the status of being among the elite was to be guarded at all costs. Not for him the horror of domestic flights, the daily shuttle run to Glasgow or Newcastle. Not for him the faded interiors of old 747s. Oh, no; his world above the clouds was gilded, exclusive. His uniform bore a designer label; his passport proclaimed Monte Carlo, New York, Hong Kong. . . .

"Is there going to be a funeral?"

Duncan blinked. "What?"

"For poor Mr. Freeland. Is there going to be a funeral?"

"It was yesterday, in New York," Duncan explained. "A quiet affair, apparently. Just a few friends and his son."

"I didn't know he had a son."

Duncan nodded. "I only met him once, a few years ago."

"You never said."

"To be honest, I forgot about it. Mr. Freeland wasn't with Louis—that's the name of his son—he was traveling alone. Well, not entirely; Louis was with one of the family's lawyers. If I remember rightly, he was being taken from the USA to Europe for a trip. A treat, because his father hadn't been able to spend Christmas with him."

"How old is he?"

"Must be early twenties now."

Rachel's eyebrows rose. "So he'll inherit his father's fortune?"

"I doubt that. Louis will have an allowance and be more than comfortable, but he's not exactly a businessman," Duncan went on, thinking back. "He's very handsome, very striking to look at, but Mr. Freeland always kept his son's existence very quiet."

"Why?"

"Louis has problems," Duncan replied, suddenly wondering who would inherit the Freeland fortune.

"What a shame," Rachel said, reopening the oven door and sliding the casserole onto the top shelf. "All the money and success in the world can't prevent things like that from happening. First his son and then that terrible accident . . . I suppose you'll miss Mr. Freeland; you liked him so much."

I loathed him, the boorish, oversexed bastard, Duncan thought but, keeping his voice light, replied, "Yes, I'll miss him. But I'm going to be working full time for Ahmed Fatida from now on. He has dealings all over the Middle East. He's twice as rich as Mr. Freeland. Bigger jet too. Triple seven," he bragged.

"That's nice," Rachel replied absently, taking off her oven gloves and moving over to the sofa. Sitting beside him, she laid her head against her husband's shoulder. "I love you, sweetheart."

"Love you, darling."

"You think you want all those wonderful things in life—luxury, money, and power—but in the end they don't count for anything, do they?" She snuggled closer to him. "Mr. Freeland and his poor son would envy us now. We're the lucky ones, you know. We have each other and a calm, untroubled life."

"Yes, we're the lucky ones," Duncan agreed. "We just have to make sure we stay lucky."

"Well, at least Victor sent me a text," Ingola said, sitting on the window seat in Tully's apartment, her thick blond hair tumbling over her shoulders. "I said I'd be in London today and wondered if we could meet up, but he said no. Said he'd call me later. He won't see me, Tully."

"What d'you expect? Sleeping with his brother's wife is hardly going to make him feel good, is it?"

"That's harsh."

He shrugged.

"I said before that you should leave him alone, and I meant it. Victor's been through a lot. Jail, then coming out into a world that thinks the worst of him and trying to fit back in. That isn't easy for anyone. And now he's involved in this case, and it's gotten out of control." He sighed. "It's too much for him, Ingola. If you really cared about him, you'd back off."

"You're a fine one to talk!" Her tone was edgy. "You ever wonder why everyone was so ready to believe that Victor was guilty? No one forgot that he'd been investigated before."

"I'd be careful what you say."

She stood up, facing Tully, not in the least intimidated. "You were responsible for that."

"What I did—"

"Was unforgivable," she snapped. "It's a bit rich all this coming from you, Tully—like you're above reproach! You're hardly the one to tell me what I should or shouldn't do."

"It was a mistake."

"You were careless with Victor," she retorted, white-faced. "You risked him. You wanted his help."

"We were friends. I would have done anything for him."

"Only Victor never asked anything of you, did he? You did all the asking. I remember it all very well. You were in the mire then, Tully, so deep in debt with your bloody gambling that it didn't matter how you paid the debtors off, just that you did. If you ever suspected that bloody painting wasn't genuine, I doubt you allowed yourself to think about it for too long."

"I never suspected it was a fake!"

"Maybe you didn't. But you knew that by getting *Victor Ballam* to organize a sale, no one would question it. He was *that* important, that influential. That vulnerable."

"I didn't destroy Victor, Ingola."

She clenched her hands to calm herself.

"No, you didn't destroy him; *you* didn't frame him for the later forgeries—but you planted the seed that corrupted his reputation and first opened him to suspicion. *You* did that, Tully, and I'll never forgive you."

He was enraged, his face red with anger. "I didn't mean it! Victor knew that. He understood."

"Well, he might have, but I never did."

Tully turned away from her, poured two glasses of wine, and held one out to her. She hesitated before taking it but did, then regained her seat by the window.

"Well, my darling," he began quietly. "You must feel a whole lot better now to have gotten all that off your chest. Nothing like pointing out someone else's shortcomings to make a person feel righteous. 'Your sin was bigger than mine.'" He sneered, uncharacteristically savage. "Yes, it bloody was, but I didn't *intend* to get Victor into trouble. You do."

"What the hell!"

"What I did was out of ignorance, stupidity. Not malice."

"You think I wish Victor ill?"

"You don't wish him well," Tully replied. "You can't face up to facts, Ingola; you never could. You were always ready to let someone else sort out your life for you. You're lazy and too quick to change sides. You came to England and needed to stay. How convenient to fall for a British citizen."

"I loved Victor!"

"I'm sure you did, my dear, but perhaps you fell in love more readily because it suited you."

Her face was waxen. "You bastard!"

"I see you for what you are, Ingola. Victor fell in love with you, and that blinded him. But me? No; I know what you're like—*you* come first. Always have and always will. It was all planned out, wasn't it? You two were going to have it all. You'd be a respected lawyer and Victor a revered art dealer. What a couple; what a lovely, pretty, witty couple to dazzle the dining tables of London." He lifted his glass to her in a fake salutation. "But then Victor was framed by the world he'd conquered. Silenced, shunted out of the limelight, and made into a criminal." He took a sip of his wine, his mouth dry. "It was *not* because of my bloody pseudo-Stubbs."

"People remembered that Victor had championed that painting."

"Dealers champion paintings every day that turn out to be fakes! If Victor hadn't been so bloody successful, no one would have remembered. Or if they had, they would have put it down to a mistake. But they remembered because they didn't want to believe that Victor Ballam had been an innocent party. No, it suited them to see it as a precursor to the monumental fraud which followed." He paused, looking at Ingola with unconcealed contempt. "You sit there and you judge me. Well, look in the mirror, my dear, and see yourself for what *you* really are."

"I have a clear conscience."

"Well, if you do, then you've got a bloody short memory."

Her head snapped up. "What's that supposed to mean?"

"You chose not to stand by Victor because your career was more important. That's how much he really meant to you. Nothing could be allowed to tarnish the stardust. Easier to marry and fuck the brother than risk failure."

Immediately she was on her feet, hands on hips, angry and shrill. "Now look here—"

"No, *you* look here," Tully replied, cutting her off. "You might have fooled Victor, and you certainly fool Christian—the poor sap—but not me. I've watched your machinations, perhaps even admired them at times. I could understand your desire to secure yourself. But now you come back and you tell me you love Victor Ballam. No. You're lying."

"How do you know what I feel?"

"Because I *know* you! I've known you for many years now. I've watched you, listened to you, seen how you work. And now you've decided that your life isn't quite how you want it, but you want what you *can't have*."

"Tully, listen—"

"No, I've heard enough lies. *You* listen now, Ingola. You want Victor because it's a challenge. Bugger Christian and what he's done for you. Sod everyone else. You're quite prepared to take advantage of someone on their uppers just to give you a thrill, to see if you can win him back. And worse, you think you can manipulate me." He laughed, the sound musical. "Well, think again, darling."

"I don't expect anything from you."

"So why are you here? I'll tell you why: because I'm close to Victor. You want me to collude with you, my dear. Want me to encourage you, smooth your path, make your life pretty again." His tone hardened. "I imagine you thought that you could get me to intercede with Victor on your behalf." He paused. "And you know what I say to that? Fuck you. *Fuck you, Ingola.*"

She slapped him hard, and Tully lost his grip on the wineglass. It crashed to the floor, and without comment he bent down and picked up the pieces, taking them over to the wastebasket and dropping them in.

"What a shame. I had a set of six of those glasses, inherited from my parents."

"Along with the fake Stubbs, I suppose."

"Go back to Worcestershire, darling," Tully said, his tone bored. "Go home and forget the past."

"I'm not giving up. I love Victor, and Victor loves me."

"I warn you, Ingola; go home. I promise I'll personally do everything I can to keep you away from Victor and out of his life forever." He smiled his wide theatrical smile. "Back off or I'll tell him what he already suspects—that you and I had an affair."

She flinched.

"You see, Victor knows about the Stubbs, knows I used him there. He knows that. But he doesn't know, he only *suspects*, that there was once something between us."

"It was a mistake!"

"You can say that again," Tully replied drily. "You wanted a safe father figure when you came to London, Ingola, and I was the perfect choice, a handy stopgap until you found someone your own age. I don't blame myself for the affair, I blame myself that I let it continue after you'd met Victor. I blame myself for being an old fool. For being flattered and letting my ego get in the way of my loyalty. You're right that I owe Victor Ballam. I do. But the difference between us is that I know I owe him, and I'll spend the rest of my life trying to make it up to him."

Something troubles me so much that I am writing it down to try to clarify my own thoughts. Maybe my imagination is moving from the canvas to real life to such an extent that I can no longer tell the difference. I pray it is so.

It is 1750 now, and Hal thrives at the Foundling Hospital. He grows very tall and has become a favourite of Thomas Coram's. I warn him not to make too much of Hal, but I know he does in secret. Discreetly spoiling a special child. For he is that, a special child. Thank God, Thomas has never been a foolish man. Not like me. I have been foolish many times. Privately and publicly. Outspoken, too quick with my opinions, criticisms, and dislikes. I would have gone further had I tempered my tongue.

But lately I had a fancy I could not resist. A whimsy, if you please. In my studio now is a portrait, newly finished. It goes until the title of Hogarth's Servants, supposedly painted as a reward for their loyalty and as a permanent remembrance of them. It is an image of good and honest people who have served me and my family well. What could be more normal for a painter than to depict the people around him?

But the sitters will never see the work, because seeing it would provoke curiosity and questions. The painting is only a reminder to me, a judicious homage to someone absent, as close as my servants but closer to my heart.

We do have a stable boy, but this lad in the painting is not he. I have not been so reckless as before. No direct depiction, as of the Prince of Wales which cost me so dear and caused poor Polly's death. No, this stable boy's image is not accurate. In reality, he is now older. No more the child that gazes out of the painting but a young man of eighteen. A farrier. Thomas Coram's favourite. The child I saved. Polly Gunnell's infant. The hidden heir.

I look at the picture—how often I forget, but many times—and see him how he was almost ten years ago. I look at the image and know that no one will recognise him because he is grown. Only I know him. Because I was present throughout his past.

And yet. And yet.

There was a storm last Tuesday night. Hailstones big as mushrooms came down and broke some windows in the Mall. Looking out, you could see the hail bouncing off the cobbles under a clamouring, portentous sky. As the storm continued a servant came to my studio and said I had a visitor.

"In such inclement weather?"

"He's waiting to see you, sir."

"His name?"

"Sir Nathaniel Overton."

He came into the studio with his coat marked from the hailstones. Taking it from him, I hung it over the back of one of the chairs and turned it to the fire to dry. My hands were shaking. As I moved back to this most unholy of men, I caught sight of the painting on the wall behind him. The painting of the stable boy who never was.

We had some little talk of the villain, Kent, my rival who had undermined me so effectively at Court. But as he spoke, Overton's sloe eyes examined my room. They rested infinitesimally on the half-finished portrait of Paul before Felix, and I fancied a stoat's smile crossed his mouth at the likeness of the dog, Vulcan.

Outside the hailstones still drummed their devil's fingers on the gutters and, no doubt, were making many a whore run for cover. I could imagine only too easily how the torch bearers would duck into the doorways or under the archways of the mews houses, their fire smoky from the damp air. And along the dark run of the Thames, the water would shudder with the impact of a million hailstones, their imprint making bubbles on an unsuspecting tide.

Then, as quick as it had begun, the storm ended. Nathaniel Overton turned his courtier's eyes on me, and—I admit it—I felt a chill go through me. Slowly he moved over to the painting of my servants, then paused. His coat was steaming in front of the grate, the brass buttons fireflies in the evening light, the pockets gaping like the mouths of martyrs.

And then he left.

Do you see why I am so troubled?

Why would a man as powerful as he come by, in such inclement weather, to pass the time of day about the scoundrel Kent? Was there more to the visit? Or was Overton perhaps just taking cover? Finding himself near to my door, was it merely sanctuary he sought? Or was there something else? As he stood in front of the painting of my servants, could he see in the stable boy's features a shadow of an old and dreadful crime? Did something prompt him, remind him of a murder many years before?

Did he see a living child surviving what he had hoped was a corpse's end? God, I pray not.

When I helped him back on with his coat, its wool was warmed from the fire, but a terrible coldness came off Overton himself. He had, as I always suspected, something of the charnel house about him. His aura spoke of ill-done deeds, of vengeance, plots, and questionable loyalties. And as I reached to put the coat around his shoulders, I felt—I tremble as I write it—that I was dresser to a devil.

Pray God he will not come again.

Fifty-One

BACK IN HIS APARTMENT, VICTOR CHECKED HIS MAIL AND HIS answering machine. Without realizing he wanted it, he was hoping for a message from Ingola, and for a long moment his hand paused over the "*Play Message*" button. But he didn't press it, didn't want to hear her voice. Or, worse, *not* hear it. . . . Confused, he sat down, switching on the table lamp next to him, bringing the apartment into focus. He no longer liked the place, not because he had signed it over to Christian—he knew he could get it back at any time—but because the man who once had lived there no longer existed. And he missed him the way he would have missed a brother, a friend, a companion. He missed himself.

Victor had tried to prepare for the difficulty of returning to everyday life, but he hadn't allowed for the fact that his life had never been everyday. He had been a master in his world. Top-billed, not a member of the chorus. His life had consisted of solos, virtuoso performances; his opinion was sought, his criticism feared. After his public disgrace, Victor Ballam could never slide back into the opera box of his life. Even the stalls were now too good for him; he would be lucky to get a peek in at the stage door.

His innocence no longer mattered, because no one believed it. The art world—except for Sir Oliver Peters—had deemed him a fraud, and the people he now mixed with, the likes of Charlene Fleet and Dr. Eli Fountain— wouldn't care whether he was a criminal. Perhaps, Victor thought bitterly, he might have greater currency in their eyes if he was a crook. Caught between the cherished world that had crucified him and the *demimonde* he hardly understood, Victor found himself disembodied, flying at half mast.

Finally pressing the answering machine, he found two earlier messages from Liza Frith, who sounded unnerved and jumpy, and one from Malcolm Jenner asking Victor to call. Apparently he had remembered something that might have been important and wanted to talk about it.

Jenner's admission that Annette Dvorski was his niece had thrown Victor. Was it true? If so, perhaps that fact cleared him as a suspect. But now Victor wasn't so sure. Perhaps, for all his apparent grief, Jenner had been merely acting. Maybe he had double-crossed his own niece, killed Annette to get the painting. After all, he knew Mrs. Fleet and had colluded with her in duping the police. Perhaps they had been working together for a while. But the more he thought about it, the more Victor doubted that Malcolm Jenner was lying. He was a hard case, certainly on the make, but no killer. That made Victor very curious to hear what he had to say now.

He dialed the number Jenner had left on the answering machine.

"Hello?"

"Mr. Jenner, it's Victor Ballam. You left a message for me."

"Yeah, I did. I remembered something. It might be important."

"Go on."

"No, not over the phone. Can you meet me later?"

"Where?"

Victor scribbled the address on the back of an envelope, frowning. "Why there?"

"I want to show you something. Something you need to see. Come at ten-thirty." Jenner rang off.

Putting down the phone, Victor stared at the address. He remembered what he had been told by Tully and remembered what had happened to Lim Chang. He wondered not for the first time if he was walking into a trap. And then realized that he had no choice.

Fifty-Two

HAVING JUST LANDED AT HEATHROW AFTER A FLIGHT FROM LOS Angeles, John Yates was surprised to find a very flustered Duncan Fairfax waiting for him at the airport. He looked flushed and out of place without his glossy pilot's uniform. His girth was obvious, with the tweed jacket and corduroy trousers he was wearing emphasizing his weight gain. Too much rich food, Yates thought to himself, making a mental note not to let himself go to seed.

"I want a word with you," Fairfax began, his tone abrupt.

Yates wasn't about to let his irritation show. He had learned early on that the blessing of a bland appearance meant that people seldom treated you with awe. And hardly ever remembered you. In his teens he had resented his nonidentity, but as he entered his late twenties, John Yates saw the positive side. People were not intimidated by him, which meant that he didn't inspire the jealousy that was the undoing of many charismatic men. His ordinariness worked with women too. They felt safe. Not excited or driven to sexual excess but safe. And John Yates slowly learned that he could get enough sex if he kept playing safe. The women mothered him. Their parents accepted him. Dogs and cats liked him. And the passengers never remembered his face but trusted the uniform he wore.

And so, hidden under this undistinguished exterior, John Yates steadily climbed the ladder to success. As a pilot he was unremarkable but had a steady pair of hands. No tantrums, no dangerous antics. As surely as the tide leaves the sand, he rose in the ranks. Until finally he became the copilot on Bernie Freeland's private jet. For a man no one envied, he was remarkably well rewarded.

But now Duncan Fairfax was hollering at him, and instead of telling him to get lost, John Yates did what he did best: he calmed him down.

"What's the matter?"

"What's the bloody *matter?*" Fairfax hissed. "You've got a big mouth; that's what."

No, thought Yates; that's one thing I haven't got.

"I don't understand. What am I supposed to have said?"

Grabbing his copilot's arm, Fairfax swerved him across the concourse and into a private room away from the departure lounge where they couldn't be overheard. Anger did little for his coloring; his skin became mottled with rage.

"You've been talking."

"To who?"

"Don't think I don't know."

"About *what*?"

"You bloody fool!" Fairfax went on, loosening his tie and leaning against the wall. "I had some man called Tully Harcourt asking me questions about Bernie Freeland's last flight. He also said that he'd already talked to the stewards."

"About what?"

"The girl who died. And the other people who were on the plane. *And me!*" Fairfax snorted. "He seemed to know a lot about me. Things no one else should know. Things I thought no one else *did* know. But I was wrong." He pulled his collar even slacker. "He talked to you; I see that now. Bloody Freeland lied. He promised that he wouldn't say anything."

"I really don't understand," said Yates, bewildered.

"You do! You understand it all well enough." Fairfax's eyes were bulging slightly. "You fucking creep, sniffing around. I know your type. Mr. Nice Guy. Never offend but stab anyone in the back to get what you want."

Exasperated and angry, John Yates turned to go, but Fairfax grabbed his arm to stop him.

"You can't just walk off! What did you tell Harcourt, hey? That Freeland was firing me? Was that it? That Freeland was about to put me out to graze and take you on as his first in command?"

Baffled, John Yates put up his hands. "Hold on!"

"*Hold on!*" Fairfax hissed. "I've been holding on for years. You think I'm going to let some little shit like you blacken my name and wreck my chances with Ahmed Fatida?"

"Look here, Fairfax; I don't know what you're talking about," Yates said firmly. "I haven't spoken to someone called Harcourt, and I haven't discussed you with anyone."

Fairfax blinked. "You haven't?

"No. After the Freeland flight I went home. The day afterward I had a vacation booked, and that's where I've been until now. Today's my first day back at work." He paused, sensible to a fault. "I've never even heard of anyone called Harcourt. And Mr. Freeland never said anything about firing you."

Feeling suddenly foolish, Duncan Fairfax paused, smoothing his hair and refastening his tie. No one was threatening his glossy life. No one was going to upset his jet-set image. No one. He had just overreacted, panicked at the thought of being demoted to a commercial airline or, worse, retired, his status over, his power ended.

Relaxing slowly, he glanced back to John Yates.

"I'm . . . I'm very sorry. I've been very worried about my wife lately. Well, anyway, I've been getting things a little out of proportion." He tapped Yates's arm in a mock paternal gesture. He tried a smile, Yates returning it. "I apologize; please forget what I said."

"Already forgotten, sir."

"I'll put in a good word for you where I can."

"Thank you, sir, but I'm already organized."

Duncan could feel his throat tighten. "Really? You're joining a commercial airline?"

"No, I'm working for an entrepreneur."

"You didn't waste any time, did you?"

"I was very lucky; just fell into the position."

Fairfax's tone was poisonous. "Just *fell in*?"

"As you always told me, sir, contacts are everything."

Fifty-Three

HEARING THE DOOR BELL RING THREE TIMES, LIZA WENT TO THE window and peeked through the gap in the curtain. With relief she saw Victor Ballam standing there, his expression tense as he spoke on his cell phone. He rang off just as Liza opened the door.

"Hi," she said, standing back and letting him in. "You got my messages?"

"You sounded worried." He followed her to the kitchen.

Still unsure of where everything was kept, Liza opened two cupboard doors before she found the coffee, then put some water on to boil. She was aware that she found Victor attractive and was surprised to find herself nervous. The clients never made her feel nervous. Special, sometimes. Cheap, sometimes. Needed, always. But nervous? Never.

"Sugar?"

"Yeah, two. Thanks."

Smiling, she added the sugar and handed him the mug, walking with him into the living room and sitting down on the sofa beside him. The collar of his jacket was slightly bunched up, and for a moment she wanted to reach out and smooth it down but resisted the urge. He wasn't a john.

"What happened?"

"I did something stupid," she admitted. "I got lonely and went next door."

His face set. "I thought we agreed that you'd stay in."

"I'm sorry! But I just got so bored, and the food smelled so good." Liza smiled her child's smile. "This woman came over with her little girl, looking for their cat, and she invited me to eat with them. She seemed so innocent and cheerful, so I went next door with them."

She could see that Victor was incensed and confided nothing else. Instead she remembered the Chinese man in the apartment next door and what he had told her. *Say nothing about me; keep quiet—or Victor Ballam will pay for it.* So she kept silent about the stranger who had sat down to the meal with them, said nothing about how much he had frightened her.

Instead she changed the subject. "You want some food?"

"Liza, you *have* to stay in the flat."

"I just—"

"You're in danger," he said insistently. "Don't you get it, Liza? There are four dead people from your flight. Doesn't that mean anything to you?"

She pushed back her hair with her hands.

"Yes! It was just that the woman seemed so—"

"I'll bring some more food tomorrow," Victor said shortly, cutting her off. "In the meantime don't open the door to anyone. Don't go out. Don't answer the phone. I'll use your cell phone if I want to call you. You have to take this seriously."

"Jesus! I ran away from Ma Fleet's because I was scared. I've been scared ever since that flight, so don't tell me to take this seriously!" She shouted; then, her voice plummeting, her head dropping onto her drawn-up knees, she said, "I knew those girls, Victor. I cared about Annette. I knew them both, worked with them both. You think I want to be next?" She lifted her head, her eyes teary. "I admit I went out. I'm sorry, I went out, I'm sorry. Sorry!" she repeated. "I'm stuck here with no one to talk to and wondering every minute if someone will get to me. I went next door because I couldn't stand it here. I went out because I couldn't listen to my own thoughts a minute longer."

He reached out and touched her arm, and she turned, leaning against him, her head on his shoulder, crying. Surprised, Victor hesitated, then cradled her. Her arms were slim, the skin warm, her hair hiding her face. If he closed his eyes, he knew he would be able to imagine another woman in another time. If he allowed himself, he could pretend he was holding Ingola again. If he wanted, he could be the man he once had been. Loved, desired, admired. If he was prepared to, he could have sex with this woman while he was in reality making love to a ghost. He could even forget for a short time that she was a whore and he was a crook.

But he couldn't do it.

Instead he held Liza Frith until she stopped crying and the evening faded into darkness. Through the basement window came the light from the street lamp on the road overhead. It was dim, but it was enough. Still holding Liza, Victor fixed his eyes on the clock on the opposite wall. It was eight-thirty. At ten-thirty he would be meeting with Malcolm Jenner. He would hear what the steward had to say.

He didn't know what it would be. But at ten-thirty he would find out the truth. Or die for it.

Part five

SITTING BY HER SON'S HOSPITAL BED, ELIZABETH WILKES LOOKED UP as Dr. Fountain entered. She had always disliked Fountain, remembered him from the days she had worked as a call girl and also remembered with embarrassment the monthly examinations. However she presented herself to the world, in Fountain's eyes she would always be a prostitute, a hooker, a working girl. Years might have passed, but something in his expression always reminded her of what he knew, and he made her flesh creep.

For a while Elizabeth had expected him to use her past against her, perhaps expose her. After all, it would have made a meaty piece for the tabloids if Kit Wilkes, always tormenting his illustrious father, turned out to have a whore for a mother. But time passed, and Fountain never played his trump card, settling for Kit as a patient instead. Perhaps, Elizabeth thought, it wouldn't be worth jeopardizing his working relationship with her sister. God knows, Charlene Fleet had been lining the doctor's wide white pockets for many years.

Bitterly, Elizabeth thought of her sister, of the time when they had been growing up. Charlene was not Mrs. Fleet then, just some backstreet scrubber who would give it to the lads free until she realized charging was the way to go. It had taken guts for her sister to come down to London alone, but then, she had always longed to leave Scotland Road behind.

So, with very little money and an old Mini, she had come to the capital. With a lack of morals and a bulletproof conscience, Charlene had started working for another madam, who never realized that within ten years she would be usurped, that Charlene—aka Mrs. Fleet—would take over Park Street. The woman died in a fall from the roof of the top-floor apartment. The coroner said it was an accidental death.

Elizabeth had never been sure of that verdict. The incident had made her wary around her sister, and like all the others who worked for Mrs. Fleet, she had been afraid of her. But Elizabeth hadn't been ready to move on. She was greedy and was making good money, and besides, she had told herself, her sister would never hurt her. Elizabeth sighed as she looked at her son. His eyelids were so fine that she could see the blood vessels under the skin. God, he couldn't die, she thought desperately. Kit was everything to her. She had lived for him, even challenged her sister on his behalf a long time ago. She had gone to Charlene and told her she was pregnant. Mrs. Fleet, unmoved, had insisted on an abortion, but Elizabeth had been adamant. She wanted the child.

"Jesus, what the hell for?"

"I want out of the business," Elizabeth had replied. "I've had enough."

"And how are you going to live?"

"I've saved some money."

"That won't last long the way you spend it," Mrs. Fleet had responded. "Get rid of the kid and get back to work."

"I could talk to the father."

Oh, how Mrs. Fleet had responded to *that* suggestion! Her eyes flint-cold, she had turned on her sister. "You know that none of my girls is supposed to get pregnant. If they do, they deal with it. They don't go and put pressure on the client." She had walked up to Elizabeth and pointed at her belly. "Blackmail would ruin my business. The client would tell others, and it would all be over."

"Not if he wanted to keep it quiet himself."

Mrs. Fleet had put her hands on her hips, her head on one side. "So who is this client? This soft target?"

"Bernie Freeland."

Laughing out loud, Mrs. Fleet had sat down at her desk, toying with the gold chain around her neck as she looked at her sister.

"Oh, you bloody fool. Only you would get knocked up by Bernie Freeland. Go on, expose him; it would only add to his reputation." She stopped laughing abruptly. "I always was the brains in our family, wasn't I?" she said.

Stung, Elizabeth had retaliated without thinking.

"*Our family*? Perhaps people would like to know about our family. It would be interesting but very bad for your business, Charlene. Think of it; all your secrets that only I know laid out for the world to see. Even for a madam, you'd be ruined." She had openly mocked her. "Mrs. Fleet, who was once

Charlene O'Dywer, fucking the boys for a few bob, blow jobs a specialty on the top deck of the bus."

Elizabeth had gone too far. She knew it, but she couldn't stop. Seeing that Charlene was shaken, knowing that she had dented her absolute confidence, had driven her on.

"And then there was the time you hurt that child."

The words had slapped down between them, but Mrs. Fleet shrugged, feigning indifference.

"She was fourteen. Hardly a child."

"She was a child! Oh, you got that hushed up, didn't you, Charlene? Who did you talk to? Oh, I remember; you were friendly with someone in the police, weren't you? Poor girl; she was sent away, wasn't she? And then it all blew over. Of course I *could* get someone to look into it again, what with my having insider information."

And then it had happened, a silent shift in the atmosphere. Suddenly Elizabeth had the upper hand, and Charlene knew it. Her one mistake had been to keep her sister close to her. At first she had done it to protect herself, but now she realized that Elizabeth was the only person who could hold her to ransom. The only person who knew everything about her past.

"You said that Bernie Freeland's the father?"

"Yeah."

"But you've been fucking others," Mrs. Fleet had gone on, thinking quickly. "We need someone who's terrified of scandal. Someone who would do anything to keep his name out of the mire." She stopped to think, then turned back to her sister. "James Holden's one of your regulars, isn't he?"

Nodding, Elizabeth had tried to follow her sister's reasoning. "What about him?"

"Tell him you're pregnant with his kid."

"But you don't approve of blackmail."

"It's the lesser of two evils, Elizabeth. It's him being blackmailed or it's me. There's no choice." She had gone on, merciless. "James Holden wants to be prime minister one day. He's married to a country squire's daughter, and he's really desperate for advancement. He'd pay to keep you quiet, and if you're clever, you could make it last for years."

"But what if he tells other people?"

"He won't. He wouldn't dare! He's one of the few clients who don't mix in the art world. Holden is all politics, so even if he did talk—which he won't—it wouldn't harm my business."

Elizabeth absorbed this in silence for a minute or two, then slowly said, "All right, I'll have a word with him."

Mrs. Fleet had sighed, then smiled her brittle smile. "Actually, *I'll* talk to James Holden and arrange everything, Elizabeth. You could bugger it up."

Surprised, Elizabeth had nodded, trying to undo some of the damage. "Look, I didn't mean—"

"What?"

"About your past."

"You lying bitch; you meant every word. Remember, we're family, and I know what you're capable of. But I want you to remember one thing: I'm only halfway up the ladder, but soon I'll be untouchable, and no one—not even you—will be able to harm me." Her eyes had bored into her sister. "This is the last time you get one over on me, Elizabeth. Enjoy your moment of triumph, because it will be the last you'll ever have."

Fifty-Five

WATCHING HER SON AS SHE REMEMBERED THE ALTERCATION surrounding his birth, Elizabeth shuddered. If Kit died, it would be the end of the gravy train with James Holden. So if Kit died, not only would she be alone, she would be poor.

You're working late," she said to Dr. Fountain, attempting to keep the hostility out of her voice.

"I have to see all my patients whatever the time."

"No point missing out on a fee."

"Well, honey, *you* never did," he said, neatly reversing the insult.

"I want to ask you something," Elizabeth said, swallowing the loathing she felt for him as much as she ever had. "Were you here when my son was brought in?"

His taut skin hardly moved with his almost imperceptible smile. "I was, Elizabeth."

"And James Holden was here too?"

"He was. For a short time. When Kit was admitted, he left."

"Was Kit already unconscious?"

Fountain held Kit's limp wrist and timed his pulse. "He'd taken an overdose."

"Was he unconscious?"

"He was," the doctor replied. "Poor boy. I was hoping he'd have pulled around by now. Sorry, my dear."

"I'm not your *dear*." She kept her voice low so no one would overhear them. "Sitting here, I've had a lot of time to think, and something's bothering me."

"Yes? And what might that be?"

"I heard about a painting." She noticed a flicker, a slight change in the doctor's expression. "Well, I didn't pay much attention at first," she went on. "After all, Kit deals in pictures, but apparently someone found a rare Hogarth, and oddly enough—you'll like this, Doctor Fountain; I know you have a taste for the macabre—everyone who knew about it has been killed."

She paused. "I don't believe in coincidence, Doctor, and seeing as how Bernie Freeland is dead—along with three people who were on that flight where the painting was mentioned—and seeing as how my son was there too and lapsed into a coma soon afterward . . . Now, what would you say to that?"

"It sounds amazing, but I haven't read anything about it in the papers. It hasn't been in the news."

"The police don't know about the painting."

"Why not? If it was so suspicious, I feel sure it would have been investigated."

Outmaneuvered, Elizabeth took a moment to gather her thoughts, but the run-in with her sister coupled with her imminent penury had sharpened her wits overnight.

"Perhaps people wanted to keep the deaths quiet."

"Four violent deaths? Honey, it would have to be a war to keep that quiet," he replied smoothly. "I think your imagination's running away with you."

"D'you know anything about this painting?"

He shrugged and laid Kit's arm back on the bed. "I'm a doctor, not an art dealer."

"But there *has* to be a connection if all the people on that flight are dying."

"Kit took an accidental overdose."

She shook her head. "He never injected himself. He's squeamish about needles."

"Kit is squeamish about many things," Fountain replied. He picked up his patient's chart and pretended to read it while trying to decide how much Elizabeth knew. Not much, he realized after another moment, or she wouldn't be pumping him for information.

"Who brought my son to the hospital?"

"I don't know who accompanied him, but when Kit was brought in, I was called. When I got here, his boyfriend and his father were here with him."

Irritated that she had learned nothing of importance, Elizabeth slowly rose to her feet and wrapped her fur coat around her. "Why wasn't his stomach pumped?"

"It wouldn't have helped. Kit didn't swallow anything."

"So that's it?" she said, her tone wavering. "He's just going to lie there and slip away? *He's in a coma!* Can't you do anything?"

"I'm doing what I can, but no one can work miracles, Elizabeth. Kit experimented. You should know that when the mood moves them, people will try *anything* once."

His inference embarrassed her. "But why *then*? Why just after a long flight?"

"Maybe he was glad to be home."

"No! Something's going on," Elizabeth, protested, her voice rising as she stared helplessly at her son.

"You really think so?" Dr.Fountain shrugged. "I don't. After all, if there was some kind of conspiracy, your boy would be dead already."

Fifty-six

VICTOR WOULD RATHER HAVE BEEN ANYWHERE ELSE.

As Malcolm Jenner drove him into the countryside and parked outside a large makeshift tarpaulin tent, he could feel the hairs on the back of his neck rise at the sound of dogs barking. He even thought for an instant that he was going to suffer the fate of Lim Chang. Jenner turned off the engine and drummed his fingers impatiently on the steering wheel. In the distance, pungent smoke rose from a hidden fire and headlights beamed from other cars swinging onto the dirt track and parking close by.

In prison Victor had never come across the brutality he had witnessed lately. Although living among violent men, he had escaped the sheer terror he was experiencing now. After all, Victor thought, who knew where he was? In a valiant attempt to protect Tully by giving him at least the advantage of ignorance, he hadn't told his ally where he was going or who he was meeting. But now Victor realized he was completely alone and at the mercy of some man he didn't really know in a place he didn't want to be.

"Why here?" he said at last.

Jenner, his eyes shadowed behind his glasses, turned to him. "I want you to meet someone; well, actually, he asked to meet you. He'll be here at eleven," he said, and changed the subject. "You know that my wife runs dogs. I never had much of a liking for it, but you can get used to pretty much anything if it's lucrative. Even the brutality—you get used to that too. I make a good living on the bets." He paused as though he was about to apologize but went on. "The bettors are all types. Londoners, tourists—"

"Tourists?"

"Yeah, tourists. You think it's all the Tower of London and Madam Tussauds? People like what they get at home or *can't* get at home. They live in places where badger baiting and dogfighting are banned, so they come here for their fix. The police might bang on about the Dangerous Dogs Act, but believe me, the breeders keep it quiet and the numbers of dogs are rising. For years my wife and I have been breeding game dogs."

"What d'you mean, game dogs?"

"You look in something like *Exchange and Mart*, Mr. Ballam, under the For Sale listings. When it describes a dog as '*game*,' it means it's been fighting. Might be a starter, a junior, or a veteran, but it's trained. They start some of them with badger baiting." He leaned down and pulled out a small metal glovelike object from under the seat and tapped it on the dashboard. "You use this to dig into a badger hole to give the dog enough room to get down there and attack. Or you trap the badger and then set the dog on it in the ring." He paused, turning away. "Some people break the badger's legs first so it's not a fair fight and it can't hurt the dog."

Victor couldn't keep the disgust out of his voice. "And you do this for a living?"

"I don't mutilate the badgers first. I've got some morals." He seemed unaware of the fatuousness of his remark.

Victor stared out of the window as more cars started to arrive. He had no idea what was in store for him and was already trying to plan an escape. He spotted a copse of trees in the distance, but with dogs after him, what chance would he have?

"You know Mrs. Fleet, don't you?" he said.

"Maybe," Jenner replied. "Why?"

"I was just wondering how well you knew her. I mean, she was your niece's madam, and you were prepared to lie to the police for her." He paused, trying to read the other man's expression. "*Do* you know her well?"

He laughed. "Charlene Fleet? All I know about her is that she gave me a lot of money to lie. I don't like the police, and it was no skin off my nose to forget there were dealers or johns on the flight."

"But you knew she was Annette's employer?"

"Yeah. So what? Everyone knows everyone. The dealers, the whores, the pilots. It's a small world."

Victor changed tack. "Tell me about your niece."

"Annette was my sister's kid," Jenner said, lighting a cigarette. "Her father was Polish, but he didn't stick around long, didn't like England. Or maybe he didn't like my sister; she was a miserable bitch."

"How old was Annette when her father left?"

"Thirteen. Already a right handful and always after the lads." He shrugged. "After the split, Annette went to live with her mother, and we didn't see each other for a long time, but I'd been working for Mr. Freeland for a while. Got to know him at one of our meets."

"I'm surprised that Bernie Freeland was into dogfighting."

"He was into everything and anything. Turns some people's stomachs. Annette could never stand it, and that wanker Duncan Fairfax."

"*Fairfax?*"

Jenner nodded. "He couldn't take the blood or the fighting. Puked outside the tent the first time he came here, but he liked the betting. Tried to keep it quiet, but I saw him talking to the Chinese and the Irish. Now, they're a rough lot, the Irish; take their dogs very seriously."

Victor pulled him back to the subject of his niece. "What about Annette? How did you meet up with her again?"

"Like I said, I'd met Freeland. He took to me and hired me. Knew I was a hard man, and I reckon he liked the idea of having someone like that around. I loved the idea. It was a great job, and it got me away from home. Then one day this familiar face appears on Freeland's jet." He laughed hoarsely. "Jesus, you could have knocked me over with a breath! When Annette saw me, she winked, bold as brass, but it took me aback, I can tell you, knowing what she was up to in the private cabin. I mean, I've got nothing against johns, but my own niece. . . . Later we talked, and she said she'd been working as a call girl for about a year."

"She wasn't bothered that you knew?"

"For someone who's been in jail, Mr. Ballam, you're bloody naive," Jenner said, amused. "I used to see Annette quite a lot. She was always generous, used to pass on all kinds of things. Money, horse-racing tips, presents from Mr. Freeland."

"And after the last trip your niece told you she had a plan?"

He nodded. "To steal a painting. Annette was greedy. She saw Bernie Freeland as her meal ticket, but she also wanted a nest egg of her own."

"Did you know who the artist was?"

"She told me, but I didn't remember." He flicked his ash out the window and stared into the side mirror.

The cigarette smoke was thick inside the car, a gray vapor, noxious and cloying in Victor's throat. He looked at the digital clock on the dashboard; only seven minutes to wait for whoever he was supposed to meet at eleven. Whatever was supposed to happen would happen in a matter of minutes.

Chilled, Victor turned up the collar of his coat and hunkered down in the seat. He could smell the scent of dogs wafting over from the back of the car and watched a couple of men pass by, nodding a greeting to Jenner. All at once, Victor knew that he was out of his depth without a lifebelt—without even a reed—to cling to; he had taken on an investigation whose roots extended farther and clung more urgently every time he disturbed the water. At any moment he could be dragged under, and no one would ever know what had happened to him. He was a long way out of London, in the countryside. After the fights were over, how many dead dogs would be dumped in shallow graves and forgotten?

And what was to stop a man from being buried with them?

Apprehensive, Victor turned back to Jenner. "What was Annette's plan?"

"Like I told you before, she was going to get this painting off Mr. Freeland and sell it for a fortune."

"It didn't worry you that she was stealing off Bernie Freeland?"

"Freeland was my employer; Annette was my niece. Whose side would you be on? She had loads of contacts, said it would be easy because the picture was painted by a famous artist. She said she'd get off the game and I could retire."

"Did she say *how* she was going to get hold of the painting?"

He raised his eyebrows. "Use your imagination, Mr. Ballam."

"But she didn't get hold of it, did she?"

"Nah," Jenner replied dully. "But Annette was determined. She was going to meet up with Mr. Freeland in New York. She was sure she could get it, but then she heard about Marian Miller being murdered and got spooked."

"She thought she was in danger?"

"Well," Jenner said evenly, "she was, wasn't she?"

Thoughtful, Victor turned his eyes back to the clock. Five minutes.

"And you never heard from your niece again?"

"Nah. She gave me her cell phone and told me to keep it and said that she'd call me on it, but she didn't. That Liza Frith girl did, but not Annette." He paused, glancing into the rearview mirror. "Looks like we've got company."

Tensing, Victor watched as two Chinese men walked up to the car. Jenner rolled down his window to talk to them. Both men were unknown to Victor, but as one of them rested his hand on the edge of the window, he noticed the man had long spatulate fingernails.

"He wants a word with you," Jenner said, turning to Victor. "Go on, get out."

"Who is he?"

Smiling ruefully, Jenner shook his head. "Look, I was just asked to bring you here. That's all they told me."

Reluctantly, Victor got out of the car. At once the first man made a gesture to his companion and then stepped back. Jenner folded his arms and watched from the sidelines.

"You wanted to see me?"

The man nodded. "You're after the Hogarth, aren't you?"

"Have you got it?"

"We *had* it."

"Did you take it from Lim Chang?"

The men exchanged a glance, and the younger of the two came forward. His eyes were pink and swollen, the skin around them inflamed. Slowly he tipped back his head and put a couple of drops into each eye, blinking slowly before he turned back to Victor.

"I want the Hogarth."

"*I* don't have it."

"I believe you," the man said, rubbing his left eye fitfully. "But I want you to find it and give it back to *me*."

"Why would I do that?"

"You know what's going on. You were hired to find out what happened on that flight." The man looked to Jenner. "That's what you told me, wasn't it?"

"Yeah, that's what I told you," Jenner replied, and moved off, unable to meet Victor's eye.

"So you," the Chinese man went on, "must have found out about the Hogarth." He paused for a moment, putting another drop in his left eye. "And being an art dealer—"

"Ex-art dealer."

"—all the more reason why, as an *ex*-art dealer, you'd want to get one over on your competitors. Don't deny it; I'm not a fucking idiot. You wouldn't have been hired unless you knew how the art business worked. Which means that you must have contacts."

"I've got a criminal record; the art world won't talk to me now."

The man sniffed, blinking slowly, then pulled his left eyelid down over his eye. "I want that Hogarth."

"I don't doubt it. Many people would."

"And quite a few of them are already dead. Cuts down on the numbers, doesn't it?"

Victor decided to go on the attack. "Who killed Marian Miller?"

"Not me."

"What about Annette Dvorski? Did you kill her?"

"No."

"Bernie Freeland?"

"No!" the Chinese man said emphatically, losing his patience. "Listen, I know I'm not the only person after this picture—"

Victor interrupted. "You killed Lim Chang, though, didn't you?"

"Yeah." He paused for effect. "With dogs."

Not far away they could hear the commotion of a fight about to start: men calling out, bets being laid, and dogs snarling, eager for the kill. Brutality was all around them in the dark night air.

"I'll ask you again," Victor said, struggling to keep his voice steady. "Why should I help you?"

"Because we have Liza Frith."

The name came out at the same moment as loud, frantic yelping began, with the thumping roar of the men inside the tent almost but not quite drowning out the bloodbath. Smoke was still rising from the fire outside, and a fox barked eerily from over the hill—but no houses, no welcoming lights from streetlamps or stores. If Victor believed that he had somewhere to run *from*, he knew he had nowhere to run *to*.

"You've got Liza Frith?" he repeated, stunned.

"We found out where you'd hidden her," he said. "Been watching her, wondering if she'd come in useful. You can have her back, unharmed, in return for the Hogarth."

"But I don't *have* it!" Victor protested.

"So find it," the man retorted. "Find it or she's dead."

A moment strung its weight out between them. Victor, now panicked, tried to play for time. "How do I know she's not dead already?"

"Oh, for fuck sake, don't screw me around! Why would I kill her when I need her for bargaining?"

"But I tell you I don't *know* where the painting is."

"You keep saying that."

"Because it's the truth. It could be anywhere in London—or in New York or Hong Kong. Or Moscow."

"Yeah, I heard the Russians were after it."

"What else did you hear?"

"That some man called Arnold Fletcher was trying to get back into their good books by finding it for them. But he's got no chance. We'll get it."

Puzzled, Victor stared at the man. "How d'you know about Arnold Fletcher?"

"There's a lot of gossip going around. Someone said there's another bloke involved too: Guy Manners." He shrugged. "Who fucking knows? Everyone's been gabby about this flaming picture. It's worth a lot of money, and a lot of people want it."

"Which is why you have to give me time to find it."

"You have to find that painting. Mr. Ballam. Fail and you might as well have killed Liza Frith yourself." He paused, listening to the commotion coming from the nearby tent. "D'you like the dogs?"

"What?"

"Dogfighting; do you like it?"

"No. I don't."

The man shrugged. "They're funny animals, dogs. You can train them to kill fast or slow. Some of them even enjoy it. Killing slow, that is. It's like they know they're inflicting pain and relish it. The dog I used on Lim Chang knew it. He liked what he was doing."

The warning wasn't lost on Victor.

"You have a week, Mr. Ballam. Get the Hogarth for me and I'll give you back the girl. Fail and I'll kill you both."

Fifty-seven

IT WAS SIR OLIVER PETERS'S TURN TO BE SURPRISED WHEN HE SAW
Victor waiting for him at ten to nine the following morning. It had been
raining in London overnight, and the streets were greasy, with puddles
throwing up iridescent colors in the hesitant morning sun. There were few
people about, only a couple of tourists staring morosely into the window of
Noble Jones and a street sweeper hurrying to finish before the morning rush.

"Victor," he said by way of greeting, opening the gallery door and turning
off the alarm. The heating had clicked in half an hour earlier, the warmth
welcoming as Oliver ushered Victor into his office. This time there were no
tea roses, no perfume that spoke of past summers or spring to come. "What
can I do for you?"

Sitting down, Victor stared at Oliver and wondered how much longer he
had left to live. The disease was working its malignant transformation, and
his thinning body had assumed a sudden aging stoop.

"How are you?"

"As you see," Oliver replied. "But you didn't come here to talk about my
health, did you?"

"No, I didn't."

"From the look on your face I assume it's something very important."

"It is. Can I speak plainly?"

"You always did."

"You're the only dealer left alive from the Bernie Freeland flight."

"Kit Wilkes isn't dead, is he?"

"No, but he's dying. Not expected to recover." Victor was surprised by
Oliver's composure, his stillness. "I've discovered that the Chinese had the
Hogarth, but then they lost it."

Oliver's face betrayed nothing. "They *lost* it?"

"Yes. Lim Chang managed to get hold of the painting, but then it
disappeared again." Victor paused, but Oliver wasn't forthcoming. "You told
me you were in touch with Lim Chang, and since you're the only dealer still
alive, I'm guessing that you have it."

"*I* didn't kill Lim Chang."

"Of course not. You wouldn't do anything like that," Victor said calmly. "But if somehow you managed to get hold of the painting, perhaps you've *kept* hold of it. I could understand why. You might want to keep it hidden away, or in your condition you might have other plans for something that could raise a great deal of money and provide for your family after you've gone."

His perception was oddly comforting to Oliver. Perhaps his decision was not so dishonorable, after all.

But he wasn't about to show his hand. "Even if I had the Hogarth, selling it would be wrong."

"Because of what it represents?" Victor asked gently. "But wouldn't that depend on who it was sold to? The right person would be someone who'd appreciate the work and what it meant, someone who would not abuse it but own it in secret. That would be acceptable, surely?"

Oliver felt a sudden desire to confide, to divide the burden whose weight was crippling him.

"It would be understandable," Victor went on, "for a dying man who had to provide for his family."

Coughing, Oliver leaned back in his seat, unable to meet Victor's gaze. "I don't have the Hogarth."

"Have you sold it already?"

"How dare you!"

Victor put up his hands to calm him. "Over the last few days I've been thinking back, remembering things like what Fraser Heath-Lincoln told me years ago about a royal bastard. The son of Frederick, Prince of Wales."

"Fraser Heath-Lincoln was an ass."

"He was a gossip but not an ass," Victor argued. "And then I remembered something else. One night we were talking, and Fraser wondered out loud if the royal bastard had survived and, if so, whether there was a living descendant."

The words bellyflopped on the still air.

"Is there?"

Oliver smiled dismissively. "What utter nonsense!"

"There *is* a descendant, isn't there? Which would account for all the panic about this painting and why I was warned off. It wasn't some thug, someone working for a dealer, or the triads or the Russians. Oh, they want the Hogarth because it's valuable, but that's not all of it, is it? There's a lot more to this, Sir Oliver."

"You're a clever man, Victor."

"There *is* a descendant, isn't there? You can trust me because I'm in as much danger as you are." Victor paused, studying the man in front of him. "I'm the one person who has no reason to betray you."

Oliver sighed a long, slow sigh and then returned Victor's gaze.

"Very well. I *will* trust you. I *need* to trust you. I don't have much longer to live, and I find myself in a terrible dilemma. Unluckily for you, Victor, you are to be my confidant, my confessor. But I want a promise from you that if anything happens to me, you'll protect my family to the best of your ability."

There was a knock on the office door, and Margaret walked in. She looked at the two men curiously for a moment and then smiled and said good morning.

"Can I get you anything, Sir Oliver?" she asked

Oliver returned his secretary's smile. "Coffee would be nice. And some of those shortbread cookies."

When she had left the room, Victor said, "You spoke up for me at my trial. I owe you for that, and I'll help your family any way I can."

"Thank you."

Victor paused for an instant before speaking again. "*Is* there a descendant of Polly Gunnell's bastard?"

Slowly, Oliver nodded. "Yes."

The admission seemed to fill the room, its enormity pressing down on both of them.

"Male or female?"

"Male."

"Does he have children of his own?"

"No. No children. He's the last of the line."

Victor took a deep breath. "Does he know his real identity?"

"No," Oliver replied sharply. "And he never will. And neither will you, Victor."

"Have you got the Hogarth, sir?"

There was no direct reply to his question. Instead, Oliver scrutinized him unblinkingly as if searching for something. "You seem changed," he said at last.

"I *am* changed."

"And you seem afraid."

"That too," Victor replied as Margaret returned with the coffee tray.

The aroma of the fresh shortbread was extraordinarily comforting to Victor. The dogfight, the threat from the Chinese men, the wood smoke, and the headlights burning in the country night seemed temporarily unreal in the placid surroundings of the gallery.

Suddenly homesick, Victor longed for his old life.

"Sir Oliver, I *have* to get hold of the Hogarth."

"It would be good revenge."

"Oh, I'm past revenge! I think I fancied a triumphant return to the fold, my banner the lost Hogarth, my power restored." He smiled wistfully. "It all seemed simple at first, but then people started dying. Suddenly all those violent, ugly deaths for a painting—even *that* painting—seemed unacceptable, not worth it."

"But you still want it?"

"I've been given an ultimatum, Sir Oliver. I have to give the Hogarth back to the triads or they'll kill Liza Frith."

Oliver frowned, his memory strained. "Liza Frith? Wasn't she . . . ?"

"One of the call girls on the jet, yes. In fact, she's the last girl left; the other two are dead. Murdered. I can save Liza's life if I swap the painting for her."

Badly shaken, Oliver stood up and walked to the window. He fiddled with the blind, the white cord a sliver of silk in his hand. Every movement of his body told of the pain he was in, of the effort to stay alive. The long legs that had so often been seen striding along Piccadilly, Bond Street, Cork Street, and the Burlington Arcade, the aristocratic bearing that had graced art sales across the globe—now he was emaciated, a candidate for a nursing home rather than an auction house.

While Victor watched him, Oliver Peters was silently weighing his options. Weighing the life of a call girl against the needs of his family. Was a prostitute worth more than his own flesh and blood? His son, his daughters, and his beloved wife—refined, respected, the perfect consort for a revered man. Was their future to be sacrificed for the life of a call girl?

"I need the Hogarth," Oliver said finally, his voice pitched low.

"So do I."

"I *need* it," Oliver pleaded as panic took hold of him. Panic and imminent loss of control. How could he relinquish the painting? How could he possibly let go of his only means of raising money? Without the picture he was financially crippled, his dependents' security under threat.

"I *need* that picture!"

"Please, listen to me—"

But Oliver cut him off. "I'm in debt, Victor. Serious debt. I borrowed half a million pounds and gave it to Lim Chang to buy back the painting from his contacts." He let go of the blind's cord and leaned against the windowsill, gripping it tightly. "I was relying on the sale of the Hogarth to clear the loan and secure my family's future. I *need* that painting, Victor. You don't know what you're asking. I'm sorry for the girl, truly sorry, but I can't give up the Hogarth."

"The half a million pounds you raised—"

"Gone! The triads have the money. They'd have the painting too, but Lim Chang had been very careful. I'd given him the briefcase to carry the Hogarth and the key to lock it. I kept a key myself, of course. But Chang had taken the added precaution of fastening the case to his wrist with a chain. The thieves couldn't get the case off him."

Surprised, Victor stared at the man in front of him. "How d'you know this?"

As if to ward off the question, Oliver put up his hands.

"Don't ask me. I can't remember . . . I can't forget. That painting made me do things, act in a way I despise myself for." He looked and sounded mortally tired, his voice wavering. "Don't ask me for the Hogarth, Victor. *Please* don't."

"A girl's life depends on it."

His face flushed. "My family's future depends on it!"

"They'll kill her like they killed the others."

"And I should trade those I love for a whore?" Oliver replied, lowering himself into his chair again. His eyes were heavy; his hands reached for the coffee, and he downed two painkillers. "Why did you have to come here? Why did I have to get on that jet? Why did any of this have to happen?" He was talking to himself, baffled by his situation and the gravity of the decision he was being forced to make. "Let me be, for God's sake; let me be, Victor. I've so little time left; let me do the right thing."

"A girl's life is at stake!"

Oliver's head shot up. "What's Liza Frith to me? Why should I save her if by saving her I penalize my own family?" He swallowed with effort, fighting the pain. "All my life I've been an honorable man. I've prided myself on that." He thought of the Hogarth painting, his father and grandfather, and Sir Nathaniel Overton. "I've borne a burden no man should have to carry. I've kept secrets for others, kept my word above all, and for what?" He wasn't bitter; he was bemused. "You look at me differently now, Victor. You despise me."

"No."

"You do," Oliver contradicted him. "And if the situations were reversed, I'd despise you. But this is my family we're talking about, the people I've loved and protected for many years and mean to *keep* protecting. How can you come here and ask this of me?" he snapped, losing control. "The triads took the money; they have half a million pounds. Why isn't that enough?"

"Because they want the Hogarth."

"And if they don't get it, they'll kill the girl." He stared at Victor, and then he saw it, the sliver of anguish. "Oh, no. You too?"

Victor nodded and bent his head, then heard Oliver sigh and the sound of a spoon being stirred in a cup. He raised his head and watched as Oliver pushed a cup of coffee across the desk to him, his hands shaking so much that some of the liquid slopped into the saucer. Victor took it and a moment later accepted a shortbread cookie. It felt like ash on his tongue.

Outside in the gallery, the phones started ringing. The working day had begun, and soon people would come to look at the paintings hanging on the gallery walls. If Sir Oliver Peters was lucky, someone would buy something. All the ordinary workings of life were just on the other side of a door, all the everyday noises and activities, while inside Sir Oliver Peters's office two men sat in silence, two lives hanging in the balance between them.

Victor was thinking that if he was going to die, he wasn't going to die ignorant. He had to know who had killed Annette Dvorski and Bernie Freeland. He knew that the Chinese had killed Lim Chang, but who had silenced Kit Wilkes? And before the Chinese got involved, who was responsible for the first killing? Who had destroyed Marian Miller and set the butchery in motion? To die was one thing. To die a fool was quite another.

"She was kind to me."

Victor looked up as Oliver spoke. "Liza Frith; she was kind to me. Asked if I was all right."

"She was in the wrong place at the wrong time."

"We all were." Oliver rubbed his right temple. "I keep asking myself why I accepted the lift from Bernie Freeland. Why I didn't wait for the next commercial flight. I can't say I had a premonition, any intimation that something was going to happen. I was just glad that I'd be getting home sooner than I thought. When I saw the call girls on the jet, I was embarrassed, concerned that my wife would find out—that *anyone* would find out—who I was mixing with. When that poor girl was murdered, I was still worried that someone would discover I'd been on the jet."

"It's understandable."

"Is it?" Oliver countered. "Pride is a terrible vice. One takes one's status for granted, but when it's threatened, it's something one fights for tooth and nail." He pressed his hands together to stop them from shaking. "I now see myself for what I am. I had hoped that by the time my death came I'd be proud of myself, but that's not to be."

"You still refuse to give me the Hogarth?"

"How can I let my family down?" he said, the words almost wailed, his anguish terrifying.

"Believe me, Sir Oliver, I didn't want to come here, but I had to. I had to ask. And I'm *still* asking."

Oliver touched his throat with his hand as though speech pained him. "You came here for help. You asked me to save a girl's life, and I hesitated. I had the power to save your life, and I hesitated. I *hesitated*. And then I refused. Men go to hell for less."

Moved, Victor watched him as he stood up, gripping the side of the desk to steady himself.

"I'll get you the Hogarth, but I need a little time."

"They've given me a week. I have to get the painting to them by then," Victor replied, his eyes never leaving Oliver's face. "Are you up to this?"

"Oh, yes."

"I'm so sorry."

"No, don't be." Oliver drew himself up to his full height, his elegance momentarily restored. "I should be the one to apologize, but I won't let you down. You can depend on that much, Victor. I won't let you down."

HAVING TRAVELED AROUND EUROPE FOR A FORTNIGHT, LOUIS Freeland was now home. The family doctor had suggested the vacation as a way to take Louis's mind off his father's death, but in that he was only partially successful. Mrs. Sheldon had accompanied the young man on his first trip to London, together with one of the family's lawyers, but later her place had been taken by Louis's girlfriend, Odette. Her demotion had delighted Mrs. Sheldon, hoping as she did that it was a sign of Louis's recovery. Perhaps his overwhelming love for his father might be replaced by love for a young woman.

At times Louis *did* show affection to Odette, but his capricious moods continued and, worse, accelerated as the little party traveled on to Italy and Switzerland. By the time Mrs. Sheldon was preparing to welcome her charge home, she had heard reports of Louis's withdrawal, and now she learned that he had banished Odette. All her hopes seemed to have stalled.

In an attempt to put a positive slant on events, Mrs. Sheldon told the doctor that they had been expecting too much too soon, that it would take time for Louis to settle down. But she didn't know. No one *really* knew how his mind worked. Only Louis did. Then, as the days passed, he seemed to slide backward, asking Mrs. Sheldon when his father was coming to visit. Her gentle reminders that Bernie was dead worked for a short time, but before long Louis would start asking the same question:

Where is my father?

And so it continued. The lad veered between utter indifference and desperate grief. At times he seemed to forget his beloved father completely, but that state lasted only for an hour, possibly two, and then there would be a massive reaction. He would talk, jabbering about Bernie, multiplying his virtues, making a faultless god of a flawed man. Then, oddly, Louis began to show an interest in the business, but that didn't last. His mental capacities were limited and erratic, and he certainly had not inherited the commitment and business acumen of his father.

Louis Freeland would live like a prince because he was well provided for, but the core of his life had disappeared and left him suspended where no one could reach him.

And so his progress faltered. His little jaunts to New York ceased, and he refused to take calls from Odette even though she tried repeatedly to contact him. The evening classes that had extended his world were abandoned. His life—always small—now shrank within the walls of the house in Connecticut, where the ghost of his dead father was ever present.

Many times at night Mrs. Sheldon would wake and go to Louis's room. She would stand outside and listen to her charge talking. There was no one there; there never was. But to Louis, his nighttime visitor was paying him the attention for which he had longed all his life. Finally Louis had all of Bernie Freeland's attention. The ghost might exist only in his mind, but to Louis his father was there, more real than he had ever been. Permanently fixed in Connecticut, listening to his son, watching what he did, a presence that would never leave him again.

It was a sweet madness.

UNBLINKING, CHARLENE FLEET WATCHED VICTOR BALLAM ENTER HER office and sit down. She had to admit that he was a handsome man. The rigors of the last two weeks had toughened him, hardened his expression. He now seemed very different from the person she had first met. Then there had been a naïveté about him even after three years in prison. Now there was no element of innocence left. She knew as she looked at him that Victor Ballam wasn't going to back off and was now prepared to play dirty.

"I know who killed your dog."

Her eyebrows rose. "Who?"

"The triads. They double-crossed Lim Chang and took the Hogarth."

"Chang had the Hogarth?"

"For a little while, yes."

"So the Chinese have it now?"

Victor ignored the question and carried on. "They killed Chang but lost the painting."

Her eyes narrowed. "And?"

"I know who has the Hogarth, but then, that doesn't matter to you, does it? You were never interested in the painting, or so you said. But that made me wonder *why* Marian Miller would be so eager to tell you all about it."

"The girls always tell me interesting pieces of gossip. Most of our clients are art dealers. Marian was just passing on information."

"But you weren't interested in the painting?"

"My business is my only concern."

He nodded briskly. "And that's why I'm here. You've lost two girls already, which must have cost you dear. And you certainly wanted Liza Frith back."

"Get on with it! Don't play around with me."

"The triads have Liza. They want to swap the painting for her. If they don't get the Hogarth, they'll kill her—and kill me too."

"Oh, dear, Mr. Ballam," she said with mock sympathy. "You *are* in a mess."

She could see that she was getting to him, but this time he didn't react.

He was getting clever, she realized, learning to bargain, to deal. She admired him for that, but what did he want? Pouring two glasses of wine, she passed one to Victor, noticing that he had changed his way of dressing; his jacket was dark, and his jeans were finished off with a pair of old brogues. Clothes than didn't get a man noticed. Clever, that.

"*You* put me in the mess," Victor said smoothly. "And I want your help to get out of it. I want to buy Liza Frith back."

"You know where the Hogarth is. Get it and buy her with that," she said briskly. "That's your deal with the Chinese, isn't it?"

"I need more than that. I need half a million pounds."

"Good luck," she said coldly.

"Give me the half a million or I'll ruin you."

Unused to threats, Mrs. Fleet blinked. If Victor had said it only a couple of days earlier, she would have laughed in his face. The death threat had obviously turned him, brought out his cruel streak. But was he as tough as she was?

"*You'll* ruin *me*?" she repeated, feigning amusement. "Are you serious?"

"I know about you."

"Really? What do you know?"

"I've been talking to your sister."

She felt her throat tighten, and a breath caught in her lungs. "I don't have a sister."

"Yes, you do," Victor replied. "Elizabeth Wilkes. Mother of Kit Wilkes. The same Kit Wilkes who's spent his life tormenting his father, James Holden, MP. Only he *isn't* his father, is he?"

"I don't know what you're talking about."

"I have to admit, Mrs. Fleet, that I've been a bit of a bastard," Victor said simply. "Having my life threatened brought out the worst in me. I wasn't expecting any of this when I started, but now? Now it's dog eat dog if you'll forgive the expression."

"Like I said, I don't know what you're talking about."

"It's quite simple. When I talked to your sister again—after she'd had time to consider the situation from all angles—she told me that she was now scared for her son's life. Elizabeth didn't know what had happened to Kit Wilkes—I'm still not sure myself—but she was very keen to make sure I had something on you. Bargaining power, she called it. You've built a business on that, haven't you?"

He paused, waiting for a response that didn't come. "Your sister's not like you, not as tough. She's afraid of you, and so she talked to me. Wanted an ally, I suppose, or perhaps she was just giving me ammunition. Who knows? Anyway, she told me that she'd passed Kit Wilkes off as James Holden's son and that you'd helped her."

"Liar."

"I have their blood groups. Elizabeth is A negative, Kit is O, and James Holden is type B, which is fairly rare." He paused. "I found that out because he gave blood for a political campaign. It's strange what stays on file, but he'd made a point of it. You know, 'Give blood—especially if you're a rare type.' Not bad for a man who made his name with beef quotas. I have to say it was a good publicity stunt, and at least he gave blood, didn't spill it." Victor paused. "Your sister also let slip that Kit's real father was Bernie Freeland. Which made me start thinking."

"Really."

"Kit was on that ill-fated flight on Freeland's jet, so was there a connection?" He paused again, watching her carefully. "Your sister says not. She says that Freeland never knew Kit was his son. I suppose James Holden was an easier target. I'm just surprised that Holden never had DNA tests done."

Mrs. Fleet flinched. Victor caught the reaction.

"You know, don't you? I checked up on that too. Holden did do a DNA test. But what a strange thing: the test confirmed that Kit *was* Holden's son. How could that be possible?" Victor stared at her coldly. "Well, it couldn't unless there was someone who could make sure the results were tampered with. A tame doctor. Like Eli Fountain, for instance."

"You *have* been busy. And thorough," Mrs. Fleet said, her rage hardly contained as she studied the man in front of her. "Let's cut to the chase. This is blackmail. You're blackmailing me. So what d'you want?"

"Half a million pounds."

"Hah!"

"You can raise it. You've got money stashed abroad, God knows how much. Half a million won't cripple you, and anyway, you can easily make it up. Hire some more girls, expand your business. Pay me, Mrs. Fleet, or I go to James Holden and expose you. He'll make sure the press gets to hear about it. All those years he was duped, made a laughingstock; you think he won't want his pound of flesh? You'll be done for, Mrs. Fleet. Your business will be exposed too, and the jackals will tear you to pieces. You'll get jail, and you won't like it. I didn't."

Standing up, Mrs. Fleet walked over to the window and looked down into the street, drumming her nails on the window ledge, rage boiling inside her. How dare this bastard threaten her? How dare this criminal try to bring her down? And yet she knew she couldn't risk exposure, couldn't risk the loss of her business and her money. Neither could she risk letting her sister talk. What pleasure Elizabeth would get from hauling out the bales of Charlene O'Dwyer's stinking laundry. Then the police would start looking into her past and other matters. Like the fourteen-year-old girl who had left the north so many years before. Or the madam who had once run Park Street.

Her eyes fixed on the road below, Mrs. Fleet felt a damp sensation of fear. All her old sins were seeping out from the graves in which she had thought them so well buried. Events she had suppressed and forgotten formed a layer of scum in her mind. She could see herself in her teens, vicious and feral, walking down Scotland Road and cursing her luck. She remembered her father, halfblinded by the boiling coffee, and how her mother had ordered her, *"Say nothing; I'll say it were me. The fucker had it coming."*

Escaping punishment, Charlene O'Dwyer had been rewarded for her brutality. And had gone on to make a career out of it. But now she was seeing it all put at risk by the one man she had never suspected would be capable of threatening her. The one man she now hated.

"You said you want half a million pounds." She turned from the window to face him. "And you *really* think I'll give it to you?"

"I think you've got no choice."

"You won't get away with this, Ballam. I'll get my own back," she said, a warning in her tone. "It might take me a while, but I will. One day. One day when you're least expecting it."

"Don't bother threatening me."

"I'm not threatening you," she said, cold as ice. "I'm *telling* you. You might have the upper hand now, but not forever. I'll get my revenge. So watch your back, Ballam; no one takes what's mine and gets away with it."

"I want the money."

Beaten, Mrs. Fleet nodded. Once. "Don't return at a later date and ask for more."

"I won't."

"Just one thing I need to know. Did Eli Fountain give me away?"

"No" Victor admitted. "It was just a guess." She smiled, almost in admiration. "I knew he'd been working for you for years and that he knew your sister. Elizabeth told me that. I bet he knew a hell of a lot about what was going on here. He's a greedy man, likes money, and I imagine Eli Fountain would do pretty much anything for it. That avarice would make him a good accomplice and buy you a trusted servant, but only so far." Victor paused, his expression unreadable. "Fountain didn't mention that he was after the Hogarth, did he?"

All the color drained from Mrs. Fleet's face. "*What?*"

"Oh, dear," Victor said with mock sympathy. "Did you really think you had him completely under control? Fountain told me he might have a buyer for the painting."

"Arnold Fletcher?"

That surprised him. "No, although his name keeps cropping up. Obviously the buyer wasn't you, was it?"

She felt as though a fist had been pushed into her heart.

"Fountain was after the Hogarth? The little bastard never mentioned it."

"Kit Wilkes told him about the painting when he got back to London. Wilkes is his patient, after all. Apparently he told Doctor Fountain that someone was picking the Hogarth up in New York."

Fire was in her throat and belly and was stinging her eyes because of the duplicity of the man she had trusted for so long. Eli Fountain had never spoken a word about the Hogarth, never intimated by look or gesture that he knew anything about the painting. After all they had shared, he had kept it from her. Double-crossed her for greed.

"Does Fountain know who the man is?"

"No. And I don't know who the killer is either. I'm unraveling the mess, but I haven't got that far."

Mrs. Fleet sat down heavily, afraid that she might fall, her legs betraying her shock. She hadn't been lying; she *hadn't* been after the painting. She had just wanted to protect her business, her investment. But to find out that Eli Fountain was going behind her back and that her sister had turned on her. . . . Her composure was melting, her instincts unaccountably sluggish. And when she looked up and saw Victor Ballam, her hatred focused on him.

"Fuck you, Ballam."

"I want the money. Tomorrow." He stood up to go, glancing at the space by her feet where her dog had once been. "You were right; your dog's death was a warning to you."

"A warning of what? Of my sister? Doctor Fountain? *You?* As for Liza Frith, frankly, if I were you, I wouldn't bother swapping her for the Hogarth. It would be a poor deal. No one's that good a whore."

"Not even you, Mrs. Fleet?" he asked coldly. "Not even you?"

I despair of this business of which I am a part.

It is 1751, and I have just published The Four Stages of Cruelty *to disappointing reviews and indifferent sales. Am I the only man repelled by the cruelties inflicted on the children and animals of this city? Indeed, this country? Is no one to talk of what is ungodly, vile? Are such matters of no purpose? Are they to have no place on public walls?*

To my rivals' glee, the prints were not as popular as my previous works, or so I was so joyfully informed. Has Master Hogarth lost his conjurer's skill, they ask, and say the public grows weary of the "brutal effects" employed. Do they thus grow weary of me?

The images I draw are too real, too like life, people complain. Too like our own steaming, stinking streets, with their threatening alleyways, dead infants, and starving, rabid dogs. Too like life to bear to look upon. Why spend money when to glance out of the window is to see it all for nothing, without the expense of a penny print?

Never learning to curtail my feelings, I retaliated, making up in temper what I lack in height. I parodied a Rembrandt, titled it Paul before Felix, and put it before the cock-a-doodle connoisseurs and public who are fascinated by the Dutchman, by his soup shadows and high themes. Down every promenade in the West End, windows parade a thousand Takings of Christ; everywhere one looks, a Jesus looms up in London streets. The talk is of Rembrandt Van Rijn, as though he, and only he, can depict the reality of man.

And fetch such high prices for the dealers.

More news came yesterday. News more than grief. Frederick, Prince of Wales, has left this mortal plain. Polly Gunnell's lover, gone to earth with every other man, his body buried, rotting like every other body in every other grave. In whispers, Thomas and I talked of the dead Prince, of his rival court, of his hatred for his father. His death should not have happened. He will not sit upon the throne when his father dies. He will not take up the spectre and orb nor feel the crown upon his head.

Together we looked out of the window and watched Hal—the Prince's son— talking to a group of other young men in the courtyard, throwing dice on the gravel and laughing under the waxy sun. His appearance speaks of his mother, denies his father. For that I am grateful. Frederick, Prince of Wales, should have inherited the throne, but now when the old King dies, his grandson will inherit and govern England.

No one will ever know of the child Polly Gunnell bore. No one will know that in London, in the courtyard of the Foundling Hospital, a boy called Hal is playing dice. That a boy called Hal—the bastard child supposed long murdered—is the unknown heir to the English throne.

The hidden, protected successor to nothing. Except life.

In a while I returned home, then took a carriage out of London to a place I visited seldom. And always alone. Here, long ago, risking my own safety I had secreted the ring the Prince of Wales had given me for safekeeping, together with my original painting: the version depicting the Prince and Polly Gunnell. As though visiting a friend, long loved, but feared, I studied the canvas I had created so many years before. He is still there, a pinch to the heart, his image smiling behind Polly, their secret hardly discernible in the swell of her belly.

He is still smiling, this man now dead. And she is still smiling, this woman so badly used, so brutally butchered. And as I gaze upon them, I bow my head, then nod a reassurance to the dead.

Sixty

WAITING UNTIL SHE SAW HER SISTER LEAVE KIT'S ROOM, CHARLENE Fleet counted to three and then walked toward it. It was past ten at night, and having seen Elizabeth wearing her overcoat, she had assumed that her sister was leaving and would not return that night. The only person in the room apart from the unconscious Kit Wilkes was the unctuous Dr. Fountain.

Pushing open the door, Mrs. Fleet slid behind a nearby screen and watched as the little doctor opened his medicine bag and began rummaging through it. A moment later he took out a vial and a syringe, carefully filled the latter from the former, and then expelled the air bubbles. At Kit's bedside, he began pushing up his patient's left pajama sleeve.

Mrs. Fleet pounced. "You little bastard," she hissed, putting her arm around Fountain's throat and snatching the syringe out of his hand. "You little shit."

He struggled in the headlock, then stiffened, listening to her.

"All these years I've trusted you, and now I've found out that you've been cheating me. After the Hogarth, are you? But you didn't tell *me*, didn't mention anything about it. But you knew about the painting from the start, didn't you? You'd been talking to Kit Wilkes about it." Her grip tightened; Fountain made a gurgling sound. "Wanted all the money for yourself, did you?"

"I can explain," he croaked in a strangled whisper.

"You'll *have* to explain and make it good." Her arm still around his throat, she squeezed cruelly. "No one cheats me, Eli. You of all people should know that. You've been with me for years, decades. We've made a lot of money together, had some real success, but you *still* thought you could put one over on me."

"I didn't."

"Why didn't you *tell* me? I trusted you; I thought you were the only person I could rely on. D'you know how it feels to find out that you've been betrayed? Do you know how that hurts?" She jerked her arm against his Adam's apple. "I could kill you."

"Don't, please don't," he begged, hardly audible. "I'll do whatever you want."

"You're right there, Eli. You *will* do whatever I want." She loosened her stranglehold. "Victor Ballam's just told me that you wanted the Hogarth for yourself, to sell it."

"I only *said* that. I didn't mean it!" he blustered. "I was trying to keep him off track."

"Really?" She glanced at the needle. "What track is *that*, you little fucker? What's this you were about to give your patient?" She waved the syringe in front of the doctor's eyes and tightened her grip again. "A vitamin shot?"

He was choking, terrified, his body rigid as Ma Fleet placed the tip of the needle against the side of his neck.

"Make one move and this will go straight into your jugular," she said, her voice low. "Now, that might not matter; it might be something to help Kit Wilkes's recovery. Or it might matter a lot. So before I jab it in your fucking neck, you tell me: Which *is* it?"

"I . . ." He gasped, trying to take in a breath. "I . . . can . . . explain."

"You *will* explain, you son of a bitch."

Slowly she released her grip, and Fountain groped his way to a chair. He sat down, rubbing his neck.

"What's in the needle?" she demanded.

"Stimulant."

"Stimulant?" Mrs. Fleet jerked her head toward Kit Wilkes. "It's not working, Doctor; he's in a coma."

"I know, I know. But it should have all worked out."

Her eyebrows rose. "What?"

"We planned it. Or rather Kit planned it and paid me to go through with it." He rubbed his throat painfully. "He asked me to keep him sedated." His voice was dry and his hands trembling as he reached for the bedside pitcher and poured himself a glass of water. "We made an arrangement. Kit called me as soon as he got off Bernie Freeland's jet. He said a Hogarth had been found. Freeland had it, and it was worth a fortune. There was something sensational about it, some story attached. He said everyone would be after it."

"So?"

"Kit was going to get it, whatever it took, but he wanted to make sure that no one suspected him of being involved. Especially the Russians. He was being greedy, reckless. He could have made a deal with them, but that wasn't Kit's way. I tried to reason with him. Why not go to the Russians? After all, he'd been working with them for months, picking up the slack after Arnold Fletcher had pissed them off. But Kit didn't want them to get the Hogarth. *He* wanted that painting to embarrass James Holden, and he was prepared to do anything to get it."

Her eyes narrowed, but she was listening. "Go on."

"Trouble is, Kit always thinks he's smarter than the other guy." Fountain coughed and took another sip of water before continuing. "He was determined that no one would know he was involved, so all suspicion had to be taken off him. He had to be put out of the running, so to speak. We agreed to make it look like a drug overdose. Everyone knew Kit was a user, so I sedated him and had him hospitalized."

"You're sure it was Kit Wilkes's idea and not yours?" Her tone was acid.

"It was all his idea!" Fountain snapped emphatically.

"It was a fucking risky idea."

"Kit was fixated on getting the painting. I just did what he asked."

"And it never crossed your mind to get the painting for yourself?"

He paused, then shrugged. "I thought about it, but I couldn't have pulled it off. Kit was the one who had all the contacts. I did what I was asked to do."

"How long was Wilkes supposed to be in his 'coma'?"

"Until the dust settled. Then I'd revive him, and he'd make a killing with the painting."

She was still holding the hypodermic in her hand, tapping it against her palm as she moved closer to the doctor.

"Kit Wilkes had the Hogarth?"

"No; Bernie Freeland had it then. Kit was arranging for it to be stolen in New York."

"By whom?"

"I don't know," Fountain replied, his eyes closing as he felt the point of the needle against his neck again. "I *swear* I don't know! That's why I was going to give Kit an injection to wake him up. I've been injecting him for the last few days, but he won't come around. He really is in a coma."

"You put him there."

"He asked me to."

Smiling grimly, Mrs. Fleet looked over to the bed. "Well, thanks to you, it appears that Mr. Wilkes is out of the running forever." She turned to the doctor. "Are you sure you can't bring him around?"

"I don't know; I've tried *everything!*" he said, panicked, still rubbing his throat. "At first I just thought it was a delayed reaction, that he would revive slowly, but he's never shown any flicker of consciousness."

Thoughtful now, Charlene Fleet realized how she could get her own back on her treacherous sibling. She might have lost half a million pounds, but her sister would lose her only child.

"I've tried everything to help him, everything." Fountain sounded desperate.

"And no one else knows?"

Eli Fountain blinked, taking a moment to understand what she was asking.

"No. I'm Kit's doctor. Everyone accepted what I told them. The rest was easy. I paid a nurse to swap the blood test results with another patient, so no one noticed anything to contradict what I said."

"You know that you'd never practice medicine again if anyone found out what you'd done? Even face a murder charge?"

"I didn't want to murder him; I wanted to help him!"

"You wanted to help *yourself*, Eli. You wanted your share. You wanted what you always want—money. Only this time you've buggered it up. You should have come to me." Mrs. Fleet went on, her tone now honeyed: "You see what happens when you try to cheat me? I wouldn't have made a mistake like this."

Dazed, Dr. Fountain kept staring at the body on the bed. "I can't bring him around! I can't wake him up!"

"So finish it."

He turned to her, eyes bulging behind his glasses, his voice a whisper. "*What?*"

"Finish him off." She passed him the syringe. "Change the injection; no one will know. End it. You could be doing him a favor. After all, he might be brain-damaged, and even if he isn't and you manage to revive him, it'll be too late for him to get his painting. Someone else has it now."

Fountain was staring at her, terrified, as she continued.

"I imagine you've lost out on a big commission, Eli, but that's nothing compared to the outcry that would follow the exposure of what you've done. Then again, doctors can always bury their mistakes, can't they?"

"I can't kill him."

"No?" She passed him the hypodermic and walked to the door, coaxing him into making a choice that would avenge her. "Your decision, Doctor. But if you *do* get Kit Wilkes out of his coma, think about what would happen. He's a vicious, manipulative brat who's made a living out of publicity. You think he'd keep it quiet? He's lost the Hogarth. You revive him and he'll want revenge."

She paused, goading him with her reptilian smile. "He'll drag your name into every paper and onto every television show. He'll make sure you're pilloried. You'll never see Park Street again, Doctor, never realize that dream of yours to retire as a rich man." She sighed with fake sympathy. "If you bring him around, Kit Wilkes will have you put away, locked up for the rest of your life. No more women, no more sexual favors, no more luxury. It'll be over. He'll cut your legs from under you, and you know it. But that's only *if* he comes around."

Fountain glanced at the figure in the bed, then back to Mrs. Fleet.

"I can't do it."

"Who will know? Only me, and what's one more secret for us to share?" She shrugged. She pointed to the immobile Wilkes. "Don't risk what you have for *that*, Eli. Do it and save yourself."

Sixty-One

"Pack it in," Tully said quietly, "while you still can."

"That was bloody awful," was Victor's response as he pushed his plate aside. "You never could cook, Tully. If that turns out to be my last meal, I've been cheated." He glanced across the table at his oldest friend. "Ma Fleet paid up."

"All of it?"

"All of it."

Whistling under his breath, Tully nodded, impressed. "You don't think she'll try and get her own back?"

"She'd love to, but how can she? If anything happens to me, it'll all come out. She's angry but not stupid."

"What about her sister? Or Fountain? You think Mrs. Fleet's going to let them get away with selling her out?"

"Again, she can't do anything. Elizabeth has the upper hand, and Fountain can handle himself."

Clearing away the plates, Tully flicked on a lamp and sat down, crossing his long legs and resting his head back against the chair.

"This time tomorrow the exchange will be over," he said quietly, staring up at the ceiling, his glance tracing the plaster center rose. "I want to come with you."

"No."

"Okay, I'll put it another way. I *am* coming with you whether you like it or not." Tully turned his head in Victor's direction. "You need backup. When you hand over to the triads, you'll need someone to get Liza Frith away safely. We'll use my car."

"Tully—"

"You *need* someone to help you."

"I was going to say that I'm using my car." Victor smiled wryly. "And you're right; I could do with you there, but it's too dangerous."

"You said it was just an exchange. The girl for the painting. A simple swap."

"I lied."

Piccadilly, bounded by the famous Circus at one end and Hyde Park Corner at the other, is a center of commerce, of expensive hotels, showrooms, and businesses, that leads to those fashionable streets where artworks are exhibited, exchanged, bought, and sold. Beneath the moneyed gloss, the sweating underside of the art world steams like a dung heap. Along Piccadilly at nightfall, the lamps are lit, the yellow lights of the London taxis move like glowworms in the semidarkness, and the restaurants are full. But the galleries are closed, locked and alarmed for the night.

In one of those galleries, in the Burlington Arcade, Sir Oliver Peters sat in his office, patiently waiting for Victor Ballam. His staff had long since left, and the clock read nine-fifteen. He swallowed a dose of diamorphine, adjusted his silk tie, and checked his reflection in the mirror. All was done, safely gathered up. The loss of half a million pounds was a body blow to a body that already had been beaten into submission, but in that instant Sir Oliver Peters looked in the mirror and smiled.

The doorbell interrupted his thoughts. Oliver let Victor in and relocked the door behind him.

"Did you get it?"

Oliver nodded and ushered Victor into the office. Under the limpid glow from an antique desk lamp, the little painting gazed back at them. Victor picked up the Hogarth and turned it over. On the back was the same slight tear at the corner, the watermark, and the grime of ages darkening the reverse of the canvas. He turned the painting over again and held it for a long moment under the light, the face of Frederick, Prince of Wales, smiling at him. A pleasant face, even—to some—handsome. But not remarkable. Not a face one would imagine capable of toppling a throne or inciting a killing. And not one killing but many. It was in the end just a man's face. The proof of the painter's hubris. The one face William Hogarth should never have painted.

Sighing, Victor slid the picture into the case he had brought with him, zipped it closed, then looked at Oliver.

"Thank you."

"I couldn't do anything else. Not if I was to live with myself," he replied, the gray silk of his tie casting an oyster reflection under his jowls. "Are you sure you can handle this alone?"

"It's just an exchange."

Oliver shrugged, his tone anxious. "And you believe they'll go through with it? That they'll keep their word?"

"I think so."

"How can you be so sure they won't cheat you?"

"Because they don't want the girl; they want the Hogarth. It's all about cash—currency to keep their business interests running. They're not interested in the painting, and they don't know its history."

"Are you sure of that?"

"Positive," Victor replied firmly. "They're gangsters, not connoisseurs. If the Russians had gotten the painting, it would have been unfortunate, and if Lim Chang had succeeded, it would have been much more dangerous. These people will just use it to sell to the highest bidder. It's a trust fund for them. A cash cow." He paused, studying Oliver carefully. "No doubt some Arab will put it in his safe and gloat over it in secret."

"Hidden before and hidden again." Oliver shook his head. "All those deaths for nothing."

"If it saves Liza Frith, it will have at least done some good," Victor replied, walking to the door and pausing. "I'm sorry I put you under so much pressure. How are you?"

"As you see." He smiled faintly.

"Thank you again for what you've done."

Oliver nodded, genuinely moved. "In the end, it was the right thing to do. The *only* thing."

Sixty-Two

IT TOOK VICTOR ALMOST AN HOUR TO REACH THE APPOINTED MEETING place, a place where he had hoped never to return. He pulled up at the knot of trees where he had parked before. Where a huge fire had once burned, a smaller fire now smoldered, throwing haphazard light on the figures surrounding it. From the copse behind, Victor heard the familiar sounds of dogs barking and squabbling but not the hysterical savagery of a fight. He was grateful for that.

As Victor approached the people with the case in his hand, he heard an owl hooting in the distance. He stopped, caught by a memory. When he was first in jail, he had struggled, fighting panic through days that were intense and blank with inaction. But the nights were the worst. That long stretch of thinking, of brooding, of remembering the trial, the witnesses, the lies that had so unjustly brought him to a prison cell. And then, one night, he had heard an owl hooting. Had almost imagined it passing close over his head, so close that he could hear the soft rhythm of its wings beating, its journey taking him out of confinement to the far, wide woods of Worcestershire.

"Ballam?"

Victor blinked, bringing himself back to the present moment.

"You got the painting?"

"Yes." He moved toward the group, and the man with the infected eyes detached himself and came up to him, He put out his hand.

"Give it to me."

"Give me the girl first."

"You don't trust me?"

Amused, Victor smiled. "Don't be offended, but no."

Annoyed, the man gestured to his companions. One of them disappeared into the shadows, then came back into the firelight holding Liza Frith's arm. She was silent, her head bowed, her dress stained. But she was alive.

"Tell him to bring her over here," Victor said, watching as she approached.

The case began to feel heavy in his grip, the handle burning his skin as he curled his fingers around the leather. But it wasn't the painting inside—

that weighed nothing—it was the weight of all that the Hogarth meant. The deaths, past and present. And in his hand Victor felt the crushing weight, the burden, of blood.

He wanted suddenly to throw it onto the fire, to watch the face of the Prince of Wales—the image that had been the source of so much misery—consumed in the flames.

But instead he held out his left hand toward Liza Frith and with his right hand extended the case toward the triad man, who snatched it, pushing Liza toward Victor and opening the case.

"Good," was all he said. Victor put his arm around a silent, shaking, and grateful Liza and turned to leave. They'd gone only a yard or two before the Chinese man called out, "Hey! Just a minute."

Victor froze. He felt Liza stiffen in his arms.

"What?"

"You did well."

"You wanted the painting," Victor said more smoothly than he felt, "and you got it. We had a deal."

Rubbing his inflamed eye, the man passed the painting over to one of his colleagues and came toward Victor. In the background the dogs were still barking, the copse a dark hump behind. Every instinct told Victor to run, but he knew he couldn't escape with Liza in tow, so he waited and watched as the man drew up to them.

"Is there a problem?"

"There's a dogfight soon. You want to watch?"

"No."

"You sure?" he asked again. "There's going to be a sideshow, something you might be interested in, Mr. Ballam."

Uneasy, Victor glanced at Liza. "I want to get her home."

"Put her in the car and then get the fuck back here!" Victor realized that he wasn't going to be allowed to go anywhere.

He walked Liza to his car and helped her in. He put his coat around her and briefly touched her cheek. Her eyes fixed on his, her lips parting for an instant. But she said nothing.

"I won't be long," he promised, sensing he was being watched. "Stay here. When I get back, we'll go home."

Straightening up, Victor followed the man back toward the fire. But they didn't stop there; they continued walking toward a large tent, both of them ducking under the tarpaulin as they entered. Wary, Victor looked around him, hearing the dogs barking frantically. Remembering Lim Chang and terrified of what might be about to happen to him, Victor felt the sweat slither down his back and moved farther into the tent only when he was pushed.

"Go on!"

The fog of cigarette smoke was so intense that for a moment he couldn't make out the figures clearly, but eventually he could see a group of men surrounding what seemed to be a ring. The dogs were still barking, and the men's faces turned toward Victor were all Chinese except for one: the face of the man being dragged toward the ring. He was English, heavyset, flushed, sweaty, and terrified. Stripped to the waist and barefoot, he was thrown over the steel enclosure of the ring, four Chinese men entering after him. Then, with speed and terrifying efficiency, they spread-eagled him, tying his wrists to two metal posts sunk into the ground and his ankles to two others. The man was struggling, screaming, wetting himself; then, as his tormentors stepped back, he began sobbing.

Horror-struck, Victor stared at the man standing next to him. "Who is he?"

"You don't know?"

"No." Victor could hardly speak. "What are you going to do to him?"

"What we do to anyone who crosses us or betrays us. Watch very carefully, Mr. Ballam; this is a warning. When our business here is finished, you stay silent. He didn't. He tried to cheat us."

"Jesus, who is he?"

"You really don't know?"

"No!" Victor said. "How could I know?"

"This is your killer, Mr. Ballam. This is the man who killed Marian Miller and Annette Dvorski."

He turned to the triad man and looked into the sore eyes and then into the blank darkness.

"This is Bernie Freeland's pilot, Duncan Fairfax." The triad man glanced over to the sobbing victim, his own face expressionless. "After they landed at Heathrow, he overheard a couple of passengers talking about something they had heard on the flight. Something about a priceless painting. And he wanted it. Needed it to pay off his gambling debts to us. He'd been playing recklessly, asking us for credit. Fat prick thought we'd never call in the debt. Jesus, I bet he couldn't believe his luck; here was a way to pay off his debts in one go! He just had to find the picture before anyone else did." He paused, watching the squirming man without pity. "It was easy for him to call by later at Marian Miller's room. After all, they were staying in the same airport hotel. She might even have thought he was the john at first. Fairfax found out what she knew and then killed her, making it look like a sex crime."

"Why the thirty rubles in her mouth?"

"That was a nice touch, supposed to point to the Russians."

"And the dog fur?"

"*What?*"

Victor frowned. "Fairfax must have done that."

Still staring at the bound victim, the Chinese man continued. "After he'd killed Marian Miller, Fairfax went after Bernie Freeland."

Duncan Fairfax's eyes were bulging with terror. As the dogs barked at the back of the tent, the pilot stared blindly up at the faces that surrounded him. He was blubbering incoherently, mad with panic.

"He went to New York, to Freeland's apartment, looking for him and the painting. Fairfax didn't like Freeland, so stealing off him to pay his debts didn't worry him."

"He killed him?"

"Fairfax denies it. He was keen to confess to everything else to save himself, but not that, and he'd have told us, believe me. Bernie Freeland's death might have just been an accident, after all."

"So why did he kill Annette Dvorski?" Victor asked, then flinched as he heard the dogs coming closer, saw the crowd parting to let the animals and their owners through. It was obvious that the dogs hadn't been fed for some days; their hackles were raised, the whites of their eyes were showing, and their mouths were working frantically against their muzzles.

"Jesus, don't do this—"

He was immediately cut off, his previous question answered.

"Fairfax found Annette Dvorski in the apartment and then tortured her to find out where the painting was, but she didn't know. He killed her anyway and then left. You were supposed to take the blame for that."

Victor stared at the man, incredulous. "You were there?"

"Not me; one of my people," he replied. "You had a close call, Mr.

Ballam. But poor Fairfax. When we caught up with him and he didn't have the painting, he got all hysterical, pleading for time to get our money back. I knew then that you probably had the Hogarth in that suitcase, so we switched it at the airport. Fairfax was still working with us then, so he organized it. It's easy for a pilot to get luggage swapped."

Confused, Victor's stared at him. "But if you got the painting . . . ?"

"Why kill him? Because it wasn't Duncan Fairfax that got hold of it; we did in the end. And we knew that if we let him go, he wouldn't keep quiet. He can't. We'd always be looking over our shoulders." He pointed to the pilot; there was foam coming from the sides of his mouth as he struggled frantically. "He's fucking mad. He's mad because of the killings, the bloodbath. He didn't have the stomach for it. The murder of Marian Miller, then the torture of Annette Dvorski turned his brain. It was only a matter of time before the police caught up with him and then us. I had to stop that."

In one sudden movement, the man dropped his hand. The dogs' muzzles were taken off, and the animals hurtled into the ring. They fell onto the bound man, one dog ripping at Fairfax's throat, another at his chest, a third at his face. Blood was spurting from torn arteries, spouting upward onto the jeering crowd; the pilot's agonized screams were piercing as the dogs, wriggling in the sand, exposed his guts and tore the flesh off his face.

Heaving, Victor turned away. At the back of the crowd he could just make out the face of someone he knew—Malcolm Jenner—watching the mauling of the man who had killed his niece.

"*No one* talks about us, Mr. Ballam," the Chinese man said quietly. "And if you ever feel tempted, remember Duncan Fairfax."

Behind them the tent had gone silent. The dogs, sated, were quiet, muzzled again. A moment later Victor could see the bloodied remains of Duncan Fairfax being dragged out and thrown into a makeshift hole. As men started to fill it in, he could see a faint flutter of movement as Duncan Fairfax was buried alive.

Sixty-Three

LIZA FRITH WATCHED AS VICTOR GOT BACK INTO THE CAR AND STARTED the engine. His hands were shaking, and there was sweat on his brow. He stared straight ahead, silent, not trusting his voice.

"Thank you," Liza said, breaking the silence. "Thanks for coming to get me, Mr. Ballam. Not many would have done that, you know . . . for a whore."

"You're human."

She stared ahead. "Most can't get past the whore bit." She rubbed her face with the tips of her fingers, then pulled her torn jacket around her.

"Did they hurt you?"

"No. They just left me in some lousy flat, but I was okay. Honestly. Scared but okay."

"Are you hungry?"

Surprised, she looked at him. "You want to feed me? You've just saved my life and you want to *feed* me?" Her voice was full of wonderment. "Why?"

"Why not?" Victor replied, reaching the end of the country lane and turning onto a main road.

When he saw the streetlights overhead and noticed other traffic moving around them, he relaxed a little, his grip lessening on the steering wheel. But the image of the mauling he'd witnessed was inescapable. He could see Duncan Fairfax in the windshield, on the road ahead, in the night sky. When he looked into the rearview mirror, he saw Duncan Fairfax. When he turned on the radio, he didn't hear music but the insane burbling of a man gone mad, the agonizing screams of a man being brutally murdered. He could still smell the blood in his nostrils and, unnerved, pulled over to the side of the road.

Anxious, Liza touched his shoulder. "Are you okay?"

Mute, he shook his head.

"It'll be all right," she said softly. "Honestly, it'll all be all right." She stroked his cheek gently, and Victor rested his head against her shoulder. Her hands closed over his as, putting her lips close to his ear, she said, "I'll never forget what you did for me. Honest, I won't. If there's ever anything I can do for you, Mr. Ballam, ask. I'll be there. I promise. I'll stand in your corner whatever happens." She held his head between her hands and smiled at him. "I've never had any man treat me like you have. You made me feel like I meant something. So remember, if you need me, I'll be there."

His eyes closed to her touch. If he asked her, she *would* stand in his corner. She had given her word and would not break it. He wondered then if Ingola would have done the same. And immediately he knew the answer. For the first time he saw Ingola clearly. Yes, she had loved him, but with reservations, with conditions, with one eye always on her own advantage.

Liza's voice was barely audible when she spoke again. "Who killed her?"

He was still thinking of Ingola. "What?"

"Who killed Annette?"

"The same man who killed Marian Miller. It was Freeland's pilot, Duncan Fairfax."

"But he was an *ass*," she said simply, her voice childlike. "We all thought he was so full of himself. Did he kill Bernie too?"

"No. I don't know who killed him. It might have been an accident after all. Maybe it was just the timing and the circumstances that made it look suspicious."

"Duncan Fairfax," Liza repeated. "God, what made him do it?"

"Money," Victor said simply, turning the engine back on. "Just money."

"So it's all over?" Tully asked, almost regretful. "I was just beginning to enjoy myself. And I got the door repaired," he said with a smile. "What are you going to do now?"

"I've got one more visit to make."

"Mrs. Fleet?"

"No. She paid up, and that's the last I'll see of her," Victor replied. "And Liza Frith's not going back to work at Park Street. She's going to work in France. Said she couldn't bear to be in London anymore. I like her; we'll stay in touch." He grinned. "An ex-con and a whore; how's that?"

"Colorful."

"We can't ever mention any of this, Tully. You know that, don't you? Never let a word slip about the painting or the Chinese. *Particularly* the Chinese. You must always be on your guard. Say nothing, not a word," Victor repeated, thinking of Duncan Fairfax.

"Not a word," Tully promised, changing the subject. "I've just heard that I've got a voice-over job—for dental paste. You know, the type that keeps your teeth secure when you bite an apple. 'For confidence with a smile, choose Fermamint.' Bastards offered me some complimentary samples, and I've still got my own teeth." He paused, scrutinizing Victor. "You must have some idea what you're going to do next."

"Stay in London, keep my ears open for work."

"What kind of work?"

"Are you my father now?"

"Humor me, Victor; you're the nearest I'll ever get to having a son. What kind of work?"

"There's a lot goes on in the art world. I've been a victim of it; I might as well try to profit by it now." He shrugged. "If I can't work among thieves, I can catch them for a living."

"Dangerous living."

"Dangerous world," Victor said quietly. "And one day I'll find out who framed me for those frauds. One day someone will slip up, or I'll hear something. It might take a while, Tully, but I'll find out who was behind it." He paused. "Everything that was taken from me *I want back*."

"Does that include Ingola?"

"No." He thought of the letter she had sent him. He had torn it up unread.

Relieved, Tully changed the subject. "What about the painting? What about the Hogarth?"

"Well, I had it in my hands, if only for a little while."

"No regrets that you gave it away?"

"None." He stood up to leave. "I'll be in touch. And thanks, Tully. Thanks for everything."

"Paid off, is it?"

Frowning, Victor studied his old friend. "What?"

"What I owe you. Have I paid it off?" For a moment Tully looked into Victor's face, then shook his head. "No, I thought not."

Sixty-Four

CRUMBLING SOME BREAD BETWEEN HIS FINGERS, SIR OLIVER PETERS sat beside the Serpentine and fed the ducks. He felt almost well. The cancer was still there, progressing, killing him, but it hardly mattered. The secret of the royal legacy was safe. He had succeeded in his duty, and that knowledge made him a happy man.

Suddenly he noticed one scruffy little duck across the water and threw some bread toward it, watching it hustle its way among the bigger birds and fight for its prize. The day had turned warm. One of those London days that act as a welcome reminder that winter is only temporary. That however dark and forbidding the weather has been, somewhere lies the first echo of spring. Grass that had been short and dark with rain now sent its shoots upward, and a few wastrel daffodils lifted their throats to the sun.

London buses cruised along the streets, newspapers vendors pinned back their tarpaulins, and a few early-season tourists shivering in T-shirts took snapshots of the Household Cavalry riding by. Hyde Park was, Oliver thought, exactly as he had seen it so often through the years since he had started running the gallery, since he had married and brought his new wife to the park. Descendants of the same trees that had populated the park then were again coming into leaf. The continuity, the familiarity of it all, soothed him. He drew some real comfort from the hope that his children would do as he had done and maybe while away an hour or so feeding the birds in the peaceful reaches of Hyde Park.

A shadow fell across his path. Oliver looked up, pleased to see Victor Ballam standing there. He patted the bench beside him. "Sit down," he said, throwing some more crumbs to the birds. "They're hungry."

Victor sat, watching as Oliver broke up some more crumbs, noticing the wasted hands, the prominent bones under his shrinking skin.

"Did the transfer go well?"

"Perfectly," Victor replied, his eyes fixed on the scruffy little duck that was fighting for its crust. "I got the girl back. And they got the Hogarth."

"So it's over?"

"Yes."

Shading his eyes from the sun, Oliver turned to him. "Did you find out what you wanted to know? Who the killer was?"

"The last person you'd expect. Duncan Fairfax, Bernie Freeland's pilot."

Oliver's surprise was genuine. "I don't even remember him."

"Which is a damning epitaph in itself," Victor said. "He's dead."

"Dear God."

"Yeah."

They sat in silence for a while, Oliver feeding the birds and Victor watching. Then he glanced around him and, satisfied that no one was watching, pulled out an envelope from his pocket and handed it to Oliver.

"What's this?"

"A check for half a million pounds."

Oliver's eyes widened in disbelief. "*What?* You got my money back?"

"No. Your money was taken by the triads. You won't ever get that back. They stole the money from Lim Chang."

"So whose money is this?"

"Yours—now."

Oliver stared at the man sitting next to him.

"I don't understand."

"You borrowed half a million pounds to give to Lim Chang in order to buy the Hogarth. You lost that money. I got the same amount from another source. I put the money in my bank, and now I'm giving you a check." He paused. "It's legal, and it's yours."

"But—"

"You told me you were in financial difficulties," Victor said quietly. "You couldn't afford to lose that much money, and now you don't have to. You can pay back the people you owe and get yourself out of debt." Before Oliver could say anything, Victor went on. "*Take* it," he urged. "It was doing no good where it was."

"But—"

"Let *me* repay an old debt," Victor said quietly. "A debt of gratitude to thank you for being the only person who stood up in court and spoke in my defense. You helped me then, Oliver; let me help you now. Let me do this, please."

Deeply moved, Oliver took the envelope from Victor's hand, tucking it into his inside pocket. He was finding words difficult, but at last he said, "You can't begin to know what this means to me."

"Oh, but I can," Victor replied, and fell silent. Several minutes passed, and then he turned back to Oliver with a smile on his face. "Like I said before, the triads are gangsters, not connoisseurs. Good thing, that, wouldn't you say?"

Warily, Oliver lifted his head but kept his eyes averted. "You know?"

"That the painting you gave me was a forgery? Yes." Again Victor glanced around him, making sure there was no one close enough to overhear what they were saying. "I didn't know when you first gave it to me, but later I had a good look at it and I worked it out. You see, it was too much to expect that you, Sir Oliver Peters, would give up the original Hogarth even for a woman's life. But then again, you couldn't let them kill Liza Frith; you couldn't have borne that. So you had to do something. And quickly."

"Go on."

"I don't know if it was because you wanted to protect the secret of the Hogarth or because you wanted to sell it."

"No, no! I admit that at one point selling it seemed the answer to my troubles, but I couldn't. I was terrified of leaving my family in difficulties, but I raised money in other ways and I've protected them as well as I can. My son won't inherit much, but enough at least to help him make his own way in the world. I've explained everything to him; he understands." Oliver paused, his voice even. "I come from what is called a good family, Victor. We've always been respected, and we respect what we have—this country and the monarchy. I couldn't in all conscience have let the original Hogarth go. Who would get it? What scandal could be caused by its exposure? The man in the painting was the Prince of Wales. The picture was a scandal in its own time. I couldn't risk anyone bringing that out into the open again."

"And besides, there's a living descendant," Victor said quietly.

Oliver nodded, his voice so low that Victor had to strain to hear it.

"Only a handful of people know who he is. It's one of the most explosive secrets ever kept, held only by the head of the government and certain members of the royal family. Now d'you see why I couldn't let the Hogarth get into the wrong hands?"

"Where's the original now?"

"In storage, where no one can ever get to it. When I die, my solicitor will confide in my wife and my oldest son, but they will never be able to sell the Hogarth, not that they ever would. It's to remain hidden as Hogarth hid it but not destroyed. Never destroyed. The future of the monarchy was under threat when William Hogarth painted that work. It's no less important now."

Silence fell between them. Victor was the first to speak.

"How did you do it?"

Smiling, Oliver leaned back against the bench.

"I've been in this business for a long time and know a lot of people with many different skills. As you said, the painting wasn't going to a collector, so I had a little leeway. Mass reproduction houses are so clever these days. They don't just have paper prints of Old Masters like they did before; now they reproduce the prints onto canvas to give a realistic effect." He pausing, relishing the skill of his deception. "So I bought the relevant print from *The Harlot's Progress* and contacted a discreet and reliable restorer who's worked for me often. An incredible man, trained at the Royal Academy and in Rome. A man I helped many years ago who finally—and willingly—repaid the favor. Before you ask, he would *never* divulge what was done."

"So how did he do it?"

Oliver smiled. "He took the replica off the stretcher, scraped away the top surface of the print, and then painstakingly repainted it, putting in the face of Frederick, the Prince of Wales."

"How could he? He hadn't seen the original."

"True. But there's an old print in the British Museum which was based on the original. An engraving locked away to which only I have access. It is not, nor has it ever been, in the public domain. He copied that. Remember, Victor, the painting's not large. The face takes up an area less than an inch. If the repainted area had been life-size, the subterfuge would have been more difficult to achieve."

Curious, Victor pressed him. "How did he get the colors accurate? He didn't have time to use oil paint—it wouldn't have dried fast enough—so he must have used acrylic."

"He did. In expert hands, it can be made to look the same. As you say, it dries quickly."

"And we had so little time."

"Yes," Oliver replied. "Layer after layer of paint was applied to achieve the muted tones, then varnished to blend with the rest. He then used a craquelure glaze to mimic tiny cracks in the surface of the painting. You know well enough that it's one of the most obvious ways of making a picture look old. Then the restorer aged it. He rolled the canvas and smoked it in front of a candle, then made the little tear in the back and faked an old watermark. And finally, he rubbed soot all over the picture." Oliver paused, remembering. "The finished painting was—"

"Incredible."

"Yes. And the beauty of the whole plan is that *if* someone ever exposed it as the original, an expert would immediately denounce it as a fake."

Victor leaned back, taking in a breath and wondering how long the Chinese would hold on to the Hogarth. Would they barter it immediately, sell it on? He hoped so. Hoped that it was used as a bargaining tool, not as a work of art. The longer the fake Hogarth remained away from the art world, the safer he would be. Under the weak sun, Victor found himself praying that the deception went unnoticed for years. That the painting would be traded across countries and continents until its history was forgotten. Until nobody remembered from where or from whom it had come.

"You did a good job," Victor said, standing up to leave.

"We both did. Take care of yourself."

"And you."

"You're a good man and a brave one. Few can say that," Oliver said, and put out a hand. Victor shook it gladly—and gently. "I won't see you again, Victor, but it was a privilege knowing you. A privilege and an honor."

Sixty-Five

CAREFUL NOT TO WAKE LOUIS, MRS. SHELDON CAME INTO HIS bedroom and placed the breakfast tray beside his bed. Coffee and toast, as always. As Bernie Freeland had always had every morning. Opening the curtains, she glanced out at the rain and smiled, knowing how much Louis appreciated such weather. The downfall was heavy. Water ran down the glass, making a puddle on the window ledge below. In a nearby tree, a recalcitrant bird shook its wet feathers; the mailman dropped a parcel into the box at the end of the drive.

"Louis, wake up," Mrs. Sheldon said, turning back to him. "Your breakfast's here."

She moved over to the bedside and glanced down at him, wondering at his extreme and unsettling beauty. Who could imagine that behind such a face was such a troubled mind? Who, looking at Louis Freeland, could fail to be impressed? And yet his appearance was a cruel joke, promising an intelligence and glamour that Louis had never possessed. The golden fleece that hid the poor unsteady lamb.

"Louis," Mrs. Sheldon said again, reaching out and shaking his shoulder gently.

He didn't move, but as she drew back her hand, she noticed a piece of paper crumpled under his left arm. And beside it an empty bottle of pills. Suddenly apprehensive, she felt for a pulse, turning Louis onto his back and realizing as she did so that he was dead. And had been dead for some hours.

Locking the bedroom door, Mrs. Sheldon picked up the piece of paper and began to read:

Sorry.

I thought he would stay with me after I made him. I thought he would, but he didn't. My father, that is.

I see his ghost; he talks to me at night, all the time.

Or rather he did; now he's gone again. I had thought I could keep him. It was the last time he lied that made up my mind. Mrs. Sheldon, thank you for being so kind to me, I'm sorry for what I did. You were always trying to get my father to care about me. I know that, I know that.

I followed my father to New York. You remember how I made a few trips to the city? I went to see him, but the last time he lied and said he was going away, and he wasn't because I saw him that day in New York.

She paused, the letter in her hand, breathing fast. She could imagine Louis seeing his father and realizing that he hadn't wanted to visit him. That he had lied again.

He wasn't going away—but he wasn't coming to see me, and I don't know why because I loved him.

I followed him along the street. I'm sorry.

He wasn't abroad; he was in New York. I followed him, and then he stopped at the curb.

I was looking at the back of his head and wondering why he couldn't love me. And then I got so angry. I saw the lights change, and I pushed him.

He went under a car and then another. He went around and over and ended up on his back, under a truck. And I watched him.

And I knew I'd stopped him leaving ever again.

I'd won.

When I came back here, my father visited every night. He spent time with me. Listened to me, let me tell him everything. He was interested. So eager to hear everything about me.

My mother lies at the bottom of the lake. But when my father was dead, he came to the house. He came in and stayed, always at night. I made a home for him, didn't even feel bad about pushing him any longer—because he was happy.

Then last night he said he was going away. He was a ghost, and he was still going away. I couldn't keep him.

I couldn't make him listen, because he didn't want to. He wanted to be gone. And so he slipped through the blinds last night, and I think I saw his plane over the house and knew he'd gone forever.

I was never enough.

I'm sorry. I'm sorry. I'm sorry.

Louis

Pushing the paper into her pocket, Mrs. Sheldon tidied the bed and smoothed out Louis's hair, laying his arms by his side, the empty pill bottle in his left hand. Then she glanced around the bedroom, checking that everything was in order and that nothing would give her charge away. Finally satisfied, she unlocked the door and returned to the bedside table.

Dialing a familiar number, she asked to be put through to Louis's doctor.

"Mrs. Sheldon. What can I do for you?"

Her voice never wavered. "It's Louis, Doctor; he's committed—"

"Oh, my God."

"You know how depressed he'd become. Perhaps we should have suspected something like this would happen."

"Did he leave a note?"

"No," she lied. "He didn't need to. It was obvious why he did it. Louis lived for his father, and with Mr. Freeland dead, he just couldn't go on." Her hand tightened around the paper in her pocket. "He wanted to be with him so much—and now he will be."

She could hear the irritation in the doctor's voice.

"The press will have a field day with this."

"No," she contradicted him. "The press doesn't care enough about Louis Freeland. No one but me ever did. That was the problem."

sixty-six

STIFF-BACKED, ELIZABETH STRAIGHTENED UP IN HER SEAT, GLANCING at the door as Dr. Fountain entered. Her expression was one of eager hope as the doctor moved over to Kit's bedside. Outside the window of the Friary's private room, the harsh and bitter cull of winter had burned itself out; before long bulbs would start pushing their dozing heads through the cold soil, vying for life in the first weak search for sunlight.

Her eyes searched Fountain's face as he turned to her with an expression of intense sympathy, his southern drawl almost a caricature in the hospital room.

"I'm so sorry."

"Are you sure you're right?" she asked, her head turning toward her son, then back to Fountain. "Are you *really* sure?"

He nodded, his action regretful, somber. "Kit has suffered irreparable brain damage."

As though the thought was wounding to him, Eli Fountain moved over to the window and looked out, his back to Elizabeth. His decision had been, to his surprise, easy. Despite Mrs. Fleet's urging—or maybe *because* of it—he had shrunk from the outright killing of Kit Wilkes. But when the madam had left, Eli had spent a long time staring at the figure on the bed and remembering what she had said. It was true that should Kit recover and realize that his plan had failed, he would exact a terrible revenge. There would be no point trying to explain that medicine was not an exact science, that it might well have been due to Kit's drug taking that the sedation had been so potent. And the stimulant so ineffective.

The newspapers would be Kit Wilkes's first port of call. He would twist the truth, expose the Hogarth painting, and tell his version of events. Eli could imagine only too easily what that might be: that his own doctor had deliberately sedated him in order to get the painting for himself. Or that he had been duped, poor gullible Kit, drugged to keep him out of the running. Either way, he would ruin Eli Fountain. As Mrs. Fleet had said, his life would be over. No more money or power. No more sordid but lucrative work treating whores, no more lascivious bonuses at Park Street. Underhanded and sleazy as his life might be, Eli Fountain had no desire to swap it for a prison cell.

"Are you sure?" Elizabeth asked again.

He nodded without looking at her, waiting to compose himself, check that the vast dose he had given Kit Wilkes only an hour earlier was working its grim magic. Fountain knew that his plan was foolproof, but he still had to be there to make sure there was no flutter, no Lazarus-like recovery. He had to remain there to check that Kit Wilkes's eyes did not open, that his mouth remained closed, that his secret would be interred within him.

In time he would leave. But not yet.

"I'm so sorry, Elizabeth," Fountain said, turning back to her. "He won't ever recover."

It wasn't like killing. Not murder . . . just suspended animation. A deep unconscious state that would lead to brain damage in a matter of hours. But in the meantime he wondered if Kit could still hear him. If in that unmoving body he could hear his own terrible fate being spelled out. That he—so clever, so vicious, so talented—would feel his brain close down, his mind crushed. And after that? Nothing. Just his lungs opening and closing for years with the help of a machine, plugged into an outlet. His whole life run by the London Electricity Board.

It wasn't really murder, Fountain told himself again. Not really. He could come and visit Kit Wilkes any time he liked and see that he was still alive. It wasn't murder; it was self defense. As for the Hogarth, the wretched painting that had started the whole affair, it had gone. He sighed, fiddling with his cuff links. God only knew who had it now. He didn't care. In truth, he was relieved. To all intents and purposes, the events that had begun in Bernie Freeland's jet had ended in a private room at the Friary Hospital.

Or they had for Kit Wilkes.

"How can I afford to keep him here?" Elizabeth asked plaintively. "I mean, how long will Kit be here?"

For the rest of his life.

"James Holden will help you, Elizabeth," Fountain replied smoothly, knowing that the MP would be celebrating the fate of his old tormentor. "He is his father, after all."

Kit wasn't dead, but he was forever *silent*, and that was good enough. With the gory tabloid spotlight taken off him, James Holden would see the path to glory open up before him. Discreetly, he would provide the hospital care for Kit Wilkes, but from a distance, and with his bastard forgotten, his past would be too. In time James Holden would be able to graduate from meat quotas, take his place in line for a medal. No longer a joke, he would finally gain respect and achieve the social standing that had been denied him by the peevish machinations of Kit Wilkes.

His private penance would be ongoing, but his public sentence was over.

Meanwhile, Elizabeth was thinking that James Holden must never—*never*—discover that Kit wasn't his son. And at the thought, she realized that she was back firmly in her sister's grip. At any time Charlene could reveal the truth, leaving Elizabeth to face years of treatment and care for her son. Treatment she could never afford, care that no whore well past her best could hope to secure. If her sister kept silent, Elizabeth could maintain her business, her life, and her son. Silence was her only weapon. Her last card.

She knew that her sister would relish the situation. Would love to see Elizabeth buckle down, remember her place, and wonder—endlessly wonder—if or when Mrs. Fleet would make that anonymous phone call to James Holden.

In her sister's hand was her future. And knowing that was a little death in itself.

Sixty-seven

INGOLA WAS WAITING OUTSIDE VICTOR'S APARTMENT WHEN HE returned later that afternoon. She was smoking to calm her nerves, not because she was enjoying it. As she heard his footsteps approach, she turned and smiled, but Victor was unresponsive as he unlocked the front door and moved up the stairs to his apartment. In silence she threw the butt of her cigarette into the gutter and followed him in, standing uncomfortably by the window.

"Whatever we had in the past is over," Victor began, his tone firm. Not unkind but unbending.

"I want—"

"No; you can't want anything from me," Victor replied bluntly. "It's finished. You're Christian's wife."

"It was a marriage of convenience!"

"God, I hope you never tell him that," Victor replied coldly. "He worships you."

Thwarted, she snapped back. "And I worship you."

"No, you don't. You just *want* me. It's a challenge for you, Ingola. You want excitement. You think I don't know what you're really like?" He paused, watching her expression falter. "You think I don't know about your affair with Tully?"

Surprised, she blustered, "That meant nothing! It was a mistake!"

"You slept with my closest friend. I could have hated him for that, but I realized that you'd have chased him, run him to ground. And poor Tully, for all his elegant charm, is a novice around women. I imagine he was flattered. I know he was very lonely, so desperate to fill the void left by his wife that he pushed his morals to the back of his mind to feel wanted. I know how he felt, because I felt it too when we made love."

"It was a mistake with Tully."

"One you *repeated*."

Flushing, she reached out to him, but he stepped back.

"It's over, Ingola. We did love each other, but not now. We can't. I always knew what you were like; it was part of your charm. It was even refreshing, knowing that you were so ruthless. No one was going to walk all over you, keep you down. I admired that in you, but not now. Now it just looks like selfishness."

"It was one mistake, Victor. I haven't been with Tully for years."

"But *we* slept together."

"You fucking hypocrite!" she snarled, furious at being rejected. "What makes you think you can judge me? Look at yourself; you're nothing. A grubby ex-con scrabbling around to find work. Whatever you can, wherever you can, mixing with crooks and whores. The kind of people you used to detest."

Stung, he retaliated.

"The only difference between the whores I've been mixing with and you is that they're professionals."

She slapped him—hard. Victor's head jerked back.

"How *dare* you talk to me like that? I could have any man I wanted."

"Not anymore," he said coldly. "You can't even have me. And I'm no one—just an ex-con, as you just reminded me. You're on the wane, Ingola; your glory days are over. Now you're a suburban wife living in Worcestershire. Oh, your career's doing okay, but the rest has soured, hasn't it?" He was being unusually cruel, unable to stop himself. "I know what you're lacking. Excitement. Sexual thrills. You always had a high sex drive."

"Listen to me!" she said desperately. "I can make this right for us. I could leave Christian. I could be with you again, like we used to be. Just us."

Incredulous, he stared at her.

"It can never be like it was. I'm a convicted criminal."

"I don't care!"

"Maybe not now, but you would soon enough. When the excitement's worn off, when you realize just how fucking tough it is without a reputation, you wouldn't like it at all," he said, staring at her. "People look at you with contempt. They don't take your calls; they make little references to what you *used* to be and what you've lost. I know you, Ingola. You couldn't take it; you always crumble when things get tough. You backed out of marrying me easily enough."

"*You* told me to marry Christian!"

"And you took the opportunity and ran with it. And now you're bored, and you want an adventure. Well, not with me, Ingola. Not with me."

She moved closer to him, touching his cheek, surprised when he brushed her off.

"You want me, Victor. You know you do. You always did."

"I want the woman you were, not the one you are now. Face it, Ingola; you picked the life you wanted. You're Christian's wife and a mother."

"Jack's only a toddler; he'd adjust to a new life."

"Are you serious? You'd just dump Christian and take his kid? How d'you think he'd feel about that?"

Her eyes narrowed. He saw the shift and paused for an instant. "You *couldn't* take a child from his father."

"Really?"

"Ingola," Victor said, suddenly unnerved. "Don't do this to my brother. It would be too cruel. Don't do it. Don't take his child away."

"Oh, Victor," Ingola said quietly. "You really *are* a fool, aren't you?" Realizing she had lost, she struck the final blow. "Christian isn't Jack's father. Tully is."

Sixty-Eight

ALL OVER THE CAPITAL THERE WERE BETS LAID AND FIGHTS FOR SEATS and standing room to see the new king crowned. Over the previous two months the final arrangements had been organized, and now, as the coronation came closer, overseas visitors and dignitaries were beginning to arrive. There was not a hotel room left vacant, and the press of tourists pummeled the London population in the heat of an unexpectedly early and blistering spring. Across the world, in countries ruled by presidents and even those with their own royalty, the interest was phenomenal.

After the extended global depression and financial downturn from which the world had taken so long to recover, the coronation was exactly the type of ceremony that united everyone. With the knowledge that the event would be covered by television and followed on the Internet worldwide, the expectation of billions descended on the regal city of London. There were huge profits to be made from royal memorabilia, from the sales of prints and commemorative items. It was an event. It was a crowning. It was big business.

In the six years that had passed since the Hogarth affair, Victor had worked on a number of cases. None as murderous as that first brutal case but a number involving fraud and the smuggling of fakes. His intelligence, experience, and fearlessness helped him to a new role and reputation in the art world in London, Paris, New York, and eventually Australia and the Far East. Instead of being a highly respected dealer, Victor Ballam had become a feared investigator.

And with each assignment, he asked himself whether this would be the one that would give him the lead to solve his own case. As he interviewed the art dealers and the dissolute runners, forgers, and petty crooks who populated its underbelly, he wondered if this would be the day, the man, the question that would lead him finally to the answer he had been seeking for so long. Would it take him to the door of the person or persons responsible for his incarceration and the theft of his good name?

After the Hogarth had been taken by the triads, Victor had often wondered if the forgery would be exposed and threaten his safety. But there was no great revelation. The painting had gone to ground. It was currency, nothing more. At times Victor found himself uneasy, but no one came after him, and when a couple of years had passed, he allowed himself to relax. But not too much.

Meanwhile, he continued his alliance with Tully, occasionally looking at his nephew and trying to see some imprint of his flamboyant friend. A friend who remained in complete ignorance of the child he had sired. But eighteen months after the argument between Victor and Ingola, she went back to Norway. Alone. Walked away from her husband and her son without looking back. But she did one honorable thing: she kept the secret of Jack's parentage. Victor and Christian—made a bemused single father overnight—grew closer, and Victor was a willing and frequent visitor to Worcestershire.

In London, Tully continued with his voice-overs; he'd even landed a part on the London stage that, regretfully, he'd had to give up because of a sudden and acute illness. Called stage fright. He continued to be involved with Victor on his cases but did only the paperwork and the research. He was too old for heroics but not too old to talk to people and uncover information that would have taken another man months. As Tully had always said, he was a pastor to the dispossessed, and his debt to Victor kept him tied more securely than a leash.

As promised, Victor and Liza Frith had kept in touch, and she reminded him often that she would help him if he ever needed her. She stayed in France for a couple of years and then came back to England. Her days as a call girl in Paris had netted her a neat little fortune that she invested in a dress shop in Cornwall, and three years after quitting the business, she married the local vet. Victor never asked if he knew about Liza's previous life, and neither he nor Liza spoke about the woman they had once known. For both of them, Mrs. Fleet was the one memory too powerful and disturbing to talk about.

Working in London and moving in the art circles that were her forte, Victor heard that Park Street had been raided. But before the month was out, Charlene Fleet was back in business. He thought once that he saw her pass by in Hampstead, more of a shadow than a person, but he didn't turn to check. She had been on the other side of the road, the traffic between them. For Victor it was close enough.

It took little effort for him to recall her in the office at the top of the house all those years earlier. Standing with the dog at her feet, cold as ice, wearing a patina of disillusionment, controlled by greed. Never before or since had he come across anyone he feared as much as Charlene Fleet. He suspected her of unnatural crimes, willing depravity, and unbending revenge. Of all the clients Victor Ballam had ever worked for, Mrs. Fleet had been—and remained— the nearest to pure evil.

For months on end he would forget about her, but then she would slither into his dreams, reminding him: *I'll get my own back. It might take me a while, but I will. One day. One day when you're least expecting it. You might have the upper hand now, but not forever. So watch your back, Ballam. No one takes what's mine and gets away with it.*

The threat had been potent and serious. Victor had never underestimated that. But time passed, and Mrs. Fleet stayed her hand.

What news Victor heard about Kit Wilkes was through his mother, Elizabeth, who had for some unknown reason stayed in touch. Older now and completely committed to her mute, unmoving, undying child, Elizabeth made a saint's life out of being Kit's companion with James Holden's remote but constant financial support. She spoke of Kit knowing she was there, in the room with him. She would tell anyone who would listen that her son might yet recover, that she was certain she had seen flickers of life: a twitch of a hand, a shudder in a foot. Nothing and no one would dissuade Elizabeth Wilkes from the belief that somehow he would come back to her.

Of course the professionals tried to stem her hopes. But Elizabeth was adamant, and when Eli Fountain died suddenly and unexpectedly of a heart attack, her initial fear that Kit's care would be threatened gave way to another feeling entirely. It took precisely one week, three days, and four hours for the last dose to leave Kit Wilkes's system, for the final injection Dr. Fountain had given him to vacate his limbs. Then something incredible happened. Freed from his drug straitjacket, *Kit Wilkes moved.* Elizabeth was there and screamed as her son tossed on the bed. At once a doctor arrived and, mistakenly thinking he was having a fit, gave the restless patient a sedative to calm him down.

Back into the dusk fell Kit Wilkes, back into twilight and the memory of something half recalled. A plane journey, a painting, a plan made hurriedly over a cell phone . . . Back, back, back into the dark went Kit Wilkes, mute again. Silenced again, his little flicker of life snuffed out. It had been his last attempt to escape. From that moment on, the man who had been sedated into a *faux* death assumed the role he had indirectly created for himself. With the last injection of sedative went Kit Wilkes's last resistance. Worn thin with drugs, his brain smothered, and half mad, he slid like a turtle under the mud of memory. And never came home again.

All this Victor remembered as he walked down Piccadilly toward Bond Street. He had been in New York and Lisbon but had returned for the coronation, some little tug of instinct drawing him home. His apartment was as it had always been, and was now let to tenants. Victor hadn't even bothered to get it signed over to him again. It was to all intents and purposes still Christian's. If he had wanted, Victor could easily have afforded to buy another apartment anywhere in the world, but his spell in prison had severed any longing for property. Having once been shorn as bald as a spring lamb, Victor had no need for possessions.

But the last thing he expected on returning to London was a call from Sonia Peters, wife of the late and sorely missed Sir Oliver Peters. She had left a message at his hotel for him and was direct, almost abrupt, when he returned the call.

"Forgive my contacting you. The last time we met was at my husband's funeral."

"I think of him often."

He could hear her take in a breath. "As do I, Mr. Ballam."

"Is there something I can do for you, Lady Peters?"

"Come and see me this afternoon, please. We can talk then."

Victor was ushered into the plush drawing room of her apartment in Regent's Park. She was wearing a dark slub silk suit; her dark hair was now stippled with white and her bearing regal, but she was clearly bordering on agitation. Behind her on a sofa table were a number of framed family photographs, several of which Victor took to be of her children, but the largest was that of Sir Oliver, taken in his prime before cancer made a specter of him. His presence, smiling at the camera un-self-consciously, jolted Victor, reminding him of a great man. And a greater loss.

Taking care that they were alone, Sonia Peters sat down on the sofa opposite Victor. Between them was a low table weighted with art books; a small spaniel was curled in the shadow underneath. Heavy curtains muffled their conversation, and the intermittent humming of a vacuum cleaner came from the rooms overhead.

"My husband always said that I could trust you, Mr. Ballam."

Victor nodded, remembering the promise he had made years earlier.

"You can, indeed."

"Good. Well, then . . . I have a great problem." She paused, putting her hand to her cheek, her wedding ring loose on her finger. It was obvious that she was in some distress and, although eager for help, was uneasy about seeking it. Her black eyes rested searchingly on Victor; then she nodded to herself as though a decision had finally and irrevocably been made. "You know all about the Hogarth painting?"

The mention of it six years after he had last seen it shook Victor to the core. It seemed as though the very name of Hogarth was unlucky, destined to bring misfortune. He wanted to stop Sonia Peters, to silence her, prevent her from bringing the painter and the painting into that room. But he couldn't. He had always suspected that the story of the Hogarth was unfinished, had often mused about when he would hear of it again. His interest had been twofold: curiosity, and an old atavistic desire to tempt fate.

"Yes; I know all about the Hogarth painting."

"I'm speaking of the original," she continued. "Not the forgery."

"I understand." He saw her touch her throat in the same defensive, vulnerable gesture her husband had once used.

"Oliver left it to me. Before he died, he had arranged for it to be hidden in a place no one could ever find it. Even I wasn't told where. All I was told was that it was safe and that it had to remain hidden. There was to be no exposure of the work, ever."

"But?"

"Then suddenly, a few days ago, I received a letter from our solicitor. My son, Simeon, is now twenty-one years old, and apparently his father had decided that he should take over the care of the Hogarth."

Victor frowned.

"You look surprised, Mr. Ballam; so was I. For six years I've been a willing caretaker of the work, but my late husband believed his son should inherit not only some privileges but some responsibility on his coming of age." She paused and smiled to herself. "Oliver had excellent qualities, but in this he was wrong."

"But if you don't know where the painting is, then your son is merely taking over a titular responsibility."

She straightened up in her seat, her head tilted to one side.

"Ah, but I *do* know, Mr. Ballam."

"You do? How?"

"Solicitors are a strange breed. They guard a person's property and family; they keep confidences and offer good advice. Those are their advantages. Their disadvantages are the same as the rest of mankind. They are human." She gazed at the back of her right hand as though the action steadied her. "Our personal solicitor, the head of the firm, died recently. His accounts were, quite naturally, passed over to his successor. I was privy to this and agreed to it. What I *didn't* agree to was that the successor should handle our confidential matters without first consulting me."

Victor was already one jump ahead. "And he found out about the Hogarth?"

"He did. Then, without realizing that I was in ignorance of its whereabouts, Mr. Graham Rundles came to see me about other matters and mentioned the Hogarth—and where it was." She caught her breath, slowing down her speech to calm herself. "Suddenly I was in possession of information I didn't want. But worse was to follow. It transpired that the reckless Mr. Rundles had already passed this information onto my son." Victor sighed as she continued. "Naturally I spoke to Simeon about it, but he shrugged off the whole matter and thought it was a joke."

"No," Victor said coldly. "It was never a joke."

"I know. But he's young—and stupid in some ways," Sonia replied, leaning forward slightly. "Simeon won't tell anyone. He won't deliberately break the confidence, but as I say, he's young, and people slip up. A man who's had too much to drink or a young man in love for the first time could brag about something to impress others. Simeon hasn't lived long enough to know how tough the world can be. This is knowledge my son should not have, Mr. Ballam. I believe from what little Oliver told me that the painting could be dangerous."

"It's deadly."

She flinched, surprised yet relieved by his bluntness.

"You did the right thing contacting me," Victor went on. "I don't want to frighten you, but your son—in fact, anyone who knows the whereabouts of this painting—is in danger. I know this from personal experience. As did your husband."

She held his gaze steadily.

"I lost my husband, Mr. Ballam. I can't lose my son. And certainly not because of a painting. If it's as influential as you say, why wasn't the Hogarth destroyed?"

"It's proof," Victor explained. "It can never be revealed. And never made public. By the same token, it can never be destroyed. One day we might need it."

"Why?"

"I would rather you didn't know that," he answered. "Your son's only in danger because he knows where the painting is. So we must move it."

"We must move it," she repeated, nodding to herself. "Yes, but to where?"

"I'm not going tell you that."

"So I—*we*—have to trust you?"

"Only with your lives. Now, what about Mr. Rundles? He hasn't mentioned any of this to anyone else, has he?"

"No. I was very angry and ordered him to keep it quiet. That no one—no one—must know anything about the Hogarth. I asked him if he'd spoken to anyone else in the firm, even his secretary. He said no, and I believe him. To be frank, I think I scared him into silence. Mr. Rundles doesn't want to lose this family's business; he can't afford to annoy me again. Or refuse to follow my instructions to the letter."

Impressed, Victor nodded. "All you have to do is to tell me where the painting is now and I'll move it. After that, you—and your son—can forget all about the Hogarth. You can't tell anybody anything anyway, because you won't know anything. And you certainly won't know where it is."

Frowning, Sonia studied the man sitting opposite her.

"But that puts you in danger, Mr. Ballam. *You* would then be the only person who knows where the painting is." She sighed and said in a low voice, "You can refuse, you know. I'd understand. Until you just explained it to me, I didn't know how serious the matter was. Now I'm wondering if it's fair to put this burden on you."

"A long time ago your husband stood up for me."

"But he didn't risk his life for you. Or for your family," she replied calmly, "So why should I expect that of you?"

"Because the Hogarth is my responsibility," Victor replied. "I always knew it would come back to me. I'll be honest; when I first got involved, I wanted the painting for myself. It was to be my ticket back to the limelight." He gave a wry smile. "I found it, then lost it, and in the end I passed off its fake, knowing that the real Hogarth was in your husband's hands and safe because of it." Victor paused. "But in my gut I knew it wasn't over. That painting has a life, an energy, of its own. It's as if when Hogarth painted it, its message was so important that no one could keep it hidden forever."

"But you're going to hide it?"

"Yes, I am."

"And if someone finds it again?"

"They won't," Victor said firmly. "Where it's going this time, no one will ever find it."

She nodded, then reached into her bag and passed Victor a small padded envelope addressed to Simeon Peters.

"I was to pass this on to my son, but I decided not to. In light of our conversation, I believe I made the right decision, Mr. Ballam. I don't know what the package contains. I don't want to know. And, more particularly, I don't want my son to know." Her gaze held Victor's defiantly. "My husband believed in honor, in serving his king and country, and he believed in duty. He was a fine man." She paused before continuing. "But that was the difference between us—he was a *man*. I am a woman and a mother. My duty is to my children. They come first. Before country, before royalty, even before personal honor."

Victor nodded. "I understand."

"Thank you. I don't expect you to approve of my decision, Mr. Ballam, only to honor it."

Sixty-Nine

THE HIDING PLACE WAS DECIDED BY VICTOR AND VICTOR ALONE. HE had wondered if he should offer the Hogarth to the royal family, considering the dynastic questions its emergence would be sure to incite. Especially on the eve of the new king's coronation. But his initial requests to discuss the matter were met with rejection. Naturally Victor was not prepared to expose the story of the painting to any minion in the royal household, and his attempts to contact members of the senior royal staff were met with a rebuttal. His history went against him. Who, after all, would believe anything a proven fraudster said? Victor Ballam had a record. Wasn't he a known dealer in fakes?

He realized quickly that his intention to do right was going to be thwarted. He neither wanted nor dared to talk about the painting and its implications, knowing that even in discussing it he would be exposing it. Worse, if he had to go through courtiers, how many others would then hear about the painting's existence? What other nasty upsurge of interest might follow? What frenzied search for the living descendant? Because he *would* be searched for—and found eventually. And how inopportune with the coronation imminent. At such a time, the exposure of a royal bastard would be a social, political, and even economic disaster.

And so Victor Ballam turned away from the court and considered approaching the prime minister. Again he was met with rejection. Finally, he realized that he and he alone must be responsible for the Hogarth. A hiding place must be found, a hiding place so clever, so discreet, no one would ever even guess at it. A hiding place where Frederick, Prince of Wales, could smile forever at his pretty Polly Gunnell and the son she carried within her.

On the morning of the king's coronation, Victor Ballam strapped the Hogarth, together with the unopened package from Sonia Peters, to his body with tape. Wrapped in a protective layer of plastic, they nestled against his skin unseen as he boarded a small light aircraft with one piece of luggage. It was to be the first leg of his journey across Europe, and as he sat in a window seat, Victor thought of the fateful trip on Bernie Freeland's jet and the greed of Duncan Fairfax that had set the murders in motion.

The weather was fair, and the city's outskirts appeared suddenly as they came down to land outside Naples. Climbing out of the aircraft, Victor picked up his suitcase, thanked the pilot, and waited to greet the new man who would take him on the next lap. No detail had been overlooked. At both stages of the journey there was to be a different pilot, neither knowing the other or his destination.

The sun was blistering. Victor stood on the runway in a heat haze that distorted the planes across the tarmac as the second pilot approached. He had put on weight since Victor had first met him and seemed to walk with a confidence that comes with being respected. With being recognized as reliable and discreet.

Tipping his pilot's cap to Victor, John Yates glanced up.

"Hot day."

"Hot as hell," Victor replied. "You look well. You know where we're going?"

"Yes, ready when you are."

John Yates had come a long way since his days as Duncan Fairfax's copilot. He was now employed by one of the top Middle Eastern industrialists but retained his interests in London and never forgot the time when he worked with the murderer Fairfax. That was why when Victor contacted him, he was intrigued and open to the offer of a simple trip. Destination to be divulged the night before. Fee excellent. No questions to be asked about the freight. One passenger. Known only to the pilot. Mr. Victor Ballam.

But there was one last, important condition: if anyone asked, Victor Ballam was supposed to be flying the plane himself, which he was capable of doing. But the deception was really for another reason. Should any questions ever be asked, John Yates would not be incriminated.

"Can we leave now?" Victor asked, climbing into the plane and putting the suitcase on the seat next to his.

As John Yates started the engine, and Victor pulled the door to, something caught his eye. Turning in his seat, his saw a stout official frantically beckoning to him from an open car parked a little way off.

Victor called out to John Yates. "Looks like they've got a problem."

The man was shouting, yammering in Italian, his arms flailing, his face sweaty in the heat. But as Victor stepped onto the tarmac, the man drove off.

Puzzled, Victor was watching the car disappear into the distance when he heard—suddenly and unmistakably—the plane start down the runway.

Surprised, he called out and began running toward the plane, but it was already well out of his reach, coming to the end of the runway and then taking off. Up into the hot white sky above Naples, up into the cloudless air, to the sun and the heat above. Still running, Victor could see the sun spark off the wings as the plane—and his suitcase—made their way across the unstoppable sky. Dumbfounded, he stood in the heat, his mouth dry. What the hell was happening? And then he realized that every one of his movements had been tracked. John Yates had been *hired* to abandon him and leave with Victor's suitcase. The suitcase believed to contain the Hogarth painting.

He continued to stand where he was, watching as the plane climbed higher and higher. Through his shirt he could feel the tape wound around his body and touched it protectively. And then suddenly—a little way off, over the Bay of Naples—Victor heard the sound of a violent explosion and stared upward into the blinding sky. The plane was no longer a machine but a white-hot flare of wreckage plummeting into a terrible descent.

What remains there were fell into the cool, deep water of the bay. It fell with the pilot, John Yates, Victor's suitcase, and his jacket, in which was his money, his passport, his credit cards, and his driving license. Everything he used to identify himself.

I'll get my own back. It might take me a while, but I will. One day. One day when you're least expecting it. No one takes what's mine and gets away with it.

Under that smoldering, unforgiving sun, Mrs. Fleet's words came back to Victor. And he knew that news would reach her in London to tell her that she had won. He could imagine her triumph, the thrill in that frozen heart, the frisson of victory. Because to all intents and purposes the plane, the Hogarth, and Victor Ballam himself had disappeared. Forever.

She didn't know that he was still alive. Didn't know that one day he would come after her.

Victor took a deep breath, exhaled slowly, and began walking. Away from the airport and down a dry, wide road. Shock was slowly being replaced by a plan. In time he would come to a town and then introduce himself by a stranger's name. He would make a new history for himself and, unwatched and unnoticed, keep the secret that had cost so many lives. He felt no fear, just a sense of absolute freedom. He had succeeded in what he had set out to do and was safe for the first time in years. As was the Hogarth. Because no one would ever know that Victor Ballam had survived.

No one looked for the dead.

Walking on, Victor suddenly stopped and, pulling away a little of the tape, took out the small unopened package addressed to Simeon Peters. The handwriting was well formed and clear, the signature that of Oliver Peters. Imagining his old colleague's well-modulated voice, Victor opened the envelope, and a gold signet ring fell out onto the dry earth at his feet.

Frowning, he picked the ring up, and began to read the letter:

> My Dearest Son,
>
> I am sorry and yet proud to pass on this duty to you. Few men are called to serve their country and their Crown, and I have always counted myself honored to be among this little coterie. You will now have been informed of the history of the Hogarth painting, why it has been protected for so long. And why its secret must be kept. The painting is proof, but also—in this letter—is more evidence. An engraved ring, from Frederick, Prince of Wales, to his illegitimate son.

Mesmerized, Victor stared at the ring, reading the engraved inscription:

> To my secret child, from his father, Frederick, Prince of Wales.

Slowly, he turned the heavy gold ring in his hand, given from a father to a son, from a prince to a pauper.

Sighing, he turned back to the letter:

> There is only one piece of information left to pass on—the name of the living descendant of Frederick, Prince of Wales, and Polly Gunnell.
>
> This secret must never be divulged, and when the time comes, you will pass it on to your own descendant for safekeeping.

I cannot express how vital secrecy is. How you hold history in
the palm of your hand.

The living descendant—pretender to the English throne and the
one man who could challenge the royal ascension—is Thomas
Harcourt.

Victor stopped reading, a sly breeze ruffling the letter in his hand.
Thomas Harcourt, Tully. Breathing deeply to steady himself, Victor realized
that in one detail—and one detail only—the gracious Oliver Peters had been
wrong. Tully Harcourt would not be the last of the line. Unknown to him
or to the powers who had protected the Hogarth secret for so long, there *was*
a successor. When Tully died, he would leave behind an heir—half English,
half Norwegian. An unknown heir, centuries away from the cellar where
Polly Gunnell had been butchered, generations removed from the boy who
had played in the yard of the Foundling Hospital. Out of the reach of killers
and conspirators, the descendant of little Hal had somehow survived.

And only Victor knew who he was: his own nephew, Jack Ballam.

Tucking the letter and the ring back into his bodystrapping, next to
the Hogarth painting, Victor walked on. Against all the odds, Mrs. Fleet's
revenge had played right into his hands. No one would ever look for him
again. Or for the Hogarth or the royal pretender. It ended with him. With a
dusty man walking down a dusty road. A man without an identity, with no
name and no history. A man who didn't exist. Who carried a secret no one
would ever discover.

What the preoccupied Victor didn't notice as he walked on was that in a side
road, a battered van was parked among dry trees. In it were two men who
watched Victor Ballam pass. And then, when enough distance was between
them, they began to follow him.

Before My God, in this year 1755, I stand in solemn witness to this end. Before My God, I take the punishment in this life—and in the world to come—for my culpability.

In my defence I did once save a child, and loved that child. In my defence, I saw him raised and safe, and tracked his every day into maturity. His life, which my own hands once saved, counted no less to me than those I call my own. His little child's triumphs and defeats moved me in equal part; his illnesses agonised over, spoken of in whispers.

His name's not his, and yet they knew him.

His name was never given by a mother, but a sham. One planned, to keep the harm away from him. Never was there such a secret born. Never was there such a secret kept. Never was there such a burden placed on such poor shoulders as my own.

In my defence, I kept the secret. And from the boy himself.

And yet my sweet Hal's gone. And all that's good has gone with him. Last night I visited the hiding place, kept secret for so long. I wanted to see the painting and the ring, but both had gone. All that remained in the hidden cupboard was a button— gold and lapis lazuli—formed into the shape of an owl. One of a set of fasteners I had seen on a waistcoat, a waistcoat that belonged to Nathaniel Overton.

How long they knew of Hal, I cannot guess. How long they watched, I cannot know. But it was done, and done well. Taken is the boy. Stolen, the last spark of pretty Polly Gunnell and her lover. For all the priests and doctors, the world's spy master, Overton, and all and everyone who sought this child, I hereby curse them. For all the villains, whores, and hypocrites who aided or abetted his discovery, damn them also. For he is taken. Gone to some other place that I can only guess at. Some other future, far from me and from the Foundling Hall. And yet I have hope for him. That those who took him, took him to be saved. Last night there was a knocking at the studio door and a man slid some little paper in my hand and then scurried off. I took it to my workplace, holding it by the candle to read better what had been written there.

It said, in all simplicity,

He is safe.

I read the message many times. I soothed myself; let my heart slow to a healthy beat; my thoughts quieten; my hopes rise. And finally I turned, fixing my eyes upon the beloved image on my wall. And he—that borrowed child of mine, that princeling with no throne—smiled back at me.

Bibliography

Antal, Frederick. *Hogarth and His Place in European Art*. London. Routledge & Kegan Paul, 1962.

Berry, Erick, *The Four Londons of William Hogarth*. London, D. McKay, 1964.

Bindman, David. *Hogarth*. London: Thames & Hudson, 1981.

Clayton,Tim. *Hogarth*. London: British Museum Press, 2007.

Paulson, Ronald. *Hogarth's Graphic Works*. 3rd ed. London: Alan Wofsey Fine Arts, 1989.

Quennell, Peter. *Hogarth's Progress*. London/ New York: Collins, 1955.

Uglow, Jenny. *Hogarth: A Life and a World*. London: Faber and Faber, 1997.

Webster, Mary. *Hogarth*. London: Cassell Ltd., 1979.